PRAISE FOR

UNDER THE CHURCHYARD IN THE CHAMBER OF BONE

"This book casts an eerie spell dark as any fairy tale, with wonderfully gruesome details and brutal moments peppered within an atmospheric setting. The story's cinematic descriptions and foreboding plot paints an irresistible tale that will grip you with claws sharp as machetes."

—KC Grifant, author of *Melinda West: Monster Gunslinger* and *Shrouded Horror: Tales of the Uncanny*

"A special, haunting work of fiction. Occasionally dreamlike, endlessly fascinating. I so loved getting lost in the universe Billingsley creates. The interludes woven through the larger narrative exploring time, death, and connection, are pure magic. A beautiful story, Billingsley's heart beats on every page. His passion for these characters and their journey, their pain and redemption, is refreshing. This book feels like connecting with an old friend. Highly recommended!"

—LP Hernandez, author of *No Gods, Only Chaos*

ALSO BY

JR BILLINGSLEY

A Mind Full of Scorpions (Eyes Only, Book One)
Observations and Nightmares: The Short Fiction of JR Billingsley

IN THE CHURCHYARD
IN THE CHAMBER
OF BONE

UNDER THE CHURCHYARD IN THE CHAMBER OF BONE

JR Billingsley

First published by Sley House Publishing 2024

Copyright © 2024 by Sley House Publishing

All rights reserved. No part of this publication may be reproduced, stored or transmitted in any form or by any means, electronic, mechanical, photocopying, recording, scanning, or otherwise without written permission from the publisher. It is illegal to copy this book, post it to a website, or distribute it by any other means without permission.

First edition

ISBN: 978-1-957941-06-6

Editor: K.A. Hough

Cover design: Ranxvrus

Interior design: Dreadful Designs

For Papa, Nana, Papaw, and Mamaw

Unable are the Loved to die
For Love is immortality…
> —EMILY DICKINSON

❧

Unbeing dead isn't being alive
> —E. E. CUMMINGS

❧

To be, or not to be…
> —SHAKESPEARE

PART ONE

Prologues & Epitaphs

PROLOGUE

As the man pushes through the snow-covered pasture, his feet growing heavier with each plodding step, he contemplates good beginnings. How to begin a story, that's the important thing. Hook the listener from the get-go.

His hands accompany other accoutrements in the pockets of his heavy coat, but nothing warms his fingers. The gloves he wears are leather and stiff—his grandfather's—good for handling barbed wire, but they permit too much air in, and he feels his digits purpling in the frosty night.

He is not old, not like the last storyteller. Age doesn't matter. He has a family. A past. A job. None of that matters, either. Tonight, he is merely Speaker, only important as long as there is a Beloved, and there is one, a ways beyond the snow that falls, faster now, thick wet flakes slapping against his coat and his cheeks and the knit cap on his head. The fence row appears in the dark, barely illuminated by his flashlight. He tucks it away in his pocket then grabs the wooden corner post and grips carelessly for the barbed wire, the gloves at least serving one purpose. On the other side, a sentry of Ozark trees stand battalion, their umbrage deep and dark and unyielding. He pushes through them, through the snow, thinner here but still falling, and soon enough he sees the first rows of tombstones in the churchyard, jagged gray molars jutting up from the white jaw of the earth. And beyond, the withered, weathered church. Still standing. Rotted and dark in its isolation.

Inside is warmer. He strips off the gloves and the coat and the knit cap, unpacks the contents of his pockets: the flashlight, a leather-bound tome, an amorphous shape packaged in butcher's wrap, its corners and its thinner patches soaked through with blood, as his vision highlights only the eigengrau.

The Speaker can hear the Beloved calling for him, but it isn't here, in the sanctuary. It is below, under the church and under the churchyard, with the twisted oak roots and sleeping mealworms and the rancid earth turned by death. It is here he must go to begin his story.

CHAPTER ONE

So many years ago:

The sod over the funeral plots had not yet had time to settle when the four of them met. The dirt beneath the sod still loose, not compacted, the bodies below still fresh.

The Dillons and the Oscars weren't old then. Older, maybe, but not old. Their children had been adults and their surviving grandchild just a baby. In fact, he'd just quieted when the four of them really began their discussion.

Outside the night had chilled, so in the front room, Elden Oscar had started a fire. He now stood stoking it, one foot on the hearth with his back to the room, the flames accentuating the lines on his face, emphasizing the shadows. His wife Aster returned to the room and said in a near whisper, "Court's sleeping now."

Court's crib had been placed in a room down the hall. The Oscar house was well-built, the walls thick, so Elden knew there was no need to whisper. He said so with a gruff cough like he was working out a clog of sputum from his throat. He knew the baby wouldn't hear them. Like he knew, believed, they were safe.

Glen Dillon started, as if reading Elden's mind, "We must assume, because it bowed to him when he showed up, that he can control it. Can keep it at bay, somehow."

"He said a word," Glen's wife, Lena, said. She sat in the other recliner, her arms folded around her torso, one hand up to her lips, one nail parting them as though she contemplated biting it.

"Maybe," Aster said, taking her place on the left side of the love seat, "now isn't the time. We just had the funerals…" She worked her hands into knots and stared at her husband's back.

"The hell it ain't!" Elden said, turning on them. Old and haggard and ashen from age and fear and trauma. *Jeesum*, he thought, knowing full well he was older than all of them. If they looked that old, he must look ancient. Lena's face pinched in frustration while Glen's eyes softened. Aster fretted over her knuckles, unsatisfied with the knot they'd become, and kept it working. "We each one of us is too old to care for a baby, but now we got to. Now we got to, cause we saw what that thing did. Our daughter." He looked at Glen and Lena Dillon. "Your son."

"What's the use?" Aster asked. "We don't even know what it was. Just some horrible—" she shuddered, her eyes closing, her lips tight as she struggled to find the right word but could only come up with— "monster."

"I might know," Glen said, "but we can't tell anyone outside this room. They'll think we're all ready for the looney bin."

Elden snorted. "They might be right."

Glen stepped from his place behind Lena's recliner. He'd had his hands on her shoulder and as he walked away, she reached out and took one, so that their fingers trailed to a touch as he left her side. She looked up at him with hope, admiration (*love*, Elden thought, for it was the same way he and Aster looked at each other), but Glen didn't look back.

"I've been at the library," he began, approaching the hearth. Beside Glen, their physical differences were pronounced. Glen was a head shorter than Elden, a bit broader in the shoulder. Where Elden was lanky even by his own observations, Glen appeared a bit thicker, but not fat. Like those guys who lifted weights all the time, though he knew Glen wasn't like them.

Elden harrumphed at this news. He knew Glen was a bookish sort.

"It's Arabic in origin," Glen continued, ignoring him, "though there are legends about it all over Europe. It haunts graveyards. It...and I apologize for the imagery...it attacks the living, and it...it eats the dead."

"What do you mean?" Aster asked cautiously. "Eats the dead?"

Glen sighed, looked to his wife who'd averted her eyes, then back to Aster. Elden pursed his lips in an attempt to hold his own tongue and focused on nothing. The only research he cared about was how to kill it. Outside, as though the universe anticipated the conversation and wanted to provide the right atmosphere, lightning flashed, and the steady pelting of rain sounded on the roof and siding.

"Just as it sounds," he said.

Lena stood and said, "I'm going to look in on Court," and left the room. Elden wondered if Glen hadn't already rehearsed this in front of Lena, and she knew what to expect.

"I can't believe this," Aster said, shaking her head and looking to some random, dark corner, but Glen continued.

"It doesn't stop with the dead. It can kill. Preys on lost travelers. It is fascinated by shiny metal and collects coins from those it kills. It...it can change its shape."

"Bullshit," Elden said, and turned his back on them again as Lena stepped back into the room. "I don't believe in haints and monsters."

"You saw it!" Glen said. "You saw what it did to my son out there."

"It looked like a dog," Elden said stubbornly, staring at the fire. "Brown with yellow spots, a weird dog for sure, but still—"

"Like a hyena," Glen corrected. "Dogs don't laugh. If you can call what that was doing laughter."

"Then it was a—" Elden paused, working the word over in his mind, "—a hi-yenna, but it still weren't no monster."

He turned back and the two men stood facing one another.

"It had the spots," Aster said, nearly a whisper, "but it wasn't no dog when it got here. It was like a man with a lot of hair."

"The eyes," Lena said, nearly inaudibly, and hugged herself as she leaned on the doorjamb of the entrance to the kitchen, as if she were afraid to fully return to the room.

Elden knew what she meant. The eyes like those you might see on a deer or a dog or something at night, all glowing. Only, not quite. A dog has the white part and the iris and the pupil, but this thing. Its eyes had been like cataracts, except all a greenish yellow color, and glowed like headlights.

"The whole head was wrong," Elden admitted.

"A skull," Glen said. "With rat-like incisors."

Rain beat against the windows. There was another flash of lightning and then thunder rolled across the pasture and hills.

"It doesn't sound like a Dracula," Lena said.

"The stories about it are just as old, though," Glen said. "The eater of the dead that lives under the earth—a ghoul."

"If this…thing…is what you say it is, how do we stop it?" Aster asked. Elden thought she looked nauseated even as his own stomach bubbled fretfully. The gruesome subject might be too much for all of them, especially if he stopped to entertain the thought of it biting into the flesh of a corpse.

Glen shook his head. Elden thought, *We're too old. We are already too old.* He was almost sixty, ten years older than Glen, and he had fifteen years on both the women. They were middle-aged and in relatively good health, but they got lucky, this time, if you could call it that, that it was only able to claim their children and the baby's older brother.

"We focus on Court," Lena said.

"And what of *him*?" Aster asked. "Is he evil? If he's with that…thing…" She let her words hang there like an executed criminal.

"*He* saved Court, according to you," Glen said. "He called it off." Neither he nor Elden had returned yet, that dark night, so the story had to be pieced together by what Lena and Aster had offered them. The creature had penetrated this well-built house. It had killed Elden's daughter, though that wasn't quite an accurate enough word, was it? They had to have closed caskets for the services. His nostrils flared and he thought he could still smell the blood. Then it found the two women, curled protectively around the baby. But before it could kill any of them, the man had appeared. He'd said a word, and the creature shrank away. Back into the darkness.

"Qissa, he'd said," Aster said. "It sounded…" She shuddered for an answer.

"Whether he controls it or is helping it or—"

Glen was cut off by Elden, who said, "It don't matter. He best never come 'round here again."

"We should go to the police," Aster said.

"And say what?" Lena countered, her tone biting.

"They said it was a dog attack," Glen reminded everyone. "They've already written it off."

"They probably wouldn't believe such a crazy story anyway," Aster admitted.

"I hope I never see him again," Lena said. Elden felt, should he come around again, it would spell the end for all of them, and a chill raced up his spine.

CHAPTER TWO

Twenty years ago, a girl crossed the grass-thin backyard from her South Texas home to the shed, which harbored something that shrieked. She'd been strumming the two chords she knew on the guitar her abuela had given her when the noises began: grating metal, squeals pealing through the afternoon. Outside, dark-coated Tia panted in the shade of the shed, and raised her massive head, her jowls quivering from the growl until she saw the girl, then went back to staring at nothing. Under the hot sun, the stone of the patio scorching the soles of her feet, the girl walked. Even the packed clay was hot. She reached up to the latch on the door, which opened to sparks spinning off a great wheel. A pair of dark glasses hid her father's face as he cradled the blade of a machete against the spinning wheel.

"Hola, papá. ¿Cómo se…?"

"No!" he snapped. "English. Practice your English."

The girl sighed and tilted her head. "What are you doing?"

"The blade of the machete must be sharp for the agave, hija."

"What about English?" she teased.

"'Hija' is a much prettier word than 'baby.'" The glasses hid his soft, brown eyes, but nothing could hide his smile. "Come," he said then. "I will show you."

He gave her a pair of gloves and lay the machete, the blade hot from grinding, in her hand, then stood behind her as she faced the wheel, the metal catching the glint of the outside sun on its arc and tip. The weight of the tool heavy but balanced, she imagined swinging it freely, beheading a cactus with a single blow. From behind, he tightened the dark glasses over her eyes, then guided her hands—one on the handle and one on the thick dull edge—and together they pushed the fine edge of the blade toward the ever-spinning wheel, offering up it in supplication to the shrieking monster spitting sparks until it was as sharp as a dragon's tooth.

INTERLUDE ONE

The Final Tale of the Last Storyteller

Once upon a time, there was an old storyteller. He had been telling stories for years, long before he was old, but he was able to tell stories because he had lived enough stories to tell. Living: the key to telling stories. Now this storyteller was a widower, having lost his lifelong companion a number of years back, so all who were left to hear his stories were his two friends, each at least as old as he—if not older—and their wives.

One day, before the cold crept in, the storyteller tried on his Marine Dress Blues. He positioned the barracks cap so it covered most of the gray, and marveled at how the uniform still fit, after all these years. Through his belt he strapped on the stainless-steel scabbard that housed his mameluke. He dropped the leather-bound tome he'd harbored for so many years into a worn and tattered knapsack. He made his way to the first of two houses he needed to visit on this, his final mission.

The first, an A-framed house in a tiny subdivision filled with oaks with street names like Camelot and Excalibur and Arthur and Gawain Way.

The friend's wife stopped him at the door. "You were there that night. You've avoided us since then. Ignored us. Left us out here to fend for ourselves. When we had Court—"

"I know," the storyteller said remorsefully. "But I'm here to explain myself. Explain a bit. I need to speak to Glen." The woman bit her lip and let him in, showed him to the den where his old companion sat, huddled and shivering under a blanket, staring at the television. The cramped, box-shaped room felt like a mausoleum.

The storyteller took his friend's veiny, purple hand and felt the cold. If he failed, it would fall to them, but, truthfully, they were in no condition. *Give them strength*, he thought with futility.

"I need to tell you something. A story. It has to do with your kids and what happened to them that night."

His friend looked skeletal. Had his friend expected this story? Perhaps he had known that he'd eventually learn what had happened so many years earlier, but he probably hadn't awakened this morning expecting the day had finally come.

"I go to a place," the storyteller said. "I've gone to this place for years. It's the same place, but it isn't, because it moves. You… Glen, you know. You were there with your son and Elden, and you saw it. Well, it hasn't come back around because…"

The den seemed to darken a little, or maybe it was the storyteller's imagination. The blinds were down. Perhaps a cloud had passed overhead. His friend's wife leaned over the love seat and took her husband's hand away from him, desperate for what the storyteller had to say. Above them, the ceiling fan oscillated slowly, quenching nothing. The storyteller met their eyes and took a deep breath, then took his time as he told his friends this story, watching their faces, knowing they would blame him, hoping they would understand. When he finished, he felt like he had been talking for hours.

"I'm going tonight," he said. "One stroke." He paused and looked at the television. They had been military men, veterans sharing stories. Stories they hadn't told their wives, their kids. Over the many years they'd shared with each other many stories, but until this day, he'd kept one story back: this story. For this moment. His friend didn't blink, only nodded. The wife showed him to the door.

"Go," she said, pointing over his shoulder toward his car with the sword in the front seat. The storyteller couldn't blame her for being angry; his story had not been what she expected. After all, she'd been hit with unexpected revelations and unanswered questions, and a new face to blame, after all these years.

CR80

The storyteller could remember when the pasture behind the old farmhouse was populated with Brangus and Charolais, but now it was overgrown wheat, dried yellow from the sun. At one point, the old man who lived here had owned over a hundred acres, upon which he'd raised cattle, mainly, but had dabbled in various critters and varmints years earlier. Working with as little help as possible, the old man had tended to the farm and his cows even as he held down a full-time job. When he retired from the public school, the farm became his full-time job until he was unable to keep it going, about five years ago. Now, creamed corn dribbled from the old man's lower lip at the table in his country kitchen. The storyteller was sure his old friend had no idea anyone was addressing him. The old man's wife sat in a chair next to him, stroking his hair with one hand as her other cradled the bowl. She was crumpled and plump, and her once-blue eyes had faded to a dull gray.

"I said, Elden, I'm going, now." He'd finished the story as he'd finished it at the A-frame house.

"One strike,'" the old man's wife echoed.

He could not hide the shadows on his face, and she recoiled.

"One's all I get," he said. "I'm out of stories."

CR80

The storyteller always found the churchyard easily enough; it was his duty to find it. He pulled off the two-lane highway onto the shoulder and stepped out, his boots crunching on the pebbles of gravel.

The headstones came into view first, even as the trees hid the bulk of the church. Only one of the double doors was open, revealing shadows he found strangely comforting.

"Qissa."

The word whispered as he entered the old church, met him as he crossed its pews, caressed him when he descended to the basement. He walked through the dark surefooted, a testament to how many times before he'd made this trip.

"Qissa."

Most might have overlooked the stone stairs in the basement, leading down further still, but not the old storyteller. His eyes always found them, even as his nose was lost to the earthy smells, the musk and stagnant air, and his ears were deaf to the things skittering in the dark, though he could still hear its voice.

"Qissa."

The stairs of slick moss and smoothed stone forced him to grab blindly at the earthen wall though there was nothing to grip onto save a prayer that he didn't stumble on this steep descent. When he finally entered the room, he shivered. He'd seen this chamber of skulls and femurs and clavicles and other bones many, many times, but he never got used to it, or the blood-blackened mortar of sinews and tendons and muscles that held them together.

A whispered voice flickered the torchlight in the chamber of bone.

"Qissa?"

"No story," he said. The darkness quivered like a heat mirage, though it was cool and damp and the smell of fetid earth, stronger here, reminded him of a putrescence he'd thought he'd forgotten. Over his shoulder he carried a knapsack, and from it he pulled the black leather tome. This he sat under the torch hanging on the wall. "For the next storyteller," he said.

"Qissa."

"I don't have any more," he said, and he heard how exhausted he sounded. He drew from its sheath the blade he had carried when he was stationed in the Middle East.

"Qissa."

"I found you. You remember that story. I found you." Punctuating this, he slapped the blade on the hard stone floor.

"Qissa."

The storyteller raised the blade as if it were a bat and studied the shadows. *One strike*, he thought, and swung. The mameluke connected, and the creature fell, curled fetal, lifeless, its blood spilling onto the bone-tiled floor of the chamber. He knelt to inspect the wound. The storyteller was amazed, sure the strength had left him so long ago for such a strike. But even in the dimness he could tell, though its eyes were closed and though the puddle spread, he hadn't successfully separated the head from the monster's body. To his dismay. The blade had not gone all the way through; it had only cleaved the meat where the shoulder and neck met. It had gone in maybe two inches, and he knew it wasn't good enough. He grabbed the handle and pulled, and when it wouldn't come cleanly loose of the gray flesh, put his foot on the chest and pulled harder. Glen would have made a reference about King Arthur and Elden would have said he looked like a man whose axe blade got stuck in a log, had either of them been here to see it.

He worked the blade loose and took a few steps back. If it had been any kind of living animal, the blow would have been good enough. If it had been a man, the blow would have ended his life. But it wasn't, though it could imitate language.

The creature rose, dizzy from the blow, and even as it recovered its feet, the wound on its neck was already mending and sewing the flesh back together. Then it flexed its claws and it lunged, and the storyteller didn't get another chance to raise his blade.

The End

PART TWO

Once Upon a Time

CHAPTER THREE

The sun had yet to climb into the sky when Court Dillon's convertible—top up; it was too cold to ride in open air— passed the last county limit sign before entering his hometown. He once again felt, ever so briefly, the apprehension of returning. Bathed in the dashboard lights as he was, his shoulders tightened as a great pressure building off the base of his skull slunk over the rest of his scalp, forcing him to wince. But this was necessary, he told himself. Even if it meant saying goodbye.

The convertible crested a hill of trees stripped of their leaves by the lateness of the season and overhead, thick, dark clouds a portent for the trip itself.

Court had been raised in Rapps Barren, Arkansas, a bucolic Ozark town just twenty miles south of the Missouri border, nested between two large lakes that fed off of and into the White River. It was a farming community, a summer vacation spot, a town of ten thousand: local blue-collar workers, retirees from Chicago, with trailer park pockets of residents peppered all through the area.

He'd been raised by both sets of grandparents after the accident that took his parents when he was a baby, an accident no one spoke of. Except for fleeting dreams that haunted him late at night when he slept, he had no memory of his parents. Faces in the dreams resembling the pictures he'd seen were accompanied by hallowed voices he'd never heard.

As he pulled onto the bypass around Rapps Barren, he spied the new library perched on a hill (new to him, at least; it hadn't been there when he last visited), the turnoff to his Papaw's farm, and even the street leading to Papa's and Nana's house. Overhead, a roll of thunder but no accompanying lightning, like a growl from a dog he'd yet to see, warning him not to trespass.

His dad's father—who answered to the affectionate name, Papa, but others called Glen Dillon—a once strong and stout man with broad shoulders, now shuffled, weakened by age, his heart ready to abandon him at literally any moment. His mother's father—Papaw, a stoic farmer with implacable beliefs, known county-wide as Elden Oscar—had been bedridden for too long by dementia, and didn't even know who he was anymore, much less what he believed.

So, informing no one, other than leaving a hasty voicemail on his girlfriend's cell and asking his dean to get an adjunct to cover his classes, Court packed up a night bag and set out at a time when most of the world was asleep.

With the gray, dreary air of the town, he could not shake the anxiety that smothered him so abruptly, and he gripped the steering wheel with both hands to keep them from shaking, his chest tightening. Rather than turning toward either home, he steered onto what he saw as a random county road to gather his thoughts. The morning fog rose low among the thick run of trees on either side of the road; shadows from the overcast sky pooled onto the asphalt and over his car. No other cars were on this desolate stretch, nor any turns or driveways in front of him, isolating him even though the highway was still in his rearview mirror.

He parked on the narrow shoulder and exited. Was it simply avoidance to seeing them again that had drawn him here? The sweat, the hindrance of breath by the weight pressing down on him, brought on by returning to this town. Or was he guided? Was it one of the nightmares: the lost loves, the time when he was little and ran into the forest? The smell of pine and something under it—something sweet—surrounded him. Calmed him. Tranquility existed in the soundlessness under the hoarfrost. The cold. No birds, no scuffling of rodent feet, no insects. He couldn't even hear what morning traffic did skirt the bypass.

Or the guilt? He'd stayed away so long, so afraid to see them age. Yes, this might be nerves, a manifestation of anxiety… but as he was creeping up on forty, the pressure in his chest could also be his heart. Stress and anxiety, the two real culprits behind modern American deaths. If either felled him now, what might he have to show for it? A girlfriend with whom he'd been fighting? Dying grandparents, the last remnants of a bloodline?

Only a few days, Dean Garson. To say goodbye.

Something scuttled in the underbrush across the street. Drew his attention. Without thinking, he crossed towards it, hopped over the ditch, shuffled through the frost-tipped Ozark underbrush, and crunched over dead leaves for another dozen or so steps before the next clearing, bramble thorns nicking his forearms. His anxiety lessened. Good, though he couldn't pinpoint why, or even what he was doing. He had to get to the Dillons' house. He had to…press further. Even when he saw the falling-down building and the surrounding graves, this false peace persisted. It was false. He knew this. He knew he should be wary of the place, that his anxiety should be ratcheting up, but it wasn't. Though he'd never been hypnotized, he'd later think this was what it felt like.

A smell of rotting leaves and mold hung in the air. The dilapidated edifice, once whitewashed, now stood faded and gray, the exposed wood crumpled in places; the steeple—fallen in—was surrounded by crumbling stones and sunken earth. Blackened windows revealed little of the inside, even where the panes were cracked or missing: a taunt to enter for anyone curious about the secrets it housed. Court was curious, but he knew he had places to be and metaphorical miles to go. "Before I sleep," he muttered under his breath.

A noise: something scurried beyond the doors. "It's an old church," he said, these words spoken louder, the sound of his voice shocking the stillness that had settled in around him.

A rustling of leaves drew his attention to the right where several old, lichen-covered stones had been threatening to topple over for the past quarter century. He walked to one of the stones and knelt, the fingers of his left hand tracing over the marker's lettering that was too weathered to read. A creak from behind. One of the double doors opened a little wider. A squatter, maybe?

The cross that dangled askew over the door gave him pause. If it fell, it was heavy enough to probably knock him unconscious or worse, brain him, and no help would come because it looked like no one had visited this place in years. Tentatively, he climbed the ruins of the front steps and pulled the door open, grating on its rusted hinges. Still the shadows yielded nothing of the interior; there wasn't near enough light yet outside to pierce the darkness. There came a slight breeze and on it the hint of things festering, that same sweet, sickly smell intensifying when he took another step in. The creak of the floorboard gave away his new position and, in the darkness, something stirred.

At once the anxiety and fear returned. The hypnosis, if such a thing had transfixed him, lay broken like a mirror, and he turned, bolted down the steps, swinging the door shut as he ran. Obsessed with flight, he missed the monument in his path, barking his shin on its rough stone, and fell to the ground. Searing pain shot up through his knee, reaching through his thigh to his groin, tears in his eyes. He winced them shut in a futile attempt to block out the pain, 'til another noise—the rusted scream of hinges—forced them open. From where he sprawled, his head now pillowed by a nameplate, he craned his neck to see that both doors stood wide open, revealing the blackness inside. Hadn't he pulled the single door shut behind him?

And now both gaped open.

Darkness beyond.

Inviting him. His chest rose in a hitch, as a thought landed on him. Cold and heavy, this single idea—that he was truly in danger—choked him and paralyzed him all at once.

The prickly weed crawling along the ground clawed at his forearms but did not register; he wouldn't feel safe until he'd reached his car and locked the doors and started the engine. Despite such a promise of security, however, the stone plaque was cool to his cheek, so he closed his eyes once more and breathed to regain control. He groped for his leg, sure he'd feel blood coating his shin but found nothing but tenderness and the start of a healthy bruise.

He rose and took a breath, and thoughts of his grandparents and of Dani and of their friends crossed behind his lids and it felt like it lasted forever, though it could only have been a minute. Their faces were frozen in various states of laughter, and they were smiling, and healthy, and he thought of what the world could be. All four grandparents stood at his wedding and at the birth of his children; names of his would-be children flitted across his tongue, and the stories he'd tell them at night to put them to sleep flashed like pictures from a book.

And then claws. Claws wrapped around his chest, digging through the fabric of his shirt and into his torso. Raked across his face and muffled his screams. Clutched at his gut and pulled his feet out from under him. Claws dragged him backwards in the dirt—there must have been a legion of hungry hands—and though he scrambled, trying to find purchase as he was pulled up the steps, gripping the corner of one of them with his left hand, the masonry crumbled in his fingers. Whatever had him was too strong. His chin bounced off the top stoop of the church and he howled in pain as the talons pulled him backward, the force now flipping him on his back. He bounced his skull off the threshold, and he lost consciousness as the church doors closed behind him completely.

⋘⋙

Two hours to the east, a young woman shot up out of bed, sweat-sheened, huffing. She felt the mattress beside her, but the shadows and silhouettes were of her apartment, not his, and they never stayed here. Her breathing eased, and the dream quickly faded to nothing, leaving only naked fear. "Court," she said, because all she could remember was that he was in trouble. In her dream.

On one of the largest Rapps Barren farms, Aster awoke when her husband's thrashing against the demons she'd come to know as dementia nearly knocked her out of bed. "Court," he was saying. "Don't go in there. You listen to me, y'hear. You do what your Papaw tells ya. Court."

She shushed him, stroked his thin, damp hair, put her arms around his skeletal frame. This normally calmed Elden Oscar, but today was proving more vexing. Normally she could tolerate this, had grown accustomed to it. But this morning was especially bad. Court had been on her mind also when she awoke, and while she couldn't recall the dream now, she felt sure it was an unhappy one.

Across town, Glen Dillon stood in the dimness of his kitchen, waiting for the coffee pot to finish brewing. No need to turn on the overhead. Forty years in this house, he knew its every nook and cranny. He hadn't been awakened by a dream, but by his bladder, and knew himself well enough to know he wouldn't go back to sleep either. Still, as Aster and Elden were waking and further off, and Dani Morales was desperately trying to remember the dream that had wrenched her out of sleep, Glen Dillon felt the tiniest of pinches in his chest and thought he heard his grandson cry out. He grabbed for the counter's edge, steadied himself, his eyes shutting from the pain. When it subsided, he looked around, expecting to see his wife. But the house was still and soundless and dark.

He poured a cup of coffee and found his seat in the study, and wondered what he could possibly do. What could any of them do? It was Court, now. Court they needed to help finish it. This darkness, this curse. It had come for their children so long ago, haunting this town. They were too weak to do anything but help, so it would need to be Court.

And what if he can't? The voice had been with Glen since he was a child. It was weak like a child and always reminded him of his doubts. He didn't suppose everyone had such a voice. Maybe Elden didn't. When he was young, the doubting voice did its damnedest to control him. As he got older, became an adult, he found ways to control it, use it to bounce his fears off of, so he could problem-solve. Now, it was finding strength again as his own heart was failing him, as he wrinkled and pruned with aged and bruised more and more easily and his breath left him more and more. As he paled, the little interior voice found new strength.

CHAPTER FOUR

*T*hree men plodded into a cemetery. Two carried shovels and one a pickaxe, and in the pocket of the one were the keys to the cemetery backhoe; access to the backhoe and the pickaxe differentiated him from the others, proved him their superior. Dawn had yet to arrive, but there was a graveside service that would start around ten, so they had little time to dillydally. There was the hole to dig and the chairs and the tent to set up, and since it was cloudy, the extension for the immediate family.

These men had forgettable names: Joe and Don and Clem, who carried the backhoe keys and the pickaxe. What they looked like was also inconsequential. They were white, of various ages: Joe, a boy in his twenties, Clem in his fifties, and Don near retirement.

They eased into their work by joshing each other, but this rite never lasted long. They all knew their jobs, so Clem headed to the garage where they stored the backhoe while the other two headed for the storage lockers behind the funeral home to get the hardware.

Ahead of Clem, the dawn light through the fog incarnadined the white garage door. Clem's mind was empty of rational thought this early, taking in the quiet. Wont guided him more often than not these early mornings.

"Clem!" It was the boy. His shrill, effeminate cry pulled the elder out of the mundanity of the predawn.

"Settle down and get to—!"

"Clem!" Joe sounded terrified. Something, Clem wasn't sure what, made him break into a run.

The boy and Don stood frozen on a knoll looking out over some newer plots, a freshly interred grave directly in their sight line. "Goddammit, Joe," Clem bristled. "Don, how dare you..."

His voice trailed off. Both men stared, tremulous, into the distance. Clem followed their gazes to a rise still heavy in shadow, but as the sun was rising, ever faster now, light slowly penetrated the umbral canopy over the graves. Perhaps it was an illusion.

The widow's grave: the funeral had been two days ago, and they'd filled in the hole perfectly, but now it looked... open?

A trick, he thought, it was a trick of shadow. He said as much and cussed them.

"No," Don said, a hushed tone, "Look."

Something fountained out around the tombstone. Clem, wide awake now and curious, headed towards the grave. Furtively, he pulled the flashlight from his belt even as the sounds of steps through the dewy grass behind suggested the other two had found their courage, albeit safely behind him. The light clicked on and indeed there was a problem. The hole they'd filled in after the funeral was back, and something inside was kicking up dirt. Sounds echoed out from the hole: scurrying, crunching, bedraggled slapping, and soppy smacking.

"Hello?" Clem called.

Whatever was in the hole fell silent.

"Goddamn animal," he muttered, but he didn't take another step and neither man on either side of him made a move.

The light trained on the grave; whatever had been spraying dirt out of the hole had ceased. Something began sniffing the air. Joe tugged on Clem's arm, but the supervisor pulled away and took a step back. From the upturned hillock echoed a low growl. Nothing small could make such a sound. The beam of light shivered over the gravestone, the grass, the dirt. Clem took a step back, but the growling only increased. Joe pawed at him, but Clem shook him off. He stumbled back into the two men who caught him, hoisted him to his feet, and all three broke into a run. From behind they heard more scuttling; Clem attempted to shine the light behind him, but he was already running too hard, and the light was more a disco strobe than an effective illuminator. The shed stood impossibly far away, but another twinkle of light or movement or both caught his eye, and they flocked together in a swarm, cutting across the grass, then the pavement, until they nearly ran into the young mortician unlocking the door, and all three men rushed inside with him.

Soon the cops were called, and Clem, his heart steadier, smoking a cigarette from the open door of the garage, watched as the deputies and that Black detective—Bullocks—knelt over the grave in the blue hue of dawn, a haze in the distance, as though the dew of the night had now settled into a lazy fog. They'd finished with the grave for the day's service, but before he and the boys set up the tent and chairs and lowering straps, he allowed them to take some time for breakfast. Now that breakfast was over, time was precious. He walked to the back of the shop where he'd left them.

"My cousin said it was old," Joe was saying. Don, proof age didn't necessitate wisdom or smarts, hung on Joe's every word. "Said it was falling down, and the tombstones were cracked, and you couldn't read the names or dates."

"I heard there's a cross over the door a hanging by a thread," Don added.

"What are you two dipshits talking 'bout?" Clem asked.

"The old churchyard," Don said, excited.

"My cousin saw it once," Joe exclaimed, obviously quite proud of his story. "He was out looking for his coon hound and he said…"

"Bullshit," Clem said. "Ain't no church out there in the woods what magically moves from spot to spot."

"There is," Joe responded. "He said he heard something inside, calling his name."

"Prob'ly your mama," Clem laughed. "Keeping it all in the family."

"Fuck you, Clem. He saw it."

"Did you see it?" Clem asked, turning on the younger man, backing him up to the wall. Clem, everyone knew, would allow for the joshing, but he had a temper. Now he had Joe by the collar and a finger in his face. His breath reflected back off the boy, a combination of cigarette smoke, coffee, the whiskey he'd stirred into his thermos before he left his house, and the egg sandwich he'd consumed as breakfast. The boy seemed to be holding his breath. "Well, did you?"

"No sir," Joe said finally. "He took me out there, but there weren't nothing there. Like it had already moved."

"It didn't fucking move," Clem growled. "Churches and cemeteries don't appear and disappear willy-nilly in different places."

Clem let him go by shoving his shoulder into the wall and walked away.

"There ain't never was nothing there," he said. "Your cousin was bullshitting you. Now, quit telling ghost stories and let's get to work. The family will be here in a little bit."

Not a word was said about it for the rest of the day, nor about whatever it was they saw at the grave. Sure, Clem thought about it, as they watered and trimmed the grass and checked the stones and, after the cops were done, filled in the hole, and he was sure the other two were thinking about it. But thinking about it was one thing. A body couldn't help what came into their mind. But because you thought about it didn't mean you had to talk about it. Talking's what women did, Clem thought, and it was as useless as gossiping or storytelling. Not much different than lying, if you want to know the truth.

Clem Willette had a reputation around the town. A lean man and a hard man, old enough for AARP, he didn't like the Black detective in his town, and he'd been married once and divorced with no kids, and he liked his whiskey and his solitude and his life. The boy, Joe, he tolerated, and he was ready for Don to retire so he could hire on someone worth a damn.

What he couldn't know, though, was that whatever was in the hole had caught whiff of Clem—not only the whiskey and coffee and cigarette smoke—but his *smell*, and it saw him for what he was: a caged hyena. It didn't like things caged up. It had been caged up. It knew, despite his temper, that Clem didn't matter much outside the cemetery walls. Well, in the coming days, Clem Willette *would* come to matter. A lot. He'd matter to the thing in the hole, and he'd matter a whole lot to those who were coming to try and stop the thing.

CHAPTER FIVE

The concrete bike path leading up to the campus was busy with morning pedestrian traffic, mostly students in a zombie march to their classes. Back in August, before the beginning of the semester, during the dog days when she seemed to sweat all the time, Dani had timed out her specific route with Court to put her in her seat right on time. In the colder weather, with more and more variegated leaves blanketing the ground, she made even better time, and was sure she'd make it with time to spare. As she walked, she found herself thinking about the checklists imposed upon her by her parents, fashioned from the parameters of small-town rubrics from conservative minds confined only to what they understood as success. Her parents weren't to be faulted, however. They didn't understand her.

When she told her parents about college, one afternoon after the New Year of her senior year of high school, they hadn't understood.

"Good," her father had said, nodding. "You can make a good living with some school. Nurses make good money, and you can get your RN there pretty quick."

Dani sighed and nodded, complacent—for the time being.

Her mother smiled and blinked like a kidnapping victim held against her will, trying to communicate nonverbally she needed help. "Nice boys at college, hija. You'll meet smart, successful boys."

As Dani walked along the trail adjacent to the railroad tracks, her cell rang; she saw it was her mother. Two cynically sarcastic thoughts crossed her mind then: *1) How fortuitous Mama's call comes, like clockwork every morning, but also when I was thinking of her, and 2) How proud she'd be to learn of my nice, normal relationship with Court.*

"Hey, Mama."

"Chiquita, how's the class?"

"Good, Mama. How's Papa?"

"Proud as ever! Like me. So, any nice boys?" There was a tone in her mother's voice: hopefulness. The expectation Dani would only be successful at college if she found the right mate.

"Not since yesterday, Mom," she answered. She hadn't told them about Court. What would they think of a professor ten years her senior? No: she knew. Her mother would ask if he were tenured, and her father would ask if he was married or had been married or if he had kids.

The disappointment in her mother's voice rang through the line. "Well, okay pobrecita."

So complacent.

"Mama," she said, walking with her head down, "graduate school is a lot of work. There is little time for anything else."

"You have time for your rock band," her mother said.

Dani sighed. Thought, technically, we're ska punk. "Yes, but the band pays my rent and the food on my table." A little white lie, as her stipend helped, as did a grant, and most of her meals anymore were spent with Court and furnished by his salary.

"Well." Dani cringed because she knew her mother's 'well.' She knew 'well' always preceded Mama's narrow view on life. "When you have a husband and children and a house to take care of, you won't have time for guitar and bands. You'll have to grow up."

"Mama," Dani said. It'd been years of this, and she was too tired to hide the exasperation from her mother. "Things don't work like that anymore."

"Oh, hija. You don't know. You'll see, when you grow up, this is the way the world is. The husband will earn the living and you will take care of the home and his children. I did this with you and your brothers, as my mother did, and you will too. You'll see."

Dani pulled the phone away in disgust. How many times had she tried to tell her mother a woman's place in the world had grown beyond the house? But her mother wore her stubbornness proudly and thought obstinance was a virtue.

An Asian girl in pink jaunted toward her, the backpack slung over one shoulder. Ahead of her, the bike trail shot up the hill toward the sky at a steep incline. Obscured by the trees on her left, the sun steadily climbed to its autumnal apex, but the air was cool, and even carrying her guitar in its hard case, Dani found the trek easy. Still, she said, "Ooh, Mama, I'm heading up the sidewalk to Kimpel. We talk tomorrow? Love you."

And hung up.

"Girl, whattup? You guys were bitchin' last night."

Dani tucked her phone into her jeans, switched the guitar to her other hand, and wrapped her free hand around her friend's neck.

"Glad you could make it out."

"Shit, wouldn't miss it," Jada said. "Whole sorority was out. You didn't stay long after your set, though." Jada squinted, eyeing her friend suspiciously.

"Me and Court wanted some alone time," Dani said. It's how it had started, anyway. She didn't feel up to telling Jada anymore.

"I bet," Jada said. "Already calling you, is he? Did you leave him in one piece? He has to teach today, doesn't he?"

"No," Dani said with a huff. They were halfway up the hill, and the sun was peeking through the branches of the trees. "My mother."

They were alerted to the sound of the oncoming train by the clickety-clack of the wheels on the tracks, and Dani braced herself for the blaring horn, timed as Jada opened her mouth to say something, then waited through the Doppler effect until they were left with the wheels whisper-clicking over the track again, the whole procession slinking off into the distance.

"You should tell her about Court," Jada said. "You guys have been together long enough. It might appease her."

Dani stopped. She'd given this a lot of thought, and hoped her logic made sense. "If I tell her about Court, she and Daddy will want to meet him, and then she'll ratchet up the pressure. She'll want me to drop out of graduate school, forget my music, get married, and get pregnant."

Jada nodded. "I get not wanting to forgo your education or your music, but the other stuff, you said you want. Right?"

"This isn't about Court," Dani said, and with a shrug turned to finish the hike up the hill. "Yes, I want kids and a family and life with him. But I want my music also. I like playing. I like teaching guitar. This is about my mother. She thinks these things are mutually exclusive."

"Your mother is old school," Jada said. "Like mine. And to make matters worse, they weren't raised in modern American culture, so they think things are like when they were young in the old country."

Dani hooked an eyebrow, a corner of her mouth. "Countries, plural." Jada looked at her, wrinkling her brow in confusion. "You do realize our moms are from different old countries?"

This got them giggling, but Jada was the first to circle back. "Point is, they don't get it. They probably weren't allowed to have dreams. You want to travel. Your mother probably never got to have such dreams."

"I want to live," Dani said. "I want my life. I want my music. My mother wants to live my life for me like some kind of ghoul."

"Mine too," Jada said. They had walked down Arkansas Avenue toward Dickson, and Jada had taken a step toward Old Main, where her first class was, when she turned and said,

"Ooh, do you think Court would look over a paper for me? It's due this Sunday."

Dani stopped and shook her head. "There's a writing center on campus. He's a professor, not a proofreader."

To this, Jada looked heartbroken but brightened quickly and waved to her friend. "I'll ask him later," Jada said and walked off.

Dani forced a smile and waved, but couldn't fight the tinge of fear, like a burning in the back of the throat. She'd gone home after she and Court had made up, electing not to stay, knowing what a fragile state he'd been in, but perhaps, she thought, checking her voicemail again and again seeing nothing, this was the wrong move. Perhaps she should have stayed with him. Maybe she wouldn't feel this fear now if she had. Under the morning shadow of the west-facing building, she contemplated firing off a text, then decided against it. If he was still mad, bothering him wouldn't solve anything. She'd let him cool; he would reach out to her when he was ready.

CHAPTER SIX

Detective Albert Bullocks exited his patrol car to find the climate more temperate than his hometown of Chicago, but it was still cold this morning. Standing among the tombstones, he watched his breath plume. The leaves popped this morning as a stiff northerly wind greeted him. Four deputies were already hunkered around the grave, and more were sure to come, as when anything of note happened in this town, they swarmed like bees. Two of them had the strained faces of third shift and the other two yawned reflexively.

"Get coffee yet," one was saying as Bullocks approached.

"Bernice's'll be open in another twenty," said another.

"I thought it was supposed to be six feet deep," said a third.

"Erroneous," Bullocks grumbled, shouldering past them. "Most states don't have burial requirements." He knelt at the grave's edge. What was left of the corpse lay in repose barely two feet below the surface. The open coffin lid could be seen well above the edge of the hole.

With the tombstone, he was more interested in the dates than the name. It was a new internment, as had been most of the others. *Still meat on the bones.* The thought forced a shiver. His knee cooled at the stain of the freshly turned earth, bracing him so he could dip his head to see better into the hole, into the open coffin. The smell hit him, sweet and putrid, hanging in the nostrils, scratching at the back of his throat with the old dust of withered souls.

The face was gray and sunken, the cheeks drawn. The eyes had been opened and there appeared to be signs of mastication around the soft tissues. The eyelids were nearly gone, as were the eyes. Whatever it was had spit the eye caps out onto the blouse, the white of the caps standing out against the cloth, a mildewy discolored yellow. The ears and loose flesh of the neck had been removed. The mouth stood open, the lips gone. He could see the ragged wound where the tongue had been removed, and Bullocks was sure it hadn't been by the mortician. The woman's face might have been symmetrical if not for the chunk taken out of the lower left mandibular. Another bite had torn through the satiny cloth on the left shoulder and had ripped the flesh from the trapezius.

Behind the pillow, the fabric was shredded. Torn and ragged strips flitted as though in a draft, intermingling with the corpse's remaining strands of hair.

Bullocks glanced up at the four deputies looking down on him expectantly, like puppies ready for a treat.

"Wild animal?" one said.

Bullocks returned his gaze to the corpse, away from their suffocating eyes. He offered a shrug as a response, like it was worth anything. The gesture was weak in retrospect; he should have had a firmer answer. They needed guidance and control. This was what he was brought in for: his experience and his ability to take charge.

"This is what, twenty?" Bullocks asked.

The sheriff's voice announced his arrival, his head tan and bald, separating the deputies like he was Moses at the Red Sea. "Twenty-three."

Bullocks sighed and looked back down at the corpse, as alien as human.

Of course, he knew the exact count of disturbed grades. Three had been found before he arrived in town. He'd followed the sheriff and the deputies to each of the area cemeteries for all of the others. Always they were dug into, and always the earth had been turned to reveal its cool, clay underbelly. And always, behind the head of the casket, the earth had been dug into a hole stretching back into complete darkness.

He reached past the coffin into the hole and felt a draft tickle the hairs on the back of his hand. Leaning in, his nose over the gnawed-on nose of the interred, he glimpsed through the shadows' deep recesses suggesting this was less a hole, but a passage that stretched long and deep into the earth and wound itself to God only knew where.

The tunnel was large, almost the width of the coffin, and he thought wildly that something had dug down to the coffin, feasted on this corpse, then tunneled away. Impossible. It was more likely…but as he connected the dots, nothing else made sense. Perhaps someone dug up the grave. "Hey!" he called up. "See if you can see anything hinky about the piles of dirt, or anything around the edges. Claw marks or shovel marks."

But what then, what bit into the flesh, for he could see the teeth marks? Maybe a wild animal jumped down in the hole after the digger left—*Why did they dig the hole in the first place?* —but something gnawed at him, suggesting human teeth. "I need a mold casting of the bite marks on the shoulder!" he said. What was he missing? He was twenty-three disturbed graves in, so obviously he was missing something.

Whatever it was had escaped through the hole, burrowing its way out. Why didn't it climb out of the hole it made? Why did it go out through the tunnel? He bent down and closed the top part of the lid and leaned further to inspect the hole. His fingers dipped into the loose mound of dirt piled under the crevice between the orifice and the casket. The deep recess tunneled back into the darkness, an artificial construction. The detective's mind worked furiously: *What if it had tunneled in, and as it worked, it needed more room, so, it had to open the lid, but then the dirt would fall in, so it had to push the dirt up and out of the hole.*

"Sheriff," he said. "Don't bother with the piles up there."

"Why?"

"Because whatever it was didn't dig in from the top. It clawed its way in and out."

From behind, snickering, muffled voices. He stood and dusted off his pants, thinking about all the white faces behind him, about his spent opportunities in Chicago and Northwest Arkansas. Was this his last chance? Bullocks wasn't sure, but he didn't have many left.

"You sure?" the sheriff asked.

Bullocks nodded. In the distance, he saw the three groundskeepers watching them. There were a lot of people like Clem Willette in the area, but Bullocks still wanted to fit in, to make it here. He had to prove to himself he could make it somewhere.

From the entrance to the main road, an unmarked beat-up pickup meandered along the narrow pavement path winding through the cemetery, eventually stopping as close as it could to the gaggle of cops and the open grave. Despite the collected dirt on the windshield, Bullocks could make out the occupants. The bearded driver, youngish, heavyset, and beside him in the cab, the withered old man

Bullocks knew as his own neighbor. Glen Dillon had arrived to witness the latest scene.

⊙⊰⊱⊙

Glen Dillon, dressed as though he'd been awake for hours, looked up to the gray sky as he climbed out of the pickup's cab, unable to recall exactly the last sunny day. As his driver walked around the hood of the truck, Glen joined him, keeping a watchful eye on the grave, up the gentle slope of the knoll, open and surrounded by cops and police tape. Bullocks was already trudging down across the grass.

He reached out a hand and said, "TJ," as TJ, Glen's driver, looked at the fingers then the palm then shook his hand. Glen offered his hand readily to the detective, who shook his head even as he shook Glen's hand. "Glen," Bullocks said, resonating disappointment. "You need to quit coming out to these."

To answer, Glen coughed. His head swirled and instinctively he grabbed for the hood, still warm. Both TJ and the detective rushed to his side, but he shook them off. Every breath he took was damp and cool, not optimal for an octogenarian with heart issues. Perhaps the detective was right.

"It's another one," Glen said. "How many now, detective?"

"You shouldn't bring him out here," Bullocks said to TJ.

"He wants to come," the bearded man said with a shrug, and spit chew.

"He paying you?"

"I ain't paying him," Glen interrupted. "I saw this boy grow up. I took him and Court fishing I don't know how many times."

"How is your grandson?" Bullocks asked.

Glen looked away, a bitter curl to his lip. "Last we talked, okay."

"What's going on, detective?" TJ asked.

"I can't say," Bullocks said.

Glen said, "Can't or won't?"

"What's your interest in this?" Bullocks asked. "You were friends with the old man dressed in his Marine dress blues we found a few weeks ago, weren't you? You and the Oscars?"

Glen nodded.

"And you and the Oscars are related by marriage?"

"You asked this back when you found him. You know we are."

"Has your grandson been to town recently? Would you tell me?"

Glen's face reddened. "Now you listen. Court ain't got a damn thing to do with this."

"But you do, right? You and Lena and Elden and Aster Oscar. It was your friend we found mauled, and here you are, sniffing around every time another grave is desecrated."

Glen laughed, looked at TJ, then laughed again. "You think I had something to do with this? Look at me, detective." There was a time, Glen knew, when he was young and strong, he'd had the back and shoulders to dig up a grave, but this observation by the detective illustrated only the bulk of his years were behind him. The next cemetery plot he interacted with would be the one they lowered his casket into.

Bullocks shook his head. "No, but if you know something—some kids doing this, you'll call me."

Glen nodded reluctantly. "Tell me something, detective. Is it like the others? Has something been eating on the corpse?"

Bullocks looked from the old man to TJ then back again. Glen knew the cop could not divulge much at a crime scene, and truth be told, Glen did not need an answer. He already knew it. Still, Bullocks nodded. "Yeah."

Glen turned back to the cab, placing a hand on the side mirror for support. TJ had been present for a number of these interactions, and Glen had been evasive in his answers, but he was not sure he'd be able to keep up much longer. As they returned to the cab and were pulling away, TJ broached the subject yet again.

"Every time. Something eating on the bodies in the grave, and you tell me not to talk about it and I don't even know what I'd say or who I'd say it to. But you know what's going on, Mr. Dillon, and that Black detective knows you know."

"I don't know," Glen said, coughing again, looking out the window as the town rushed by. "I got an idea, a crazy one, but I don't know for certain."

"You know enough," TJ said.

Though the morning was stretching on the sun would not break through the clouds. It hadn't in how long and today would be no different. They were under a spell, Glen thought. The town was cursed, and part of the curse was the sunlight had been stripped away.

"I know I need to get Court back here," Glen said.

Nothing from the other side of the cab. The radio hadn't been turned on, so only the hum of the engine answered him.

"What?" Glen said finally.

"I know I grew up with him, and I know he means well and it's his life, but it ain't right, him not coming around. I don't mind driving you here and yonder, Mr. Dillon, and I always liked you and Mrs. Dillon, and the Oscars too, but it ain't right. He ought to be here, Mr. Dillon. He ought to be here taking care of his family. If I knew how to reach him, I've half a mind to tell him so."

A part of Glen knew TJ was right, but he also supported Court and his life in Fayetteville, teaching, spending time with his girl, Daniela. She was good for Court, and besides, Glen was sure his grandson would come when he was needed most. Court wouldn't let them down.

They pulled into the circular drive of Glen's house and TJ shifted the truck to park so it wouldn't idle too hard for Glen as he climbed out the cab. He thanked TJ and began across the yard, avoiding the flat river rocks spaced across the lawn as stepping stones, seeming more like an accident waiting to happen. His house shoes sank into the dewy grass and softened dirt, his eyes cast down as he watched his pale, vein-scarred feet shuffle. When he heard the front door open and heard the truck roll away across the gravel, he looked up and saw Lena standing in the doorway, still in her robe, holding a cup of coffee. The look on her face was one he knew of disappointment and of powerlessness to keep him from doing something foolhardy.

He braced himself for an ass-chewing, but too many years had passed, and he knew she knew it was futile to castigate him now. Not like he'd start listening anyway.

"You mad?" he said with a shrug.

She motioned for him. "Get in here before you catch your death."

He did as he was instructed, telling her about the cemetery and what he and TJ had found, as she ushered him to the den. He paused at the corner, gripping the wall, doubling over. The coughs came forceful and tasted like copper, but he saw no blood. Still, his nose was inflamed, and he was reminded in this moment how every inch of his body ached. The veins and arteries felt stretched, and his joints felt rusted. His muscles ached.

"Go on," she said, guiding him around the corner when he settled to his leather recliner, removing his house shoes and getting him his afghan. "Hang on," she said. "I'll bring you some coffee," when he was but a sentence back into the tale. As she walked away, Glen thought about the open grave. It had been fresh, the ground still soft.

"And ol' TJ brought me back here. Like every other time," he finished.

"You can't be out in this weather," she said finally. "I'm not ready to lose you."

The coffee warmed his throat and loosened whatever phlegm caught back there he had been hacking on all morning. "You ain't gonna lose me yet," he said.

"Well, we'll get Court here," she said. "But I'm afraid if the girl comes."

Glen nodded. "He'll probably want to bring her."

"It isn't safe," she said. "Look what happened to the others."

"I know," Glen said. He had nothing to add. In order for Court to understand, in order for him to believe, he'd have to be here, to see for himself. If they tried to warn him beforehand, he might not listen. He'd think they were nuts, in fact.

"When you get back, we should talk about it. When do you and Aster need to be there?"

"About an hour," she answered. "Won't take long. You sure you're okay with this." It wasn't a question.

He nodded but wouldn't look at her. "Got to be done. Better now than after I go. You won't feel like making such decisions then, I imagine. I know I wouldn't if it were me."

"No," she said, and bent and kissed him. "No, I wouldn't." And then she was back in the bathroom, getting ready.

CHAPTER SEVEN

*A*ster Oscar read from a book of poems their grandson had published, a poem Elden had been proud to see on the printed page.

> In age your wisdom comes strong like the winds
> Now blowing this December morn', and you
> Readily call on what you know, for friends
> And your kids, fools in youth to knowledge true.
>
> You've helped us all more than you know, been there
> When we're down or hurt, no need to ask for
> Grandpa knows, and you come not asking fair
> Repayment for deeds…just love abound more.
>
> The life you've lived allows you more than we
> Can yet attain, and you share your wealth with
> Us as much as you can, a legacy
> Richer than ever bestowed—heartfelt myth.

I say myth for in years to pass, no one
Will believe what you gave could be so done.

○○○

Aster set the book—*Sonnets and Thoughts of Family*, by Court Dillon—down by the bedside and picked up a cookie from the plate under the dim bulb of the bedside lamp. The cookie was dry and crumbled in her lips and on her tongue, and bits and pieces fell to the gray carpet. Oatmeal raisin: the best parts excluding the batter dissolved in her gullet as the crumbs ground into the carpet fibers beneath the soles of her orthopedic slippers.

Court's words seemed to always soothe him, but even as she held the cookie's uneaten twin to Elden's lips, he began his fits. What happened at sundown mirrored only the dawn, and this morning was particularly rough. He tossed and turned and his eyes flitted. Under breath, he mumbled in a language only he understood, the few words she could make out were spoken with new inflection and order. Aster put the cookie back on the plate and leaned in close.

"There is goodness here," she said. "I don't know where you're lost, but there is good here. You are safe here." But his eyes, listless, continued to search and seemed vacant, devoid of him, of his soul.

His hand shot up like a flare and snatched her by her wrist, his eyes wild and unfocused, forcing his head to roll on the pillow as he searched for something to settle on. While she wanted to scream in pain, it was only the agony on his own face keeping her in check as she snatched her arm away.

"I'm right here," she said. This settled him some, and she sat back in her bedside chair and when he settled back down, she reached for his nearest hand and caressed it. "We got to go to the doctor today, Elden. Dearest. Am I doing right by you?" This bothered her. The doctor had given her some literature on dementia, but she hadn't read it, too afraid of what it would say. This summed up her whole life: afraid of being wrong. There was a time when she could talk to him about her fears, and Elden might say that she's being silly or something, but he'd support her and help her through it, and comment about how she was so disciplined and inspiring. It's who he was. Her rock. He'd always made sure they were secure and supported, easing her worry. Worked his butt off to provide for her, in fact, but in the end, today as she looked after him, finances or her own security were not a worry for her.

"What, dear?" she asked. He'd been mumbling again.

This time his words were clear. "It's eating the dead."

CHAPTER EIGHT

The young mortician pulled the hazmat suit over his dress shirt and trousers, adorned himself with his gloves, face shield, and goggles, then walked through the door. The embalming room was cold, sterile, and filled with steel; the floor tile sloped gently to a drain. Two bodies lay on separate steel slabs.

He preferred the suture method to keep their mouths closed. The gray hand of one had been frozen up as if petting a dog or a child's head, so he moved it down across the torso, then adjusted its other hand, and then repeated the process with the other body, crossing the hands over the chest.

"Suture method," he said. "Tendons are weak. The mandible is much stronger. The cartilage in the nose will not degrade as fast as the flesh, the muscle." The needle might be a wasp's stinger if the wasp were three feet long.

"Your hands in prayer. How nice, they'll say." He wouldn't normally work on two bodies at once, and if both were being prepared for a wake and a service, then he definitely wouldn't.

"So why you'n not her?" as if he were repeating a question from the corpse, his southern dialect thick. "Well, she's no skin slip. No jaundice. But more 'portantly, she's no family. No one'll miss her when we drop 'er in the ground. You, however, you'll be missed. So, we must preserve you. We must correct the imperfections for as long as they'll last, at least up 'til the viewing. The viewing is the only thing that matters now. The viewing is what the family and friends will take from this process."

He'd heard once hearing was the last to go. Wondered how long it lasted. Reports on brain activity after death, both medical and metaphysical, indicated the person was in there, still, for quite a bit of time after. Even after he took the large-bore needle to the femoral artery and sucked out the blood, a profession-wide measure to ensure death was final. Couldn't have them wake up on the embalming table, after all. So, he talked to them. All of them. Even the ones he didn't prep. They were all relegated to this last lot on this earth as provender.

"Now, you're old and have some slip, and there's a bit of yellowin' about the jowl, so we must account for such in the mix. It's all chemistry, from here on out. Your body rots and smells and infects, but it mustn't infect the soul. For the soul must leave, to fly, and the body and soul are to remain separate. But I have never seen a soul. I have never detected a difference in the weight of a body. I've interred the nearly deceased and the long since gone, and all are the same sickly, lifeless, pallor as you.

"So, let's prep the chemicals that'll scour through your veins, and infect your muscles, and purple your flesh. The very chemicals we'll then vault the world against, because the dead outnumber the living, and woe betide anything which encumbers nature…"

He turned to the table next, where all the chemicals were stored separately, muttering to himself various calculations, naming chemicals.

What breaks up clots, seals the bonds, preserves the tissues, neutralizes the pH? How much cavity fluids? To dye or not to dye is the question. Concentration: one gallon of mix to three gallons of water.

The embalming machine. Like some steampunk stainless steel invention, gauges and knobs and tubes every which way. "Steampunk?" He stopped, pondering. "Or Victorian Gothic contraption, still in use? Something out of Dr. Frankenstein's laboratory." The word *laboratory*, pronounced in as close to British proper as he could muster, sounded funny from his lips, used to pursing out the South Arkansas dialect.

Another needle injected into the femoral artery.

He cut into the flesh of the neck to raise the subclavian vessels, so he could get into the jugular vein and the carotid artery. Cleaned the connective tissue. Pulled the clots out to open the drainage.

"When we cleanse, does the heart still pump the fluid? Alive? Maybe I should go into the femoral. Maybe the radial artery."

The trocar into the lungs. Happy with the thoracic area? Now into the lower abdomen.

Aspirating finished?

Trocar button. Now close the incisions. S Kurt needle.

The procedure took about an hour. The police were there, investigating a break-in, and he had an appointment coming up, but he had time for this one procedure. Luckily, he didn't need to do two.

The process finished, he sluiced the runoff down the drain with a hose, disrobed the hazmat suit, and was washing his hands when the door opened.

"The Black detective wants to talk to you," one of his older coworkers said, and, not waiting for an answer, allowed the door to close to keep the chemical smell contained.

The young mortician from South Arkansas waited to be sure the door was closed, then walked over to the untouched body. She was young. Eyes open. Did she see? He often wondered if the other senses lingered, not just the hearing. He positioned his face in front of hers, hovering over her, bracing himself with one glove on the table and the other on her thigh, high up and to the inside. Too intimate a touch for strangers, but they were only strangers in life. In death, he knew everyone intimately.

Her face had been mangled in the wreck; a deep gash split open her right cheek and had torn the jaw from its hinge. The blood had long since been cleaned away. Her dark hair, wet from the cleaning they'd administered upon her arrival, was thick and curled in life, as her ID picture showed, but now the deep cleft of her scalp could not be concealed. He'd already sutured some to keep the brains from spilling out. He thought of *it*. It liked the soft meats, liked the brains.

"Suppose it's my fault," he said. "It weren't supposed to come in here, but it did anyway. I hadn't been feeding it proper. It don't like the taste of you all when I embalm you." He pointed to the other table. "Like her over there? Might get some muscle. Thigh. Latissimus. Pectoral. But the soft meats: your brain, your heart, your liver, all ruined by the process."

He returned his hand to her thigh, caressed it. "But is it? My fault? I can't help it people dying all have loved ones who want to see them one more time. I got a job to do, after all."

He straightened and looked down on her, his mouth turned down. "I don't envy you. Not how you died, and what you're about to experience. Even though you ain't got no one to mourn you, I'll be here doing it, and maybe as the last bits of you waste away in its stomach, maybe some solace will come knowing you are finally completing the circle of life."

A second of silence, all he could afford, and then he was peeling off the PPE and looping his tie back on in a half Windsor, brushing the sleeves of his suit coat and turning out the light to the embalming room. Through the shadows, he took one last look back. At first what he saw startled him, until he reminded himself that bodies were capable of a number of functions after death. Settling gas offered up strange sounds, and muscle spasms caused all manner of movement, from blinking to limb motility. Liquids shifted and settled. So, a tear rolling out of the left eye of the young car accident victim was nothing more than another example of this. Certainly not remnants of a soul. He'd never seen no soul. Still, it saddened him enough he took another minute to compose himself before rejoining the living.

CHAPTER NINE

Lena's white Toyota Avalon pulled slowly off the state highway and turned down the slope through the open wrought-iron gate to the expansive yard with single-lane paths twisting between the headstones, guided to a stop right in front of the red brick and white wood-trimmed building with plantation style columns holding up the flat roof over the brick-lined porch. The cemetery stood more ominous with the trees bared for autumn, the plots of grass dry and dun. A cool wind threatened to topple each woman as she exited the car, Lena from behind the wheel and Aster from the passenger's side. Lena gazed to the distance, where a group of men labored in and around a collection of open graves; a couple of the stones had fallen over, but all the graves were opened.

The two women linked arms and walked into the building. Inside, they removed their outer garments, the head scarfs and gloves and their overcoats. Both had lived nearly the same years, and a lot of years between them. Lena was tall and thin, an energetic nurse who wore her age well. Most who looked at her told her they thought she was twenty years younger. Aster stood shorter and squatter, and the years had been less kind, Lena thought, cruelly but truthfully. Aster's cheeks were sunken, thanks to years of dentures, her pallor lighter due to heart issues, and her hair much grayer. If Lena looked twenty years younger, then Aster added ten years to their median age. Still, both women were in better condition than their husbands.

The young mortician entered. Barely old enough to shave. He bowed like Court used to when he was ten and was taking karate, (*Not karate, Nana: Shotokan*) and folded his hands in front of them without saying a word, but his smile spoke volumes. It attempted to be consolatory, but it came across as ghoulish. Like he had the opportunity to use flexible state laws and lax funereal regulations to fleece these two grieving widows-to-be. "I 'pologize. I was just comin' outta the prep room. Gotta meet with the detective soon, but y'all a welcome distraction from that grisly business."

He ushered them into a side room and sat with them at a large oak table. Around them on the walls were framed portraits of eagles and cardinals and nature scenes. Lena took the time to look at each of the wall décor while letting this boy in a suit with his molasses-thick South Arkansas accent talk at her.

"We have caskets 'n vaults 'n everything ya need. Y'uns both made the right choice, coming in now. It'll be so much easier to do this now than… How are they?"

Lena and Aster exchanged a glance, and Aster looked down at her phone. Lena knew how apprehensive she had been to leave Elden, even though TJ's wife Britta had sat with him plenty of times before. "If something happened to him while I was gone," she'd told Lena many times, "I couldn't live with myself."

"There will be insurance," Lena said, ignoring the question.

Aster nodded. "Yes, for me too. And we have a trust."

"Everything should be covered for each of our husbands," Lena said. "They are both military veterans."

"Then let's take 'em each in turn," the young man said with a grin he thought would be reassuring. "We'n talk caskets, vaults, 'n we have the mausoleums. We offer a coach for the pall bearers and a limo for the family and a fire truck. Of course, the military will cover a lot of the expense."

Both women stared at him.

"What kind of truck?" Lena asked, confusion causing her to stiffen in her chair, her voice unnecessarily accusatory.

He smiled; his blue eyes flashed a bit. "The *fire* truck? It's where you put the *fires*."

Lena and Aster exchanged a glance.

"The fires?" Aster asked. They were both from the Natural State, but his accent was thicker than either had heard in a while. Lena and Aster began to work out the word together. He was of no help.

"Flowers?" one finally said.

"Yeah, the *fires*. Sorry, it's my Stuttgart accent getting in the way. "You can get a truck for the *fires* to take 'um up to grave site."

Lena patted Aster's hand and thought of what she'd seen upon exiting the car.

"There were some men out by some open graves."

His lips twitched a bit, and he blinked. "Oh, it's nothing. Some landscaping. But we got lots to discuss here, and some of the extras can get expensive. Are either of you interested in cremation?"

The two looked at each other and squeezed the grip on their hands and shook their heads. It was to be internment, then.

CHAPTER TEN

The mortician waved goodbye as the Avalon pulled away. He didn't envy the women and what they were going through, but he did see it as a commonality shared by anyone not desperately alone in this world. Suffering was as much a part of life as love and security.

Inside, the older coworker stood in his perpetual stance: head down, hands folded together.

"You finally ready?" the coworker asked, then turned and led the young man down the hall. "That detective ain't gonna like you blew him off." They walked into a cement room with no windows, with what was left of a body on the table, entering through the door hanging off the hinge by splinters. Down the hall, a uniformed police officer was taking pictures of the back-exterior door, a heavy metal piece dangling loose from the hinge, strips of metal like torn flesh. In the embalming room, Detective Bullocks stood staring at the corpse. The other two bodies had been removed, like some gruesome magic trick, while he'd been in speaking with the two women.

"Thank you for coming," the young mortician said. "Sorry I had to help those two ladies. I'd forgotten they'd made an appointment.

Bad situation. Both might lose their husbands at the same time. Related by marriage. My mother lost…"

"You found it like this when you arrived this morning."

"Yessir. After my groundskeepers told me 'bout the grave. Called you and then them ladies showed up." It had been three weeks since the groundskeeping crew had discovered the first desecrated grave. Since then, there'd been several, but this was the first time a corpse had been violated inside a building. The mortician knew he'd talked with it about not coming inside.

Bullocks mumbled something like, "this one's worse," but when the young man asked him to repeat, he refused. Still, the mortician had been out to the affected sites in the yard and had seen firsthand the mutilations. This one was worse.

The soft flesh of the facial area had been devoured, as had the upper shoulder areas, but the thighs and meaty parts of the arms were also nearly gone; the considerable torso, bloated from fried foods and beer—contributions to the middle-aged man's fatal heart attack—completely eviscerated with large portions of organs missing. Strips of flesh had been cored away from muscle, and the only meat left on or in the body seemed to be only the stringiest and toughest of morsels. For all this destruction, though, the mortician had noticed something else when he'd found the body upon opening: a surprising lack of blood.

"Where were you in the embalming process?" the detective asked.

"We hadn't begun," the young man said. "Only picked him up from the hospital late last night at the family's request. Was gone get started after this morning's appointment."

"So, you've done nothing whatsoever to the body."

"Yesterday was a long day, sir. I was tired. We got him here, removed his clothes, and gave him a quick once over kind a cleanin' before we locked up for the night. And yessir, before you ask, I always make sure to lock up. No way something could get through the metal door back there."

"But it did," Bullocks said, "Or it was made to look like it did."

"Now hold on! If you're accusing me or one of my employees of…"

"I don't think one of your employees could have ripped a heavy metal door from its hinge so violently." Bullocks pointed to the ceiling. "Before I go get a warrant, can we review your cameras?"

The mortician motioned to the elder one, who left the room. "It's all on the cloud," the young man said. "Won't take too long to download, but it's an off-site server with a third party, so we'll have to contact them. Don't like it, but we're owned by this conglomerate out of St. Louis, and they make all the decisions. I for one would prefer we were local. Helps with building trust and respect in the community—"

"Trust? You overcharge people for unneeded services under the pretense of the law and prey on the grief-stricken to turn a profit," Bullocks said. "You're a ghoul."

The elder returned and whispered into the younger's ear, who translated for the detective. "We're reaching out to them now. My associate here called. They a bit backlogged, but as soon as they can email us the footage, we'll download it to a thumb drive and rush it right over.

Bullocks nodded, his lips curled in disgust.

"As to your condemnation of our profession," the younger began, his voice shaking. He knew there were people who held this view of the funeral industry, but he'd never been confronted with such hostility on his own turf. The attack had caught him off guard and he'd been struggling to find the words; he felt his face wash white with fear. When the words came, he spoke up, his voice abandoning him in squeaks. "Now listen here, sir…"

Bullocks, unfazed, turned and walked out of the room. "We'll be in touch."

The uniform from the back door entered and began to snap pictures. Tired and overwhelmed by what lay ahead of him, the mortician left the crime scene and returned to his office. He trudged up the stairs as a middle-aged man might approach his career, slowly and wearily, and locked the door behind him. The office chair was plush leather, a gift to himself, and it gave itself to him readily as he settled into it. As the reality of the condition of the body sank in, as the shock of the morning wore off, he began to cry.

What kind of deal, exactly, had he made?

INTERLUDE TWO

The Tale of the Lost Little Boy in the Forest

Once upon a time, there was a little boy named Court, who was staying with his grandparents. The boy's full name, much to the chagrin of his Nana, was Courtney, which she'd never felt was a proper name for a boy, so she'd shortened it to Court when she addressed him and hoped this would catch on. Her name, for the record, wasn't actually Nana, but it's what Court had called her (or more to the point, what she wanted Court to call her as it isn't proper for a child to call their elder by their given name).

So, Court was playing with his toy dump truck on the cement patio out back while Nana stirred the homemade chicken noodle soup and Papa worked at staining the privacy fence. Court, too young to understand what Papa was doing besides "working in the yard," only thought it looked fun, running a brush over the wood after dipping it in the tray. Court could smell the food from within the house and smiled because Nana's cooking always tasted good. For lunch she'd made him a bologna and cheese sandwich with the crust cut off and lots of mayonnaise and he'd eaten it so fast and drank his chocolate milk not because he was especially hungry, but because the way Nana made it was so good.

"How much longer?" she called out.

Papa stopped and surveyed the fence row. "About ten, fifteen minutes. When we have to meet the contractor?"

"Final walk through at five. Will the kids be back to pick up Court, or should we take him?"

Papa put the brush down and walked over and knelt in front of the toddler. His rough hand ran through the boy's fine blonde hair, and he smiled, and to this Court smiled. "We can take him," Papa said. "He needs to see where his Nana and Papa are going to live." He looked at the boy with a broad smile and a deep sigh of contentment. "It's a big house shaped like an A, and it's got lots of trees and stairs and a big basement. Lots of room for you to play."

Court smiled and clapped. He was still too young to grasp the architectural amenities Papa had listed off for him, but the house was new, and so an adventure.

Papa said something about cleaning up and walked into the house, and Court resumed playing with his truck.

All in all, this had been a pretty good day. Nana had made him eggs and toast and bacon and then they'd watched Big Bird talk about letters and counting and then they played and he'd gone to the bathroom like a big boy like Mommy and Daddy wanted and then he'd played some more and then Papa came home and they all had lunch and then Court watched 321-Contact and Captain Kangaroo and Bozo, and then he came out to play again.

And then, and then, and then… Court looked down. He'd only gone to the bathroom once, a long time ago. And now…

He stood up and felt the sag of his britches, then sighed and looked around to make sure no one else had noticed. Nana was going to yell at him (why he thought this, he couldn't tell you, because Nana didn't have a record of yelling at him). His mommy and daddy would find out and they would maybe swat him, and he didn't like swats. (There was a record of swats.)

So, he peeked inside and saw Nana was busy stirring the pot on the stove. He scurried through the kitchen and looked down the hall, where he heard water splashing in the bathroom a ways away. The screen door, weighted heavy against the spring, was still easy enough to open, but when it snapped back against the wood frame, he heard Nana say his name.

And so, the race was on. His bare feet moved through the trimmed Bermuda of the backyard until he found the neighbor's yard, and though a low concrete retaining wall gave him a little trouble, Court managed into a third, then a fourth yard. From somewhere behind, Nana screamed his name, but he dared not turn around, lest she caught up to him. He didn't want no more swats.

After the fifth yard, the grass ended, and Court knelt to touch the hot pavement of the porous asphalt and said, "Ouch!"

"Court! Baby! Come back here!"

Across the street, Court saw the tree line. The street was deep, but he had to chance it. Besides, wasn't Mommy over there? A lady seemed to be dancing between the trees, and she motioned to him with a big smile on her face. Maybe it wasn't his mommy, because this lady had red hair it looked like, but she seemed nice, so he trotted across the street and climbed through the shallow ditch and up the embankment to the trees.

The woman was gone.

"Court! Glen come on! Court!"

"Hi Court," he heard, but it sounded like a young girl, and he still couldn't see her. He took a few more steps, then stopped. The birds were silent. Nothing scurried, and the trees were still, like a wind couldn't even penetrate the forest. The dirt was hot against his feet, and he smelled something. Whether it was a skunk or something dead, he wasn't sure. But the smell grew stronger whenever he heard his name whispered by the young girl.

"Nana," he said. His lips trembled, and his brow furrowed. He didn't like the smell and something in the pit of his stomach turned. Court was scared.

"Follow me, Court," came the voice. He looked to his left, and deeper into the woods where in the distance he could see some gravestones and, beyond, the hint of a building with a cross over the door.

"Church?" Court said. Then, "Nana? Nana I'm here!"

"Come see my home, Court."

And then he was snatched up, his eyes wide as his world spun in a great blur, and Court screamed, sure the girl had grabbed him, but when he looked on the face of the body holding him, he saw only his Nana, and though she did give him a swat (it didn't hurt), he hugged her neck tight and said, "Nana, you found me."

"Of course, dear. I always will."

And she carried him home.

The End

CHAPTER ELEVEN

Elden had made a success of raising cattle. He'd worked his way up through the public school system, from bus driver to assistant superintendent of maintenance and buses before retiring. His rental houses, acquired over the years, brought a steady income, and he never carried a loan, not even on the hundred-plus acres on which he raised the herd. He wrote checks to buy his pickups or Aster's Cadillacs, so haggling was never off the table for him. While Glen had made good on a white-collar life, Elden had been one of the few to reach the pinnacle of the blue-collar world, and so neither man nor their family wanted for anything.

⊙≾⊙

Home Health arrived later that morning, well after Aster had returned from the funeral home and dismissed TJ's wife Britta with a hug and several thank you's for sitting with Elden. She prepared them each a cup of coffee under an obligation of politeness and hospitality despite how tired she was and how little she cared, then she poured herself a cup of coffee and added some cream and sugar until the coffee was the right color of tan and the right amount of sweet, and glanced in the direction of the back room as she took a sip. Nearly ten, and Elden was sleeping; he never used to sleep in. She sat on the couch across from the two young men in their green scrubs, both smiling like the young mortician she and Lena had met at the funeral home. Outside, the clouds stretched across the firmament, oppressive, weighty. She felt breathless by everything weighing her down, from the choices at the funeral home to the questions these young men brought.

"I can't give him the care," she said.

"Have you thought about assisted living?" one of them asked.

"You won't get him to leave this house," she said.

From deep within the dark bowels of the hallway came a voice which could no longer cross any kind of distance: "Mamaw!"

"He was so strong," Aster said. The cup trembled in her hand, sloshing coffee all over her floral print pants. She'd have to wash them. She couldn't have them stain.

"Mamaw! I got to pee!"

As one of the young men looked at her, concerned, the other looked in the direction of the back room.

"Should we?"

Aster shook her head. "He thinks he has to pee, or he thinks he's hungry or he thinks he's not hungry. He's never hungry. That's the problem, isn't it? He never knows anymore what he wants. He can't know." She took a sip, studied their faces. Were they furrowing their brows out of sympathy? Were those looks of pity or of silent judgment? "I'm not mistreating him," she added. "I love my husband. But I can't do it on my own."

CR🙰SO

Pressure on the bladder, down in his gut. Elden looked to his left. The door to the bathroom, the sink, the tile, the light streaming in through the window. The pressure increasing, like a goddamn cat was sitting on his lap and kneading his flesh with its paws, claws barely retracted. A hint, another hint, and adjusting its haunches for maximum pressure. Ever increasing. Ever increasing.

When no one responded when Elden called again, he knew this task was all up to him. Fine. He could do it himself. His whole life he'd been doing it himself. Like now, reaching for the bedside table, the lamp, the digital clock. Rigid surfaces all, but what he needed was a brace. He rolled to his left and with his right hand finding purchase on the edge of the mattress, gripped and pushed with all his might, and slowly hoisted himself upright enough until his left hand could contribute. Soon he sat at the edge of the bed, his feet dangling off, his arms buttressing his thin, pale frame.

The bathroom was so close. Then he saw his scraggly thighs like bundled tufts of straw. If he could stand, would his legs support him? They used to be so strong. One time he'd thought they were so strong. He couldn't remember when, exactly, but he hoped now they were still strong enough.

He pushed off with his hands and found his feet, rising unsteadily, knees wobbling, his gaze focused on the tile before him. Balance returned to him after some vacillation; he took a step, and when it didn't falter, he took another, raising his hands to the side like he was traversing a high wire. Another tentative step, and he found himself a foot away from the cold tile, the room he needed to be in to relieve the seismic pressure in his gut. He took another step and then another.

The cool of the tile chilled the pads of his skeletal feet. Here he found support with the walls, the counter. Around to the left of the shower enclosure, the toilet. He smiled and prepared his boxers for the release from his overstuffed bladder, but as he adjusted his seams, his vision blurred, and he swooned, and his face numbed. A kaleidoscope of images swirled and swirled and sang to him, called like a nymph to him, and he saw Aster waiting on the porch for him with a cup of coffee in hand—he could smell the half & half and sugar—and he smelled the bacon and the buttered biscuits and the stewing gravy and the yolks of the eggs and…

His weak thighs gave out from under him, and his head smacked on the counter; he issued only a yelp.

⊗

The men were in the middle of letting her know which services were covered by her insurance when Aster perked to a sound. Distant, barely audible. When one or the other tried to speak, she shushed them and rose from her chair, turned to the kitchen. She said nothing as she walked to the back bedroom.

The bed was empty; she moved instinctively to the nearest room—the bathroom—the home health nurses right on her tail. One caught her as she stumbled and the other rushed to the bathroom. Elden lay prostrated on the tile, his eyes listless, his breath rapid. The nurse leveled him and began chest rubs. Elden's eyes had rolled back in his head. Aster saw, and her scream drowned out his words of "I'm drowning" as the other home health nurse joined his partner and snapped at Aster to call 911.

⊗

The ER doctor approached Aster and took her hand, but it wasn't until he smiled that she began to relax. The concern in his eyes as much reassured her as told her they weren't out of the woods.

"Can I see him?"

He nodded. "I must tell you, first… your husband had a seizure, but we're convinced it was due to an electrolyte imbalance. We've got him on some IV fluids and he's resting now."

She nodded to him like she understood.

"We don't know yet the extent of the damage," he said.

"What did I do?" she asked, more to herself than to the doctor.

"Mrs. Oscar, you couldn't have prevented this."

She shook her head. "No. I should have been with him. I shouldn't have taken the meeting then." She recalled then about hearing him. "Oh god," she wailed. "I should have believed him. He said he had to pee, and I told them he doesn't know what he wants."

The doctor touched her shoulder, but she didn't want to be consoled. She wept, slumping her shoulders, her eyes open only enough to see the doctor motion for a nurse, and the pretty young thing ushered her to Elden's room.

When the doctor said it was okay, Aster pushed through the privacy curtain and saw him, withered and transparent, tubes connecting him to beeping machines. The nurse helped place her into the nearby chair, and she took Elden's knobby hand and studied his pallid face. His breathing was shallow, and his agape mouth seemed to be desperate to pull into a rictus; she prayed it didn't, as she trembled.

"I'm here," she said, not knowing if he heard, like he would remember, and her tears continued to fall, silently.

CHAPTER TWELVE

Once TJ had dropped Glen off, he drove to the boat factory. He parked and entered by the front office, walked into the clean room after showering and put on the white hazmat suit, then walked into the spray yard.

The spray yard was the size of a hangar, an aluminum-sided and wood-studded area encased in plastic where the fiberglass was sprayed on the parked boats inside with little interference.

TJ walked the gang planks over the boats, watching his men work the insulation in their masks and suits. Was this the future for his kids? The eldest had already enlisted, and this made the old man proud, but the middle kid was an artist, and she was looking at colleges in Arkansas and Missouri. The last kid hadn't any aspirations. There was music, if you could call what he listened to music. When he took his ACT's, he'd done marginally well. His father's work interested him, and this bothered TJ because he didn't want to subject his boy to the fumes. Funny, he hadn't been worried about them back when Britta questioned if he ought to take on the job there back when they were graduating, but now his son might be breathing in the fiberglass, thoughts of lung problems and cancer and all sorts of horrors kept TJ awake at night.

After lunch, he returned home to the double-wide they'd placed on five acres back when they were entering their thirties and thinking they had life all figured out. The gravel drive was empty save her white Cherokee. He expected her to be either folding clothes or sweeping or vacuuming, vegging on the couch with one of her shows like Jerry Springer or Steve Wilko, or curled up in bed with one of the migraines that had plagued her since adolescence.

As it was, Britta stood in the kitchen, stirring at a pot, and so TJ knew what he'd come home to. Still, he walked up behind her after closing the door audibly in case she didn't realize he was home, and he kissed her ear.

She shrugged.

"What you pissed about?" he asked, shouldering her as he reached for a beer in the fridge.

She was chopping carrots into thin strips. Other vegetables were laid out for the sacrifice: red onions and kale and romaine and cherry tomatoes and cucumbers.

"I sat with Elden Oscar today," she said. "He spent the whole time calling for Aster."

TJ said, "Well, I drove Glen out to one of those grave robberies."

She spun on him then.

"He's sick, TJ. They're all sick. They're dying."

"So what? We should ignore them?"

She returned to her salad. "Course not. But we cain't let them consume us, either. We cain't forget about the kids."

"What kids?" he asked. The frosted glass window over the sink suggested light and greenery of the trees, but the world outside was blurred and tinted gray. "Our enlisted boy or our surly girl or our littlest who's going to end up like me?"

"They ain't all bad," she said, but she had doubled down on the salad.

"Who's the salad for?" he asked, a meat and potatoes man.

"All of us."

"What do you want?" he asked. He wasn't sure why he asked it then, but it felt right. She was distant. Was she distracted? Disinterested? He wasn't sure.

"I don't care anymore," she said, and continued cutting.

TJ stepped back into the living room and saw all the windows darken, but were the clouds outside or in his head? His world felt darker. There was a shift in power. Britta wasn't like she was before. She'd been about them all: her husband, her kids. But now, since sitting with Elden this most recent time, she was different.

"What's the matter?" he asked.

She hovered over the counter, chopping. She cut into the lettuce and tomatoes and onions and carrots and the hard-boiled eggs and didn't turn back to face him until it was all sliced and tossed together.

"It's going to eat us all until we're rotten," she said.

He knew it was true.

CHAPTER THIRTEEN

That his wife of fifty years could be content to sit beside him on the couch watching HGTV was enough for Glen Dillon to know Lena truly loved him. Early on in retirement, when he was still strong enough to get out and do things, he worried a day spent in the den watching television might bore her—though he could read her fine features like he was some expert human lie detector—but now he, with his heart issues, didn't have such worries. He would be eighty-five this year and was thankful for every day he had with her, knowing full well those days were numbered. Still, there were too many days when it felt like he'd just met her, and he desired another fifty years by her side. Perhaps then it might be enough, the 'it' as indefinable as 'time' or 'love.' Or perhaps he'd crave another fifty… and then he'd worry about getting greedy and devaluing the meaning of the life he had.

He lifted his Bible off the side table and began to read about Jesus and the wild man who broke his chains and ran through the graveyard. Earlier this morning he'd finished a novel, and he wanted to reread his grandson's latest book of poems. How was Court doing, he wondered not for the first time and not for the last, and closed his Bible and spoke with a raspy near whisper, "How were the Oscars?"

Such a loaded question. He knew Elden wasn't doing well, but the look on Lena's face told him how bad his old friend was. Bad enough for hospice yet, he wasn't sure, but bad. His gaze fell to his faded blue robe, the color of the veins that scarred the back of his pale hand. "Don't spare me details 'cause you don't think my heart'll take it." He knew she wouldn't do no such thing.

"Aster and I talked. We'll get Court back here."

"We'll have to tell him all of it, I suppose."

"I can do it," she said. "Aster and I can."

"You weren't there at the churchyard. Elden and I were…"

"We were there when it came calling for his mother. You don't get to own the nightmares." On TV a young couple, very attractive, were ripping up a bathroom floor. It all looked messy and arduous. When they'd remodeled their bathroom fifteen years earlier, he'd hired a contractor.

"I'm sorry," he said. A smile crept to the corner of his mouth. "You mad at me?" He hoped she wasn't, even as she took his clammy hand and noted his translucent skin and the flush of his cheeks.

"I'm going to the kitchen. You want something to drink?"

He thought about it, shook his head, and stood. "I'll come with you," he said. It might feel good to get up and move around. God knows he needed the exercise. But in the effort of standing, sweat poured out of him and his face flushed even hotter.

In fact, he was burning up, could feel it before she inserted the thermometer under his tongue. He snatched at the quilt that overlaid the back of his chair and covered his lap and legs and pulled tight up to his shoulders. Sweat continued to drench his collar and forehead.

Lena gave him a smile. She still looked perfect and young and…

"You're shaking."

"I'm cold." He cinched the covers to his chin.

"Over one hundred," she said.

He looked at her, his breaths coming in great emphatic spurts.

"Your chest hurt?"

Glen coughed, a jaundiced and phlegmy blob spewed onto the lapel of his robe. His eyes vacant; his palpitations shallow. He threw an apologetic look her way, blue eyes once shining now dull. But he was worn down.

She took his hand, for him a moment of intimacy, but he knew for her this was an opportunity at clinical evaluation. With but a glance she saw his blue nail beds and could not dam the sigh or the look on her countenance. He coughed into his lap and let go of her hand.

She took up the phone and called their family doctor.

⸎

She parked in the closest spot to the ER entrance. Though clouds hung low overhead, the day was warmed by the thinning sunlight desperately assaulting from above, and nearby she could smell the autumnal aroma of burning leaves or wood. The air was cool, though the leaves were starting the slow turn to autumn. A slight breeze blew under the gunmetal sky, clouds boiling in the distance. She hoisted Glen up and tried to help him toward the door, but his body was like jelly, folding under her support. By the time she made it to the foyer, she knew they were exhausted, and Glen collapsed. The fluorescents were harsh and the A/C cool, the smell of antiseptic and medicine, chemical artificial smells permeated the halls.

On the table he convulsed. Her fist pressed against her lips to stifle a scream as they dragged in machines and shouted orders in acronyms. Analytically she understood them, but emotionally she was his wife and everything else was foreign. She recognized his prolapses for what they were—he was having a heart attack.

CHAPTER FOURTEEN

As the day wore on, Dani had expected some kind of response from Court. A text. A voicemail. Hell, even an email. Something. But not only was there no word from him, there was no sign of him on social media, either. The dream in all its vagueness from the night before had returned, and worry set in. After her last class, Dani rushed across campus and set down her guitar case at the base of Kimpel Hall. She scanned the front entrances, but of course, his class had already started. She blamed her professor for running long, and the unusually cluttered sidewalks on her hike from her class, for her delay in catching him beforehand. Now she'd have to wait until his class was over.

Stalker, she thought, only to argue with herself. They were adults. He was nearly forty and she was nearly thirty, he working towards tenure and she in grad school, and they had been seeing each other for a year now. She deserved to know at least he was okay. *You're being silly*, she thought. She was putting too much stock in a dream, but she'd had the feeling something was wrong all day. And not hearing from him had only made it worse. So, if she went upstairs to his class and saw him teaching, that would be enough. She'd at least know he was okay, and he wouldn't have to know. They could talk later. Snatching up her guitar, she hurried upstairs, rounded the corner, and inched closer to the classroom until she saw the closed door.

From behind, voices. She pressed closer but couldn't discern his voice. The doors in Kimpel were mostly wooden, but had long narrow rectangular windows in them, through which she chanced a glance, then fell back, sinking into a nearby chair as a voice rang through.

"You might try a doggerel," the professor said; it wasn't Court's voice.

"You don't get me at all!" the student wailed.

The workshop stretched impossibly long. When the doors opened, a little after five, Dani had run the gamut of emotions, from fear to guilt and anger and back again. She stood as the first students exited, then caught the older professor as he walked out, the strap of his leather satchel over his shoulder.

"Excuse me," she said, reaching for him, getting his attention. "I was looking for Court Dillon. Isn't this his poetry class?"

The older man gave her a smile. His salt and pepper mustache matched his hair, and his eyes were a deep green. "Yes, dear. But Professor Dillon is out. Some kind of family emergency."

He didn't stay for her to finish her thank you, a mumbled jumble of words she spat into the hall as it filled with murmuring students and random laughter and the noise of bodies exiting the building. She dropped into the chair again and stared at the tiled floor as students herded through the hall. Not until it emptied, and the only sounds were the buzzing overhead fluorescent lights and the hum of the old furnace through the vents did she raise her head. Not until her name was called, did she push herself to her feet, expecting Court. What she found instead when she turned was an insipid little man primly approaching. Dani hated the way Dean Garson carried his briefcase at chest level with both hands on the handle, pinkies up, as his black wingtips skidded across the tile. She hated his thin, white hair and bow tie. The dean was a rhetoric man and had a partnership with some of the STEM departments. This relationship left little room for the creative arts, and Dani knew he was bitter that Court—a poet—was nearly tenured faculty.

"Evening, Dean," she said. "I was about to head to your office."

"Ms. Morales. A bit far from the music building, aren't we? How may I help you?" He wore the thinnest of smiles, something meant to resemble an invitation but worn more like a warning not to approach or take his time.

She was intimidated by this little man, as most were. There were few graduate students, in her opinion, who weren't at least a little unnerved by university deans. Those attracted to those positions were political animals who enjoyed the power they wielded. "I'm looking for Professor Dillon," she said. She knew full well the dean was aware of their relationship. Court had talked about it at length, how the dean lorded the relationship over him when they were not even violating university fraternization policy.

The dean's smile looked especially reptilian. "Ah, yes. *Professor* Dillon did inform me he was going to be out for a few days and asked me to recruit substitutes for his classes. Something about family business. He didn't tell you?"

Careful, Dani thought. *He's fishing.* She watched him flick his tongue out to moisten his lips.

"No," she admitted. Started to blush and dropped her gaze to the floor after a young man, pale and bony and effeminate in his posture and the way he waved his arm, called out to the dean, who turned and waved.

"Well, Ms. Morales. I must go. I hope your studies are going well. I recall you were a strong student of literature as an undergrad. I'm sorry you didn't apply for graduate school with us."

He turned to leave, and before she realized what she was doing, her arm shot out and she grabbed his shoulder. This action shocked her, and from the look in his eye, shocked him too. But she couldn't hide her desperation: eyes wide with fear and unblinking, mouth trying to form a question she hadn't yet figured out how to ask.

"Ms. Morales," he said, his voice wearing exasperation as thin as his smile "I'm sure everything is fine, although I do know Court is worried about his family. If he didn't tell you, then maybe it is a sign this is a family, and so a private, matter."

"I..." Dani trailed off. What was she going to say? She *was* family? She was his girlfriend and they'd been together for a year. She cared about him and he for her. The L-word was still relatively new, lip-service reserved for something to say after sex. He adjusted his grip on his briefcase and locked his gaze on hers. His smiled widened.

"There is little leeway given to a professor going for tenure, especially when they are not a PhD, but *only* have an MFA. This, Ms. Morales, is true at the university level. Now, if Court wanted to work for a community college, then NWACC is up the road, but I assure you, my dear, he doesn't want to trade teaching two classes here for five there. I don't even think *you* are worth such a professional compromise."

Not only the words, but the hoity-toity tone of voice he intimated to talk down to her, felt like a punch in the gut, and Dani took a step back. "What are you saying?" she asked.

The reptilian smile was back. "I'm saying Professor Dillon is—and should be—focused only on tenure right now, so maybe, maybe his not telling you about this family emergency is his way of getting some distance from a relationship that might do more harm than good to his professional career. Now, if you'll excuse me."

Dean Garson turned on a heel, his wingtips clattering on the tile floor. He put an arm gingerly around the young man's waist and escorted him around the corner.

Dani felt rage build in her chest like a burning under the skin, flushing her skin up to her neck and cheeks. Fuck him. She glanced at her watch. *Fuck. Fuck me*—she was late. If she ran, she might make it to her car, and then if she caught the lights right, to her one tutoring appointment for the evening, on time. But afterward, she knew where she'd find answers.

CHAPTER FIFTEEN

The glass partition reflected the familiar face even before Lena entered the waiting room, its gray and hard chairs and its wall of windows opened to the complete blackness of night, but she wasn't reassured by Aster's presence. How could she be? Just another woman losing the love of her life. Aster's chin had dropped to her chest and her eyes were closed, like she'd worn out sitting there. Lena sat down next to her and took her hand; Aster's head jerked up and her eyes shot open.

"Oh," she said when she saw Lena. "Did someone tell you Elden's here?"

"No," Lena said. "Glen has pneumonia." She thought about tacking on the heart attack, but pneumonia at 85 was good enough to explain her presence now. "What's wrong with Elden?"

"We think a seizure." Aster's gaze, like her voice, trailed off. Lena followed it toward their mutual inevitable outcomes as widows.

"When I first met Glen, he never even got a cold. He had stomach issues, but otherwise he was so healthy. So strong."

Aster nodded. "You hear from Court?"

Lena shook her head and squeezed Aster's hand. "We all messed around and got old." She laughed a little. "It's what Glen said on his eightieth birthday. He told Court. I heard him say it."

"What if it's come back? We can't stop it now." Lena thought, it didn't take Aster long to bring that up, but in truth it had been in the back of her mind as well.

"I'm afraid of that too," Lena said. A part of her marveled at the simplicity of the fear, even as she recognized it in herself.

"It's evil," Aster said with a huff. Then, "What else are you afraid of?"

"Being alone. Nearly fifty years I've been with him. Longer than when I was single. I don't think I want to know what it's like to be without him."

"You depend on him," Aster said, nodding.

"No, it's not about dependence. I stood on my own before and I can do it again. It's not that. He's become…it's him. I don't want to be without *him*."

"I know what you mean," Aster said. "The house will feel so empty once he's…"

Lena cast her eyes toward the ceiling tiles in an effort to dam the tears. "Yes."

"But at least Glen has his faith," Aster said, a comment meant to be reassuring. "He was our deacon. All those years he taught Sunday School."

"Elden went to church too," Lena tried.

"Not but for my needling him incessantly. And after I retired from the church, he didn't like the way Brother Howe treated me—some pastor, didn't even come visit when I had my first heart attack."

"Wasn't too Christian."

"Elden preferred being out with the cows or whiling the afternoon away at the catfish pond."

"Glen had his moments, too. But he always turned to the Bible in those times."

"Did he have those moments often?" There was something desperate in Aster's voice, a yearning for solace.

"No. The last one I know of came the night Court…our…his parents. Glen said to me the next morning, asked, 'Would God allow such a thing? I don't believe it. If such a thing could live in this world, then life has no meaning.' I could hear the doubt in his voice. I saw the look in his eyes. Like what he was staring at wasn't something tangible, like the floor or a table or something. I knew he was questioning his own faith. He built his whole life around his faith."

"Did you have an answer for him?"

"I just said, because God allowed such thing was reason enough, we had to believe." A beat. "Court took us to lunch not too long back. Glen told him he knew where he was going when he died."

"He tried calling me."

"Me too," Lena said, as a nurse entered and motioned toward the women. For a brief second, they wondered for which of them she'd come. A grim reaper in cerulean scrubs.

"Mrs. Oscar, you may come in now. Elden is asking for you."

Aster rose, and patted Lena's hand one more time, then followed behind the nurse. Good news. A bit. Now if they could have one more piece…

She stopped before rounding the corner and turned back.

"I sent out a package the other day," Aster said.

"To Court?"

Aster nodded. "A story. Show him what's coming. Or what's back. He needs to see the evil. Needs to be wary of it but needs to know it all the same."

When the nurse returned and waved to her, Lena thought for a moment, if it had come back, they'd need their husbands, and they needed them strong again. But they'd already been given another day, and she didn't want to ask for too much. They needed to get ahold of their grandson and go from there.

In the hospital room, Glen looked up at her weakly. An oxygen tube trailed from his nose. He was pale and his eyes seemed like they wanted to close and stay closed. Still, he offered her a smile and reached out with his hand for hers. She sat and took it and thanked God for one more day.

CHAPTER SIXTEEN

Dani's final student packed up her guitar too slowly. Her methodical placement of the instrument in the case, and the careful return of all notes and tab sheets in their proper order usually didn't bother Dani, and the two would often chitchat about the girl's school or about a boy she liked, but today Dani was preoccupied with Court's whereabouts and her own turbulent emotions.

"Is something wrong, Señorita Morales?" the student asked, studying her. "You look worried."

She shook her head in frustration and muttered, "Yo no he pegado un ojo."

"You can't strike an eye?" the girl responded, wrinkling her face in confusion.

Dani smiled. She'd forgotten the girl was in high school Spanish. "It's an idiom," she said. "It basically means I haven't slept a wink."

When the student pressed, Dani made it clear, as nicely as possible, that it wasn't something she would talk about, but it was on her mind. They had put everything on the table during the fight. Had spoken their wants and expectations for this relationship. And now he was gone, and she was worried, and embarrassed, because what if he was getting a little distance, and here she was acting like a little schoolgirl with a crush. But she'd also known him for a year and disappearing like this was out of character. Yes, he drank a lot, and yes, they'd had their arguments between their pleasant times, but he didn't ever run away. He didn't disappear, and he didn't clam up. She might not always know what he was thinking, but he never ran away or disappeared.

After the student left, Dani loaded up her car and drove to Court's loft apartment, letting herself in with the key he'd given her. His place. The other night, he'd met her at the door and kissed the top of her head. It had started so simply, the fight the night of the concert. He had said, "Food's here," and this was all either said until they were halfway through dinner.

The loft was dark, cool. It felt like a cave, something vacuous and haunted. Their ghosts danced around her, reliving that night. There they were at the table.

"So, I've been spending a lot of time here," she had said, wiping her lips with her napkin and staring at the plate in front of her, now containing only a smattering of morsels and arcing streaks of red sauce and butter.

"You have." He set his fork down. Looking at him was difficult. His eyes were so kind, a deep blue with only the hint of creases around the edges.

"You're drinking a lot," she said after a moment. "I've been here, and I've seen it."

"If you'd rather be elsewhere—" he snapped, but he cast a sideways glance at the beer to the left of his plate.

"I like being with you, but I don't like the passive aggressiveness or the self-destructive behavior. Remember when we first met and you'd brag about all the women you slept with, the pot you smoked, the drugs you've tried? And now the drinking?"

"Where is this coming from?"

"I've been thinking…"

"You're afraid of missing something. You're afraid. If you get too close to someone or something, you'll miss out on a better opportunity."

"I told you I'm not ready to settle down yet, but I think you are. I think you are so scared of—"

"—of what? Of how my only family, my grandparents, are dying and I can't do damn thing to stop it? Or of how the dean has it out for me and my job is in such a precarious state right now? Or of how my last two books haven't even raised an eyebrow at the Pushcart Committee?"

"When's the last time you talked to them?" She reached out and took his hand, squeezing a bit in support or solidarity. She knew he loved his grandparents, and she knew about their failing health and how scared he was. The job…the committee, these things didn't help matters. But what fueled his fear was losing the only family he had and being totally alone in the world. God, she didn't want him feeling like that.

"I can't," he said. He stood and walked the bottle over to the recycling. "I see them, and I see they aren't the same. Hell, I'm not the same. I…they…we are getting older." With each modified pronoun, his face grew longer.

"So, you drink instead?"

"It numbs me. It stills my mind so I can sleep at night and not think about all this shit, like my job and my poetry and how they might not ever see me with a wife or kids."

"You knew who I was when we met," she said, and stood to clear the table.

"You mean impulsive, and before you cast stones about my drinking, you've kept up with me on more than one occasion."

"I have been self-destructive, also," she admitted. "But we have to stop." She walked to the sink and turned on the faucet, then drizzled dish soap over the plates and utensils. There was a dishwasher, but it was old and at best, merely sterilized the dishes and dried them (kind of).

"So, this is the talk you want to have, right? This is the status-of-our-relationship talk? Where you remind me about how you want nothing serious and I'm a bastard?"

"I said 'we.' We're both self-destructive. But if you want those things: kids and a regular life, *we* must stop."

"So, let's stop," he said. "Go. I'd hate for you to miss out on anything." He grabbed another beer out of the fridge and popped the top, raised it to his lips and began guzzling.

She dried her hands and reached for his arm. "I didn't mean *us*. I don't know what I want. I like being spontaneous and adventurous, but I know I want to experience these things with you."

"You call it spontaneous, but you scare me sometimes, Miss Morales. You get—"

"Manic? My mother used to say the same thing. She'd say, 'Slow down, *hija*. You're a blur through life.'" At this Dani laughed. Her mother's English had never been great.

Court allowed a laugh too. "A blur through life? My grandfather had one of those, my mom's dad. He'd say, 'It's like a bird in a tree,' when he meant, 'a bird in the hand is worth two in the bush.'"

They let the ease of the moment pass between them, smiling long past the humor so the grins hung on their lips, until Court said, "Jesus."

She rubbed his arm. "What is it?"

"I referred to him in the past tense," Court said, and he slid slowly down the fridge until his butt was on the tile and he could lay his forearms over his knees. He buried his head in his folded arms and let out a sigh that echoed between his legs down to the floor. She sat beside him on the cold linoleum tile and put an arm around him, being by him quietly while he stayed motionless.

"You need to go see them." She kissed his cheek, and he pulled her in close, sniffed into her hair.

"Will you come with me?" The thought of meeting his family terrified her even when he clarified. "I don't mean so you'll meet them in an official capacity. I'm terrified of losing them."

She swallowed hard and caressed the back of his head. "Yes," she choked out.

This was how things were left until after the concert, when they'd returned to his loft and had sex, and she straddled him and played "Malagueña" on her classical guitar and then "Autumn Leaves" until he fell asleep, and she slowly dressed and snuck out the door back to her place. Normally she would have spent the night, but at the time she thought they'd both needed some space. Now, reflecting as she sat at his computer desk and started up the desktop, she realized she had been afraid. It was a good night, and it would have been ruined by sobriety the next morning and the resuming of their conversation. If it went further, she thought, they would break up, and she wasn't ready to break up yet.

While the computer warmed up, she walked to his bedroom and rifled through his dresser, searching for anything that might give up the numbers to his grandparents. She opened various drawers in his room, in the kitchen, searched his closet, even the spare (which was empty), but found nothing. Back at the computer, it took her three tries to get through his logon (she smiled when she realized it was her birthday), but found nothing in his documents and his email had her completely locked out. Same for the social media accounts. As a last act of desperation, she searched Facebook for people he'd friended, but found she couldn't DM Glen or Lena Dillon unless they were friends, so she sent them a friend request. Those grandparents were relatively easy to find in Court's 3,000-person friend list, but she could not for the life of her remember the names of his maternal grandparents.

She hated being stuck. Hated not knowing something, and she hated not knowing what she wanted. Her indecision kept her in this static state. As the evening pressed on and the ghosts of their lives flitted through the apartment, Dani thought again about speaking her mind, and hairs on the tongue.

CHAPTER SEVENTEEN

Clem Willette had made a habit of spending his evenings at Sally's Suds, out near the bypass almost every night it was open—save for Sundays, when there weren't any liquor sales in the county, and the only establishments able to serve it also had a kitchen. Sally's wasn't such a place. Run by a guy named Bob, who Clem knew from school—there had never been a Sally—it had become the de facto watering hole for most locals and any bikers who passed through and the occasional Chicago retiree who'd moved to the area and wanted a taste of that Ozark lifestyle. Clem didn't much care for the company, but he hated drinking alone at home; his pappy had told him alcoholics drank alone, so Clem drank the suds and the whiskey every night but Sunday, his drying out night.

His work never suffered. The stiffs at the cemetery would never complain. The holes got dug and the grass got watered and the hedges were trimmed. His nights at the bar began in solemn reflection of the day's events, watching whatever was on the flat screen—(Bob had had a small TV box on a platform up in the corner for years, but had finally upgraded to a 55-inch with Hi-Def, though

Clem couldn't tell a difference in picture quality from the TV he had at home; he was just happy he could see the screen)—usually sports or Fox News. Whatever was on television usually dictated which topics were rolling off Clem's tongue to whoever would listen as the alcohol kept flowing and the hours passed. On this he was in good company; most of the patrons agreed with his philosophical outlook on life. Still, few engaged him, and most of the time it was only Bob who was forced to listen to him.

The bar was slow this particular night, with only Clem and a few other patrons, Bob behind the bar, and Sean Hannity on the screen, educating those Americans smart enough to listen on those godless Dems and their latest efforts to undermine the best president to come along in years.

"…I'm saying," Clem was saying, "I ain't never seen any building up and move itself. Can you believe such foolishness? My pappy told me about some weird things he saw during the war. Said the Nazis were into some weird stuff over there. You know," he paused for a drink, finishing off the tumbler of whiskey, "'nother'n, Bob."

"Do I know what?" Bob asked with all the enthusiasm of someone who didn't give a shit.

Clem leaned over the bar as though he had some secret to impart, only to let out a fart as he strained across the bar top. "You know, I saw walking down College the other day like there weren't a care in the world. A ni—"

"Get off the bar," Bob said flatly. "You know I don't want such language in here."

"My pappy used to tell me there weren't nothing wrong with speaking your mind, especially when they called each other the same or worse," Clem snapped, his voice a little too loud, sitting back on his stool. Bob slid another tumbler of ice and whiskey over to him, and Clem took a drink and made a face. "You waterin' this shit down, Bob?"

"You watched me pour it," Bob said.

"Well, I seen more of 'um in town. And some Spics, too. Now, I know they got some good people, but you know a lot of 'um come over here hate America and wanna rape our women and steal our jobs. Like them Blacks up in Chicago living off the government. Must be nice. I tell you what if our president isn't going to put an end to such crap."

He went on for a while, spurred onto a tangent by whatever word he overheard from the TV or another patron. Eventually, his ramblings became mumblings, then finally silent soliloquies, when he was too drunk to articulate.

His world philosophy had come mainly from his father, a World War II vet who had also hailed from this small, Southern white community, who had gone off to see the world and only saw horror, and believing this view was all there was, brought it home to his son. In his fifty-five years, Clem had never wanted to leave the town, and so he was comfortable in believing his father's world view. He'd married once but divorced not long after. The prospect of the Willette lineage dying with him never ruffled his feathers until he remembered that he had two brothers he never spoke to. His sister had kids, but her last name was Juniper or some shit now; he hadn't talked to her in over a decade. All three of them had left him to take care of their father and their mother, left when they were young, and never came back to this town until it was time to stick the parents into the ground and then talk to the lawyer, so Clem couldn't give two shits about them anyway. They didn't want to be here, good for them. His pappy had told him all he needed to know about the outside world. The retirees he'd met down from Chicago seemed to support the theory, as did Sean Hannity and the half of the TV news that wasn't a mouthpiece for the liberal left.

After last call, Clem stumbled out of Sally's Suds and took a long hard look at his truck dancing thirty paces in front of him in wide, rotating undulations. He lurched towards it, hoping it would stay still long enough for him to reach it, 'til he remembered Bob had taken his keys again, offering him a lift home, and like almost every other night, he'd left indignantly, sure he'd find his way by foot.

Guided by the moonlight, the wind's teeth biting through his inebriation, Clem stepped slowly down the shoulder in as straight a line as he could walk, leaning forward a bit too much, pushing each step in front of him as he swung his arms vigorously and furrowed his brow, an old Patsy Cline song on his lips issuing forth as an alien-drunk whistle.

"I'm getting more drunk," he said to no one in particular, continuing the stream-of-consciousness pontificating, "because alcohol takes time to enter the bloodstream, so even though it's been a while since my last drink, I'm getting more drunk." He said this after he found it nigh impossible to form the necessary embouchure to continue the tune, bleary as he was. It was then he heard the song being carried on the wind through the trees to his ears, originating from somewhere deep behind the tree line a sound ensnared between a whistle and words, drifting across the night air. His right foot found a particularly forceful placement, and he looked between two oaks on his left; the song paused briefly, and the playful laugh of a young girl reached his ears, and then it began again.

"Girly," Clem said, stepping to the tree line, clinging to a waif of a pine like it was his prom date, the bark cool and rough against his gristly, pockmarked cheek. The song invited him a few more steps and he took them willingly; the melody was intoxicating and as inviting as a bottle.

Finding new supports with each twisted and knotted oak and maple and elm, he pressed through the forest until the trees fell away and he barked his shin on something sharp and unrelenting. Muttering a curse, he glanced down to it. No blood. It didn't hurt now, but it would sure smart in the morning. Clem knelt and traced his fingers over the grainy stone surface, the carved letters, but he could do little in the dark and in his state to decipher them.

It was when he stood that he noticed more stones breaching the darkness, familiar shapes taking form as his eyes adjusted to the nighttime, and beyond, abandoned ruins with a steeple roof and a cross that looked about to topple over, and the double doors ajar. From inside came the song.

"Girly?" he said. "You shouldn't be out here. This ain't no place for a lady."

He blinked, looked around at this old, dilapidated building surrounded by these ancient stone markers of the long since interred. But he'd lived in this area all his life and he knew there was no church here. Not normally. Still, here it was now, its lines hazy and trembling, ill-defined. The air heavy and suppressive, moist in his lungs, nearly choking him.

The playful laugh. The next verse of the alien tune singing upon the heart. Something scurried to a dark corner to his right; he imagined a rat or a squirrel and took another tentative step inside the pitch black and otherwise deathly silent church. The tune had stopped. He wasn't sure when it had, but there was no sound now.

"Girly," he said again, but doubt had crept in. He'd seen no one. The whistle and hum and girlish laugh had faded, and something guttural issued from the darkest recesses of the churchyard's belly. He tried to pinpoint the sound, finding only a blur of something darker than the night, flashing in front of him as it smacked him in the chest, knocking him on his back; he hadn't the breath to scream for the pressure on his chest. A shadow, featureless save for the glistening yellow orbs of its eyes. A great gasp escaped with a breath and the thing laughed like a little girl. Clem pawed at fur as it bent over him, rancidly hot breath on his neck, and he felt its teeth, a legion of tiny daggers, dig into his flesh. He screamed.

And then it said, "Qissa?" and reared up and glared at him. Clem prayed it would get it over with. His neck burned from the wounds as blood trickled down to puddle under his back and this thing was straddling him, and he cried out but some of it was muddied as he spit up blood.

It reached its other clawed hand into his pants pocket and pulled out some coins—spare change from the day's random transactions—lunch at Debbie's diner, a Coke at the Kum N Go.

"Shiny," the thing said, and ran the coins through its fingers, allowing them to drop with a dull thud to the dirt. "Live," it said.

Clem realized it was asking a question. He nodded, his head light and the blood trickling from his neck. "God, yes." He coughed up more blood, a gelatinous iron spherule he spat beside his cheek.

"Help," it hissed, put its face next to his, and Clem turned away and closed his eyes because of the stench of its breath and the horror of its true self, but he kept nodding as he silently sobbed, the weight of this thing pressing down on him, his pants soaked now from urine and his back and shoulder wet from the blood draining from his neck.

※

In the little town, cars stopped for the most part; yes, a few crossed the bypass, but morning would come early, and the town slept hard, rousing for nothing, not even the stars twinkling above, vanished now behind the curtain of clouds that hung low over the Twin Lakes area.

The elderly were always the first to turn in, followed shortly by the children, then their parents, and finally the teenagers. A few people gathered on porches to sip beer or whiskey, to talk and laugh about whatever there was to laugh about in this small, pitiful town: usually the calamities of others. An undercurrent of meanness stretched through Rapps Barren, permeating every hour of every day through nearly every person, except for Sunday mornings, when the majority of the town tried to pray it away and begged for forgiveness for their transgressions before they began again the next week. Some, at night, voiced their prayers and grievances so as to absolve themselves before the morning, muttering their litanies and invocations and requiescats to whatever slinked through the night wearing the coat of deity.

But because the town slept didn't mean all her denizens rested easily. The laborers were more likely to slip into coma-like states, not rousing until it was time to ready for their next shift. The elderly would awaken multiple times, as did the parents of all children. Only the drug-toxic bodies of the addicts crashed harder than the laborers, passed out from the nightly influx of mind-altering substances wearing their bodies down, their sleep the sleep of the dreamless, an empty void through which they floated until the dawn returned them to sobriety.

Generalizations, with plenty of exceptions as rules were wont to have, but by and large this was the state of things at night in Rapps Barren.

Neither Lena nor Aster slept on the cots the hospital had provided for them. They'd shut their eyes in the guest chairs that they'd pulled up to their husbands' bedsides, but there was no quality of sleep. Both steadied themselves for what they were sure would come next; widowhood was the only reward for a long life spent with a soulmate.

Detective Bullocks slept dreamlessly and fitfully. He arose several times. Once, right before the witching hour, he got up and stepped out on his balcony and looked toward the Dillons' dark house, unnerved at how empty it appeared. A shell, like a corpse, haunted by an unnatural stillness.

How Clem made it home was lost to him. He awakened in his bed, clothes and boots still on, his inebriated brain working overtime to convince himself what he'd experienced was a dream, even as he dreamed of his father, long since dead, coming back to him.

These were but some of the exceptions, and none of them were disquieting enough to rouse the town from its slumber, so Rapps Barren slept, and the thing which feasted on the dead crept through the shadows, looking for the next weary traveler.

⊂⊃

There used to be a lot of stars out, but Tommy couldn't see them through the blinds. He blinked, pulled his thumb from his mouth, and frowned. Mommy had told him only little boys sucked their thumbs; she had said this again at breakfast this morning, while he was eating his cereal and she caught him sucking his thumb. She told him often. Big boys of five and three months don't suck their thumbs, and they don't need binkies, and they don't sleep with blankies.

"Tommy…"

The voice was distant, almost buried in the darkness. When it called again, he decided it sounded like a nursery rhyme. He knew he shouldn't get out of bed, because Momma said a boy should have no reason to get out of bed after dark, especially if he uses the potty before bed, and he had.

With the bedroom door opened, he could stare into the living room, cool and dark and filled with shapes and shadows he didn't recognize. It didn't look like where he played NASCAR or watched Bugs Bunny. The silhouette of the Tonka truck looked like a Tyrannosaurus Rex with its jaws unhinged. The scary night wind made the singsong sound of his name again, and he jumped a little when he heard it.

"I want to play with you," the night sang.

He walked up to the sliding glass doors of the rear deck. He could see the dark, the stripped trees, the immediate yard in the moonlit darkness. But the source of the voice calling his name was still lost to him. Still, he heard it…

"Tommy… Come play with me."

He lifted the latch and looked back across the living room and the kitchen, afraid the snapping sound would wake his mother in the bedroom beyond. But no light came on; no sound came. He pushed one door back across the rollers far enough to ease his little body through to the balcony and found the wood deck cold against the soles of his feet.

Though he scanned the darkness when his name came again, he couldn't see from where.

"Where are you?" he called softly, and glanced back again to make sure he didn't wake his mother. She wouldn't like that he was outside this late. Now was the time for boys to be in bed.

"Here," it called. Something like a dog—but with cat ears and dark spots on its tan fur—walked around the other corner of his trailer. It stood under the light of the utility pole, casting a gilded shadow over the dun blanketed, a permanent grin on its face.

"Doggie!" he said. He took a few steps down from the deck. The doggie approached. It looked at him, head cocked to the side, blinking at him with its black eyes.

The child, ever so trusting, reached out a hand to pet the animal on the head. It laughed, high-pitched but mirthless. *Dogs don't laugh,* he thought for a second. And then it lunged at him.

Tommy reached for the banister, and he stumbled backwards up the stairs, but his hand slipped across the frost of the rail, and he nicked the riser with his heel and sat hard on the deck. The dog-thing crept toward him slowly, its eyes locked on him. It opened its mouth and Tommy heard his name, whispered on the nocturn wind, and then he saw the thing gnash its teeth. As it sprang, he looked up to the stars and screamed.

INTERLUDE THREE

The Tale of the Bored Poet

Once upon a time there was a man who wrote poetry, and when he wasn't writing poetry, he was teaching others to write poetry. One might think he had a life full of music and song, but they would be wrong.

This man, this poet, had grown dissatisfied with his life. A lot of women shared his bed, and he published his books, and he went to work every day and he wrote at home, and he drank copious amounts of alcohol in between, but still his life felt empty.

So, he hopped from bar to bar, and he picked up pretty women with his pretty words, and he ignored the thing he wanted, more than the publishing contract and the secure job and the adoring readers paying attention to what he had to say. He ignored what his grandparents had. Glen and Lena Dillon had led quiet lives making sure he was happy and healthy, and Elden and Aster Oscar had given back to the environment as farmers even as they made sure he had a future.

Back when he first told the Oscars he wanted to study poetry, he might as well have told them he wanted to prance through the fields and blow dandelions all day.

"Are you sure?" Aster had asked.

Elden harrumphed around the room, arms folded over his chest.

"I know what I want to study at college," the young poet had said.

Elden waved his hand in the air like he was swatting away a fly. "So, poetry. After all we given you. You want to get your degree in poetry?"

But they loved him, and supported him, and neither balked when it was time to write the tuition check. They understood and had worked out with the Dillons who would pay for what; years earlier, Elden Oscar had started a trust for the baby and added to it regularly, and even the Dillons contributed, and this money paid for the poet's undergraduate studies.

"What's a stipend?" Elden had asked, though Lena and Aster and Glen all understood the word meant that the poet's graduate education was paid for, all because of his talents.

"You that good?" Elden asked when they explained.

The poet nodded. "I am, Papaw. I am."

So, the poet went to graduate school and got an MFA and began teaching at his alma mater and publishing, first in literary journals, and then he found an agent and a small press who wanted to publish a book of poems.

And all the while the poet continued writing. He wrote essays and guest posts on blogs and entered contests and won and got published. He researched an old mentor and wrote a biography of her life, even as she got sick, and her words began to fail.

This was all he ever wanted, for his words to be heard. For someone, other than these doting grandparents whom he thought were obligated to hear him, to hear his words, his stories. It was what he wanted and, like some magic spell answered, the world responded; this little orphaned kid from a small town in North Arkansas had a voice that mattered to the rest of the world.

But still it wasn't enough. He drank, as the darkest shadows settled over his loft, and contemplated how one half of the puzzle was complete, which meant he was still incomplete. For all his words, and all his stories, his heart was empty.

So, he filled it with friendships and acquaintances and meaningless sex. Even the deepest of friendships couldn't fill every intimate hole, and acquaintances only served to temporarily silence the void of loneliness whispering in the still moments when he realized the life he'd chosen. The sex only feigned intimacy, shallow metaphors barely lasting 'til dawn.

Then he met a girl. And she smiled at him, and she listened to his words, and she allowed him to seduce her, this girl ten years younger than himself. How could he have known how eager she was, and interested and willing for him to take her? How could he know she saw it not as an occupation but as an alliance, which she strove to solidify? He didn't realize 'til later that she had designed this as much as he had, encouraging him to pursue his desires.

There was nothing illegal in their union. They were both of age, though the semester before, she'd been his student. If she were still his student, it would have complicated things, but because she wasn't, the university policy against fraternization was satisfied, though the poet knew the dean, who didn't like the fact he was on a tenure path, watched him like a hawk. But he was close to this woman and felt it and knew it. When he held her, he felt his emptiness, his loneliness like a hole, filling. What he'd always wanted was coming to fruition.

He was scared. Thought, because his parents had left him and because he'd strayed so far from the path his grandparents had illuminated, maybe he wasn't deserving. Maybe he deserved to rot and die and fester in immorality until the worms ate out his eyes.

And in those moments when he thought such things, he felt her firm thigh caress his thigh, and her arm wrap around him, and her lips on his ear. This forced from the poet a great sigh, as he released himself into the mattress and loosed all rigidity, and he felt in such moments he could succumb.

The End

CHAPTER EIGHTEEN

Grubhub had brought Dani a burger and fries, and she'd fiddled around with the computer and then, when she got nowhere, her classical guitar, which she'd left the other night (intentionally, she realized now), until she fell asleep. When she awoke, morning light streamed through the skylight-high windows of the second story loft, and it tiger-striped through the vertical blinds, spreading across the two great bay windows on either side of the front door. She'd slept in his bed, the guitar in his spot, and she carried it with her now, into the living room. She checked her phone, but there were no texts, no voicemails, and no friend acceptances on Facebook.

While she was sipping her coffee, her phone lit up. Frank Torn, the screen said—her drummer. They talked about next gigs and he mentioned again the studio recording time, but to this she remained tight-lipped, as usual. She wasn't sure what her next move was. She liked playing, she liked performing, but she couldn't see herself doing this forever. She wanted to teach music, maybe even open a studio, while the rest of the band seemed unanimous in their desire to book gigs and record an album. They'd brought up this topic before and she'd successfully skirted it in the past, but this morning Torn was not letting it go.

"We've all been talking," he said. "You don't seem keen on recording. We're wondering what the hell is going on with our lead singer."

She sighed, closed her eyes, rubbed her temple. "This isn't a great time—"

"It's never a great time, but we got to know *something*. We got plans. But if everyone isn't on board, plans could get derailed."

"You know I love singing," she said. "I love the band, I do. But I'm not convinced it's my life. We've had some fun on the road, but it takes a special person to live on the road, and I have to focus on school. I can't tour and finish my graduate work."

This time, the sigh came from his end. "So, you want out."

"Don't put words in my mouth, Frank." Most people, including her, called him by his last name, or called him 'F Torn.' Using his first name was tantamount to a child being scolded by his mom.

"Then what do you want, *Dani?*"

"I don't know," she answered, and realized this was the truth.

"Listen," he said after a pause. "Bobby's back with Sheila." Bobby was their lead guitarist and Sheila was his on-again, off-again girlfriend. They were toxic, like Sid and Nancy toxic, when they were together, but she did have a voice, and Dani knew what he was getting at.

"Look, give me a few days to think about it," she said. "I've got stuff going on over here, but I didn't say I was out yet. Okay?"

"Okay."

There was a knock at the door.

"I gotta go."

"What stuff? If we can help…"

Another knock. More persistent. "Thanks. I'll let you know."

She hung up as whoever it was knocked again. Probably the manager, she thought. Maybe Court asked him to check on his place, and he's wondering why she's here. Well, she thought, okay. Perhaps Court was backing away, letting her down by taking a step back. If it's what he wants, then she wouldn't lose any more sleep over it. She'd—

Opening the door, she found not the apartment manager, but a uniformed police officer.

He nodded and said, "Ma'am."

She frowned instinctively. Police don't come to your door. They don't show up for no reason. Leaning against the frame, her eyes moving up and down the visitor out of suspicion and even a little fear, she swallowed a lump in her throat before she found the words.

"Can I help you?" The officer stood on the front stoop, the parking lot and stairs leading down were visible behind him. Invisible to her was the traffic filing up the hill on the street to the left and what sounded like the engine of the old panel van owned by one of the neighbors firing up.

"Does Court Dillon live here?" She tried to read the cop's face, but he was stern and young enough his forehead didn't wrinkle when he kneaded his brows together. In fact, he looked fresh out of high school, his brown eyes sharp and expressive.

"He does."

"Ma'am, Rapps Barren police asked me to come and see if he lived here with anyone."

Her stomach dropped. She gripped at the door frame to support herself. "What…" Her voice failed.

"They found his car this morning in the ditch on a county road near the town. Didn't look like he wrecked, only parked the car, but there was no sign of him. When they ran the plates, it came back to him and this address."

"Oh, dear God," she muttered.

"Are you his wife? Girlfriend?"

Her voice completely gone, all she could do was nod.

"Any idea what he was doing there?" the young cop asked.

She was trembling and felt lightheaded. Waving him inside, she retreated into the kitchen and sank to the table. "Family," she got out. The cop was studying her when she looked up at him, a look of concern on his face. "His grandparents live there. He went to see them. They haven't been doing well."

"Do you know their names?"

"Glen and Lena Dillon. Those were his dad's parents. His mom's, last name Oscar, I think. They have a farm."

"And his parents?"

"Dead. Years ago. Is he… Are they going to find him?"

He nodded. "Yes ma'am. I'm sure of it." He'd been writing down the names in a little notebook, and now stuck it back into his pants pocket and returned his pen to the pocket on his shirt. "I'll get them the names."

Her phone pinged. A Facebook notification. The officer headed for the door. She pushed herself up and followed him, again leaning on the door.

"It'll be okay, ma'am. We'll find him. I promise."

She thanked him and shut the door. When she returned to the table and opened the app, she saw Lena Dillon had accepted her friend request. She quickly shot off a DM: "I'm a friend of Court's. He was coming over to see you. Have you or the Oscars—" yes, she was sure their name was Oscar— "heard from him?"

Had she expected an instant response? Worry had returned to her like a tidal wave, washing impatience over her. Fear he had suffered some accident suffocated her. In her heart of hearts, she knew what the response would be. No one had seen Court. He had vanished.

Still, no response had come from Lena Dillon when Dani stopped by after class. Outside, clouds moved in quickly and the wind picked up, a chilled easterly blast from across the plains bringing the clouds. Dani could smell the coming rain when she opened the door for Court's friend, Rong, and hugged him.

"I'm glad to see you," she said, then sat down again at the table to tell all she'd learned.

Rong sat stoic, eyes unblinking behind the thick glasses. When they spoke, it was without accent, the voice level at a bass monotone. "We'll find him," Rong said.

CHAPTER NINETEEN

The sun still on the rise behind the vast expanse of clouds blanketing the area, Detective Albert Bullocks sipped his coffee while sitting on his back deck, staring out at the expansive wood behind his house, the slow changing colors of the leaves, the dewiness of the early morning over everything. It was well after Labor Day, which in the Ozarks meant any day the weather could shift from late summer to early fall, so it was right on schedule, and he was enjoying his attire: short-sleeve polo and slacks. To his right he heard a door shut. His neighbor, the nurse, stepped onto her own deck across the breezeway, coffee and paper in hand. Today she wore a haggard, sleepless look. He thought for some reason she was usually dressed at this hour and not still in her pajamas and a robe and slippers. When she saw him, she did her best to smile.

"Mrs. Dillon," he called, raising his cup.

"Morning, Detective."

"How are you and your husband doing this morning?"

She stopped in her tracks, taking a sip of coffee as she regarded the question. "I haven't slept much. Glen is in the hospital."

"Oh God, is he…?"

"He's got pneumonia and he suffered another heart attack."

"If you need anything," he said. He'd seen her only yesterday, and how spry she was, but this morning she'd seemed to have aged ten years.

She smiled and gave a little wave and said, "Thank you," then walked back into her house. He couldn't help but worry for them, even as he realized he'd probably interrupted her one chance at solace out on her deck. Why, she'd brought the paper and the coffee, and he'd interrupted her, recriminating himself sharply under his breath as he returned inside and washed out his own cup. His mind shifted gears to the more pressing work matter:

There had been nothing on the CCTV recording he'd been given, and it didn't take him long to figure out why. The tape he was given was on a loop from the evening before, after they'd received the body and it was undressed and laid out. The time stamp showed how early in the evening it was, so at least Bullocks knew the break-in had occurred later. He'd watched the whole thing in regular time then slowed it down, scanning the seconds. Death had been his coworker for a number of years, but it still disquieted him to watch the still room, the motionless body. What disquieted him more, however, was how the mortician had deceived him. At least, that's what it felt like. Like the young man hadn't disclosed all he knew. But why cover this up?

He retrieved his phone from where he'd left it on the bathroom counter and saw he'd missed a call from the sheriff. The voicemail ordered him out to a county road and said not to bother going to the office first. His stomach did a little roll.

ೕೊ

Detective Bullocks knelt at the edge of the forest, the day humid and warm. The temperature had dropped a few degrees after sunrise, but had since climbed steadily, and Bullocks could feel it in the sweat beading up on the hackled hairs of his forearms. Still, he shivered, despite the weather. A couple of guys behind him were trying to hide behind their toughness and not succeeding.

"A kid."

"Dear God."

"There ain't no god, man."

Further off, a rumble came seemingly from the hills themselves, but Bullocks knew a storm was roiling over the horizon. "We need to get him to the state ME," he said. It was all he could think of.

"We need to notify his mother," the sheriff said.

"I'll do it," Bullocks replied. Not waiting for a response, he returned to his car and pulled away. Staying at the scene any longer only bordered on the obscene.

The mother he found under police surveillance at the station. Numb, lost in a fugue, she stared at the floor, cradling a Styrofoam cup in both hands when he entered, and she didn't look up until he sat beside her.

He saw the hope wash over her face and then ebb away, as her mouth dropped open and her eyes widened and a low moan escaped from deep down, as if her very soul had been ripped from her. The plan was to be matter-of-fact about what they found, but hesitant on the details. Let her start the process of grieving. But now he was here, sitting beside her, with a look on his face like he figured the plan was trashed.

When she broke down, he held her and tried to shush her, but she could not be consoled, and she shouldn't be, he thought, and when a female officer approached, he retreated because he knew he wasn't good enough; and he excused himself.

Outside, he walked around the corner and thought about all the things he saw up in Chicago and then about what he'd seen when he transferred to Northwest Arkansas, and then he thought of the little boy and he retched up the previous night's dinner, dry heaving when his stomach was empty. Above him, the indifferent gray sky stared blindly down, no solar pupil to laser its focus on his beady little head.

CHAPTER TWENTY

Aster had only slept in spurts when Britta touched her arm, startling her. Still, she had the presence of mind to glance first to the man in the bed whose hand she held, still unconscious, or sedated—she wasn't sure. The doctor had told her which, but his words were a lifetime ago.

"I was resting my head," she said, sure Britta had seen her head on Elden's thigh. She looked over Britta's shoulder to where TJ stood in the doorway, arms crossed over his chest. "How'd you know?" she asked, but then remembered she'd called them the day before, as the ambulance was carrying Elden to the emergency department of Ferrous County Regional Hospital.

"How you doing?" Britta asked.

"You call Court?" TJ said from the door.

"Fine, fine," Aster said, and took another look at Elden. Sleeping, yes. She was sure. He'd been sedated. It was important to remember these things. "Lena's calling him about his grandfathers."

Britta and TJ exchanged a glance.

"What do you mean?" Britta asked.

Aster blinked, then looked at both of them. "Glen is here too."

CHAPTER TWENTY-ONE

Area Graveyards See Spike in Vandalism
by Staff

Rapps Barren police and the Ferrous County Sheriff's Office are baffled by a series of grave desecrations in local cemeteries over the course of the past few weeks. Overnight, graves have been exhumed and coffins opened, with the desecrations found the next morning, exposed to the elements and various corpses eaten on. When questioned, officials have cited vultures, coyotes, or wild dogs as possible culprits, but this has done little to comfort citizens who are worried about the remains of their loved ones.

Others suspect the vandalism is the work of bored teenagers and have asked the sheriff to instate a curfew and increase patrols around cemeteries. Members of the community met Tuesday at the town hall with the sheriff and his lead detective, Albert Bullocks, fielding questions from the audience.

The sheriff and the mayor have promised to do everything in their power to catch whoever was responsible for this; however, when our office reached out for a statement, neither the sheriff, the lead investigator, or the mayor returned our call.

❦

Rong had been more successful hacking Court's desktop, but it had been a stroke of genius on their part to research from their own laptop, Dani hanging over their shoulder. Together they found a dozen articles that covered the grave desecrations over the past few months, and when Rong found access to the newspaper's archives, a longer history unfolded.

Born in Hong Kong, Rong had been brought as a baby to Missouri, and like a good son studied engineering. But Rong's mother was old school and couldn't understand having a son who identified as heterosexual and nonbinary, so she was the only person in the world who referred to them as 'him.' Rong was a Chinese name for either a boy or a girl, meant 'prosperous,' 'glory,' or 'honor,' but as a child meant bullying and tormenting on the playground. Rong didn't like American sports and didn't care about fashion. Rong buried their nose in books despite the fact in the small town they grew up in, boys focused on sports and girls and farming. So Rong was wrong. Rong, for all their years on this earth, had been wrong, and now, a senior in college, Rong embraced the wrongness.

"It's sporadic," they said now, scrolling the older articles. "But there is a history of graves being exhumed and bodies desecrated going back decades. Look at this."

❦

An old article, back from the 1830s, when the paper was about the only form of entertainment in the settlement of Rapps Barren, before the town was incorporated. The picture accompanying it was faded from the years, a sepia-toned daguerreotype of a steepled, white washed church surrounded by cemetery stones, a large wooden cross hung perfectly over the double doors. It was the epitome of an old country church like one might see in a Norman Rockwell or Edward Hopper painting. If it had more rooms than the sanctuary, they were few and small. The article, Rong recited for Dani, talked about the church as one might whisper to a neighbor about a salacious affair.

"The preacher was run off, it says, but I wouldn't be surprised if he were killed. They talk about unnatural sermons, bodies in the basement. Necromancy."

"Jesus," Dani said.

"Not there, sounds like," Rong responded, though neither laughed at their attempt at humor.

"What does this have to do with Court?" Dani asked. Rong's lips whitened when pressed together, as though they were forcibly keeping words from escaping.

"Maybe nothing," they finally said, but Dani had known Rong long enough to know when they were holding back. She also knew she couldn't press them; they would only clam up more. "But as a part of the whole strangeness of the town, it can't be good. And since you haven't had any luck reaching anyone over there…"

Their voice trailed off, leaving the thought unfinished, perhaps intentionally. This was true. As the afternoon had pressed on, Dani had continued to try and contact his grandparents. Lena had accepted her friend request, and she'd sent a couple of DM's with no reply, so she'd quit, fearing what the woman might think. She'd also found an Oscar—Aster Oscar—on Facebook: the profile pic was a sweet, smiling older lady with short, white hair curled into a loose perm, thick bifocals over her eyes, chubby, pale cheeks. From what she could see of the profile, she was confident this was Court's maternal grandmother, so she'd sent out a friend request to her too but had yet to hear back.

"I should go," Dani said. She stood and crossed to the windows, pulled the vertical blinds open, looking outside and to the east to the parking lot where the evening shadows stretched longer. "I could get there in a couple of hours." When Rong didn't respond, she turned and faced them. "What?" They wore a pensive look, brow wrinkled, finger to their lips.

"You have class tomorrow. Tutoring"

"I'll email my professors. My students."

Rong nodded but still offered a pause. "Your students and their parents might understand, but your professors might not."

"They'll have to," she said. She'd made up her mind.

"Think about this," Rong said. "You email them—a graduate student skipping class due to an emergency you can't even classify as a family emergency, no matter how much you care about him. Your boyfriend has run off. Might sound a bit sophomoric, don't you think? You told me your Music Theory Prof—Carlyle, was it—said all absences were unexcused because 'student problems are personal problems and so have nothing to do with the class.'"

The shadows grew longer outside, and in the distance, she heard a few rumbles of thunder. The clouds had been inching their way over the area all day and seemed about ready to unleash the torrent they carried.

"Wouldn't a true emergency warrant more than an email?" Rong continued. "After all, you can't convey pathos in an email. It's grad school, and you are concerned, so it should at least necessitate a face-to-face conversation. Not to mention, you've been unable to reach anyone over there, so before you show up on someone's doorstep, you should probably let them know who exactly you are and why you want to come over. They are probably aware now of Court's disappearance, and it sounds like the police are involved."

Damn their logic, Dani thought, but outwardly she could only nod. None of this added up to solid proof. Court could have had car trouble—a flat, or something—and his grandparents could have come and picked him up. They could be focused on health issues and getting the car repaired. It was easy to jump to conclusions, but there still wasn't enough information to go on. Not until she heard from the grandparents would it be prudent to act.

Dani moved to the kitchen but knew instantly she wasn't hungry; the thought of food repulsed her. Her stomach rolled and grumbled loudly, so she pulled a gallon of tea from the fridge and poured herself a glass. Rong set down their laptop long enough to pour their own glass, then returned to the couch, staring again at the screen. Scrolling.

CHAPTER TWENTY-TWO

Clem Willette didn't go to the bar that night. Instead, he broke his cardinal rule: he bought a twelve-pack of pints and sat in his living room as he watched One America News and drank slowly, savoring every drop. For dinner, he got a deli sandwich, made by one of the Mexican ladies behind the counter at Walmart, the lettuce wilted and the tomato rubbery and the bread like Playdoh. Still, it was enough to soak up the beer. He drank well into the night, not giving a shit what time he had to get up, sure he'd be excused for missing a day if he so chose because he'd never called in a day in his life. Outside, thunder rumbled somewhere far away, over the television volume, and the air smelled electric. On the tube, a reporter was praising their current president and his conservative policies. Clem felt his head droop and the lights around him seemed to dim, and he didn't mind. Hell, he could fall asleep right here and be okay, and he was about to when he heard a bang and roused himself long enough to see his front door slapping against the kitchen cabinet and the screen door flapping against the trailer siding.

He started to rise, but the couch cushions sank deep, swallowing his ass, and he had to brace against the arm to stand; even still he swayed as the trailer opening danced in front of him. Stumbling, grabbing for the doorjamb, holding it for dear life as he leaned out over his front steps, he fumbled for the screen door, pulling it closed when he found the lever. Tripping backward now, he shoved the wooden front door closed, locked the deadbolt and the doorknob and slid the chain home. He turned and came face to face with his father, who'd been dead for twenty years.

"Lousy drunk," his father said.

Clem swayed a bit, caught hold of the back of the recliner he'd inherited from his dad and said, "So were you."

"Excuses are like assholes, Clem. If I'd jumped off a cliff, would you have done it too?"

His father looked the way he remembered him. Unaged. His voice was what Clem heard when he dreamed of his father and he even smelled the same, like Hai Karate and Jack Daniels.

"I'm tired, Dad," Clem said. He reached into the fridge for another beer (four left) and looked over his shoulder to ask if his dad wanted one. Never mind this was probably a hallucination brought on by nerves; he'd play it out and see it to the end.

"No, son, I'm fine. But you got to get your head straight. Things are about to happen."

Clem snapped the tab and took a long pull, his throat working up and down like a firing piston until he smacked his lips as the last of the beer washed down his throat. "Like what?"

"Well, an important person has come to town, and he's been restrained. Now, I took care of him, mind you, but you need to run a diversion."

"A diversion? What is it?"

"It's a fake play to draw your enemy's attention away, but that's not important right now." Clem chuckled because his dad, as mean as he was, could have the best jokes.

"Airplane!" Clem said.

"Now listen, boy!" his dad snapped, and Clem straightened up. He didn't want the belt again. No sir, the buckle smarted. "This important person I handled, well, he's got friends. And they'll be coming. And they'll want to meet his family. A lot of people won't like what we're doing. But Clem, we got to do it. For this town. For God. For what this country stands for. You hear me, boy?"

Clem took another pull off the can and nodded slowly, realizing this might be the most important mission of his life.

"We got a lot gone against us, Clementine. And its only gone be you and me, and we'll likely be outnumbered. But it means we got to do all we can to win."

"Okay, Daddy." The middle-aged Baby Boomer was an adolescent again, caught under the thumb of his father.

"I mean it. To protect our way of life. To safeguard what we know is right. You cain't pull no punches. If you got a shot, you got to take it."

"Okay, Daddy."

His father looked to the wall. Clem finished off the can and crumpled it in his hand then followed his father's gaze to the shotgun he kept mounted on the wall. It had been his father's before it was his and it was his grandfather's before him, but it still fired, and it still held buckshot. It was a twelve-gauge—and it would do fine.

Clem tossed the beer in the trash, then fished another out of the fridge. When he turned around, his door was open again, the screen door was banging against the siding of the single wide, and the wind was driving something fierce in over the hills from the west. His father was gone, but he knew what he had to do.

CHAPTER TWENTY-THREE

A storm assaulted the night, lightning flashing on the western horizon as thunder shook the windows of Ferrous Regional. Aster had tried the cot but found it even less comfortable than the chair. She sat up and stretched, then moved to the chair next to Britta who slept with her chin on her fist, her left leg kicking at some nightmare. Aster imagined TJ was down the hall with Lena, as she hadn't seen him for some time. Not since the two of them had gone to the cafeteria and brought her back a sandwich which she barely ate, the bulk of it still partially wrapped in the cellophane on the bedside table.

Aster studied the sandwich for a time, half expecting it to move, entranced by it, thoughts emptying from her head as she stared at the fibers of the bread, the way it all meshed together with mayonnaise like glue sealing it solid. Outside, the thunder rolled, and she heard the hint of wind, but it was the flickering of Elden's wrist, the twitch of his fingers, which woke her up completely and focused her attention.

"I'm here, baby," she said. "I haven't left you. I won't."

She couldn't know Lena was also roused from sleep, a few doors down, alerted to Glen's twitching. Both men would begin in somnolence uttering the exact same phrase.

"Not yet, not yet, not yet, not yet."

Both Glen and Elden sounded so weak in their pleading, so feeble with the tubes hooked up to them. Both of their heart rates spiked. Nurses came in to check on their vitals. All of Lena's nursing knowledge emptied as she held her husband's hand; Aster didn't have such knowledge but held on to Elden as tightly as possible, even as both men uttered the same thing over and over again, and outside the winds raged and the lightning flashed and the thunder shook the world and the rain came down.

"Notyetnotyetnotyetnotyetnotyet."

INTERLUDE FOUR

The Tale of the Poet's Loves

Once upon a time, there was a poet who loved women and wrote about love on the pages of his journal, but love was a fleeting thing and the women the poet loved all met tragic ends.

His high school sweetheart went off to college in the exact opposite direction as he, and she started a new life in this new town, even dating. But she never lost contact with the poet and agreed one Christmas to meet him during their break. Her car skirted the icy Ozark roads, hugging the hills and skating the ridge lines, 'til something darted out in front of her car and forced her to jerk the wheel and slam on the brakes.

When the poet attended her funeral, he couldn't know he was watched from the tree line by the very thing that had forced her to steer into the ravine, killing her instantly.

For it had a purpose. It had known for some time he would become a storyteller, the very storyteller it needed to satisfy its hunger.

The thing watched him from afar, calling on its darkest magiks to spy on him as he studied at the university, hours away. It saw the pretty auburn-haired thing he courted the fall semester of his sophomore year. It saw him try to study and focus and it saw this girl intrude upon him and harass him and impose herself on him.

Oh, how it hated this girl, like it hated the one he'd taken to the high school dance. He ought to fall in love with the girl it showed him way back when he was a toddler investigating the tree line, and the dancer in the forest.

But she was easily rectified. It took a knife and a mugger on a sidewalk not far from her apartment to appease it, and soon enough the young poet sat morose again, welcoming the shadows, the darkness.

He took some time to recover from her death, but he met a pretty blonde with tight cheekbones and emerald green eyes in an Irish themed bar on Dickson Street a year and a half later, and she latched onto him good. They were both English majors and she had an intellect she taunted him with, and perhaps they would have ended up together if not for the landing leading up to his apartment.

She'd left early one morning for class, you see, and tripped on nothing the cops could find—but tripped nonetheless—and her neck snapped on one of the concrete risers down to the landing between the first and second floors.

The poet wept. He went home and his grandparents consoled him. It watched.

But don't feel sorry for him, and don't think this was the sum total of his dating life. He had other dates and he slept with other women, and most were fine, though some also met mysterious ends, but these three deaths affected him greatly.

The End

CHAPTER TWENTY-FOUR

The voicemail appeared as she checked her email on her phone while the coffee was brewing, like some illusionist's magic trick. She had awakened in his bed after a night of fitful sleep, her stomach roiling so much she barely made it from the bed to the bathroom before vomiting into the toilet. Outside, the rain fell steadily, pounding on the tin roof of the loft like eighth notes on a snare drum. Morning light streamed into the loft dim and blue, the shadows thick in the deepest corners and recesses, the bedroom nearly pitch. She rinsed with mouthwash and splashed water on her face before walking into the kitchen, before picking up her phone. The message was hard to hear over the rain, but it was Court, and seemed to be from a couple of days earlier.

"I thought you'd stay, after the concert. When I woke up, I never thought I'd see you gone. I don't want you gone. I'm heading to my grandparents. My grandfathers aren't doing well. I'm taking your advice, going to say goodbye. To see if I can... I don't know, do anything. I'll call you when I get there. I promise. I hope you'll answer." There was a pause, but no indication the message was through. In fact, the ticker still showed twenty seconds left. "I love you, Dani. I know we haven't said it yet. But I do."

She dropped the phone on the table, pressed her palms into her eyes. "Fuck," she said, processing the message instantly. Had she missed his call? Had the goddamn service provider dropped his call like it apparently dropped the voicemail? She called customer service, the IT person on the other end apologizing for the interruption, saying no other calls had come from his number. She hung up and called his cell anyway, hanging up only when his voicemail kicked on. All the while, the rain continued unabated its drum solo on the roof. Dani took a long sip of coffee and called Rong. Rong promised to call Blue and Dani, before jumping in the shower, called Jada. The closest friends to she and Court, now all in the loop. Rong and Jada said they would come this evening. As she hiked to the campus, Rong texted and said Blue was bringing along Chuy. She read this on the steps up to the music building, muttering as she pocketed the phone after reading the text. "The more the fucking merrier."

Professor Carlyle sat in his office, listening to a composition on his desktop which Dani could hear from the hall. She paused to knock, recognizing the piece: chamber music by Nino Rota. Gathered her nerve. He intimidated her.

"Come."

The professor was a thin man with prominent cheekbones, dark, thick eyebrows that joined completely over the bridge of his nose, and large ears that stood out even through his unkept mane of thick gray hair. Today he wore a black turtleneck, and his thin rimmed glasses were perched low on his nose. "How may I help you, Miss Morales?" He waved a hand as though to usher her to the guest seat, at once an invitation and permission.

"Thank you," she said, sitting. She folded her hands in her lap, wondering where to begin. He didn't have unkind eyes, but he wore a stern expression. Upon her entering, he'd paused the performance, and she was sure he was eager to get back to it. "I won't take much of your time. I need to go out of town for a few days," she started, after taking a deep breath like one might take a shot of whiskey. "I am not going to miss today's lecture, and I don't anticipate being gone past the weekend, but in case I am, I wanted to let you know." Notify him especially, as he was her graduate advisor, the head of the department, and one of her instructors this semester.

He sat back in his chair, its parts squeaking. Folded his hands behind his head, studying her. Overhead, a vent kicked on. "I see," he said after a moment. "Might I ask the purpose of this trip?"

It's personal, she contemplated saying, then, "I've been seeing someone. Another department. Court Dillon from English."

"Ah yes," he said, nodding. "I know Professor Dillon. I enjoy his poetry. I'd heard you two have been spotted around campus and Dickson Street. I hope all is well."

She bit her lip, shook her head quickly. "He had a family emergency and had to return home," she said. "I don't think he made it."

The squeak of the chair echoed through the room as he leaned forward, this time accompanied by a gasp. "What do you mean?"

She told him about the cop coming to his apartment, her inability to reach anyone. Recalling these events yet again, on top of a fitful rest in his bed the night before, finally brought tears to her eyes. He handed her a tissue.

"I know personal excuses are just excuses," she said in closing, wiping at her eyes, "but I need to know what's going on. If he's okay."

"You suspect he isn't, correct? Isn't your fear part of what you aren't telling me?" Goddammit, did he have to sound so robotic?

She nodded, took another tissue when he offered it.

He pursed his lips. "Are you even in any condition to attend the lecture?"

Unlike the wave of his hand, this was not an invitation. Merely a question, asked out of annoyance. To this she nodded. Blew her nose, wadded the tissues into her fist.

"Very well," he said, leaning back again, hands back behind his head, squeak of the chair, all this a regal pronouncement like a king granting clemency. She knew him well enough to know that despite his outward appearance, he was concerned. "You may leave after your courses. I do hate to hear of another faculty member's troubles. Hopefully you'll turn up some good news. But I expect you to email me if there is no word by Sunday. We'll have to figure out your classes for next week, as I can't assume you'd return until he's discovered, especially if law enforcement is involved."

No emotion. And though she'd heard his lectures and spoken with him on many occasions, she still wondered who spoke in such a manner. Someone pompous. Someone who regards himself above others. A narcissist, she might have imagined had she not known him better, hating she had to come and beg when something could have happened. Perhaps if he could only show some emotion, she thought, and she muttered her thank you and was rising to leave, tossing the wad of tissue into the nearby waste basket, when he spoke again.

"We put a lot of faith in our graduate students, Miss Morales. This is why we are so strict with our policies, as cold and unfair as they may seem. Especially a student in your position, earning a stipend to compensate for tuition. Your responsibilities to this program are of the utmost importance, and there is no room for leeway in this regard. You are, in our eyes, an investment, a valuable piece of property to this distinguished program, something we have poured time and money and energy into because we believe in you, your scholarship, your talent, and your promise."

He removed his glasses and cleaned the lenses with more tissue, never taking his eyes off her. Something in his eyes softened, and his voice lost a bit of the robotic tone while gaining some emotion. "But I do understand when students are hurting. And I do appreciate your feelings. Professor Dillon is a talented poet and a respected colleague. I ask only that you keep me updated on the situation."

Dani swallowed the lump in her throat out of fear it would raise more tears. "Thank you," she said in a near-whisper, then closed the door and stepped into the hall, reserving the outpouring of emotion for after the closing of the door.

CHAPTER TWENTY-FIVE

After Lena had forced down a cracker and half an apple for lunch, she found the house too empty, so she returned to the hospital. She'd walked its halls so many times as a nurse of nearly fifty years and as a friend or family member of the sick, so that now the tiled linoleum and fluorescent lighting seemed like a second home, the beeps and bells and whistles and overhead announcements breaking the silence that sat undisturbed at their empty house. This wall and its crack here. The uneven plaster against the elevator there. Hadn't they joked the subcontractor had come in too cheap? What about the drip on the third floor? The leaky tile?

But this building was so mundane in its peculiarities. These imperfections had been noticed for a lifetime, now, and so, as she entered and ascended, they were old hat. Like the imperfections of her house. Long since forgiven, they were amusements now shared between her and Glen.

The med-surg waiting room showed no sign of Aster, so she made her way to the nurse's station, where a young LPN at the desk gave her a feckless smile. Lena continued on down the hall and pushed the door open to her husband's private room.

So many machines. How could anyone rest with all the beeping and humming? She knew their purpose, as a nurse, but as a wife wishing her husband peace, these impediments squawked intrusion. His eyes flitted as she entered the room, and he turned his head, smiled at her, then squeezed her hand tightly as she sat at his side. In his visage now she saw a glimpse of the young man she'd married. This was neither an indictment against his age nor an accusation he'd had the audacity to get older, but merely an observation. Time pancaked age onto the faces of the youth like too much cheap foundation.

"I gave you quite the scare." Raspy, gravelly. His voice.

She offered him a smile as feeble as his vocal cords, and prayed a tear would not spill down her cheek, but then Glen did something she'd thought impossible: his arms braced behind him and he scooted up, sitting bolt upright in the bed as the doctor entered.

"Your preliminary labs indicated pneumonia," the doctor said, and while he saw Glen sitting up, he didn't share Lena's surprise. "But we've had to double check your most recent monitors for glitches." This last he said, glancing at the iPad in his hand.

Instinctively Lena looked at the machines and frowned at the numbers. As a nurse she knew what they should suggest. An eighty-four-year-old white male with such a low pulse and a BP rating below 40% would not have saturation levels so elevated after such short-term intravenous interaction, would not have respiratory function this restored. She looked to the doctor for answers as Glen swung his legs over the side of the bed and kicked his feet.

The doctor shrugged. In her fifty years as a nurse, Lena knew a shrug only meant one thing: he had no clue what was going on.

"How do you feel?" she asked, retaking his hand.

Pensive first, as though he considered the question, Glen offered the smile he'd displayed their entire marriage. "Good," he answered, his voice clearer, stronger.

She looked back to the doctor for reassurance, mindfully preparing herself for jubilee, but the frown he wore kept her in check and called into question all they knew. She addressed his grimace resolutely, prepared for any dire prognosis, for any outcome other than the one he gave.

"This has to be a mistake. This can't be right. Heart function…" and the next few words the doctor mumbled, before remembering he wasn't alone in the room. "I'm sorry. The cardiologist has said for the past few years, your heart has had an ejection rating of forty-five percent. Piss poor for a younger man, but for an octogenarian with your cardiac history, not too bad. You've kept active and have managed to lose some weight, which has eased the burden on your old ticker, but the numbers have stabilized."

"I've monitored him closely," Lena said.

"We look out for each other," Glen said.

The doctor shook his head. "Mr. Dillon, what I'm seeing here is impossible. Your cardiac function has improved, according to what we've been monitoring while you've been here. In this short time, you've improved to seventy percent ER. Sir, such a refraction is normal for healthy, active, young adults."

"Maybe the IV helped," Glen joked.

The doctor didn't join in. "No, sir. It doesn't. Not this kind of improvement, without changes to medicine or surgery. In a man your age, this level of improvement is unheard of. This is a miracle."

"The pneumonia?" Lena asked.

"Gone," the doctor said with another shrug. "All traces. I'd like to hold you another day or so, to be sure, but…"

Glen motioned for his clothes. "Nope," he said. Lena handed him his wadded-up khakis and he fought to get them on under the gown and over the underwear.

"These results are preliminary. We should monitor…"

"Feeling better, doc. Thank you."

The doctor furrowed his brow. "I didn't do anything."

Glen took the gown off and put on his tee and then his short sleeve button-up. He straightened himself on the side of the bed and took a deep breath. The socks and loafers, he pulled on, and considered them for a long moment, with a look as though he had something to say, until he straightened and stood and turned and smiled at each of them in turn.

"Once when my grandson was around eight, we were getting ready for Sunday school, he asked me why we called them penny loafers, and I told him we put shiny pennies in each shoe—you remember?"

Lena smiled and nodded.

"So, before Sunday school that morning we put brand new pennies in his shoes and in my loafers. In these loafers." He lifted his leg toward the doctor and flexed his foot to show off the shoe. "We polished them when we got back from church. I showed him how to care for them so they'd last for years."

The doctor eyed the pennies in the loafers, but before he could ask, he met Glen's easy grin.

"Same exact ones we put in."

"Mr. Dillon, we need to monitor you more. At least to find out the reason behind this marked improvement. Men your age don't generally get healthier. Not like this."

"You read the paper, doc? You know what the cops been finding in the local cemetery?" He didn't wait for the doctor's inevitable silent nod. "My grandson is coming back home and we're going to get to the bottom of this. We got work to do."

He looked to Lena and took her hand. "We got work to do."

CHAPTER TWENTY-SIX

As the grandparents were leaving the hospital, Dani left her morning class thankful her lectures were finally over, and with her acoustic in hand, she hoofed it to her car in the parking lot on Dickson St. across from the Walton Arts Center and drove down College Ave. to the music shop where she gave her lessons. With her she'd brought a small salad and a couple of hard-boiled eggs, the latter of which she sucked down as she sped down College. She opened the salad when she was set up in the tiny room, her laptop opened to receive the next Skype call. Only then did she rip open the packet of Italian dressing and dump it over the romaine and kale and cherry tomatoes and olives and sweet peppers. As she ate, she scrolled through her phone. Still no DM, no text. It wasn't the cellular data, which she turned off, or the Wi-Fi connection. Her thoughts threatened to carry her to dark places without proof or evidence before the first of her students entered, lugging an acoustic Simon and Allen.

"Okay, so we left off with the pentatonic scale on the seventh fret." She blinked, then smiled at the girl of twelve who'd started lessons only a month earlier. "I'm sorry, Liv, how are you?"

"I'm fine, Señorita Morales. How are you?"

"Muy bien," Dani said, setting her phone down with one more aggrieved look. Still no voicemail; still no text.

CHAPTER TWENTY-SEVEN

Aster ran the saucer under the faucet 'til all the crumbs washed down the drain and still she watched the water, the clear stream, swirling, washing away into the plumbing buried underneath the house. Elden had installed those pipes himself, just like he'd built the other rooms to expand this small farmhouse in the years before he met her. His hands had touched every inch of this home, skin to skeleton.

Behind her, Britta wiped down the white gas stove, having already finished with the countertops, and she reacted quickly when Aster started crying, rushing to her side to put her hands on the older woman's shoulders.

"He's been my rock," Aster said, her voice barely breaking. "He's been my whole world."

"Shh. Let's finish so we can get back up to the hospital."

"What will I do?" She looked at Britta with a desperate, pleading look. "What will I do? What can I do with myself? I've spent most of my life with him as my partner. I don't know if I can go it alone."

"Let's not talk about this, now," Britta said.

"Lena is strong enough. She doesn't define herself by Glen. She'll miss him like the dickens, but… I can't be alone."

"You aren't. You got Court, and you got TJ and me. And Elden isn't gone yet."

"What will become of me?"

Britta didn't have an answer, so silence followed until the old rotary on the wall rang and the two women jumped. Britta reached for it instinctively, wondering aloud who it was, but Aster interrupted. "I've got it." She picked up the receiver. "Oscar residence," she tried in her most pleasant voice. "Yes… I see… Okay… We'll be right there… Thank you."

Britta said, "What was it?"

"You… you have to go get your kids—I'll… I can drive myself." There was something Aster was trying to piece together. The words she'd heard made little sense, and with a glance she could see she was scaring Britta.

"What's wrong?"

"It was the hospital," Aster said.

"I'll call TJ. He'll pick up the kids. What did they say?"

"It's Elden," Aster said, but she couldn't say more because she couldn't believe it. She dared not believe it. As much as she had thought about it, to be confronted with it now seemed impossible.

CHAPTER TWENTY-EIGHT

The friends arrived together, oohing and ahhing over Court's apartment, all but Rong having never been there before. Dani found it odd, given the number of times they'd all hung out, but Court had only ever met them at bars on Dickson or visited their homes, so they hadn't the opportunity to see the 1,400 square-foot loft with the expansive front room, the exposed beams and vaulted ceilings. They were talking nonstop. Outside, dusk was settling in quickly, the air turning crisp; it smelled like fall.

Dani ushered them in: Rong; Blue, Court's old friend and a local singer, her dark hair short and curly, her thin frame clothed simply in jeans, a tee, and Birkenstocks; Chuy, an engineering major, short and dumpy but affable, his black hair coiffed and his black goatee trimmed, a thin line of beard racing up his jaw; and Jada, Dani's sorority sister, looking amazing as always in pinks and purples and blacks, her cell permanently attached to her left hand. Dani had a couple of pizzas ordered for when they arrived, feeling the need to feed this crew who'd come at her beck and call. Still, the thought of telling the story again felt exhausting, so when Rong spoke up and offered, Dani let them speak for her, and only jumped in when they were all sufficiently caught up.

"So as soon as I get a hold of his grandparents, I'm probably going to head out tonight."

"You want us to come?" Jada asked. She had already mixed herself a drink and was nearly done with it—Dani wondered if she would be able to drive.

She shook her head and checked her phone, more of a habit than a hope. "No. You all stay. Have fun. Relax. I'll keep you informed."

"You gonna call them now?" Rong asked.

Dani scratched at her chin. "In a few. Wanna make sure they had time to get home." They let this settle for a few minutes before the ho hum conversation began. Reflective, Dani sat back and listened. The conversations existed outside of her and her current state. She didn't see them as uncaring. In fact, their faces masked in worry, that tone dictated words that, in another setting, might be flippant or even jovial, but their words suggested an ease of companionship. They were all friends with each other, as well as Dani and Court, and it showed now clearly as she sat on the outside looking in.

Chuy: So, I'm the running for this grant, and I should know something in a couple of weeks.

Jada: Where'd you get the shirt, Choo?

Blue (to Rong): I'm saying she's losing her identity to him. I hate it when women pull such shit. So, fucking weak.

Dani: Love isn't weak, Blue. How's your sister doing?

Jada: Fine.

Blue: Like sister, sister or sorority sister?

Jada: Sister, sister.

Blue: What's wrong with her?

Jada: Surgery.

Jada: They think the big C. Ovarian.

Blue: Jesus. Sorry, J. I'm dealing with the C with my aunt. Not Ovarian, but who the fuck cares the difference. Cancer's cancer.

Jada: Where'd you get the shirt?

Chuy: There's this boutique on Block Street…

Dani: You want something else?

Rong: Water's fine.

Blue: You've been awfully quiet.

Rong: I'm gonna go smoke.

Chuy: He can smoke in here.

Blue: 'They' not 'he.'

Chuy: Jesus fucking Christ.

Dani: Besides, they smoke cloves.

Jada: Yeah, take that shit outside.

Rong returned a few minutes later, bringing the smell, like spicy incense, with them. Dani's focus kept finding her phone, letting her friends' words become a jumble of inane noise. Eventually, she stood and began to pace. Jada picked up her drink—something sugary and colorful with lots of alcohols mixed into it—and paced with her, talking at her about whatever drama currently consumed her; Dani wasn't listening.

"Quiet, y'all," Rong tried. This did nothing. Dani still paced and Jada still followed, drink in hand, and Blue and Chuy still tried to talk over one another.

Dani was scared. She was scared of not knowing and scared of what his grandparents would think. Her cheeks were flushing, and her fingers were trembling as she typed, checking Facebook to absolutely no news.

"Call," Rong said, a bit louder. They stood. "Dani, call."

Dani turned and pointed, and Jada, her question lost in the chatter but now with an answer, retreated to a door on the other side of the kitchen island, into a bedroom. Presently, a faucet could be heard.

Blue was about to counter Chuy's argument of, "But what about neoclassicism," when Dani's phone buzzed. Dani found she was shaking, and she fumbled a bit to answer. "Yes."

"Is this Dani Morales?" A female's voice. Older. A bit cool.

"Yes." Her breath hitched in her throat, like a hiccup almost.

"I'm Court's grandmother, Lena Dillon. You were trying to reach me?"

"Yes ma'am. I'm a friend of Court's—"

"Friend?"

"His—his girlfriend, actually. He left a couple of days ago to go see you. You and his other grandparents. Is he there, Mrs. Dillon? I haven't heard from him."

Silence on the other end. She thought Lena was talking to someone, but her voice was muffled, like she was covering the mouthpiece of the phone. Someone might have responded, but it could have also been a TV on in the background. Or perhaps it was her husband.

"Dani," she said finally. "When did you say he left?"

"Early morning a couple of days ago."

More muffled speaking.

"Mrs. Dillon," she said into the phone. "Mrs. Dillon!" she repeated a bit louder, hoping to get her attention. The room around her had quieted and the friends had stiffened, all watching her silently with faces drawn with worry and fear.

"Yes, I'm sorry."

"The police were here, at his apartment. They found his car abandoned in Rapps Barren. You haven't heard from him?"

"No, dear…" A shuffling of the phone, banging against the speaker, mysterious thuds and noises.

"Mrs. Dillon?"

"I'm here, dear."

"The police didn't contact you?"

"No, dear. I'm sorry. I've been at the hospital with Court's grandfather. Actually, both grandfathers were in the hospital. It's possible we've missed the police if they came by either of our houses."

"Mrs. Dillon, I would like to come over. I'm worried about him, and if he's missing, I'd like to help."

More muffled speaking. A raised voice. Desperation must be setting in at the Dillon household. How much panic had she stirred up?

"Mrs. Dillon. Mrs. Dillon!"

"I'm here."

"I don't want to be an inconvenience. I can stay in a hotel if need be."

"Don't be ridiculous. We'll expect you in a couple of hours. I'll text you the address."

The call died.

Dani hung up. Her hands shaking worse than before, she tried to stop them by gripping the phone tightly, walked over to the sectional and eased down onto the cushion nearest the armchair. Where Court always sat. Jada walked up behind her and began to rub her shoulders. Rong sat back down between Blue and Chuy.

Dani met Rong's eyes and shook her head.

And Rong said, "Whatever you want from us, tell us."

"I don't know," Dani said.

"When are you leaving?" Rong asked.

When Dani sighed, her whole body shuddered. She bent at the waist, her hair falling around her face. When she finally looked up, her face was red and there were tears in her eyes, which she wiped at furiously. She blew a tuft of hair out of face and took a few more deep breaths. "I need to pack a bag."

When she stood, it was Jada by her side. "C'mon," her sorority sister said. "I'll help you."

◊◊◊

The sun finally disappeared into the western horizon, glaring through the rear windshield and refracting into her rearview mirror as she entered a predominantly white town in an area with few decent radio stations, someplace heavily Evangelical, rural, and poor. There a Baptist church. There a gravel-lot dealer of single-wide mobile homes. Then there was the billboard that rose above the town limits: a photo of a little blonde-haired, blue-eyed girl with the caption: "It isn't racist to love your own kind."

But there was something else she felt as she drove. An odd feeling, as she looked at the trees standing sentry at the shoulder, their colored leaves in the dim light of sunset and the low, dark clouds hovering ahead of her on the horizon, the dying grass. She wasn't entering another season. She was entering another world. It felt like a dark fairy tale. A place under a spell, shadowy and cold.

The state highway widened as she entered the town of Harrison, the midway point between Fayetteville and Rapps Barren; she passed a few dealerships and a couple of banks, and then she took the bypass entrance on the right and wondered bitterly if she wasn't good enough to see the town proper. She might not be good enough to see the family even. Certainly, she'd posited this line of questioning a week earlier, during an autumn storm.

"What will they think of me?" she had asked him after sex, as he held her in bed.

"My grandparents?"

She bit into the nails of her free hand and stared out to the trees, darkened by shadows, stretching long into the fresh night. And when would the deer dart across the highway, and wreck the car, and smash into her rescue? Pastures and trees stretched out before her.

"What if they see me like some Spic whore not good enough for their little boy? Not white enough."

"Dani…" he'd said.

"I know towns like this, Court."

"You think I'm racist? I'm from this town."

She shook her head and turned east onto a two-lane state highway, flanked on either side by oaks and maples and elms.

"I know towns like this, Court," she had said. "Of course, you aren't. You got out. But the people here didn't get out. Your grandparents…"

"This town is isolated, Dani," he had said, "but it doesn't mean its citizens are." His paternal grandfather had flown all over the world in the Air Force; he'd served in the Korean War. His maternal grandfather had enlisted in the Army and fought in Europe in World War Two on the ground. His paternal grandmother had studied nursing in St. Louis in the fifties.

"And your maternal grandmother?" she had asked him. She'd been counting. He'd missed one.

"They aren't racist, Dani. They're old. Set in their ways. The world has changed and sometimes, it leaves people behind. But they'll love you."

"You don't have to wake up every morning and think about being white, or a man. You think about breakfast and lectures and when you can have your first beer. I'm never allowed to forget I'm a woman or I'm Hispanic. I think about these things almost every second of every day, because I'm constantly reminded by everyone who sees me, every white person and every male, regardless of color, who checks me out."

"So, you work out? Because your femininity and your race define you to this world? Because you think it makes you vulnerable?"

"It doesn't make me vulnerable; it makes me susceptible."

"Well, either way, your thighs look amazing."

She'd punched his bicep, but it was playful. "I'm serious, Court. Imagine a world where you have to think about what you'll encounter when you step outside the door because of the color of your skin or what is or isn't between your legs."

"I can't," he admitted. "It sounds… exhausting."

"It is," she said.

She passed the deep, deep forest filled with shadows, where anything could happen, and they wouldn't find your attractive body for days. She was pretty, and she knew it, her black hair curling past her shoulders, her figure, her full lips and her deep tan skin, her wide hips and ample breasts. Court was aroused by these things, as most men would be. But while he spoke of strength in her spirit, his perception was still based on sex. Her strength protected her. Her strength, past being a woman and a Latina, was that she knew she was an individual who could defend herself in a world which cast her as 'other' because of those classifications.

The north-central Arkansas wilderness stretched around her, the meager path of the two-lane road the narrow trail carrying her from civilization into the other realm, the realm of deep shadows and fog, where animals lurked at the edge of the forest's expanse and monsters were everywhere. It was nearly pitch black as she turned down another highway, cresting a hill; her headlights shone on the path until it vanished around another bend. She remembered conversations with Court and focused on the road, on the potential of deer running out in front of her, on the potential for other cars.

Still, though she emptied her mind, she couldn't escape the feeling she was traveling into another land, haunted. Or cursed. She'd entered some dark fairy tale, an idea heightened by the mid-twentieth century stone rainbow arch bridge she crossed and then a roadside cemetery. But more than ghosts and goblins and shadows and monsters, Dani knew in this land *she* was different. Some of the people, perhaps even Court's own family, may not tolerate her, and what then? How would she find him if no one cooperated with her, if everyone shunned her?

Court's stories about his grandparents didn't suggest they'd reject her. On the contrary, the few times they talked about meeting family, he said they would love her.

Still, his grandfathers were both dying, and she knew his grandmothers were preoccupied with this, as well as with Court's vanishing, so Dani prepared herself for the possibility they wouldn't be able to help, that she'd still be left alone.

CHAPTER TWENTY-NINE

Once Rong had returned home, they began to pack immediately. For Rong, it didn't feel like a choice. They truly wanted to respect Dani's wishes to go alone, but something sat foul with this whole mess. For Court to vanish didn't make sense. Either his grandparents were hiding him out and away from Dani, or he'd up and disappeared. But those news reports stuck in their brain too. They were reminded of them as they checked email on their laptop—most of the world papers to which they subscribed had delivered fresh news to their inbox.

Rong picked up the cell and asked, when the call was answered, "What kind of mpg does your Xterra get?"

Jada was on the other end. She was used to Rong, whose openings and salutations were abrupt; still, she said, "What?"

"We need a vehicle with enough room for all of us that's easy on gas." Then a thought clicked, and Rong said, "No. We should caravan. At least three vehicles. Come over."

Rong hung up and dialed again, wondering where they'd stored their travel toothbrush.

INTERLUDE FIVE

The Tale of the Girl and the Guitar

Once upon a time, a girl received an acoustic guitar from her grandmother. Wanting to please her, the girl learned a few chords. She learned to strum, then to finger pick, and learned a few more chords after that. She stretched her fingers across the frets and played until the callouses formed. When her grandmother passed away, the girl clung to the neck of the guitar, sobbing, until a song issued forth. Playing became a source of comfort for the girl. She listened to old records on the grandmother's antique wooden record player, and the girl scratched at the strings as the vinyl scratched out the songs.

The songs were bandolero ballads and mariachi sounds, until one day they weren't. The girl discovered an old vinyl of her grandmother's and, intrigued by the cover, put it on. An angry Latina played power chords and sang about things the girl had never heard a woman sing about. The singer cursed and spit into the microphone, and the drums pounded to keep up with the fast guitar riffs. Might there be a hint of the bandolero or mariachi? Yes, under the current of angry punk, there was this identity. The identity she'd known. The devout, humble woman who always wore a smile and hated to speak English unless she absolutely had to.

"This record," the girl said one day, showing her father.

He smiled and nodded. "Your grandmother introduced me to punk when I tried to tell her about the Dead Kennedys. I'd come home from school, and I was very excited, but your grandmother just shook her head and asked if I wanted to learn the true history of punk, and she put this record on."

The girl practiced power chords. She got faster at scales. Her time in high school was as confusing as anyone else's, so in that way she was not special. Her outlet, playing the guitar, was what was special. And how she played it. A few years after her grandmother gave her the acoustic, she'd bought a cheap solid body electric. Working at the laundromat for her mother in high school provided her the means to upgrade the cheap solid body to a G&L and a nice amp.

The girl played first for family, then for friends. The high school had a band, but no guitar instructor, sticking strictly with percussion, brass, and winds. The girl played mostly alone, until her father (now working at a local restaurant), convinced her to play one Friday night for the patrons of the restaurant. It wasn't until the strangers rewarded her with applause and tips that she considered making a living playing guitar. Up to that point, her parents had been successful convincing her to major in something safe in college. Like nursing. There was nothing safe about guitar. Not especially the way she played it.

The girl researched music programs and liked especially what the University of Arkansas offered. She showed her parents the brochure for the nursing program. Of course, her mother didn't want her moving so far away, and the girl expected this. What mattered more was that the girl wanted to move away. Especially if she wasn't going to follow the path they were laying out for her. She loved her parents wholeheartedly, but she'd come to feel she could not breathe. If she pursued nursing as they expected her to do, she knew she may never breathe again.

So, she moved north and enrolled in the music program. She took her guitars and played and made friends and dated and joined a band and played and aced her classes. While that is the end of this tale, it is not the end of the story for the girl, who met a professor of English during a faculty Arts mixer and thought, *he has a nice smile.*

The End

PART THREE

The Carriage of Immortality

CHAPTER THIRTY

A lone, narrow stretch of blacktop led into the night. The threadbare trees silhouetted against the gray-black clouds choked out the headlights and dimmed the small pool of illumination in a nearby drive. In the study of a house sitting off the road and away from the drive, a lamp caged in the window spilled gold light out onto the yard. The outside, cold and dark, seeped in through the sealed trim around the edges of her sedan, the windshield fogging up.

Dani gripped the wheel, staring into the void. She was here. About to meet one of Court's grandmothers. A woman probably consumed with her dying husband and her missing grandson and Dani was to—what? Console her? What if the woman didn't want her help?

Google Maps flashed at her: 0.2 miles 'til she turned right, and her destination was 0.3 miles away on the right. Arrival time: two minutes. She had already decided that if Lena Dillon rejected her, she wouldn't go home, but find a hotel and keep searching for him on her own.

She shifted into drive and steered her car the remaining 0.3 miles, turning right into the gravel circular drive in the front of the house. Three maples and an oak filled the semicircle of yard in front of the A-frame whose face wore a stone porch, a wooden balcony above. How very inviting, Dani thought.

The window by the front door was lit. She thought about beeping the lock and about grabbing her bags. No. Too intrusive. First, she let go the wheel, prying her sweaty fingers from the leather. Shocked by the cold as she exited, she shut the door gently. Habit screamed at her to lock it, but she knew the beep would draw attention to her, and she felt so naked out here now. As her eyes adjusted to the dark, she could make out the stepping stones spaced across the yard to the front porch. She took them as if she were crossing a pond, as though if she fell off them onto the yard, she might drown. She felt like drowning now.

As she reached the front door, she realized for the last time it wasn't too late. The car was just right there, over the stretch of yard. A hop, skip, and a jump over those flat stones. And then she could drive away into the darkness, back to…

A TV was on somewhere in the house. She couldn't tell what program, though the volume was up.

She rang the doorbell and paused, listening. Then, nervously, she knocked.

The tv muted. Footsteps. Dialogue. A man and a woman.

The door opened. An older man with thinning hair offered her an inquisitive smile, looking her up and down, but not in a lascivious way: more out of curiosity. He was short (her dad's height) and trim, with bright blue eyes and a face easy on the wrinkles, without blemish or blotchiness or even the splotchy paleness of the elderly. She'd seen his face in pictures before when Court had showed her and knew him immediately.

"Glen?" she said. It popped out. He wrinkled his brow at this and cocked his head.

"Yes?" He squinted and looked again, taking her in.

A tall, dark-haired woman appeared over his shoulder. She was slim and proper and wore a stern countenance. If his skin was unblemished, hers was pure marble. Her blue eyes pierced as furiously as the cold outside, her black hair in a Pompadour.

"I'm so sorry," she said. "My name is Dani…"

Glen beamed. "You're Dani!" The stern woman over his shoulder—Lena, Dani realized—relaxed her gaze some, but the lips remained tight. The door opened wider. "Come on in!"

As she stepped across the threshold, Glen wrapped her in a hug. "We were glad you called," he said.

Lena held back, a bit more reserved. "And you actually came," she mumbled."

Glen added, as if correcting his wife, "We're glad you're here."

Dani pulled away slightly so she could look at both of them. "Any word from…?"

They exchanged a glance and shook their heads, frowning. Lena said, "We'll find him." Emphasis on the "we." Like she was excluding Dani.

Glen said, "You'll stay with us."

Lena's smile was forced, full of apprehension, and worried Dani more.

Glen peered over her shoulder to scan the front yard. "Don't you have bags?"

"I'll get them in a minute." She paused and looked at each of them. Lena still looked rigid and stern, but Glen appeared relaxed, and he still smiled eagerly. "Court said you were sick."

Again, Glen and Lena exchanged a glance. Glen simply said, "I'm better now, and just in time it seems. Come, let me show you around the house, and then you can get your bags."

The floors were pine. A leather-trimmed wooden buffet stood by the front door. A glance to the stairs, dark with carpeted risers leading up to no one.

As they walked down the hall, Lena said, "Now, Dani, we aren't broadcasting Court's disappearance. There is… a lot… happening in this town right now, and we don't want to cause a kerfuffle." Her voice was cold. Even. When Dani looked at her, Lena's eyes narrowed to icicles.

Dani dropped her gaze to the floor, her face flushed. The room they had entered—the den—was cozy, small. The hall continued on past it, to two doors perpendicular to each other. Across from the den, another door partially open revealed a bathroom. On the whole, the rooms and floor were clean, well furnished, and decorated nicely. Homey, but not overly cluttered. A definite sense of refined style and fashion.

"I should have told you I was coming. I was worried. Court's friends are, also. I don't mean to be an imposition. If you want me to stay elsewhere."

Lena pursed her lips in thought. Mumbled. "Several hotels in town."

Glen: "Nonsense. We have the room. We insist."

He shot a glance to Lena, who dropped her eyes and tightened the pucker of her lips further, forming lines at the corners.

Dani: "I know I'll stand out here." She thought a little more, then added, "Not to seem presumptive or indelicate, but from what Court's told me about the town."

Glen led her back toward the entry. Said, "We have a lot we have to tell you, but I don't think tonight is right. I don't think you'd…"

He hung his head and sighed heavily. "We have a lot to tell you. But not tonight. You need a clear head."

"But Court—" she said, and at the sound of his name, Glen nodded.

"We called our neighbor. He's a detective. Court is… we think he's…"

"He's okay," Lena said. "We think for right now he's okay."

At this news, Dani felt the first tears roll down her cheeks. Her shoulders slumped and she let the tears fall and she couldn't catch her breath and she felt Glen's arms around her yet again. In his embrace, she felt warmth and security.

"We'll find him," Lena said.

Glen said, "We'll find him together."

But their voices seemed to shimmer like a heat mirage over hot pavement.

⁕

Dani retrieved her bags from the trunk, noticing the trepidation between the elder couple. She was worried that they would never tell her everything. Glen gave her a tour of the house, Lena following primly along behind them. He showed the two bedrooms at the end of the hall and, leading her back to the other side of the stairs, showed the kitchen and breakfast nook and balcony, then the laundry room and the garage off it, and the stairs leading down to the full basement with its own garage entrance. Glen showed her his armaments, stored in the closet of their master bedroom: a shotgun which had belonged to his father, and a Ruger, a .22 single-shot rifle, and the machete he'd bought during his tour in Korea.

"She doesn't want to see such things," Lena said. "You must be exhausted. Let's show her the upstairs."

Glen shouldered her bag as they trudged up the risers, and Dani, despite herself, felt the day finally catch up to her, and she yawned.

⊗⊗

Soon enough she was unpacked, then undressing and putting on her PJs, still wondering about the last thing they'd said to her. Lena seemed cold, distant. Cautious even. But Glen was warm and welcoming and healthy. More than healthy: he was strong and able bodied, certainly not dying. Had Court been lying about his grandfathers being ill? Had she been conned? Was Court secretly married and his grandparents skilled at breaking the news to his latest conquest? *Here's your bacon and eggs and biscuits and gravy dear. Hope you slept well. Court's back in Iowa with his real family.*

Ridiculous, but the fear of learning some undeniable truth about him and about them which would forever change her trajectory, felt true, and her shoulders pinched from this so that a great weight settled on her spine. She rubbed ferociously at the base of her neck, pushing her hair out of the way.

She could still go. Gather up her keys and quietly pack her things and sneak down the stairs and catch her car and phone her friends and leave this godforsaken town. After all, Court thought she wanted an unsettled life, so maybe she did, right?

Why wasn't Glen sick and dying in the hospital? Why was he okay? And where the hell was Court?

With these questions, she realized she couldn't leave.

The upstairs was the tip of the A-frame, where the ceiling followed the roofline. There were a couple of walk-in closets and a full bath as well as full door access to the attic. Even with a TV cabinet, a bed and trundle—a queen—a sewing station, and a computer desk, the door out to the balcony wasn't blocked.

She curled into bed. There was warmth up here, so the dark didn't seem so lonely. The patterned quilt fit the queen so nicely; it hugged her form pulled into the fetal position. Her eyes fluttered as she thought of her friends, so understanding, and how Glen at least had welcomed her. But they seemed to know something about Court and where he could be and yet, they'd shared nothing. They would tell her soon. In the morning. They must, she reminded herself, her thoughts fixated on Court's whereabouts and safety and things left unsaid, even as she drifted off to sleep.

CHAPTER THIRTY-ONE

Clem popped the top of his seventh pint and pushed open the hollow aluminum door to his back deck, a sagging wooden structure with graying beams and joists that creaked with each step. This led to his expansive backyard, whose barbed wire fence roped off the perimeter, marking his property from the wheat-filled pasture abutting.

The clouds hung purple in the night sky, blocking out the stars. Clem wondered if he could remember stars. Were they the ones what sparkled or was it the planets? Christ almighty. The song always reminded him. *Twinkle, twinkle little star...* his ma used to sing to him, back when he was a toddler, before the cancer ate her up. Twinkle, twinkle, like those fairies over in Eureka Springs and Northwest Arkansas. His dad and his ma had driven the Harley over to a bike rally in Eureka Springs years and years ago, and left Clem's siblings in charge, and when they got back his mother went to the doctor and they said she had the cancer and then she died.

"They're here," the voice sang in the darkness.

"Court's friends," Clem responded, and pounded the beer, then sat the empty can on the railing and looked out across his yard. Something—he could feel it— was there; he couldn't place it.

"And Court's girlfriend."

It walked under the light shining over his deck, wearing his father's skin.

"I know you ain't him," Clem said, snatching up the empty can in his hand, crushing it, and carried it inside, only to return a second later with a full pint and the thing that wore his father's flesh sitting in the chair across from him.

"You drink too much," his father said.

Clem sat and popped the top and took a good long pull off his eighth can. It was Lite and so mostly water anyway, and wasn't it important you stay hydrated?

"Good for him he's got friends."

"What are you going to do?"

Clem shrugged. "Finish this pint and a few other'n, then hit the hay."

"It's more than the girlfriend and his grandparents and some of his friends. The detective is also involved." The sneer on its lips, the curl of its tongue, told Clem which local law enforcement official the thing wearing his father's skin was talking about.

"The nigger detective? Bullocks?"

"None of them will listen, Clem. Someone must make them listen. What would I have done, if a couple of chinks, a dyke, a couple of wetbacks, and a nigger detective stood in my way?"

Clem surveyed his beer and imagined each of them as the thing dressed as his father had named them. They were the horrors of the world he'd been sheltered from for so long, creeping in now. Pappy hadn't stood for it. No sir, he'd done his damnedest to keep his kids from the outside world, and he sure as shit wouldn't have let such an element into the town, by God.

Clem stood and the figure stood also, smiling. As Clem walked back into his trailer the figure stood out on the deck, smiling as though it could see through the tin siding of the single-wide, as though it could see Clem walk up to the mounted twelve-gauge and lift it off its hooks, cradling it in his right arm as his left hand stroked the barrel. The thing on the deck smiled as Clem sat on his couch, the shotgun laying across his lap. He stared at the gun and its mechanics and wondered where he'd stored the gun cleaning kit.

Time had come to clean the gun.

CHAPTER THIRTY-TWO

The bed was stiff and hot and TJ, stifled by the covers, kicked them off, crossed his arms, and turned his back towards his wife. By her breathing, he knew Britta was still awake. She huffed and snorted like the Labrador they'd had a few years back, when it thought it was being ignored.

"Christ," TJ mumbled.

"You 'wake?" Britta said.

"You know I am."

She huffed again.

"Jesus Christ, woman, say what's on your mind."

"Don't take the Lord's name in vain."

"Well, what else?"

She huffed again. He imagined her staring up at the ceiling in her flannel pajamas. He'd felt her kick off the quilt also; the small room held in both heat and darkness well.

"Glen don't need to be gallivanting around. Probably what put him in the hospital."

"Don't you think I'm worried about them? I sit an' stew on it all day, how my driving him around might've caused this episode."

"None of 'em's good," Britta said. "Elden don't know what day it is, or who's president. And Lena and Aster ain't too far behind them."

"You go and sit with him."

She huffed. If she thought he was throwing it back in her face, her involvement, he was. How dare she blame him when she was just as entwined with Court's family.

"We got to stop it, TJ. For us. For our kids. We got to take back control of our own lives."

His cell began to ring. He ignored it and rolled over to face her.

"You and I love those old folk like they was our own. We always have and we always will."

"You gone answer it?"

"Not 'til we're done."

"We're done," she said.

He rolled away and reached for the phone, finding Lena Dillon on the other end. Lena spoke quickly and passed on a lot of information, some he couldn't quite grasp, but only left him time to say an occasional "yes" or make other affirmative noises, and meanwhile, curious to the conversation, Britta let go her rigid hold, turned on her side, and watched his shoulders and back.

When he dropped the phone on top of his jeans, which lay crumpled by his side of the bed, he bounced on the mattress to face her, his look solemn, his eyes bright in the night, still haunted.

"Court's girlfriend is in town. It appears he's missing. And Glen…"

CHAPTER THIRTY-THREE

Consciousness returned with an inhalation of the rancid effluvia floating through the air, crisped by a soundless darkness. Court had the immediate sensation of floating in the murky depths of death. Rot surrounded him. Decay flowed through his nostrils, slithered down his throat, and curled around his tongue. The sweet smell of blood clung, tacky, to his clothes and flesh, wrapped through his hair, kissed his lips. A pain shot through his shoulder, even as he caught a dim light out of his periphery. His left knee and calf also stung, and the whole side of his body felt grainy. When he swiped at his leg with his right hand, he heard pebbles ricochet off a distant wall or part of the floor still cloaked in shadow. Only when he stood did he find he couldn't put pressure on his leg at all. He groped blindly for some purchase and, finding none, fell onto the unforgiving floor. Absently, he wiped at his face as he took in his surroundings.

The air stale, tinged with something rotten he could taste on his tongue almost instantly. He forced a spit though saliva was in short supply, his mouth cottony. When he coughed, he heard an echo, then forced another cough. The light he saw was brighter, but he still had no bearings. There was moisture in the air, which he tasted every time he took a breath; it weighed down on his lungs, and he was already so weak.

Court blinked until his vision cleared and he saw he was focusing on a single torch mounted to a wall, and as he continued to blink, his periphery cleared and he saw more torches, flickering all around him. The room appeared circular, but... The light stretched up to shadow, but the walls didn't seem to meet a ceiling. Rather, they rose and arched together somewhere above in the cavernous darkness. So, it was a kind of dome-like room—a chamber—or something similar.

Eyes were on him. He felt them watching him. He must have been dragged in here by whatever it was that had stalked him in the old graveyard. Slowly the incident returned to him, reminding him of what happened before he'd lost consciousness, but he wasn't clear how much time had passed.

He closed his eyes, struggling for more, but his mind would allow nothing else. Beneath his crouch, the pebbles and stone of the floor cut into the palms of his hands and pressed uncomfortably against his thighs and buttocks. Then a single question rose to fill the void.

What are you afraid of?

"What are you afraid of?"

The voice ran like molasses out of the darkness overhead, seeping thick and dark down the walls.

"Who's there?" Court asked.

Above him he heard scurrying, nails on thin tile. He staggered toward the nearest torch, where, in its glow, he found familiar angular carvings in the white walls. An arch here, a rectangular cutout there. He reached for the wall as the scurrying sound closed in, still distant but gaining, suggesting the room was larger than he'd already guessed, extending his hand to feel the texture of the molded shapes before his eyes, the rounded arches jutting out and deep crevices for the rectangles and...

"Oh god!" he said, stepping back. He'd dipped his fingers in the dark gunk holding this room together and wiped them on his jeans, imagining the filth and rot and bacteria clamoring up his arm, the smell infecting him. "Oh god!" he spat, because while he didn't know where he was, he knew in what kind of room he stood. As his eyes cleared, and he smelled the rot and earth and fetid, sealed off air, he saw a skull here, there a femur, and securing this joist a humerus, or a rib bone, or a scapula as a brace. The torchlight showed that the curved walls encircling him were of all the same material. This was a room shaped by the bones of humans.

"What are you afraid of?" it asked again, the thing scuttering along the bones above him out of the reach of the torchlight.

"Where am I?" Court asked, his voice dry and cracking and hollow in the dimly lit chamber. The whole left side of his body ached until half of him was numb. This wasn't new, but the pain finally had caught up with him. He felt dirty and sore, his clothes clinging to him as if to smother him. As large as the room seemed, he felt claustrophobic and wanted nothing more than to wrench his shirt and pants away so he could truly breathe.

He could see movement above: a shadow descending, growing larger from a strange mass to an oblique spider, just crawling into the torchlight. "Fuck," he muttered to himself as the thing neared. Horripilation broke out over his stiffened body. There was nowhere to run, not that he could run. He could only stare as this nightmare descended the wall, its gleaming eyes trained on him.

"You are home," it said.

"No," he said to himself, shrinking away. He could smell it now, the source of the rot and stench of decay wafting off the creature as it neared. "No," he said again, falling back to the stone floor. "Oh

Jesus, God," he muttered, staring up at the bone-lined wall. How many humans had this thing used to craft this place? "No," he said again as the thing crept closer.

"No way out," it whispered. There had to be, he thought wildly. It had dragged him in here, so there had to be a way out. But what that might look like, or any levelheaded thought abandoned him for terror.

"No way out," the thing said again, from the darkness.

Court closed his eyes and pressed his cheek against the bone-stone floor to feel the coolness. Clarity came slowly, as it did for a drunk leaning on a toilet after a midnight vomit. If it were going to hurt him, it would have already. He was weak and injured and in no condition to fight or run, but still, it did not approach more or make any attempt to intrude upon him. Yet. That doesn't mean it wouldn't, but as of yet, it hadn't.

○○○

Autumn arrives slowly in the Ozarks, taking her sweet time. She teases some cooler days in August and September, enough to make the denizens curse the heat that dominates the landscape. But when she does come, she is swift; her arrival is a shock to the system, bleaching leaves of their chloroform, so overnight there is a change in the foliage canopying the world.

Bullocks witnesses the transformation while drinking a beer on his back deck. Next door, a girl moved in with the Dillons, and the birdie on the street is that she's their grandson's betrothed. Good for them. More word on the street is Court is now missing.

Bad for them.

The first frost comes mid to late October. Enough to shock the leaves to slumber, from which they can't wake until spring.

Those are the rules. From here on out, it's all dead.

INTERLUDE SIX

The Tale of the Wandering Lawman

Once upon a time, there roamed a lawman, all around the Midwest. Born on the tough streets of Chicago, the lawman made his name there with a series of cases so gruesome one of them would have cracked the steadiest of cops. But the lawman was no ordinary police officer, and he stood against five such cases, each more disturbing than the last, 'til one so gruesome and so personal came along it took all the resolve he had to bring the culprit to justice.

After, the lawman moved south, and ended up in a college town working for the local police chief. For a time, he found peace; he was happy in the Southern community, and he bought a house and thought, for once, he'd found a place to cast aside the demons of his past so he could look to the future.

But this would not be the case.

A woman was murdered, and the lawman had to decide if it were her jealous husband or her lover, the husband's best friend. As murder begets murder, soon the lawman faced the inconceivable, an evil far worse than anything he'd experienced before, and the lawman was once again called upon to draw on his strength to protect the innocent.

But he realized then there would be no solace in this town, either, so he moved again. His chief had connections in an even smaller town, deep in the Ozark hills of north Arkansas. This is where the lawman moved. Selling his old house, he bought a new one next to an elderly couple, befriended them and did his job, investigating meth makers and small-time drug exchanges, and fished and smoked his cigars. Each evening he sat out on the back porch and watched the stars through his telescope while he drank scotch and thought about love and loneliness and how, for many reasons, he didn't fit in this particular town, all the more reason he should try and make it his home.

Then one day, he got a call. Someone had broken into the local cemetery, they said, and could he get right down there. Someone had dug up a grave, they said. Then, well, he better get on down there.

He hung up the phone, and put on his tie, and took a sip of his coffee. A few of the local teenagers might be brazen enough for such a prank, sure, but something gnawed at him. This time he'd stumbled back into the darkness. And as he drove, he realized he'd never escape it.

The End

CHAPTER THIRTY-FOUR

Morning came. The clouds above hung low and gray. The sky melted into a low fog draping over the land like a curse, pulling back to reveal only the closest of objects, as though it would strike the constitution too severely to bare the entirety of the community, all at once. The overnight temperature hadn't changed much; it hung in the forties, cold but not so cold to effect change. Not enough to retain the hoarfrost or cause a breath to crystalize, but cold enough to force a shiver from a county detective standing over one of five new grave openings. Even as Bullocks hugged himself inside his wool peacoat, he prayed the smell didn't permeate. God, if the smell got against him, against his skin or trapped in the fibers of his coat—

He shuddered and felt phlegm clog his throat, so he cleared the passage with a grating sound, spat a yellow spherule into the mud.

"Goddamn smell," he said, feeling it crawl into the back of his throat.

He didn't have to poke and prod at the corpse—a cursory look showed where the chunks had been removed from. Major muscles.

A bite out of the pectoral, the latissimus dorsi, the quadricep. A nibble at a bicep or the triceps from an especially fresh corpse.

A couple of deputies and the mortician behind him, and the sheriff at his side, Detective Bullocks took a step back from the fifth grave and stroked his chin. He'd offered the same examination to each of the corpses, and still wondered one thing.

The chemicals. They'd each been pumped with chemicals after death and before burial. Chemicals to make them look alive long enough for family to say goodbye. So, how long did it take those chemicals to affect those muscles?

"You pump the blood out, and you pump these chemicals in," Albert said, turning to face the mortician. He pressed his palm against the damp, dewy stone that labeled the grave. "Without blood flow, how long does it take these chemicals to reach these larger muscles?"

Stuttgart took a breath before answering. The look on his baby face suggested he was still bothered by the detective's disdain for him. "About two hours," he responded. Bullocks could tell the mortician wasn't even sure why he was concerned with such a question, so he sighed and stepped away from the hole in the ground.

"You sell them things they don't need, because you claim there is an environmental hazard."

"There is," the young man stammered.

"There is an environmental hazard because of the crap you put in them."

"Their bodies are degrading."

Bullocks waved his hand. "Like deer. Like possum or the armadillo. Like any other fucking animal."

"But we aren't like any other animal."

Bullocks turned his back. "You're ghouls. You show up at every dead body. You start performing unnecessary procedures, and you then charge for them. And then, because of those procedures, those chemicals you dump into those bodies, you charge more to seal those bodies up so those chemicals aren't released. You destroy those bodies, and you pillage those families. You are a ghoul." He felt their eyes on him. They already judged him so much, he knew he didn't have much latitude. The sheriff. The deputies. They were just looking for an excuse, he knew. He decided then he wasn't going to give them one.

He walked away from the graves, the brisk air chilling every intake of breath which he was afraid to deepen for fear of inhaling the putrescence. Above, a flat gray sky hovered over deadening trees, the leaves falling like fodder for seasonal gods through the curtain of fog, and someone nearby was burning leaves, completing the sensory overload of Charon's arrival.

A hand clasped his shoulder. Bullocks didn't react to the cheap cologne and the scalp oil worn religiously by the sheriff. The sigh he heard sounded like fatigue and disappointment. There had been too much happening here lately, more than enough to exhaust a lazy county sheriff.

"The mortician boy's beside himself."

Bullocks nodded. "Their whole profession is a scam. They prey on people who can't afford it, and act like there is no other choice."

"Is this about your dad? Chief Prader told me."

Bullocks hung his head. "What kind of decisions are those for a thirteen-year-old to make?"

"Your ma?"

Bullocks shrugged. "Chicago Black woman. Single. Big whoop. News flash of the day there." He sighed, something heavy on his chest. "She was in no shape. They loved each other once, 'til his job took him away, then took him for good. She was heartbroken. Devastated."

"It isn't fair to you," the sheriff said, finally. "It's too much for a kid. And for you to go on and find his killer and… you took too much on."

Bullocks let his shoulders relax. He stared at the ground and thought about his time in Chicago, and then his time in Fayetteville, and now here, in the whitest town of all, where he found a home in the least likely place.

"There has been a thread of evil I feel like has chased me all my life. It nearly caught me a few times, but it's always been there. I'm afraid it's here again."

The sheriff sighed. His scalp oil and his cheap cologne offered the only hint of solace. His hand on Bullocks shoulder squeezed: all the reassurance the young detective would get.

CHAPTER THIRTY-FIVE

God, he was thirsty. The sun sparkled against his closed lids; Clementine Willette blinked and saw the parted blinds, the sun streaking into his bedroom, and smacked his lips, tasting salt and a whiff of beer and something sweet like whiskey. Goddamn, he'd tied one on. Sure as shit last night.

He sat up and felt his head throb in response to the change in direction. Supporting himself on his left arm, he reached up with the right and rubbed at his temple. Jesus, it was one hell of a bender.

He frowned at trying to recall his return home as he pulled himself out of bed. What the fuck time had he come home? He'd jingled the door and crashed fully clothed on his mattress, and...

But he wore his boxers now, and not much else. Absently he scratched an itch on his gray-haired chest.

There was a voice.

He shook his head; God, it pounded. No voice.

It soothed him, when he was undressed and under the blankets. Goddamn, he hated not remembering. Coffee helped him remember some, thought it also helped ease some of the hangover.

Last night was a blur. A lot of nights had been a blur recently.

He shivered, reached for the remote but didn't turn on the TV as was his normal routine. Instead, he supped his coffee and stared ahead at the wood-paneled wall, hoping it would warm him, but it did little to ease his disquiet, the voice in his head echoing into his subconscious.

You made a promise.

What was it? A blur, a whisper. He couldn't exactly picture it, but he could feel it and he remembered, nodding.

His fingers, in an effort to drown out the voice, fumbled for the remote and turned on Fox News, and he listened to the day's stories. Jesus Christ, the Dems were destroying this fucking nation. Family values were fading. It's what he'd been saying for some time now. Not that any goddamn patron in the bar would listen.

They're coming.

Clem frowned. The voice was stronger than ever. It brought pictures. There was a fit Hispanic girl and a lesbian and a Japanese girl who reminded him of the stories his dad had told him and his siblings about being stationed overseas with the Marines and a creepy Asian kid who could pass for either a boy or a girl.

"They're coming," Clem said.

"No. They're here." The voice was his father's, but it wasn't. It existed both inside his head and outside. It was a part of him, and it wasn't, and it terrified him and thrilled him to know he wasn't alone.

But they can't be here. The borders are secure so they can't come in. We're supposed to go back to the way things were.

"We can," the voice said. "But we need you."

He stared at his wood paneling and sat on his couch and listened to the voice. It told him many things about those kids coming to his town and it told him other things too, about a guy who destroys the fresh food, who corrupts the dead.

CHAPTER THIRTY-SIX

Glen had the sausages sizzling when Dani walked into the kitchen. He smiled as she rounded the corner, her feet padding on the hardwood, timid in their approach. Offered her a cup of coffee, which she politely accepted.

"Cream and sugar on the counter," he said as she sipped at it, watching him work over the stove, stirring some batter as oil popped in a cast-iron skillet.

"How do pancakes sound?" he asked.

Dani said, "Good" without the enthusiasm to accompany the word, and Glen studied her with a frown for a second before setting down the bowl and pulling a key from his pocket.

"What's that?" she asked.

"To the house. You might be here awhile, a few days, anyway, and you shouldn't have to rely on us to let you in or out."

She turned the bronzed house key over in her hand. "When did you have it made?"

He smiled. "Oh, we've had a few extra over the years. Court has a key. I don't remember who it was made for, maybe his folks at one point. But it's yours now."

Dani, thinking of the level of trust this man must be extending to offer up something so personal, so inviting, to a girl he'd just met, squeezed the key in her hand and said, "Thank you."

He served her a plate of sausages and pancakes and lay another setting for Lena, who entered shortly after.

"We have a full day planned," Glen tried.

Dani nodded, her mouth full of a mix of pancake and sausage.

"We need to go see the Oscars first," Lena said.

Dani frowned at this. Oscars. Plural.

"And then Aster and I are going to take you to the farmer's market," Lena said.

Dani couldn't fight the look on her face, like a six-year-old on Christmas who'd received socks.

Glen seemed to anticipate her reaction, and said, "Our neighbor, the detective, is already at work, but the market is on the square near the building. He said he'd meet you there." He reached over and patted the back of Dani's hand. "It'll be okay," he said, smiling warmly. "I promise."

CHAPTER THIRTY-SEVEN

Breakfast finished, they all dressed quickly. Dani stared at her reflection in the mirror in the upstairs bathroom, studying herself under the lights, looking for blemishes, wondering what they might see, searching for lines of worry for Court. She applied some makeup and brushed her hair and checked herself again. Still, hoped neither had heard her vomit after awakening. Told herself it was merely nerves. Glen, she could tell, liked her. Approved. Lena was a different story. She could feel the coldness exuding off the woman, from her gaze and her voice. If the Oscars treated her the same way, it might be too much.

No, she corrected herself, sternly and with deep breaths. No. She was here for Court. Not for them. She joined them at the bottom of the stairs and followed them down to the basement-garage to where Glen's Aveo was stored. Soon they were out of the drive, then on the bypass, doubling back the way Dani had come the night before. To her right, a fenced-in pasture, the wheat tall and firm without the livestock to keep it trim, an old gray gambrel barn in the main pasture, a newer looking pole barn halfway up between it and the main house.

The night before, her headlights had failed to illuminate any of this, so this became the first time she could really look at the farm. The Aveo turned off the bypass and followed the road up to the drive of the main house, a single-story L-shaped building with cream-colored siding and a rusty metal roof. Glen pulled into the gravel drive and exited the car, leading the way to the door.

"Elden, my mom's dad, is the oldest of the bunch," Court had told her once. "He was born in 1920."

"He's almost a hundred?" she had replied, a bit of a shock.

"He got rid of the last of his cows about five years ago." This conversation had occurred early on in the relationship, after they'd first slept together. The afternoon broke through the blinds in his apartment. Outside was cold, but his bed was warm.

The door opened to a short, plump woman with an easy smile and warm, gray eyes, and she hugged Lena and Glen each in turn and thanked them for coming, a thick Southern accent curling from her lips as she said in a voice nearly squeaking, "And who do we have here?"

Dani smiled. "Dani, ma'am." She held out a hand. "Daniela Morales."

Glen said, "Dani, this is Aster Oscar, Court's maternal grandmother. Aster, this is Court's lady friend."

Aster pushed Dani's hand aside to wrap her arms around Dani in a tight hug. "Welcome, dear. It is so wonderful to have you," and Dani thought she meant it. "We have heard so much about you. Come in, come in."

They walked through the door into a large living room with a fireplace already going, the smell of burning wood and dry heat filling the home. To their left was an archway to the kitchen, and beyond a smaller room with a television, a recliner and loveseat, a gas stove, and a sliding glass door leading out to the back patio. This little den shared a wall with the kitchen and the living room, but it also had a cutout like a little window with a shelf and knickknacks adorning the opening. Dani needed only to shuffle a few steps to see all three rooms and the strange architecture. Aster had begun to pour cups of coffee, as Lena helped her, but Glen had followed Dani into the den as she looked around.

"It is a window," he said, following her gaze to the cutout in the wall between the living room and den. "Aster," he called.

"Out in the toolshed," Aster was saying. Then, "Yes, Glen. You take your coffee black, correct?"

"Yes ma'am. Mind if I show Dani around?"

"By all means. Dani, sweetie, do you drink coffee?"

"Yes please," Dani said. "Black also."

"Elden bought this land back when he was in his twenties, right after World War Two," Glen said. "He got over a hundred acres, the old gray barn out there, and this house, which at the time was only two rooms, the living room and the kitchen. He worked for the school district, at first driving a bus but then making his way up over the years to maintenance supervisor. He'd get up early to take care of his cows, then go to work, then come home and care for the cows again, then work on the house."

They were facing south, toward the window between the den and the living room. He turned her around. "He built this dressing area, closet, bathroom, and bedroom next, then added this hall to the left." A long hall stretched behind the kitchen then made a right angle toward the back of the house. "He added these back bedrooms later, along with the utility room. Most recently," he said, opening the door to show her, "he had someone build this back master suite and two car garage."

"Impressive," she said.

"Other than this final addition, he did the work himself. Framed, drywalled, wired, plumbed, and roofed the house, bit by bit, working every evening after tending his cows and working at the school."

"That is impressive," she said, realizing the scope, recognizing in this story a work ethic she hadn't known in another save her father.

"He gave that to Court," Glen said. "That grit. We all shared with him the best pieces of ourselves, as much as we could. It's how I know he's still alive and that we will find him."

Dani met his reassuring smile and nodded.

The front door opened and closed, and the screen snapped shut. Elden Oscar stood tall in the archway from the living room to the kitchen, his bright eyes shining a cool gray that matched the overcast autumn morning. His gaze settled on Aster, the Dillons, then Dani, then back around, finally settling on the young girl and taking her all in. Dani stood aghast. Had Court intentionally lied to her about the health of both his grandfathers? This man seemed even trimmer than Glen and was far from infirm. He carried himself with the air of a man half his age, and when he spoke his voice was stern and strong and commanded life.

"Is this Court's lady friend?" he asked.

"She got in last night," Glen said, but as Elden Oscar didn't seem surprised by her arrival, she suspected he'd already been informed.

"You ready to go?" Elden asked him.

"Aren't you coming with us?" Dani asked.

Elden crinkled his mouth and narrowed his eyes at her. "We got things to do, me an' him."

Aster sat her empty coffee cup on the counter by the sink. "Actually, dear, you, me, and Lena will speak with an officer while Elden and Glen work on other avenues to find Court."

Dani nodded; it all sounded reasonable enough, but still she was bothered. She watched the women kiss their respective men and followed them out to the car. There was something simple in the domesticity of married life as it was presented by these two couples, and Dani wondered, as they drove off from the farm, if such bliss were for everyone.

ଔୟୠ

Though the fog lifted some, the clouds remained as they made it to the market, and once again Dani imagined this town existing in a bubble or caught under some dark spell. It felt isolated from the rest of the world. The two women spoke of people she'd never heard of, nearly ignoring her. They parked off the square in a law firm's tight parking lot and led Dani out to the square itself, whose name was deceptive; the town square only had three sides.

The courthouse stood in the center, surrounded by a moat of grass and sidewalks like a cross bridging out from the limestone edifice. On three sides it was surrounded by buildings of similar construction, tight little streets now filled with vendors and a small crowd piddling through the wares, laughing and talking, all white. She felt she stood out instantly—her skin bronzer than anyone else's, her hair darker. The eastern side of the square was the five-lane Highway 62, which snaked through town.

All these white faces. She wondered which one was the detective.

"Do you see him?" Dani asked.

Lena turned a shrewd eye on Dani. "So, dear, Court tells us you are an adventurous type."

They'd stopped in front of a vendor selling flowers. Around them people clamored and laughed and talked.

Dani frowned. She wasn't sure of the point of this. Court must have told them about her. Slowly she nodded.

"The detective," she said.

"He'll be along in a bit," Aster said, otherwise seemingly oblivious, her attention turned to the vegetable stands and flower and craft peddlers.

Lena squinted her eyes. She wore a smile, but it was thin and full of mistrust. Dani shivered. "Court needs to settle down," Lena said. "Once we're past all of this, once we find him, he'll want a sense of permanence."

"You're younger than he is, dear," Aster piped up, then resumed her ogling.

"What does this have to do with finding him?" Dani asked. She was aware of the tone of her voice, the rising lilt, but she didn't care. She'd come, hadn't she? She was here and looking for him. How dare they question her motives and poke into her relationship with him.

"Everything," Lena said, still stoic and prim and proper. "We have much to tell you, much you need to know if you are to help us, but if you are some fly-by-night trollop, we aren't sure we can trust you with this information. We need more than a good-time gal."

Dani stammered, a flush rising on her cheek. "What...?"

"Now, now," Aster said, stepping into referee between the two, the conversation snagging her full attention. "She didn't mean it, dear." She shook her head reproachfully at Lena.

Truthfully, Dani felt like slapping Lena. Instead, she said, "I can't promise you I'm going to marry Court, or we'll have all the babies in the world, but I'm here because I care about him. I do love him. I want to see him home safe. What happens later, no one knows. I don't know, but it will be between me and Court."

"'Court and me,'" Lena corrected. "Dani, dear, we both understand you care about him, but he's too old for the sock hop. If you're looking for a boy to park with on lover's lane or take to a dance, you need to find someone more befitting your age and social class."

Aster stood back, mouth agape. She might have wanted to say something, but Dani could see she was as dumbstruck as she herself felt. Dani took a beat to gather herself, lest she showed her own ass.

"How dare you," Dani snapped. Her voice had risen, and she'd seen in the periphery a few heads snap around towards them, but she didn't care.

"You aren't good enough for him, dear," Lena continued, her voice soft and soothing, her eyes never leaving Dani's, never blinking, never yielding. "So perhaps you should run along home and let those who care search for him."

Dani balled her fists. Another glance around: all the white faces watching anger flushing her cheeks, forcing the tears to well up. She reached into her pocket and pulled out the key Glen had given her and dropped it at Lena's feet.

"You don't want me to stay with you… fine," she said. "I'll stay in a hotel."

She stormed off.

Aster whirled on Lena, who refused to meet her eyes, instead scanning the broad expanse of the crowd. "How dare you treat her such a way, Lena Dillon? What's gotten into you?"

Lena's lip trembled. "This is something best left up to family, is all. Besides, it's not safe for her. You know that. It's better she leaves now."

"Not like this. Maybe we should tell her and let her make up her own mind, don't you think?" When Lena didn't answer, Aster bent and picked up the key, and held it out for her friend to take. Lena shook her head and nodded toward Dani, who'd found a stand with tomatoes and cucumbers and lettuce upon which she was feigning interest. In the distance, the dark scalp of the detective bobbed and weaved between the crowds.

With her free hand, Aster grabbed Lena by the wrist and jammed the key back into her palm, then followed her as Lena approached the girl. If Lena hadn't taken the hint and walked, Aster was prepared to drag her over.

Dani turned when she heard a clearing of the throat over her shoulder. Lena stood there, holding the key out to her, but wouldn't meet her eyes. Aster tried her best to smile for the three of them. She kicked Lena's ankle.

"I apologize," Lena said. "I'm afraid we've gotten off on the wrong foot."

Dani looked at the key but didn't take it. She didn't say anything, but she needed more.

Lena finally met her gaze. "I know how I just came across. I don't really believe...I'm sorry, Dani. I know you're worried about him. It's just, of the things we have to tell you, some of it is about the previous women in his life. What happened to them. I was trying to run you off to...to protect you. But it isn't for me to decide. Let's speak to the detective, and then you hear us out, but of course, should you choose, you are welcome to stay with us."

The haughtiness had abandoned her. The erect, prideful, and rueful woman looked sad and old. Dani thought about asking Aster if she could stay with her, but then wondered how this might all be explained to Glen—he'd been so sweet to her—and how it might affect their dynamic moving forward as a group with one goal: to find Court.

Dani reached up and picked the key from her fingers. "What do you mean, 'what happened to them'?"

"Detective Bullocks," Aster exclaimed, and both Lena and Dani turned.

Dani's jaw dropped. In this white town, at this white farmer's market, she wouldn't have expected to see a Black cop. He was tall and wore a nice suit, fitted well to his lean frame. Shook the hands of both elder women before turning his attention to Dani.

He dipped his head in a bow, took her hand, and said, "Enchanté," and Dani blushed a bit. Surely, he wasn't coming on to her.

"Hello," she said. Then, "Hola."

"Hola señora. Lo siento. Estamos con ustedes. Lo encontraremos pronto." There was a bit of a struggle in his delivery, but it was as though he was out of practice and not ignorant of her language.

The redness on her cheeks brightened a bit and she bowed her head out of respect and amazement to hear her language in this community, the last place she'd expect. "Gracias," she said simply.

And then he recited the facts. He let go of her hand as he let go of the artifice and spoke to all three professionally, reciting what he knew. Court had left the day before to visit his grandparents and never made it. His voice nearly monotone, there still existed a lyricism in his cadence. He could have been a podcaster or audiobook narrator, she thought.

He spoke about the recent cemetery vandalisms as coldly as possible, using as much police-speak as he could to appear completely detached despite the gruesomeness of the crimes. Still, he choked back something like contempt for the subject and this was evident to Dani, herself dysregulated by the topic. What this had to do with Court, she wasn't sure, but she was again losing patience and felt like she was drowning. She let her attention wane, her eyes meander over the crowd, until she settled on a vendor selling duck eggs and she spied two women she never expected to see in this little Ozark town.

"Jesus Christ," she muttered, then realized then the detective, Lena, and Aster had stopped their conversation to look at her.

"Excuse me," she said, and touched Lena's and Aster's arms as she did a half-bow to dismiss herself. When she'd closed the distance by half, she looked back, only to see Lena and Aster were again engaged in their conversation with the detective.

Dani slapped Jada on the arm of her jacket.

Jada, who'd moved on from duck eggs and was looking at some polished stone jewelry, jumped at the assault, as did Blue. She had spied them with their backs to her, which spoke to how much they stood out in this marketplace.

"Dude, what the hell?" Jada said.

"You're following me?"

Blue and Jada exchanged a glance.

"Well, we wanted to see you're okay."

"And we wanted to help," Blue chimed in, acting a bit tougher than Dani thought she might actually feel in the moment.

Dani closed her eyes. She saw welcoming blackness and took a deep breath. Still, it wasn't enough. "Go home." Why she said it, she wasn't sure. Something unsettled her. She felt it was dangerous for them. Probably for all of them.

"We can't," Jada said. "We're all here. Rong, Chuy…"

"The actual fuck," Dani muttered. There came a tapping at her shoulder, Blue poking at her and then pointing behind her.

"You're being summoned," Jada said.

Dani looked back and saw Lena and Aster looking her way, Aster smiling and waving, and the detective studying her. "Go home," she ordered the girls again, then turned to rejoin her group.

But there were more eyes on her, the feeling of being watched. She scanned the crowd to find a boy standing alone on the courthouse steps, staring at her. The boy, about six, had brown hair, wore overalls and an OshKosh B'gosh striped polo and a frown.

"You want to take him," the boy said. His lips moved, and he was too far away her to hear him over the crowd of the market, but she heard him nevertheless. His voice had been in her head.

"I don't," Dani started to say, then added, "Who?"

The boy furrowed his brow some more and turned his back as the crowds amassed.

"It's time to go," Aster said. Dani blinked. Had she crossed the marketplace to rejoin them? She must have, but she thought for a moment she had been moving (floating) toward the child, but when she turned back to where the boy had been standing, he was gone.

CHAPTER THIRTY-EIGHT

Court's time no longer measured in days or hours or minutes. When the thing had left the last time, he got a sense the hour was late, but he had no proof. No window to look out of, no clock to tell him. Time didn't exist down here in this chamber of bones. So, Court fought the fatigue and continued to search for a way out. He examined what felt like every nook and cranny—but found no escape—until he could stand no longer, and he collapsed near a lit torch, its soft flame flickering.

Ideas like 'awake' and 'asleep' became as vague as time, no matter how much he tried to give them significance. Laying on the ground, under the soft light of the torch, he listened to his own breathing and a far-off drip of water, until its clawed feet clicked on the bone-lined walls and floor again, and the creature hugged the shadows.

"Your friends are here," a voice said. "Your girlfriend is here. Yet you are alone."

Court stood and scanned the darkness. "Here?" Of course not. The thing didn't mean they were here, only they were in town.

"They have come to help," the voice said.

Court didn't like that Dani was here, or their friends, but what could he do? "Please," he said, his voice cracking, his throat dry, "I need to see her."

From the shadows the voice came again. "You sleep for days. What happens when you sleep forever?"

Death? "What do you mean?" He was trying to get his bearings. The room was spinning, and his head was spinning and was he drugged or was it something else... from this... *creature?*... this voice.

"Your grandparents will sleep soon. Then you. And your friends will live, and your story will matter to no one. Because no one is like you, anymore. You have become—"

"Irrelevant," Court muttered. It had ended its sentence with an idea of transcendence, and Court had finished its thought with an idea of hopelessness. He was irrelevant.

The voice from the shadows came like a leaking gas line: a hiss. "Yes."

Sound echoed through the vacuous chamber, and the torches illuminated only a little, not everything. Whatever it was crawled in the shadows, along the walls of skulls and mandibles and clavicles and femurs, out of reach of the light. The thing was dangerous, and it had strong jaws and tight claws meant to pull the flesh from the bone and cartilage. This thing had cleaned the gristle from every bone wallpapering this room. As it moved, he could follow its eyes: the pupils like laser tracers, always aligned, moving with the sound of the claws across the black expanse above him.

"What do you want?" Court asked. A flood of emotions thrashed at his spirit. Anger. Fear. Exhaustion. None of it good, these feelings only served to beat him down further. Perhaps that's what it wanted.

"Qissa." This was not an answer. And yet, it was all the answer Court would get. All the answer he would need because soon enough it was gone again, the sound of its nails retreating though the blackness, hurried clicks carrying the eyes away.

This creature, whatever it was, must be keeping him alive because it wanted something from him… whatever this 'qissa' was, but he had to wonder if, once he knew, and once the choice to grant it was presented to him, if he'd grant it. He couldn't imagine he would, no matter his condition now. If he couldn't escape, he'd die before helping this thing.

A sound, from far off.

"Hey!" Court called after it, and he reached for his throat. "Hey. Tell me what this 'qissa' is. Hey!"

A soft sound, a whimper; had it hurt itself, or was it a trap? Court grabbed one of the torches off its base and scanned the darkness. The sound grew closer as he followed the wall, limping, his leg throbbing with every step, and the torchlight illuminated a low overhang and a small bend. This was new for him, and he tried to redraw the map in his mind of where he actually was. Not a single room, but a cave-like system, perhaps. A spark of hope lit up in his mind. A cave might mean another tunnel, and perhaps an exit. He switched the torch from right to left and, bracing his right on the bone outcropping, knelt as best he could to see a small cubby and a mass of red, tangled hair.

The torch light shone into a crevice and flickered with the current of air. What he saw as the curtain of darkness shivered into strands was a bright brown eye that flashed in the torchlight—and then the girl screamed.

"It's okay," Court said, though he'd jumped back when he realized she was alive. Fire shot up through his leg from the sudden movement and he breathed out a curse. He reached in to help her out into the main chamber and shone the light as she looked around, and as he studied her. Her face was dirty, and she was emaciated. Still, he thought she was pretty young. Maybe a teenager or in her early twenties. Her dress looked as though she'd lived in the dirt, torn in some places, great holes in others. She was trembling and backed away from him when he reached for her.

"It's okay."

"The creature. You're with it," she said.

"No. It got me too. What's your name?"

Her eyes darted all around, her movements jerky. "Sarah," she said finally, hugging herself. "I'm so cold."

He nodded. Still holding the torch, he had forgotten how cold it was down here. *Down. Were they down?* "I'm Court. Where do you suppose we are?"

She turned and walked into the chamber of bones, still trying to warm herself, staring at the walls. "Under the church, probably. Way under." When she breathed, he saw plumes of something like smoke. It wasn't cold enough to see breath, so what had that been?

"Way under," he said, a soft echo mumbled under breath.

"How long have you been here, Sarah?" he said, not realizing he was studying her until she caught his gaze and looked away. She sank by the wall and hugged her knees.

"I don't know. I saw the churchyard and started looking around, and thought it would be nice, and then…"

"Me too," Court said. He shifted the torch in his hand and felt the weight of it. "Sarah, is it okay with you if I put this torch back up on the wall and sit down?" It was heavy and didn't provide much in the way of warmth or light, especially if they weren't moving.

"You can do what you want."

He was sure not to sit too close, but Court could not shake the feeling he knew her. There was something familiar about this girl, but he couldn't place it. He racked his brain, wondering if this girl knew his grandparents, or if he'd seen her at a gas station, or maybe she lived in the same neighborhood as the Dillons.

"Maybe we're dead," she said. This got his attention. "Time doesn't matter down here. There's only darkness and the vaguest drops of awareness. This is what death is like, until the brain rots away."

"We're not dead," he said, but he couldn't help but hear the lilt in his own voice, the rising question bubbling up from his dry, scratchy throat.

"I bet your wife and kids miss you," she said.

"No wife," he said. What a thought, to die down here so alone, after a life so unfulfilled.

"A man your age," she said. "You aren't married, no kids. Not much of a legacy." He flashed a look at her. She was focused on something on the floor, but on the corner of her lips crept the faintest hint of a smile.

"I think about that," he said.

"Are you afraid?"

"Of love? Or of leaving a legacy?"

"Of dying down here without finding either." She turned her gaze up to him. Her eyes shined brightly, nearly cutting through the shadows.

"What about you, Sarah? Husband or boyfriend or parents who'll miss you?" Or already missed her. He sensed it now, something off about her.

"No, Court. Everyone I know is dead. You avoided my question."

"I feel like I know you from somewhere." His mind raced for an answer.

"You do," she said. She raised her head and offered him a chance to look into her eyes. The pupils looked almost golden under the torch light. "You still haven't answered my question."

"Yes. I don't want to die. I'm not ready yet. I want to find a way out, back to see her."

"I thought you weren't married."

"I'm not. Not yet. But I want to marry her. I want to have kids with her." He stood with a grimace and looked around then screamed, his voice echoing through the chamber, piercing the bones. It was a scream of frustration. Of anger. Of not giving up.

"Feel better?" she said, standing up herself.

"There has to be a way out. It comes and goes as it pleases, so there has to be a way out."

She said nothing to this, but slowly began to turn in circles, fluttering her arms slowly as if they were wings, twirling, as if dancing, a soft hum pouring from her lips.

"Who are you?" he asked.

She continued dancing, spinning, humming, almost floating across the floor.

"Maybe, Court, we'll get out of here when you give it what it wants."

"Who are you? How do I know you?"

"I'm the girl of your dreams, Courtney Dillon." Her hair swirled around her, hiding her face, and the humming was replaced by a mirthless laughter, something high-pitched and psychotic.

He grabbed her shoulders. "Stop! How do I know you?"

"Think, Court," she said, raising her gaze to his, her pupils narrow and gold where they reflected the torchlight. "You can't see the forest for the trees."

"Trees?" he mumbled, then backed away. He remembered then. Glimpses of her dancing through the trees and vines, singing out to him. Calling the little boy away from his Nana. "You're the girl I dream about. When I was two. You were in the tree line. But how?"

"I have wanted you for a long time, Courtney Dillon. I have wanted you and watched you and have followed you. You are a poet, Courtney Dillon. And your words I cherish if only you'd speak them to me."

"What are you?" he asked.

The girl shed the dress and stepped backward into the shadows, each step issuing a click on the bone floor, her body fading slowly until all he could see was the gold of her pupils, and slowly the mirthless laughter began again. Court's blood ran cold. His heart pounded in his chest.

"Qissa, Courtney Dillon. Or I kill them all and I'll feed on them and then feed them to you until you choke on their blood."

"I don't know what Qissa is!" he yelled, but his voice was drowned out.

The laughter again, a godawful sound like ripping sheet metal, a cold sound, and then scampering, carrying the thing away, carrying its laughter away, the light in its eyes, until Court was again all alone.

CHAPTER THIRTY-NINE

Damn farmer's market. Ben Derringer shuffled his weight from the ball of one foot to the next. The Razorbacks would be kicking off soon, and he thought of boneless wings and pizza and beer and his couch. But he stood here at the farmer's market as his wife investigated flowers for an eternity. He scratched his crotch and deliberated supporting a free-standing post that was keeping the tent up.

His wife bent over a batch of petunias, her gargantuan ass so much wider in his lens than it had been when they were dating… a bitter pill he'd yet to swallow. When he looked away, he found himself smiling at a boy not more than six or so who was playing coy a ways off.

With a glance back, he saw that his wife had moved on to exclaim over the bunches of irises. They were pretty and perennial, and so timeless. The boy cocked his grin a little as if anticipating this observation. He was a dirty kid, dirty cheeks, thin, his clothes dirty and ill-fitting. Parents probably live in the nearby trailer park, Ben supposed, as he approached him with a smile and knelt—his knees creaking—and tried to reassure the boy with a reach to his cheek with his palm. The boy recoiled.

"I'm not going to hurt you." His statement sounded even to him a bit pedophilic.

"I want to go home," the boy whispered. Ben sensed a bit of trust in the boy, in the eyes or in the words.

"I can help you." Ben said, to which the boy glanced at the hefty woman evaluating irises at the cash register as though their selling price was up for bargaining. Ben followed the boy's gaze and conceded, "We can help you."

"I want to go home."

"We'll help you," Ben assured him.

His wife needed little convincing. Barren herself—a private shame she'd feared for years would drive Ben away—her motherly instinct kicked in upon meeting the child. She stroked his cheek and beamed to her husband. They were obligated.

When they drove away down the state highway, with the boy in the back seat, there rose no objection from any occupant that they were heading down the wrong road.

"Stop here," the boy said. His voice was calm and matter of fact like he wasn't nervous—or like he'd practiced the line a million times.

Ben pulled the car to a shoulder. Both he and his wife looked around but saw no house. The road itself was encroached on either side by the Arkansas wild: autumnal colors and drab blades and a few stubborn smatterings of green, but not enough to alleviate the cold and empty feeling of a wilderness dying. Cold penetrated the car's interior, and Ben's wife visibly shook; he fought the chill creeping up his spine. The emptiness manifested like a hollow in the chest, as if someone had sucked his breath away. His mind grasped for rational thought but found no anchor, and he lurched into the cold and the breathless emptiness with only a strange, irrational fear to guide. But it wasn't unknowable. He'd recognized it for what it was as soon as he'd shifted to park on this desolate stretch of country road. There were no houses. They'd been led into a trap. The eyes on him peeled away any defense he might've had left. With his wife, he looked to the back seat, where the boy sat primly, hands folded in his lap. And smiling.

Had there come a passerby, they might have seen windows fogged opaque—a chemical reaction catalyzing in an instant—or the jolt of the car as though two lovers were testing the shocks in the backseat. They wouldn't have heard the screams, unless they were on foot, but if they were on foot then they would have turned away from this stretch of road. The cold would have penetrated their clothes, and a sense of emptiness, of isolation, would have robbed them of their breath. Instinct would have driven them away. For Ben and his wife, however, instinct hadn't come quick enough, and the only passerby who watched from the ridgeline was the older man who'd agreed to help the beast feed.

Clem looked on and made sure it fed uninterrupted.

CHAPTER FORTY

The diner was filled almost exclusively with white Boomers, the leather booths torn in places so the jagged edges dug into their backs. Still, the detective seemed at home, called the waitress by her first name as she called him Albert, and asked if he wanted his coffee and a western omelet. He said he didn't like to eat breakfast so late and ordered the patty melt with fries and, hungry as they were, Chuy and Rong ordered the same. As she started to walk away, Bullocks reached up and snagged the waitress's sleeve.

"Hey Rosie, how about three strawberry malts?"

These came first, and Albert Bullocks looked like a twelve-year-old sucking the strawberry milkshake through a straw, topped with whipped cream and a couple of cherries.

"Thanks for meeting with us," Rong said.

"Got a small army in town, I hear. I met your friend, Dani. You all here to help look for Court?"

"We care about her," Chuy said. "Her and Court."

"This is a police matter, kids. Rest assured we're all over it."

Bullocks had watched Dani and the grandmothers leave when the Spanish kid and the Chinese kid walked up to him, asking if he could help them. As the only resident minority in town, it had shocked him to see the two and wondered briefly if they sought him out because he was the only minority, or if they sensed he was a cop, but he had maintained composure and announced someone at the station could help them, and he was going to lunch. The Chinese kid introduced himself with, "I'm Rong, they/them. It's you we need to talk to, Detective Bullocks."

Bullocks considered both for a long minute before nodding his head and inviting them to join him.

"There's something you need to know," Rong said.

The waitress reappeared with their patty melts—hands full and one plate balanced on her bent forearm—as Bullocks took another long sip of his strawberry shake.

Bullocks picked up his burger and took out a big chunk. Chuy and Rong each took a sip of their malts and exchanged a glance. Rong said, "You've got a lot going on in this town."

His mouth full, he said, "Court's missing. We have something desecrating graves in the area. Some people have gone missing."

"We know," Chuy said.

"I've been following the news reports," Rong said. "We think it's all related."

Bullocks used his napkin to dab at the corners of his mouth. "Why would you think so?"

"Because nearly every girl Court has dated, every girl he's been serious about, is dead."

Bullocks squinted, studying the college student. "How did you…?"

"A lot of time at the library, and a lot of time online," Rong answered. "Trust us. When you find the graves, have you noticed anything else?"

Bullocks nodded. "Something has been digging into the fresher graves and…" he gave a pause, looked down at his half-eaten patty melt, and pushed it away. "Eating. It's been eating."

Both Rong and Chuy recoiled, dropping their forks mid-bite. There existed a moment of silence, hanging between them all like a dark cloud. Chuy saw it on the horizon. A challenge. A will to his determination. It was an invitation for the kids to join the man, the seasoned warrior, the holy quest. Chuy felt like throwing up.

"I need to go to the bathroom," Rong said, and forced Chuy out of the booth so they could evacuate.

Chuy stared at the salt and pepper shaker. "So, the people who've gone missing?"

"Missing is what we've told the paper. We've found some of them. Parts of them, at least."

"Jesus," Chuy said.

"So, you think, because Court is missing and he's lost girlfriends, whatever is eating these corpses and killing these people has him?"

"It's why we came," Chuy said. "When Rong showed us all this, we all knew Dani was in danger, so we came."

Bullocks smiled. When his thin lips pulled back, they showed deep creases around his mouth. His eyes tried to condone the emotion his mouth wanted to show, but, unblinking, he could only shake his head.

"She isn't the only one in danger," he said.

"What do you mean?" Chuy asked.

"There's a lot of white folk in this town who don't like a Black man here."

"Yes."

"They don't like I'm a detective, neither."

"So, they won't like people of color traipsing around their town."

Rong returned from the bathroom, and Bullocks, breathing out, sat back and finished off his malt. The waitress came back also, calling him, 'sugar,' asking if he needed anything else, and he asked her to box up their leftovers. She looked to all three and said of course, then left.

"If you aren't white and straight, you aren't welcome here. I'm neither, though this town doesn't know about the latter. They tolerate me because they see me as a Big City Detective, but make no mistake, it's more than this thing here putting Dani, and all of you, in danger."

"We're not leaving," Rong said. "Not until we have Court."

"Then maybe it's time you meet his family," Bullocks said.

CHAPTER FORTY-ONE

Oster and Lena had found them a table near one of the stages where local musicians were setting up, and Lena paid for a glass of iced tea for each of them, telling Dani they had one more person to meet here today. They waited in near silence, only sipping at their tea and listening to the bluegrass music. Plenty of time for Lena to expound on her apology, though she didn't bother. Dani assumed it was guilt or pride or both that kept her silent. It wasn't long before the woman came, youngish, dressed in yoga pants and a tee; she hugged both women and studied Dani up and down before shaking her hand. Lena introduced her as Britta, a school friend of Court's.

"Oh," Dani said, as they all sat.

"I married his best friend," Britta confided. Dani tried to imagine hanging out with this woman, and realized Court never spoke of any friends from back home, just his family.

"It's nice to meet you," she said to Britta, then turned toward Lena. "So, you're going to tell me about these safety concerns?"

"If I'd have known you were coming, I would have told you on the phone when we spoke," Lena said. "You would have stayed away."

"I love him," Dani said. "Nothing is going to make me leave. Nothing is going to keep me away. Not until I find him."

Lena and Aster exchanged glances with Britta. "Then there are things you need to know," Britta said finally. "About other women who loved Court Dillon."

So, they began to tell Dani everything.

CHAPTER FORTY-TWO

Farming was especially hard in Rapps Barren. Many people, like Elden, chose livestock over crops. Elden's farm had once stood at over a hundred acres, and at one time, long before Court was born, he had horses and pigs and chickens, as well as the cattle. But as he got older, Elden culled out the animals every other season, until he had only chickens and cattle. While he'd eventually raise Angus, he started with Charolais, Gelbvieh, and Hereford.

The chickens he kept until Court was a toddler. Toddler Court had meandered into the calf lot behind the house on his way to see his grandfather, who was working on the tin roof of the old barn. When the rooster jumped in front of him, Court had yelled at it, but rather than frightening it away, the cock leapt in the air and dug its claws into Court's scalp. Elden could hear the flogging, could hear Court's screams. He leapt off the barn and raced up the lot, catching hold of the old bird and tearing it off his grandson, choking it, throwing it on the ground and kicking its remains as Court stood back and watched, crying.

☙❧

Glen got out to open the gate as Elden steered the flatbed Ford into the calf lot, shutting the truck off at the white washed shed inside the gate. He opened the shed's hollow-core wooden door to a dry smell, like a tomb, the air all closed off and stifled, and led Glen halfway down the shed to a step-down addition with a dirt floor. There, amidst all the wood and paneling and rolls of fencing, Elden spied what they came for: some fifty-pound bags of salt meant for the cattle who no longer grazed on his farmland, and spears of rebar gathered in a clump.

Glen's library internet and microfiche research told them they'd need both; wordlessly, the two men began collecting up the items. It would take several trips.

"There's a couple of kids in the yard up there with the detective," Glen said, motioning over his shoulder as he tossed another fifty-pound bag of salt onto the flatbed of Elden's pickup.

Elden dumped three six-foot lengths of rebar beside them as he nodded. "They've been nosing around the farm. I saw them when we got back from the library."

"Wonder how long."

For Elden, this was an unimportant question. He put his hands on the side of the truck and stared at the flatbed, the rebar, the salt.

"We were dying, you know."

This caused Glen to stop. He nodded, placing his hands on the truck as well, mimicking Elden. "And now we're all better."

"Why?" Elden asked. "For how long?"

Glen shrugged. "Maybe 'til we stop this thing?" He posed it as a question, but perhaps he meant this as an answer to both of Elden's questions.

"It was dark. Cloudy. It was like I wasn't even connected anymore."

"Like you were a ship anchored to this beach, and all around you was this hurricane, and then the anchor lifted, and you were pulled out to sea, and all of a sudden the whole ocean was open to you."

"Death is an ocean?" Elden asked. "No wonder I don't like boats."

Glen smiled, but Elden could see his gaze drifting off, lost in the horizon.

"Don't you believe in clouds and heaven and such?"

"I have my moments, like when I lost my father. Then when I lost my mother. When I was in the hospital, when I was young, right before I met Lena, I was suffering some of the worst intestinal pain of my life, and there were nights when I laid in bed and prayed for the pain to go away, and when it didn't, I began to wonder."

"And what do you do during those moments?" Elden asked. He was honest with this question. He'd grown up with the Bible. It had taught him that, when he went hunting, not to shoot at doves, but much beyond, he hadn't any practical use for the book.

Glen shivered. "Pray harder," he said.

Elden nodded. It wasn't much of an answer to help him, but it was an answer, and it was honest. They finished packing the truck, then drove it back into the yard, where they parked and exited the vehicle, staring at the Chinese kid in the thick glasses and drab clothing, who sat on Elden's porch alongside a Hispanic boy who'd prettied himself up, and the Black detective, who seemed to be gazing at one of the oaks in Elden's front yard.

"You fought in Korea, right?" Elden asked.

Glen nodded. The Chinese kid was studying his smart phone with some intensity.

"You get the Jap, then," Elden said.

As both men approached the porch, Rong looked up from their phone to match their gazes. Chuy did as well, and Bullocks turned, nodding to the old men.

Behind them, the gravel popped, and all eyes turned to see the Aveo pull into the drive, followed by an economy SUV Elden had never seen before. Next, TJ's truck pulled into the far drive, and got out as the women were gathering themselves out of the cars.

When the Chinese boy spoke, Elden noticed the near monotone and accentless timbre. "So, the gang's all here," Rong said.

CHAPTER FORTY-THREE

When it returned, the chamber filled with a fetid stench. Death clung to it. It reeked of festering, of decay, of rot, like freshly turned soil filled with mealworms and maggots and nightcrawlers, like what he and Papaw dug up when they used to go fishing.

Court didn't know how long he'd been down here. He'd sipped at a trickle of water leaking in through the black marrow cracks of the walls out of thirst. Because the Ozarks were filled with caverns and underground springs, it was easy to find a rivulet of water trickling across the floor from a small hole where the stone met the calcified wall. Despite its source, he drank eagerly, finding it cold and tasteless. He couldn't remember the last time he ate. His stomach rumbled and his leg hurt. He had, in fact, uncovered numerous sores and fresh pains: scabs, flesh burning from scrapes, joints aching, muscles sore. These things preoccupied him and kept his mind off the hunger, and to block the pain he wondered what his life might be like once he got out of this place. He wasn't prepared to consider the alternative yet.

Scenario One: He'd get a call that his grandfathers had both died. He would fall apart, probably spiral into a bender. In scenario 1-A, Dani would cradle him through the heartache. In scenario 1-B she'd leave, and he'd lose his job and impregnate some... some random woman he could not love in an effort to not be alone.

Scenario Two: He'd come to town and his grandfathers would be fine, and he'd remember how loving and tender they were with each other, and he'd go home to Dani ready to commit only for her to laugh him off and shoo him away, ready for her next adventure.

Kissing the cold stone, deep in the dark, dank earth, he couldn't imagine either reality. No alternative granting him a happy ending could exist because *it* was there, lurking in the shadows, its voice like a whisper that, when it spoke, came from all over.

"You avoid," it said, "because you're afraid."

Court raised his eyes and scanned the dim chamber. Torchlight still flickered, but the monster was concealed by too many shadows.

"I'm not afraid," he said. He rose with a grunt, fresh pain shooting up through his body. "You're the one hiding in the shadows."

"You avoid them." Its voice slithered through the darkness, oily and snakelike.

"No."

He scanned the domed walls. He thought he had it, could pinpoint its location. But then what? What would he do if he caught it? This thing had defeated him so easily and dragged him down below the earth. What could he do to stop it?

"Why do you hate coming here?" The question knocked him back against the wall. Court did not want to answer. He did not want to talk about such things with whatever this was. But the simple question was posed efficiently, because even this creature understood that he did hate returning.

"Because every time I come back," he said, his breath hitching in his throat, "they are older."

"Time is borrowed."

"No, time is finite. It's all we have, and I don't want to remember them old and dying. But the rest of this town, it can all go to hell."

"No," it hissed.

"Yes," he snapped and tried to peer through the darkness. In the shadows above the torches, he saw a form scurry. Its long limbs were hairless; it was grinning. And had he seen rows of teeth, and eyes that glowed greenish yellow?

"They remind you," it said. It spoke with a sense of wisdom Court did not want to attribute to it. He sensed that beneath its words, it was at once inquisitive and mocking. Mocking him for his ignorance, this poet, this man who'd come thinking he was so smart. However long this thing had lived, it was smarter.

"Of what?" he asked, even though he did not want to have this conversation. He especially didn't want to have the conversation with this thing, but in truth, the conversation had taken his mind off the pain and hunger that gnawed at him incessantly. His stomach rumbled and a wave of weakness folded over him. He felt cold. "What do they remind me of?" he asked again.

"Of what you aren't. Of what you don't have." *Imperious monster, terrific*, Court thought.

It leapt to the floor and instantly morphed from its hidden form, sliding into the image of a stripper Court had met three years ago, then into Dani, then into his high school crush Becky Tomlinson, with her dirty blonde hair and big breasts and her infectious smile.

"You aren't real," Court said, and the thing laughed.

"And you are?" it asked with the lips, the voice, of Becky. "You're a playboy. You're afraid of growing up."

"You're wrong," Court said. But this thing was mirroring the conversation he'd just had with Dani, and because it was saying nearly exactly what she was saying, he knew it was true. But he also knew it was true because deep down, he knew these things about himself.

"Because you don't want to be like them."

Court sat up, bent his knees, and hugged them; he stared at the stone floor. "That's bullshit. I do. I—" Did he want a marriage? Kids? Did he want the stress he'd brought his grandparents? Did he want the constant worry whether or not his child would turn out okay? What if something happened to him?

The thing wearing his ex-girlfriend's face shook its head. "You see where it gets them."

"They live happily ever after," Court said, but even then, he knew the truth.

"No," it said, and leapt back up to the shadows, morphing again into its alien skin, but its voice still echoed down. With its last words before it scurried away, it sang a truth Court couldn't deny, which left him weeping on the cold, dark, dank stone floor.

"No, Court," it said. "It leads here… to them dying."

Court was alone again. He could smell it in the air. The creature had gone back above ground, to feed or to hunt, maybe both. Somewhere out there, his friends were dying, and his grandfathers were dying, and he was here.

Because he was too afraid or too selfish. Their aging and dying inconvenienced him, so he couldn't watch it, certainly couldn't live it. He was the consummate playboy, the alcoholic, the partier, older than all his friends. Like Peter Pan, he wouldn't get older nor face his mortality. And if he didn't come around, then he didn't see them age, so in his mind they'd always be young. And they wouldn't face their mortality either.

In his mind.

He was selfish.

But still there was the idea that Dani wouldn't run, and she wouldn't reject a future with him. Oh, it was the best possible scenario, and it brought a smile to his lips. As he rested his cheek on the stone floor, he thought of cementing his future with her.

INTERLUDE SEVEN

The Tale of the Devil's Choice

Once upon a time, the Devil cornered a man at a crossroads. The man was nothing special, but like every other man he had a choice to make, and the Devil knew it—he walked right up to the man and held out both his hands, palms up. He offered the man a sly smile and a wink, and said, "What if I could offer you what you want?"

"Go away!" the man said. He didn't have much, but he was a good person, who knew the Devil when he saw him.

But the Devil knew the man was traveling two paths. The man walked this road because he had a promise to keep, and he had to make it to his destination. But deep down in the places he talked about with no one, the man harbored intense feelings for a young woman with whom he hoped to walk this path, someday…

"You know who I am," the Devil said, and the man nodded. "And I know what you want. I know why you are on this road, and I know how alone you are. I know that right now, you can't imagine a scenario when the love of your life is on the trail, walking by your side, and you can't even imagine making it to your next destination as you so desperately must."

The Devil was right. The man had already faced so many tribulations on this journey, and the thought of reaching his destination seemed like a long shot at best.

"I can help you," the Devil said. "But you must choose."

"Choose?"

The Devil's grin broadened. He had the young man, now.

"Aren't you tired of walking this path alone? Wouldn't you like a companion? Not just any person, mind you, but someone who understood your every desire, your every wish, someone who shared your every dream."

"I would." The young man seemed almost hypnotized.

"Your journey has been fraught with danger. You have fought every inch of this trek. Why is it you need to see this sojourn through?"

"Family," he said. "Sick. If I don't do this…" His voice trailed off.

"So, you must find your destination? Not for yourself, but for them."

The young man nodded, and the Devil, still smiling, held his arms out at the crossroads to showcase each available path.

"Choose," the Devil said.

At the end of one path, the young man could see his journey's end, where lights from the town arced in the distance, lighting up the horizon. He could see his family happy and healthy, the curse of ill health lifted. At the crossroads where the man now stood, facing the Devil, this path veered off to the right.

To his left, the path showed darkness save one beacon of light. A girl—his girl—stood there, dressed alluringly, beckoning to him seductively, her lips pursed. Her arm extended, palm up, index finger curling as though she were reeling him in.

Straight ahead, there lay only darkness and the promise of unforgiving mountainous terrain somewhere in the distance. Lightning flashed at the horizon. Thunder rolled lazily down the valley.

"Choose."

The End

CHAPTER FORTY-FOUR

*P*ositive. That's what two stripes meant. Positive. Dani dropped the stick into the trash and turned on the faucet. First reached over to flush what Aster had called the 'commode,' though Dani detected nothing but a thick Southern accent, when the elder woman had pointed to the little room again. Perhaps no one noticed her gone. Perhaps. Through the eastern-facing window, long shadows grew across the backyard, empowered by the setting sun. In the trash can were chunks of toilet paper, a cardboard roll, and some makeup remover cloths. Dani delicately tucked the pregnancy test under the other detritus, washed her hands, and opened the door.

She was in the front bathroom, and when she exited, she found herself in a little alcove between a bedroom, the den, and the hall. On the dresser sat a picture in a silver frame, a photo of a young couple with two kids: a toddler and a boy several years older. She frowned. The older boy looked familiar to her. A recent face, and that she couldn't recognize him right off bothered her. Until she could. The boy at the farmer's market? Similar. No. Same. She scanned the eyes of each member of the family, staring as they were into the sun, into the light, into the camera. All of them so familiar, but so foreign.

To the boy in the picture again. His clothing: OshKosh B'gosh. Same shirt, pants, as at the farmer's market. It *was* the boy from the market, those same eyes staring through the lens, right at her. A child of six with his parents, and a baby with the eyes, the stare, she'd come to know. Court stared at her that way. Here, he was a baby, his features a blending of the parents holding the kids in the picture. It was his parents, she knew, because she could see the resemblance in the photo. How had she not seen this picture before? This question was followed immediately by the simple act of touching her own stomach. How might their child look? Court's earnest gaze? Her hair?

"Oh dear," she muttered.

"Dani," Aster called from the kitchen. She spun in place like she'd been caught, but there was no one in the den; she settled a bit. But when she looked to the right, to the long, dark hall, she thought she saw something blinking from the deepest recesses. But Aster called again, and Dani straightened.

"Yes ma'am."

"Your friends are here."

Her friends. Terrific. And, she was sure, the cop, and Glen and Lena. The whole gang. And who could she tell about the pregnancy test? Maybe Jade. For sure not Court's family. God, Court. She ought to be sharing this with him. But the fact she wasn't sharing it with him conjured up fresher dread, and Dani found herself shaking and sweating and on the verge of fainting. She gripped the dresser and nearly crumpled under the weight on her chest and shoulders.

The framed picture toppled to the floor, Dani watching it, frozen. The sound drew Aster, who came immediately then knelt beside the upside-down frame. She examined the picture of the young family with the two boys, picked it up and placed it back on the dresser.

"You okay, dear?"

Dani nodded. Whatever knot in her stomach loosened a bit and she offered up a smile.

"The glass didn't crack," Aster said, nodding to the picture.

"Good," Dani said.

Aster looked from her to the picture and back again, then reached up and patted her shoulder. "Come, come. Your friends are here, and so are the Dillons and their cop friend. They might have word on Court's whereabouts."

Dani forced another smile. "Yes ma'am."

She followed Aster into the kitchen; she approached the corner cupboard and peered into the living room, unseen. Her friends and Court's grandparents sat, spaced out around the room, between the four recliners on either side of the fireplace, facing each other, the sofa staring at the hearth, the dining table in the corner with its chairs pulled out and angled toward the conversation.

Dani helped Aster with the drinks. When Aster sat in the recliner next to Elden, Dani took her seat in the opposite recliner.

Scattered around the room like pieces on a chess board. Her friends. Court's grandparents. The detective.

"So, what's going on?" he asked. He turned his gaze to each one of them. Was Dani the only one to notice the grandparents exchanging glances?

"It's as you said, Detective," she answered. "We're all here looking for Court."

"But there's also the thing digging up graves," Chuy said, his words directed to the cop. Bullocks nodded in confirmation.

"And people are being murdered," Rong added.

"And graves have been desecrated," Glen said. "The corpses eaten on. But it isn't a wild animal, is it, Detective Bullocks?"

"We know all this," Lena said.

"It's good to make sure," Aster said. "Everyone on the same page."

"It's all related," Dani said. "Court's disappearance, the grave desecrations, the murders." It was a hunch; it was all she had, but she knew she was right.

Rong cleared their throat, and the room focused on them. "I called the sheriff and the mortician."

Outside, beyond the bay window, orange and yellow light filtering through the curtains reminded them all of the coming night. Rong seemed to focus on the glow, but the others focused on the dimness.

"Yes?" Lena asked.

And so, the stories began…

೫೬

The Tale of Rong and the Sheriff

"It was a dim, gray afternoon. Rain-filled clouds squatted fat and pregnant over the land."

"Hello, Sheriff? So, when did you first notice the graves?" Rong squinted outside; despite the overcast, the shadows, and the cooling temperatures, and still they sweat some.

"Who is this?"

Rong stammered. "My name is Rong, sir, and I'm friends with Court…"

Laughter. So loud Rong pulled the phone from their ear. Their clothes stuck to their slick flesh even in the shade under the library awning where they stood. To their right, a mom led her daughter out by the hand, books in the little girl's handbag. Mom and daughter, both dark-haired, were Caucasian and regarded Rong with forced grins, suggesting they didn't belong.

"What's your real name, son?" the sheriff asked. Rong had swallowed hard, and their vision blurred. The laughter continued, until the sheriff said, "I don't have time for stupid pranks. Good day, son."

⊗

The Tale of Rong and the Mortician

"Rong, you say? What an unusual name. You say you're a friend of Court. Court Dillon? How do you know him?"

Rong cleared their throat. "He's a professor at my university. I mean, I go to the University of Arkansas. I mean…"

"Well, um, Rong, was it? Rong, we've told all we know. There's been some grave robbing and other things, but I don't know anything about your friend Court or anything else. Have you called the sheriff?"

⊗

Dani felt her own throat seize up. The experience for her friend, she realized, illuminated how difficult it would be for any of them to penetrate a Southern white community.

"First, let me apologize to you on behalf of the sheriff," Detective Bullocks said. "It wasn't right of him…"

"Don't apologize for him," Rong said calmly. "You didn't do it. Let him own up to his own behavior."

"I thought I could get my hands on CCTV footage from the funeral home, but the file they handed over was a loop that revealed nothing."

"So, you need to go back and get the real tape," Elden said. He pointed to himself and then to Glen. "We'll come with you."

Bullocks waved them away. "No, no. You all sit tight. Still, I could use some help." He looked to Dani, and Dani only. "Which of your friends are good with computers?"

Jada and Britta each raised their hands. Rong thought of joining them, then thought better of it. Dani thought, as Rong must have, their talents would be better served elsewhere.

"Fine, you two come with me."

"Stakeout," TJ said. "Some could go stake out a couple of the cemeteries. Like the two or three places most recently hit. I can go with my wife here and we can look at the video."

"What are you doing?" Britta whispered.

TJ pulled her tighter and leaned into her ear. "Court's missing, and these…people are here. We go with this cop, it might help us understand what the hell is going on."

"Not alone," the detective balked.

"Of course not," Britta said, much too loudly, pulling away from her husband. "Everyone should pair up, keep an eye on things, and if they see anything, call you."

Bullocks seemed to consider it, before he said, "I can't risk putting you in danger. You all stay here. We'll go to the funeral home and look at the tape. And besides, we'll be able to watch that cemetery also." He ushered TJ and Britta out the door.

"Court's grandparents," Rong began, when the door closed. "Other than the cemetery and funeral home where the detective is heading, how many cemeteries are there in Rapps Barren?"

"Three major cemeteries in the city limits," Elden said.

"Yes, but another three or four in the surrounding county," Glen said.

"So, we tackle the three in the city, first," Rong said. "If you gentlemen would give us the names and locations. Chuy and I can take one, and Jada and Blue, would you take another?"

The girls exchanged a glance and nodded in acquiescence as Elden spoke up.

"Glen, you care to take a ride?"

"Sure," Glen said. He leaned over and kissed Lena. "Why don't you and Dani and Aster stay here and coordinate things. See if anyone calls or we get word on Court."

And before Lena could answer, Glen and Elden shared the details of the other locations, and everyone was out the door.

CHAPTER FORTY-FIVE

Court's muscles had settled into a kind of numbness, and a dull ache throbbed in his temples, something akin to white noise; he was now used to it, but it wasn't soothing, the discomfort was still there, underneath the surface.

He was tired. His circadian rhythm wasn't off: he knew it was night because his body told him so, and the aches and pains subsiding to a dull throb suggested his body would allow him to sleep. Sleep wouldn't come, though—another visitor darkened the passage.

It wasn't his captor. This simulacrum walked upright, bipedal. On the floor, and not crawling along the walls. This one wore a bit of swagger in its lanky gait, and as it closed in, Court smelled whiskey.

The torchlight illuminated a man in his sixties, his hair still dark but the wrinkles on his face, especially around his eyes and mouth, gave away his age. He wore a jean jacket and jean pants and a Conway Twitty concert T-shirt. When he knelt, the mud-crusted work boots close to Court's nostrils allowed the poet to smell shit and fetid dirt. The smile on his lips bothered Court.

"So," the man said.

Court was sure this guy wasn't here to save him. When the man stuck out his hand as if to offer Court a gentleman's welcome, Court looked at it as though it'd bite him.

The man's derisive laugh cut through the rancid air. "Just trying to introduce myself. It ain't gonna bite."

Court occupied his hands in bracing himself to sit up.

"I'm Clem. Don't worry. You ain't mine to kill. I'll leave it up to her."

"What do you want?" Court asked. His voice was hoarse, barely a whisper.

"Well," Clem said, settling into his squat, casting his eyes skyward as the torchlight caught his salt and pepper grizzle, "it's a real conundrum, now ain't it. I been searching for years. What I want, I don't have the faintest idea, Mr. Dillon. Guess I been drifting along, you might say. My daddy once told me… you… you wanna know what he said?"

Court wasn't sure why he nodded. This man talking was keeping him from sleep, but also, thankfully, from the throbbing.

"He said it don't matter what you want. Life will give you what you need. So, you need to work on living life, and the rest will be provided."

"He sounds like a wise man." Court strained to speak.

"He was," Clem said, then rocked back on his haunches. He rubbed his hands together and looked up at the torchlight. "Daddy was part of the greatest generation. Like your Pawpaw."

"Papaw," Court corrected, then coughed.

Clem wrinkled his brow and curled his lip. "Well excuse the fuck out of me," he said and raised and lowered a hand in one fluid motion, slapping Court across the jaw. "I was talking, boy."

Court spat something red from his lips that tasted like pennies as his jaw throbbed in pain. Clem regarded him for a moment before continuing, as though he were allowing Court to wallow.

"They had a greater calling. Weeding out evil. Weeding out the scum of the earth."

"How long you been trying to live up to your father?" Court asked.

Clem raised his hand again. Court didn't look away, but stared him down, and eventually Clem lowered his hand.

"Your friends are here, boy. The ghoul has something special planned for you, but I'm going to take your Spic girlfriend and your weird, colored friends, and I'm going to slaughter them all. And I'll take my time with her ass. And then I'm going to gut your grandparents. Think of it. Think of all the blood and flesh she can lap up at her leisure."

Court mustered up enough spit to form a bloody, gooey globule, and spat it onto Clem's boots.

Clem considered the lump on his boot with an odd smile, then backhanded Court, knocking him to his back and sending his head ricocheting off the stone floor. Stars danced in the periphery and Court's vision blurred then briefly darkened. When he saw Clem again, the man's face danced over him. A lump was forming on the back of his skull from the impact, a pain emphasized when Clem grabbed a fistful of hair back there and yanked Court's head up.

"She wants me to offer you a deal. Give her what she wants, and she'll leave them all alone."

"So that's why you're here," Court said. The pain ringing through his head sounded louder than the church's bells on Sunday.

Clem made a clicking sound, winked, and nodded. "But," he continued. "She didn't ask me about no such deal."

"So what?" Court asked, raising his head. "You gonna kill me too?"

Clem belted out a laugh. "Not tonight, old friend. Tonight, I have a date with your friends. With your girlfriend."

He rose, knees creaking as if on rusted hinges, and gave Court a swift kick in the gut, the fresh pain forcing him into the fetal position. Clem stood, turned and moseyed back toward the darkness, his laughter echoing through the chambers long after he was gone.

Another bloody spherule languidly spilled out of Court's mouth, and he looked around the room, his vision fuzzy and doubled as he forced himself to stand. There was no inch of his body not in pain and he could not help but whimper as he drug himself to his feet. When he tried to focus on a particular torch, it overlapped with its wall. Fresh fire burned through his ribs.

His eyes closed, but he didn't succumb to the darkness. Instead, his mind began to race. The redneck had gotten in here somehow, which meant there was a way out for him. Court spat another globule of bloody saliva, this one trailing to his chin, and tried to shake off the oncoming concussion. When his vision started to clear some, he rose and began to scan the dark, bone-lined walls.

CHAPTER FORTY-SIX

Night settled in, sealing Dani and the grandmothers into the farmhouse with a kind of completeness only fear could provide. The friends gone, the detective gone, Court's grandfathers out and still no clue as to Court's whereabouts, she felt isolated, even more so in the darkness. The world beyond the artificial light no longer existed. Looking out the sliding door of the den, there was no more a backyard, no ricked cords of firewood at the north end, no barbed-wire fence and no pasture laying beyond. Merely black and empty with a cold seeping in around the seams, making her feel hollow. *Death is bleak and empty and cold and dark and hollow*, she thought, and she couldn't stop the single tear from rolling down her cheek as such an existential thought jumbled with her worry for Court's safety, and for the little test she'd tried to hide in the bathroom wastebasket. Behind her, the grandmothers sat in the kitchen, expressing their own worries.

"We should have stopped them," Lena said.

"You know good and well," Aster said, "I've never been able to stop Elden once he gets an idea in his head. And I doubt you'd have better luck."

"Fool-headed, the two of them, going off on their own."

"Damn fools," Aster added and sipped her coffee loudly. They'd offered Dani a cup, but she'd politely refused. How could anyone drink coffee so late, even if it was decaf?

"Pushing their luck," Lena continued. "As sick as they were, and to be given another chance like this, only to rush out and tempt fate again."

"Do not tempt the Lord your God," Aster half-quoted. "It's what Jesus told Satan on the mountain."

Still, Aster's words reminded Dani of how well the two men looked. They certainly weren't dying as Court had said. She returned to them in the kitchen and when Lena did not immediately respond to Aster's proverb, Dani spoke up.

"Court was coming to visit because he said Elden and Glen were dying, but they seem fine to me." She left the question inferred, looking from one woman to the other.

Lena and Aster exchanged a glance before Lena spoke. "We aren't sure what happened."

"They were sick, both of 'um," Aster said. "In the hospital. And then…"

"How sick?" Dani asked.

"Court was not exaggerating," Lena answered.

"But they ain't just better," Aster said, slapping her palm on the table, but not so loudly to startle either woman. "It's like they're stronger. Younger."

"Not just them," Lena said, nodding.

Dani narrowed her eyes. "What do you mean?"

"I feel it too," she said then to Aster. "Don't you?"

Aster nodded.

"Whatever helped them, helped us too. I don't know what it is—"

"God," Aster interjected. Lena only slightly nodded her head before continuing.

"But it's like we were meant to be here. To face this…thing."

Dani pursed her lips and folded her hands as if in prayer.

"Where they found Court's car…"

"County Road 157," Aster said.

"Where is this county road?" she asked, lowering her hands to the table as the old women exchanged a glance; neither, she gathered, was great with directions.

Lena answered. "On the way to the lake, up the bypass from here, in fact. It's a spur, only connecting the bypass to the old Rapps Barren homesteads and Panther Bay Marina."

"What, about a five-minute drive?" Aster said.

And before anything else could be said, Dani was up and had her keys in hand. She was gathering up her purse when Lena spoke again, something like, "You can't go."

But Dani had to. She opened the front door and looked back to the two women. "I can't sit here, either," she said, not waiting for them to decide if they'd accompany her. Them traipsing around the forest after dark would only impede her, so she shut the door, and by the time she was in her car and it was started, she'd had the county road programmed into her GPS; setting the iPhone on the dashboard charger, the bright screen the only beacon in the black of night, she pulled out of the drive and headed towards Court's last known whereabouts.

CHAPTER FORTY-SEVEN

It was too late in the fall for cicadas by at least a few days, which Blue found weird. One night the noisy little things could be heard, a symphony of sound on Night's Plutonian shore, but with a drop in the temperature, and a few nights later, maybe even one night for the more observable listener, and the sound was gone. Autumn was dark and deaf, and Blue was stuck in her vehicle looking at a bunch of tombstones with Jada the bobblehead as her companion.

Her silent companion. Jada was enthralled with something on her phone, texting, from the looks of it. Blue sighed and focused on the cemetery.

She didn't know where she was, only that this was where she was asked to go because there were people vandalizing graves, and it could be related to Court's disappearance, so she went, not knowing where she was in relation to the rest of the town or her friends or Court, wherever he was. Not here, where somewhere in the dark distance someone was burning leaves, by the smell; the air was cool and dry.

How quickly things change.

Aunt Adelaide had had such high hopes for them. "Samantha," she'd said, back when she was the only one not to call Blue by her chosen name, "he's such a good boy. You'll like him."

Blue had tried to like Court. They'd hung out and drank and made out a few times. She told herself if she let herself get drunk enough, she'd let him do whatever, and she reminded herself he was a good-looking guy, and they had a lot of fun together.

And what if you do "whatever" and get pregnant and then he wants to get married, can you live the rest of your life knowing that you are not and never will be attracted to him? To any man?

Fucking rational mind. Used to only speak up in those times when she was alone, and silent, at first. But as time went on, her inner voice had gotten louder.

It was a night much like this so many years ago, when she noticed how quiet it was, when the cicadas had stopped chirping, and he had pulled away from her, a look of doubt and worry in his eyes, and something else. Concern. Her face revealed how unhappy she was.

"What is it?" he had asked.

"The cicadas have stopped," she said.

"What?"

She raised her eyes to him and wanted so desperately to explain her feelings. And she tried her best to emphasize that the feelings she had were there long before they'd ever met.

"With you, I guess I wanted those feelings to go away, and I wanted you to be…"

"You can't change who you are, Blue."

He'd asked her if she'd been afraid, and she said not of her aunt, but of others; in those years, few people came out of the closet for fear of how others would act, especially here in Arkansas.

She grabbed them each another beer and they went from canoodling to hugging, and from kissing to him placing a kiss on her forehead, and promising to support her, and slowly, as the evening drifted on, they found something funny to watch on television and when they went to bed, he crashed on her couch. When they woke up the next day, they were friends. He accompanied her to the lunch when she told her aunt and was there at her apartment when she returned from the long trip to tell her family. Their core friends began to revolve around them, pulled into their orbit, spinning through Northwest Arkansas across the years until Dani came into the picture. Both had found her attractive, but Blue knew Dani wasn't attracted to women, so she encouraged her old friend and this pretty Latina, and now here she sat, staring through the dark at an empty cemetery, noticing once more the chill and silence of the night, and how the cicadas had once again gone silent.

"Blue," Jada said, and Blue snapped back to reality. She'd been so lost in her memory that now as she returned, she wondered what she'd missed, and jerked up.

"What's wrong?" she asked, looking around.

"I saw," Jada said, pointing into the darkness. Blue looked, but the night was still and thick, and nothing moved.

"What?" Blue asked, a heat rising to flush her cheeks as a tingle of fear prickled the fine hairs on the back of her neck.

The night was still and silent, and that was all the answer Blue needed, for whatever Jada had seen, there was nothing now.

CHAPTER FORTY-EIGHT

Britta sat at the computer in the office on the second floor of the funeral home, having been led along with her husband and the detective up the narrow, carpeted staircase through the dimly lit building, a floral smell with just a hint of the chemicals used in embalming under the surface.

She followed the young mortician's cues, pulling up the file for the surveillance footage and scrolling until she found the right file. TJ yawned loudly and she stifled her own in response. It was getting late; she wanted the mystery solved so they could sleep easily. They'd been busy all day and it felt like they hadn't slowed… but Court was still missing, and the girl, Dani, was beside herself, and if this could give them any new answers, then no matter how much Britta shared TJ's desire to crash, she was in it for the long haul.

"Yessir," the young man said, pointing. "The one with the shadow. Click on it."

Britta did as she was directed, highlighting then double-clicking the icon and bringing it to full screen.

They saw a hallway. What looked like a heavy metal door exploded off its hinges, and then something blurry swooped inside. All soundlessly; the silence gave it an even more ominous feel. Britta was sure she didn't want to watch anymore, but she could not look away.

"There." The young man pointed, and Britta clicked on another icon.

A new camera. Showing the embalming room. A shadow, some indistinct form, slinked around its walls, circling this table in the middle of the room upon which a body lay, perfectly still, a bit gray. Britta prepared herself for the inevitable: the body would jerk and move, and she'd see the dead come to life. She steeled her index finger over the mouse, tightened her lips.

The blur crossed the room, then climbed atop the table. Behind her, her husband gasped, something she was sure she'd never heard him do in their years of marriage. In her periphery, the mortician jerked reflexively. The detective muttered something incomprehensible, but she was sure he must have uttered a lamentation. The shadow became a humanoid shape, but it moved all wrong to be human. Its appendages were exceedingly long and lanky, and there appeared to be claws on its hands. But blurry as it was, they didn't need a clear picture to know what it did once it straddled the body. They could tell very clearly it was eating the corpse.

"Jesus!" TJ said and turned away. Britta couldn't watch either, and as she averted her eyes, she noticed the detective's face had lost its color, though he would not divert his gaze. Neither did the young mortician, though he looked pale also. Absently he'd put his fingers to his mouth.

When Bullocks phone buzzed, he didn't look away from the screen when he answered. "Yes," he said, matter-of-factly. Nothing, she imagined, could shock more than this footage. Then his eyes went wide, and Bullocks said, very clearly, "Oh, God."

CHAPTER FORTY-NINE

The car was cool; Chuy had shut off the engine. The tombstones in front of them were confined to a space identified by a perimeter of stone walls and streets and buildings, concrete and mortar, all around. This graveyard, so old its tombstones were nearly illegible, existed towards the center of town, as though death did not want the living to forget. Dotted with trees, it existed between houses and an old but still functioning schoolhouse, between the elms and oaks busy shedding their leaves now, and near businesses where people worked and near churches where people prayed. The girls had been sent to a fresher graveyard, but even they weren't in danger. Rong knew this was by design: The grandfathers would have taken the most dangerous spot.

Before everyone departed the Oscar homestead for their various locations, the small group had staked out the most recent desecrations and they'd determined that of the three primary graveyards in the city limits, the most obvious choice was Meadowlands, where the grandfathers went. The graves were too old at Shady Grove (where Chuy and Rong now parked), and because

Rolling Hills had been desecrated frequently, the group assumed Meadowlands would be the focus.

"I think whatever is doing all of this," Glen had said, "is aware someone, perhaps even us specifically, is on to it."

"Then why go to these other graveyards?" Chuy had asked.

"Yeah," Blue chimed in. "Why go where this thing probably isn't going to go?"

"Because we don't know," Elden said. He was in his rocker and loading a .410 with buckshot. "We don't know, but we suspect."

Dani spoke up then. "You've seen it before, haven't you?"

The old people exchanged a glance.

"You more than suspect," Rong said. "You know whatever we're looking for took Court, and has killed those people, and is digging up graves."

"It could be all related," Glen said finally. "But we don't know its patterns. We're pretty sure it isn't going to hit those places, but it might. So, we've got enough protection here for anyone who wants it. If you're going to go, you might as well be safe."

Jada stood and pulled something black from her purse and held it in her open palm. The handle and barrel were all the same shade, and the dainty pistol fit nicely in her hand.

"My daddy bought it for me for protection," she said.

"A Smith and Wesson 9mm Luger," Glen said.

"I have two loaded magazines for it," she said, nodding.

Blue slapped the table. "Then you can't ride with me. I don't like guns. I won't have one in my car."

"Dammit, Blue," Jada said. "You are so overly critical. This isn't about you. I'm going, and I want to be safe."

"And I don't want some prissy pink little sorority girl shooting that thing off at every scary noise she hears in the shadows."

Jada turned on her, her features pinched in anger while she tucked her pistol back into her purse. "I'll have you know I'm certified concealed carry and I went through the extra training to carry on campus. I've had this on me every time we all got together and none of you knew it. And I go to the range every weekend. I am a damn good shot, and I know how to treat this thing better than most gun owners."

"Guns are dangerous," Blue said, a bit quietly and her voice trembling.

"If there is something doing all of this, if it has Court, then it's dangerous," Jada said. "Look, Blue, I won't load it. Both magazines will be in my purse, and I'll only load it if we're in immediate danger."

"If you're out walking around, it could be too late," Elden said. "'Sides, guns probably won't kill it. Might slow it down some, enough to get away."

"Is anywhere a good vantage point of the cemetery, where we could stay in the car?" Blue asked.

Consulting the maps, they figured out the best entrance, and from which street to approach it. It was settled then: they would stay in the car.

"I don't like guns either," Chuy had said. The group's attention shifted to him. "Can I use something else for protection?"

Rong had pulled mace out of their jacket pocket, then approached the coffee table, where the arsenal had been laid out. Glen was preparing his own twelve-gauge. On the table there lay a silver .357 revolver and two boxes of shells. One said .38 and the other matched the caliber of the handgun. Rong picked it up, felt the weight of the gun in their hand. It was heavy, a dead weight. They picked up the boxes of shells marked .357 and looked to the grandfathers for approval.

"That's my gun, boy," Elden said. "You be careful with it, ya hear?"

"Yessir," Rong said. "If you're okay with me taking it."

Elden nodded. "You wanna take the .38's also?" This he said, nodding to the box of shells nearby.

Rong examined the gun, then shook their head, picking up the box of .357 shells instead. "No sir. These others are more powerful." They turned the gun over in their hand, found the safety, and clicked it back and forth. Then they opened the chamber, checked and saw it was empty.

෪෨

In the car, they repeated the action.

"I don't like it," Chuy said. He was staring out the window from behind the steering wheel, having cast a sideways glance at Rong in the passenger seat.

"I know," Rong said. They took the shells out and loaded six into the chamber. They too had asked the old men about an optimal place to park, but Shady Grove only had one entrance, so they were parked at the gate; their view was blocked by the concrete walls and smattering of oaks through the five-acre plot of land. Rong unlocked the door and opened it, placed one foot out on the gravel with a crunch. "You coming or going?"

"Difference between a condom and a coffin," Chuy said, smiling. Rong cocked their head, then smiled also.

Chuy cracked the window. "I'll stay." As Rong closed the door, they heard the muffled sound of Ska from Chuy's Bluetooth flowing out of the dashboard speakers and wondered if this was the first time such music was played in this town.

Rong held their gun to the side, smelling the oil and feeling the weight, and entered the old cemetery. The large oaks cast long shadows over the already darkened land. The few streetlights did their best to illuminate the tombstones, but without the moon or stars, these were shades of gray silhouette-spotting the area randomly. Using their free hand to rearrange their glasses to help them see better, Rong's eyes began to adjust, and soon could identify the tombstones easily enough to avoid barking their shin on them.

An autumn wind blew through the grounds, sending a shudder through them, rattling the dead leaves still on the limbs and scooting the others across the ground like audible footsteps. Rong had wandered aimlessly, and now couldn't see the car or the headlights for the cemetery wall, though when they turned back, they could identify a pool of white light and the batwing silhouette of the arched open wrought-iron gate. "Damn," they said aloud, wondering how they could have been so preoccupied to lose sight of Chuy and the car.

They turned and continued to walk, their left hand in their coat pocket already tightened on the mace, their right chilling to numbness as it clenched the gun. Their thoughts were fluid, considering their friends, Court, the old people. They liked the old people. They didn't see the need to correct them on their political incorrectness; they knew they wouldn't change them. They were nice to them and their friends, and the detective was decent despite their first interaction, and they would do anything for their only grandson. All of them were risking their lives for Court.

Quiet so as not to be nervous, as everyone was congregating, Rong had slunk through the Oscar's house. Not the personal rooms, but around, and had seen the pictures. The young couple in a frame, with a little boy and a baby. In another photo, the same foursome with four other people—younger versions of the old people—at what looked like a picnic. So where had the parents gone, Rong wondered. Where had the other boy gone?

They had looked like they were keeping something between them, Rong thought. This... whatever had Court now, could they have encountered it before? Could it have...

Their thoughts were interrupted by an explosion of sound, a flash of light in the periphery. Rong jumped and turned, stumbled back against a tombstone and fell back as the glow of the headlights illuminated a tall, lanky silhouette with a long rod on its shoulder passing through the bat-winged gate, and as Rong's arms pinwheeled, their gun went flying. Rong cursed and smacked their head on a root, thick and rough, as they saw stars for the first time this night, and their head swam.

The hunter leveled the rod on its shoulder and then there was another explosion: first in sound and muzzle flash, and then in the tombstone over which Rong had tripped, as pellets of concrete speckled Rong's cheeks, cracking their glasses, slapping playfully at the dirt as they ricocheted off other nearby monuments. The figure stalked closer.

"Where are ya, ya bastard? Come to my town, do ya? After all y'all done."

Rong scrambled behind a tombstone as a flashlight clicked on. They were sure its pool pointed the direction of the rifle. From their hiding place, Rong saw the beam scanning the ground, caught a glimpse of an old oak limb, about six feet long, and a glimmer of silver beyond, next to a cross and a carved image of a baby. The gun was too far away, but Rong still held the mace in their pocket.

The crunch of footfalls was closer. The assailant's voice closer.

"We ain't changing. You freak. You and your friends ain't nothing but freaks and I won't let the world go to y'uns. You godless, sinning lot. I'll kill every damn one of you before I let you corrupt my country with your ways."

The pool of light was well in front, and Rong saw through the darkness the first footfall of a boot and rose silently from behind the waist-high monument that had been concealing their thin frame.

A flash of light. His hunter was older—middle-aged, not as old as the grandparents—and thin and pale. The mace caught the man directly in the face, and he spun wildly as he screamed and fired again, the noise echoing off the cemetery walls, deafening Rong even as they felt a sharp pain in their right side and bicep. The mace fell from their hand, and they lurched under the barrel of the rifle, coming up wielding the oak branch. Some of its bark flaked off on impact, but thankfully the limb was still thick and not rotted and hollow. Heavy enough. They planted their left foot forward and swung hard, catching the assailant in the side of the head and sending him down. The rifle went flying. The man's head bounced off another tombstone and the oak limb cracked in half as the larger piece flew into the dark.

Rong dropped the remainder of the limb, pulled out their cellphone and clicked the flashlight app, their fingers shaking. They cast it around 'til they found the revolver and drew it back on the prostrated body. From the form came a soft moan, but whoever it was didn't get up. They tried. Their left foot kicked at the ground, but soon stopped. Still, Rong wasn't taking any chances.

"I'm calling Detective Bullocks. I have a .357 revolver pointed at you. If you move, I will shoot you."

What came from the collapsed form were weak, hate-filled mutterings. *"Gook, Chink, slope, Antifa, nigger cop..."* Whoever it was, was in pain.

Headlights flashed over the wall. Rong heard a scream and saw the body twitch then roll over, muttering something unintelligible. The man grabbed at the back of his head, started to rise, caught sight of Rong and growled, working harder to sit up. Rong cocked the gun and aimed the barrel right at the man's face and called out, "Over here!" as he heard Bullocks say, "Keep her back."

Rong winced at a flashlight and turned their eyes away to focus on the man as Bullocks neared. Their own cellphone flashlight blinded the middle-aged man, illuminated clearly his deep-set dark eyes, the wrinkles and crow's feet, the overall pallor and the ruddiness in the cheeks and nose. They put him in his mid to late fifties or early sixties, and probably an alcoholic.

Bullocks was talking into a radio as he approached, ordering backup patrol and an ambulance, his flashlight bobbing with each step. He took one look at the man, bent and hoisted him to his feet with one hand, a seemingly effortless show that made the assailant grunt but didn't even rattle the detective, who pulled a pair of cuffs from his coat and yanked both arms behind the attacker's back. "Hi Clem," he said. "Clem Willette, you're under arrest for murder and attempted murder."

"Fuck you," Clem spat.

"You're bleeding. Do you require medical assistance when we process you?"

"Fucker got the drop on me." Clem said.

Rong stood back, swallowing hard. *Murder and attempted murder? No*, Rong thought, *I'm fine*. But their eyes narrowed and try as they might, they could not take a deep enough breath. A breath deep enough might shake this feeling. They followed several steps behind the detective. As they approached the gate, the flashing lights of an ambulance pulled up, joined by three patrol cars, whose headlights were trained on Chuy's car. Court's school chum, TJ, was there, holding his wife tightly as she cried. TJ had tears in his eyes as well but couldn't steal his gaze off the crime scene.

Rong staggered behind the detective, who was passing right by the driver's side door, where the window had been shattered by the blast. While their glasses were cracked, they could still see pretty well out of the left lens. Jagged tiny fragments still clung here and there to the frame, but the window was gone, and the seat and passenger seat and window, lit by the headlights of the patrol car, were all soaked in blood. Something darkened and bloodied slumped in the front seat, but it was no longer their friend. It wore Chuy's shirt, but there was no sign of his head, only a mass of blood and chunks of meat. Chuy's hand—bloodied—lay palm up on the center console.

They turned their head away. A toneless, consistent ring screamed at them from their inner ear, so Rong closed their eyes and doubled over. A nauseated heat swept over them, and Rong was sure they were going to throw up. A patrolman asked Rong for their revolver and they handed it over willingly without facing the officer and the car he stood beside.

"Find his shotgun," Bullocks called to another officer as two others took the prisoner and slammed Clem Willette into the back of the furthest car.

Rong recognized TJ and Britta with the cop. They were standing outside the gate by another of the several patrol vehicles that had responded. Rong could not bend their knees or elbows. The married couple reached out for them, but Rong stepped back. Because they didn't know this couple, their solace would not be enough. They followed Rong's gaze to nothing, saw nothing but Clem hunkered in the back seat. He looked out the window, his face turned up to the streetlight so that it highlighted his yellow teeth and his gnarled grin.

Rong felt a tear. "It was a shotgun," they said. "I thought it was a rifle, but it was a shotgun." Not that this mattered. Shock numbed them and their mind struggled to process what had just occurred. It didn't feel real. It couldn't be real.

"Are you okay?" Britta asked. This didn't matter either. Physically, they were sore, and they'd just walked past the remains of a close friend whose death was violent and graphic.

"You're lucky to be alive," TJ said, and this didn't matter either. Rong didn't feel lucky.

From afar, one of the patrolwomen said she'd found the shotgun. One pulled away with Clem in the backseat. Rong noticed something in the older man's eyes. Wild, hate-filled and predatory, it suggested it wasn't over. In fact, it was only beginning.

Bullocks approached, still on the radio; a voice spoke. "Found the girls. They're okay. We'll send them back to the Oscar house."

Another: "That's a negative detective, no sign of Glen Dillon or Elden Oscar here, or their truck."

"Find them," Bullocks said.

Another: "Mrs. Dillon and Mrs. Oscar are safe. No sign of Ms. Morales."

"Find her!"

Same voice: "They say she went looking for Court Dillon." Static. "Car."

Bullocks' eyes cleared and met those of Rong and the married couple. Around them, two cops were bagging the shotgun and the EMTs clustered in front of the open driver's side door of Chuy's car, blocking their view of what was inside.

Bullocks was speaking, and there were other sounds, but Rong now only thought about Chuy and how they should have stayed and if they'd stayed then they'd be dead, and they began to weep as a patrolwoman approached and Bullocks ordered her to drive the three back to the Oscar farm.

Rong was only vaguely aware of the ride, of the town's businesses and homes and gas stations and schools passing by, of the Church of God whitewashed with the steeple and the bell, of the the farms and the low-water bridge over the creek and the trailer park with a sign that read "residents with children need not apply," and then the Oscar farm and house. Rong hadn't the legs to walk when they arrived, so TJ and Britta helped, each taking a shoulder, and it was as TJ pulled up Rong's shoulder that they winced. Inside in the living room, with the grandmothers and Jada and Blue looking on worried, the female officer helped Rong off with their coat and then lifted their shirt. Speckling from the shot peppered their torso and erupted surface abrasions on their face. Another ambulance was called, and Rong and Jada passed several hours in the emergency room. Rong gave a statement, but the shock and the painkillers had long kept them in a daze, with all the blood.

Eventually, they returned with Jada to the house. One of the last things Rong recalled was Aster Oscar showing them to a spare bed and turning down the sheets. Undressing in the dark, Rong wept silently until sleep overtook them.

CHAPTER FIFTY

Dani parked. The woods surrounding the two-lane county road were dark and silent. With nothing but a hunch, she'd chosen the spot on the shoulder to stop and shut off the engine. She exited, looking around. No marker, no indication that this was where Court had been. Except, she knew he had. She could feel him. The feeling was weird and something she'd never experienced before, but it brought her a tinge of assuredness and she knew it was right. He had been here. She focused on the feeling, and even though she could see little, she closed her eyes to drown out any potential distractions. And then, just as sure as she was that Court had stood in this spot, she knew he crossed the road. She did as well, and with but the briefest of pauses, she entered the tree line.

She knew this feeling driving her instincts now. It went by many names. Love was a familiar one. It fit well into abstract parameters, like sensing another's presence because you are close to them or knowing their movements, their choices, because you know them so well. She knew Court and she loved him, and this feeling was strong and guiding here in this Ozark forest, as bright as the flashlight on her phone that spotlighted bits of terrain and a trail.

An ancient worn path cut between the weeds and undergrowth as a trail of dirt winding deep into the forest like a worm between the flora, only to disappear into the shadows. Perhaps over the years kids had beat the path down in ritual and custom, dragging their bikes and their heels along the trail. No kids would be out now, surely: the dark and the cold would have sent them home to the warmth of their beds. Hers would be, by God.

Hers. It wasn't the first time she thought about her own offspring, what they might be like. Part her and part Court. She'd teach them Spanish. Teach them guitar. Court would read them poetry; they'd have a nice library in their house. They'd have a house. Something big enough for them, a couple of kids, a dog. Not a little yippy dog, either, but a big dog, like an Alano or a Basque Shepherd or a Mastiff. When she was a kid she'd had a Presa Canario, and she'd wept when they had to put Tia down.

A scoff or a cough, something from the all-consuming shadows. If she jumped, it was only to look the way of the sound. Under normal circumstances, she might appreciate a scene like this. Explore by bike the mysteries of the forest. Hike with a knapsack full of supplies, out exploring the wilderness, a frontiersman or some Wildman, perhaps some aboriginal denizen of the lush growth—a mystery to herself, or one secure in the forest's secrets.

But now as she walked, these childhood feelings took a back seat to the fog and mist and starless black night, the fear in her stirring deep down a longing for her youth, tugging at her as though she could still become a lost girl. She remembered all of it, smelled the pine and heard the rustle of leaves, not now as an adult might experience these things—though she did—but through the lens of youth, with all the mystery and possibility only a child could behold and appreciate. It had become once again for her a playground whose details were concealed under the canopy's penumbra, not a place of outer, of alien and cold, but a sanctuary of wilderness, a natural labyrinth walled and shaped and roofed by oaks and maple, paths carved from granite and thin topsoil, shaped by holly and crabgrass.

A whisper, from deep within, begging her to focus. Suggesting this was what it did: put travelers under a spell, forced them to get lost, isolated them before it sprang.

In Mexico, the more prominent voice came, the flora might be different, but the feeling here was the same. Court's words came to her as she took a deep breath into her lungs. *Come forth into the light of things, let nature be your teacher.* Wordsworth. She turned in place, eyes cast down, remembering, remembering… failing to remember. The path they'd carved, like her childhood, had vanished. Court had quoted her Kipling. *"They shut the road through the woods seventy years ago. Weather and rain have undone it again, and now you would never know."* How easy it had returned to her, the line when the path was lost. If Kipling or Wordsworth were still on Court's syllabus, then in early spring, after the bloom but before the weather turned for the warmer, they should invite his students out on a hike to Devil's Den and feed them some lines. Winter break would leave the students starving for nourishment so that only such as these could satiate them.

She reached to the rough bark of a barren apple tree. *Where are your mossed cottage-trees?* Home. With Court. Or with Nana and Papa? Mamaw and Papaw. Our friends. Had it been so long since she'd thought of him? Like an alien nightmare she didn't recall.

The weaker voice returned: *You aren't focused. This is dangerous.*

Then, to the empty forest floor: "*Fill all fruit with ripeness to the core; / To swell the gourd and plump the hazel shells.*" She knelt to examine the husk of a shell and the air near the ground felt cooler, moist. What she rolled between her fingers was a sheathed pecan, or possibly a walnut. Her cellphone had shown her the current temperature—lower fifties—and as she recalled Keats' next stanza, she recalled also the previous spring as the temperature rose and how much warmer fifty had felt then. Like a promise, and not like the breach she felt now. Like spring, it was all left behind, and she didn't like the path she'd found.

A sound above. Dani cast her eyes skyward through the canopy and recited the last of Keats' ode: "*And gathering swallows twitter in the skies,*" as a murder of crows scattered and squawked overhead.

A scuffle in her periphery. She rose to her feet, her knees popping as a figure vanished behind a grove of trees, a ripple in the darkness. Had she recognized it or merely found its shape familiar? Either way, it was enough to pique her curiosity, and enough to push her forward, deeper into the woods.

The thing is, she was sure she recognized it from the stories she was told by her own parents and grandparents, coupled with the flashes of vague images from her childhood, she thought she knew the figure traipsing through the foliage. She'd pictured her so many times.

Cradled by her, a lyrical voice singing nursery rhymes with warmth and love, and she imagined all she'd been denied as an orphan, raised by his grandparents. No, not herself, Dani realized. Court. As Court was raised. This time she was aware of her mind fogging again, of a spell being cast to keep her unfocused.

To clear her mind, she blinked. In the darkness, in the beam of her light from her cellphone, the forest cleared some. Old yellow and rust-colored leaves, having lived their short lives, now fell beneath their gargantuan parent or clung on, flapping in the wind, holding to their ancestor… the trees were too old, by and large, to cater to a child's needs, but they never loved them less. In fact, they couldn't imagine their life without them. Sans parents, they were all he had.

Court, or the leaves?

She gripped herself. Was this what Court was feeling right now? He was cold and he was alone. Alone. But alive?

She stepped around a stone, then another, her downcast eyes rising to survey the surroundings. More cement markers circumventing a forgotten building.

"This loam serves as my guerdon." The voice, like it came from the foliage.

Dani, her thoughts fuzzy, felt the voice must be connected to Court. "Is it all you're worth, or what you think we're worth?"

Dark, lyrical, the voice came from the forest, from the bark, the reeds, the crabgrass, and the shadows. Kneeling again, Dani ran her fingers through the loose soil. This tactile action broke the hum in her mind and allowed her to contemplate what she was hearing and where she was. For to consider this meant she was to consider her own insanity. As the voice had come from all around her, it also came from within.

The voice rang with familiarity, though she couldn't place it, sounding feminine and warm and pleasant. In contrast, somewhere in the distance, a lone raven cawed. A slow fog snaked along the ground, whitewashing the ruins with a kind of pale transparency that existed only in dreams, the haze of the subconscious. Was she floating? She didn't recognize her feet moving or the passage of time, but still drew closer to the church in the center, the door widening slowly to reveal more of the darkness inside. Maybe she fell asleep; this was too much like the recurring nightmare which plagued her almost nightly for years, well before she knew Court or his family, back when she was swaddled against her mother's bosom.

A woman appeared to Dani through the fog. She had freckles and her auburn hair fell in waves down to her shoulders, and Dani could see the flecks of green in her eyes. Her voice angelic, what infant ears might hear. In the threshold of the church, she beckoned and smiled.

"You want to be his mother," Dani said.

Across the night-strewn yard, the figure evanesced, and there echoed over the churchyard a laughter, but mirthless. Joyless. A mimicking thing from something unable to grasp the human reasons for the sound. This luring mock meant to entrap, like a web. It was a sound belonging to the darkness, high-pitched and tinged with evil.

Dani scanned the fog-thick banks and flat lands, marked with toppled tombstones and the abandoned, ruined church. Nothing moved. Like a painting or a charcoal sketch, monotone and lifeless. When she glanced back to the church, both doors stood open and only blackness yawned forth, holding fast the secrets inside.

Another laugh.

Dani felt the fog in her head. Her thoughts felt sluggish, her vision blurred. Delayed. She hadn't felt like this since the days after she'd met Court, and Blue had told her over lunch how good a guy he was, but he was a bit of a player, and he'd come out with her friends on Dickson Street and charmed them all, and then he was a part of the group, and they barhopped like they were still twenty-one and before her walk home, Court beside her like a gentleman, the night swam before her like a filtered aquarium.

Aquarium. Like tonight. The woods quivered in front of her. She tried to organize her thoughts, but there was the laughter. It rattled from all directions and did not reveal its location. Hid things unapologetically. Not a rustling leaf and not a chirping bug. Everything dead and motionless save for the incessant laugh.

"What are you?"

Heh-heh-hee-hee-hee.

"Where are you?"

To the left. To the right. Straight ahead. Directly behind. Still beyond the open doors of the church in the darkness. Dani took exactly three steps before the next round of giggles shook the landscape.

In the periphery, movement. Dani looked in time to see a shadow bolt and a few leaves rustle to a whirlwind from a stir but heard nothing.

At her shoulder came two audible clicks, like the sharpening of claws. Her spine stiffened with a chill and her breath caught in her throat, and she straightened up. The trap had been set behind her and she'd fallen for it. Her eyes closed. She thought of Court and her parents, and her siblings and her friends, but she tried to bring Court's image back to the forefront before whatever was stalking her attacked.

"Dammit girl, don't sit there looking stupefied."

Dani opened her eyes. She smelled familiar scents: cologne, deodorant, aftershave.

From either side, Court's grandfathers approached. Glen cradled his own father's Browning double-barrel 12-guage and Elden held a short-barrel .410. Then the detective appeared as well. The laughter had faded into the distance. Between the doors was now a lazy gray luminescence and the hint of pews and further in, the podium.

"You were asleep," Dani said. It was all she could think to say. Around her, the fog retreated and a howl rose and fell and all she could focus on was Glen's Browning.

"Did you hear the laugh?" Elden asked.

"We should leave," Glen said.

The detective pushed forward, gun drawn, gaze intently focused on the open church doors. "What's in there?"

The grandfathers reached for her, but it was Dani who screamed "No!"

The fog burned away, and everything was backlit by a yellow luminescence, as though the moon had been dropped behind the church. Then... gone. The church and stones faded with the light, until they were left in darkness and the cold, unyielding wilderness.

"What the fu..." the detective's voice trailed away, staring not at stone and mortar, but trees and undergrowth and the night.

Glen stepped up, crestfallen. Patted his shoulder. "Let's go, let's go home."

"We can't leave!" she said. "Where did it...?" She couldn't register what she'd seen, so couldn't form the words to ask what would only be an insane question. *Where did it go? Buildings don't vanish. Where did it go?*

"We'll come back," Glen said. He propped his gun against a tree trunk and grabbed her, holding her shoulders in his hands, forcing her to meet his eyes. "Dani, we'll come back."

Dani looked at him, dumbfounded, then back to where the church should have been. "Where did it go?" A mad laugh rumbled deep in her belly, threatening to erupt. Buildings and tombstones don't vanish. *Jesus Christ, they don't up and disappear. What the actual fuck is going around here?*

She let them lead her away. Soon, they were at the road, and Dani saw Elden's pickup behind her car. The detective led her to the passenger side of her own vehicle, then he asked for her keys. Tires spun on the gravel shoulder and weeds spit under the tread and they headed back toward the Aster farm and away from the wilderness, away from that strange old church that had just vanished, like the night had consumed it again. It was then she reached into her pocket and felt only the cloth; she turned back toward where the old church had been with the sinking realization that she'd dropped her cellphone, her only lifeline to her job, to Court, somewhere out there. Fear billowed in her then: whatever had been hunting her, whatever had been laughing at her as it stalked her… something told her that thing had Court.

CHAPTER FIFTY-ONE

The mortician hadn't been able to sleep. Outside, the temperature had dropped to nearly forty, so he dressed accordingly, albeit slowly, contemplating what had awakened him, a realization so jarring his own dog had jumped as he shot out of the bed, staring into the darkness. In the dream, he'd been in an amphitheater back in school, listening to an old professor lecture an introduction to funereal practices. When he realized he was alone in the room, the professor had pointed at him and said, "The answer is in the book."

There was nothing pressing that required him to be at the funeral home at almost four in the morning. The bodies there could have waited a couple more hours. Still, he blinked through the early dawn, unable to shake the voice in his head. Ever since he saw the first graves, and later saw it confirmed in the video footage, he knew what was out there, and he knew the detective had no idea what he was up against, and he knew he was the only one who could stop it. So, had he called out to it? He wasn't sure. But he was convinced it was answering him now.

The night showed no sign of the coming dawn as he parked the car at the rear of the building. An autumn mist flurried around the lamplight and kissed his cheeks. On the highway above, a lone car passed then faded into silence. Behind the funeral home, on a side street serving as part of a neighborhood, houses darkened and silently slept through the last hours before the sunrise.

He unlocked the side door, then punched in the keycode. The interior lights were few, spaced just evenly enough to illuminate dimly the funeral home's interior. While the funeral home was hardly noisy during working hours, the silence was thick now. He could hear the hum of embalming equipment behind closed doors on standby, the buzz of the HVAC. The carpeted hall led him past the staging room, where a coffin stood open, the body prepared for the visitation later. Another retiree. Because of them, business was booming; this town, or one like it, had always been his destination. From the doorway, he peeked. Nothing. Silence. Normally he wasn't bothered by the persistent silence in the funeral home, but this morning, perhaps because he'd awakened so quickly and so early, he felt the hairs on his arms stand on end. Even the slightest sound alerted him, and his imagination was still feeding off his frenetic, melatonin-fueled dreams.

By the storage room in the back, he unlocked then opened the door to the embalming room. The older gentleman he'd helped to place on the slab the night before lay, awaiting the mortician's touch. Exhaling each whispered number, plumes of frosted breath helped tick off each count of the still-closed drawers. Somewhere behind him, there came a noise. He turned, pulling the embalming door closed, desperate to identify the sound. Something had been kicked. Or someone had stubbed a toe. It was a quick thud, a sound muted quickly. Because of this, he couldn't be sure where it had come from. It meant, though, that he was not alone in the building.

Hurrying on, he found the stairs and started up. Behind him, closing in, muted by the carpet but not completely silenced, the sound of soft footsteps. They advanced down the hall toward him. He chanced a glance back and scanned the hall, but the few lights that were on showed nothing.

The young mortician reached his office at the top of the stairs, shut the office door, and twisted the tiny nub in the center of the knob, a feeble lock all he had to separate him from the encroaching steps.

His office had only one reserve light, just barely bright enough to lead him to his desk where he turned on the brass table-top lamp and moved it closer to the bookshelf behind his desk. The name of the class escaped him but not the name of the text: *A Comprehensive History of the Funeral Sciences*.

There had been a whole chapter on myths and folklore, some of which had inspired early funerary practices, like leaving bells with strings in the coffins. But the section of the chapter—of that entire course in fact—he'd been most fascinated by began with an engraving of a creature skulking amongst tombstones. He reread the passage for the thousandth time, so immersed in the legend that it might have been the first time he'd seen the text. So drawn in, he missed the doorknob turning behind him. The phrases came as he remembered them. *Salt and iron and steel... takes the coins... calls to lost travelers... must behead it with a single blow... eats the dead... churchyards... shapeshift...* and... "Qissa," he said, looking up as the door opened with a force. The feeble lock had failed.

Still too dim for details, but the form had shape. It slinked into the room, crawling around the walls, the smell of decay wafting from it. As it approached, it halted, sniffed the light of the lamp, then retreated, clinging to the shadows.

"You called me," it hissed.

The mortician whimpered, his voice faltering at first. "You shouldn't have come inside," he finally squeaked out.

"Hungry."

He couldn't see it for sure. A blurry shadow in the furthest corner from where he stood. He closed the book so that his right middle finger served as a bookmark. "You can't— you can't keep doing this. You have to stop."

"You defile the food," it replied. A claw reached up and scratched the wall inquisitively.

"Not all," the young mortician said, voice trembling. "What about the girl I buried? And the freshest ones? I show you the freshest ones."

"No!" A sound so loud he jumped. The voice wasn't in the corner but came from all around. "You fill with nasty liquid. The meat putrid," it spat. The man jumped, afraid the spittle would touch his flesh and burn through him like acid.

"I have what you want," the young mortician said. "If you stop, I'll give you what you want. *Qissa*, right? Stories. I've got a ton of stories. I know the stories of everyone I've helped here. I know about their families. I can bring you lots of stories."

Silence. He glanced around the room, eyes wide, wishing he could get a glimpse of its location (not of its image—*God* no!—the engraving was bad enough; he couldn't stomach seeing this thing for real).

"You think I want stories from defiler of food," it said, derisively.

The mortician dropped the book. A low growl rolled around him like a fog bank, deafening him to its location. When it sprang, his body stiffened, as though he could feel it in the air, and though he tried to brace himself from the impact, he was unprepared, and its claws and its teeth dug into his flesh. He screamed, with only the dead below to hear him and laugh mockingly because now, it was his turn.

INTERLUDE EIGHT

The Tale of the Chamber of Bones

Once upon a time, deep under the earth, there existed a chamber of bones. This was the home of a strange creature that haunted churchyards and skulked through the night, searching for travelers and children with which to decorate its den. You see, the bones weren't of mere animals, but of people.

Some of the bones came from people who died naturally; the creature would exhume the bodies by digging through the mud and clay with its sharp claws, and it would taste of the soft meats of the freshly dead before the bugs and other things rotted them away, and it would peel the skin in long thin strips and devour the muscle, snapping the tendons and cartilage 'til the bone was free. Of the whole of the skeletal structure represented in the shelter, femurs were the fewest, for as a dessert of ice cream and cake satisfies the tooth of men, so also the marrow satisfied this creature who sucked the femurs dry.

This creature lived a solitary existence, and it watched from the shadows the people bustling about. It watched families playing outdoors and lovers kissing in the moonlight and children skipping and playing in great droves; and always it existed alone. It had no one to walk with, no one to share in games, no one to talk to. Sometimes it would sneak to the houses where the people lived and listen outside the windows of the littlest children for their parents to come and tuck them in and tell them a story. It liked the stories. But it knew mankind well enough to know if it were caught, it would be killed, so it ran and devised a plan for those times when no new soul was buried in the grave.

There were always wayward travelers, or little boys and girls, who wandered off alone, and the creature enjoyed its fresh supply, eating the soft meats and muscle 'til it got its fill, then carefully peeling the flesh as though it were peeling a tomato, and removed the face so precisely it could be worn as a mask.

And what masks it collected! There is a special place in the chamber of bones for all its masks and suits, and the creature—not of this earth, not like a man or dog or bear or lion—found when it adorned a suit and its corresponding mask, it looked like the person, kind of.

Once, after a little child went missing, villagers claimed to see him out playing by the river, and of course it was the creature playing dress-up, but none of the villagers were the wiser. Another time, some relations came to visit an older woman who hadn't been to church the past couple of weeks, and she said she was fine and invited them into her house for tea. While they noticed, they'd later say, an odd smell and a droopy inflection in her voice, they thought nothing of it. The smell was of the creature; since it hovered around death it also reeked of it, and it hadn't quite figured out how humans, in all their languages, exactly spoke. But it spoke close enough, borrowing the old lady's voice as it had borrowed her face and flesh, and even those who knew her best were ultimately none the wiser.

In this way, the creature had figured out how to leave its chamber of bones and engage with humans, and it was no longer always lonely.

The End

CHAPTER FIFTY-TWO

Sunday morning came with the slow clarity that the world outside was dying, that anything in the light was temporary and fading fast. Winter was coming. The sun hadn't been seen for days, and this affected the mood of the town. The sky overhead remained the same overcast gray, the trees continued to shed their leaves, and the grass continued to brown, with only a smattering of green about the drab lawns. The low-hanging fog blended the sky and the ground, a thick soup forbidding visibility, leaving all within its range isolated, alone.

Dani awoke with a sense of hopelessness. Didn't speak much to the Dillons as she drank her coffee, ate the breakfast Glen had prepared. Neither Glen nor Lena spoke. They'd listened to her melancholy guitar playing up in the guest room the night before, the notes filtering down, her mournful voice lamenting loss.

CHAPTER FIFTY-THREE

Elden listened to the radio and slurped his coffee as Aster made him a breakfast of oats and toast, and bacon sizzled in the skillet. Elden thought about the foolishness of the girl going out there all alone. He was sure something was there, and, more than likely, Court was there too. But Elden knew the old church's peculiarities, how it tended to change location.

Sure, you might stumble upon it, hiking off County Road 87 off the bypass, but someone else might encounter it in the woods off 5 North, and someone else might find it, much as Clem had, on the southern tip of the town. But by and large the population ignored it because most weren't aware of the old legend, and those that were didn't believe in it. Not really. Elden had been born in this town, and he had spent the better part of his 90+ years in this town, so he knew all about the legend. There were few of his generation left. Hell, Glen had moved here about forty-five years ago, already a grown man with a family, and he sure as hell didn't go traipsing about the woods.

But those who did never talked about it. As Elden sipped his coffee, he thought back with his sharper-than-ever mind and couldn't recall a single conversation about the abandoned churchyard, but he remembered his own encounter with the mythical place, a memory he hadn't recalled in the many decades that had passed since he was a youth romping through the Ozark hills. Until now.

He'd been twelve, been out squirrel hunting with his .22 lever action rifle when he'd stumbled on the old church. It had an empty, haunted feeling to it, something cold and dark, but it beckoned him in, and, perhaps bored and a little curious, and even a little mischievous, young Elden had walked into the church and felt its coldness, its dark. It forced a shiver down his spine, and he steadied his rifle as he pressed in between the rows of pews, sure no one else had felt this in a church ever before. There was something evil lurking in there.

He could smell it, taste it nearly, the something inviting him into the church itself, though it wasn't whatever inhabited the thing now, he realized, looking back. No, the creature came later, was probably drawn to this place. Perhaps it was the location itself, but he knew that wasn't right either. There'd been rumors about an old church and cemetery, long since abandoned, circulating since forever even when he was a boy, but some of his elders could remember it clearer then because they lived it. They spoke of an old preacher who'd found the place once the town proper had moved away, a fire-and-brimstone kind of guy, a snake handler, some said, though others claimed he could work miracles. He had lured some of the townsfolk out to the old churchyard, along with followers he'd brought with him from wherever he came from.

"I've lived here all these years," Aster said, "and I never heard about that preacher." Elden started a little. He'd been rambling his thoughts and hadn't realized they were out loud. Was this his mind slipping back to the dementia then, he wondered. He performed a self-cognitive check, reminding himself of the day, the president,

Court's age, and even Court's girlfriend's name. Satisfied, he leaned back in his chair and offered a sigh.

"Aren't many around who know it anymore, besides me. Maybe a few others. Like I said, this story was old when I was a kid, and we both know I was a kid a very long time ago."

He'd told his mom about finding the church when he got home, and she slapped his jaw and told him never to go back. It'd be almost a month before he'd learn the full story from his father. They were out splitting some firewood and his dad told him about the church. About the preacher who'd come once and set up shop in the church and of the evil things he did.

"What kind of things?" Aster asked.

Elden sighed and leveled his gaze at his coffee cup. Something swam behind his cloudy blue eyes. A memory. Perhaps he'd left his own body and slipped back into the past. His lips parted, his jaw slack, he stared at his cup, breathing shallowly, not blinking.

Presently he smiled, let out a "heh." Then he looked at her. "They say he did spells there. Called up the devil, called up the dead. They say he let the snakes bite people and the whole congregation would watch the people die and then he'd raise them back, claiming to be like Jesus raising Lazarus."

"What did you see when you were out there?" Aster's hand was trembling, so he reached over and squeezed it tight.

A deep, regulating breath paused his response. The past was something he didn't want to focus on. Still, he saw the necessity.

"I'd forgotten this. I mean, not since my mind was going. I think even then, when I didn't know where I was, I'd find myself back there even if I didn't understand where it was. No. I'd forgotten about this even when I had my wits about me. Back when the kids were young, and we were working, back before the thing came after our family, when I was still at the school. I'd forgotten about it."

"You repressed it, honey," she said.

A smile crept to his lips "Re-pissed?" and this made him laugh. She laughed too.

After a minute, the quiet returned. "No. I heard my name. I think I saw..." but his voice trailed off and he shook his head.

"What?" she prodded.

"Shadows, had to be."

"What did you think it was?" she asked.

"The preacher, maybe. Like maybe he hadn't gone, but he was waiting there. Calling up more of the dead. The churchyard's been bad, long before this thing got here. I think bad attracts bad, and I think Court is there. Glen thought so too. After we met the Chinese boy yesterday, we drove around, trying to find the place. But we couldn't."

"But you said it moves. Like disappears or reappears? How?"

Elden shook his head. "I don't know. Maybe, it don't rightly exist here. Not all the way. Like, maybe it's more spiritual than real. Maybe it ain't really the place, but the ghost of the place."

Aster shivered. "I don't like that," she said. Elden knew she didn't cotton to stuff like that. He didn't either, truth be told, which was probably why he'd bottled that story up for so long.

"Irregardless," he said, and sipped his coffee. "Court's probably there, and we got to figure out how to tether it so as to get in there and get him out."

"We'll find him," Aster said.

Elden nodded, then bent and resumed breakfast. Still, the urge kept rising in him: this story was important, and Court should know it. He knew Aster would tell the boy if he asked her to, and he knew of the four of them, Glen was the storyteller—but he felt this story was his, and Court should hear it from him. With everything going on, though, there was a real possibility he would never see Court again.

"Ma," Elden said, and Aster looked up from her bowl of porridge. "Might I use your writing desk for a bit?"

This was a novel request; he expected she'd take it as odd and she did, setting her spoon in her bowl, then folding her hands together and leveling her eyes at him. She studied him for what felt like forever before she nodded, her face tight and serious.

"Might I ask what for?"

He set his own spoon down and dropped his gaze to his coffee cup. "I gotta write it down. While I remember it." He took a breath, then looked up at her. "For Court."

"Of course," she said, and he knew she wouldn't lurk, and he knew she wouldn't goad him with questions, but he could see she was worried.

CR͟SO

And the morning pressed on.

CHAPTER FIFTY-FOUR

Each awoke the day after Chuy's death, taking time to mourn, all gathering in Rong's hotel room, staring at his empty bed. Tears came quickly and plentifully, and there were hugs and whispers. None of them spoke aloud about leaving. Court was still missing and if they left now, Chuy's death would mean nothing. But each in their own way was terrified. Surely, they thought about the possibility that if Chuy could die, then any of them could, that of course more deaths would come. They had been weakened by losing Chuy. Each of them felt taxed and numbed by his murder, and that Court was still missing only helped to slow their logical minds. So, they mourned, and wondered what the next move would be.

※

Detective Albert Bullocks knelt over the body of the young mortician, the second scene he'd been called to. There was no sign of a break-in, but the alarm had been turned off and the front door was unlocked. Had he come to meet someone? Half his face was gnawed off, his heart had been dug out of his chest, several ribs had had the meat removed, his left bicep was torn out and missing, and the meat of his right thigh was gone, right down to the bone. His shirt lay shredded and bloodied on the remains of his torso, and the carpet below was soaked through. It reminded Bullocks of some of the gangland slayings he'd investigated up in Chicago. Even though they stopped resembling the living, he never got used to seeing such sights. It disturbed him how quickly and easily a body could go from speaking and having a personality to being a bloody shell devoid of all consciousness. He stood over the body, his right fist sealing his lips, his eyes poring over the details.

A book lay upside down and open near the body, a bit of blood spray across the cover. A bit, the detective noted. Not much, enough to reaffirm directionality. With a gloved hand, he picked it up, regarded the cover, then the pages, some bent. The title and chapter headings suggested a textbook for funeral sciences. With his index finger, he held open the page the book had been opened to: an illustration of a woodcut church surrounded by a cemetery. The blood was dry on the cover, he noticed, as he tucked the book into his coat pocket, looking around to make sure none of the deputies at the crime scene had noticed his acquisition.

The sheriff poured two cups of coffee and sauntered over to the only occupied cell. One cup he stuck through the bars. He pulled up a folding chair and sat, then took a long, thoughtful sip from the other and smacked his lips.

"I ain't gonna lie to you, Clem," the sheriff said. "You're gonna go away for killing that Mexican. A long, fucking time."

"Little swisher faggot had it coming, like all his friends."

The sheriff took a good long look at Clem Willette. A man he'd known all his life, the two were in elementary school together until Clem failed the sixth grade, and then the seventh. Way back then, Clem had been a bully. At almost sixty, he still was. His father had been a hard drunk, a lonely man who'd been rough on Clem, and Clem had carried such traditions into adulthood and beyond his father's grave. But the look on Clem's face now was something the sheriff had never seen before. The man sat holding his coffee cup but didn't drink; rather, he held the cup in both hands between his knees, his torso hunched forward a bit, his eyes unblinking, and a slight grin on his face. He'd more or less maintained this position since the sheriff had first entered a few hours earlier, and by some accounts he'd been seated thusly since they brought him in. Still as a statue.

"Why'd you do it, Clem? Why'd you shoot him?" He'd been planning to lead up to the question, but looking at him now, he felt confident Clem might blurt it out. When he spoke, the sheriff had to do a double take to see if his lips were moving.

"Our town hasn't changed in a lot of years, has it, Charles? It still looks pretty much the same as when you and I were young'uns. I mean, some businesses come and go, and some new buildings come up, and some people die, and some people are born, but it's pretty much the same."

"I suppose," the sheriff said.

"Well, some others have tried to come in. Families who don't belong. Sure, we let in the Chinese family 'cause they opened the buffet, but we been good about keeping out people who weren't like us."

It was true. The few minorities in the area hadn't been welcomed. The sheriff had dealt with a number of white nationalists in his tenure and tried to make this an inviting area. The retirees from Chicago who migrated down here to live might have invited diversity, but so far it had only fueled the racist undertones of the area. Sure, people of color came, but they also went pretty quickly. The sheriff had come across Clem and a number of others plenty of times during such altercations.

"But then we got that Black president and we was all forgotten. And things started changing. Now the gays are everywhere kissing and fucking in public, and showing their asses, and the coloreds are running around like they uppity, and people don't identify as male or female anymore, whatever the fuck *they* means.

"So, when he came, and his friends, I wasn't going to have it. Our town hasn't been tainted by such shit, and I won't stand for it. You say I committed murder. I say I'm standing up for our values."

The sheriff drained his Styrofoam cup, shook his head, and stood. "Look, Clem, I don't like it any more than you do, but murder ain't the answer. You cain't take anothern's life."

"I didn't," Clem said. "I killed an animal." The sheriff saw the hardness in the man's eyes, the blackness of his soul, and it left him speechless. He shook his head, tossed his cup in the trash, and walked away.

Clem didn't think about anything. Eventually, he drank his coffee in short sips, but a plan was forming in his head as a series of images like puzzle pieces, and only when he'd seen all the pieces fit together did he finally understand his role in it all.

The morning stretched on. Time passed, and he listened to his belly rumble. He was about to yell out to a guard about lunch when a patrolman walked up to his cell.

Clem studied the patrolman for a minute or two before smiling. It was in the eyes. It couldn't hide the eyes.

"But I thought you could only look like dead people?" Clem said.

"Keep your voice down," the patrolman said, looking at the guard. "No one's found him or his wife at home yet, so they don't know he's dead. I made a little stop after visiting the mortician."

"How'd it go?" Clem asked.

"I'm no longer in the mood to deal with his kind. He thought he could change our agreement, but his refusal to give me fresh meat, untainted by his process, sealed his fate."

Clem laughed. In the distance, the guard looked up. The patrolman offered the guard a smile and a wave, as if to say he had this, then turned back on Clem.

"If I let you out, will you fulfill your promise to me?"

"Yes," Clem said, his eyes gleaming. "I'll kill them all."

The patrolman glanced over his shoulder. Clem followed his gaze. The police station stretched out as a long room before him, sectioned by a few cubicles and more desks, filled with patrolmen, a couple of paramedics talking with the sheriff in his glass-partitioned office, the few secretaries and civilian workers assisting with the office work, a drunk still in handcuffs getting a mugshot, and a woman who looked like she was on meth sitting at a desk with a patrolman, scratching incessantly at her scabby arm. Lots of bodies, Clem thought, and lots of guns. But *she* wouldn't have any problem. When the patrolman faced Clem again, its face had already begun to morph from the cop's visage to something else. Its mouth stretched impossibly open, its teeth revealed rows, dripping saliva. When the attack came, Clem didn't avert his eyes from the bloodshed; he didn't block his ears from the screaming and the pleading. The guard had gone first. Clem wasn't bothered by the carnage; he couldn't see everything from his location. Blood fountained darkly up from the bodies, the overspray casting against the walls and up to the ceiling, tinting the fluorescent lights until the room glowed crimson and reeked the iron-rich scent of death. He heard no gunshots, which meant no gun was drawn. The action was so dizzying it was almost hard to follow. The thing was fast and methodical and as much as Clem was smiling, he imagined the creature enjoyed the carnage even more. The sheriff had stood in horror at the thing filing toward him, having forgotten about his pistol. No one escaped.

When Clem's door swung open, he waded between the bodies. He stepped over the scabby forearm of the meth woman and skirted a secretary who'd been bisected. He approached the nearest window and drew the shades, then moved to the next window. When all the shades were drawn, he took the phones off the hook. The room was silent aside from his movements and actions and the drip of blood from various points. It sounded like a rainforest, he thought. He crouched down over the sheriff and stared into the man's blank eyes. Clem wondered if people really went to Heaven. He hadn't entertained such thoughts since his pappy had taken him to Sunday school years ago. But this would be as existential as he would get. He took the keys out of the sheriff's pocket and used them to lock the front door behind him. Should buy him a little time. Maybe even enough time to get set up, because they would be looking for him soon, that detective and the others. And he had to be ready. First, he needed to get his daddy's gun.

CHAPTER FIFTY-FIVE

Dani hadn't blinked in a while, though her right hand moved, stirring the jug of iced tea, dissolving the sugar little by little as the ice clinked against the glass, her face focused on the drab and dreary day outside the window. Even when the sun was supposed to be out, it was so dark.

"Does it ever get sunny here?" she asked, her words snapping her to. She stopped stirring and pushed the glass jar back on the counter until its spout dangled over the edge. As she grabbed one of the glasses already holding ice cubes, Lena attempted an answer.

"It's been cold forever, feels like."

The grandmothers were busy at the kitchen table, assembling sandwiches from a platter holding the assemblage of deli meats and cheeses and pickle and lettuce and slices of purple onion and tomato, surrounded by packages of bread, opened bags of an assortment of chips, and jars of mayo and mustard. Normally, Dani would not turn her nose up to such a buffet, but her stomach roiled, settled only some with gentle sips of the tea.

The rest ate, scattered about the front room, some at the table, some in the chairs. Dani settled in the recliner, watching them all, one hand gripping the cool glass and the other resting on her stomach.

"I hope it wasn't breakfast," Glen said, leaning over to her.

She shook her head and smiled. "No," she said, "Breakfast was good. I woke up not feeling well."

The detective had also refused food, but he'd been open about his reasons: finding the murdered mortician earlier this morning had killed his appetite.

"The poor boy," Lena had said, and Aster had nodded.

Sensing the meeting was getting underway, Bullocks ignored the ringing cell and tucked it into his inner coat pocket. Still, he could feel its incessant buzz against his chest.

Glen faced the group, after speaking in whispers with Elden. "We had a mutual friend," Glen said, "who died not too long ago. You found his body, Detective, if I remember you saying."

Bullocks remembered the old man he'd found. It felt like months ago. "Right before you both went into the hospital on death's door and came out supermen."

"We think we came out like this to put a stop to this thing," Glen said.

"What thing?" Dani asked. "You keep alluding to something like you know what has Court."

"We do," Elden said, "but we ain't exactly sure where."

"We think it's the same thing what's been grave digging," Glen said. "It's probably been killing people."

"A little boy," the detective said. "A couple at the farmer's market the other day."

"And the mortician," Jada said.

"It's what we saw on the videotape," TJ said.

Glen sighed, looked to Elden as though he wasn't sure, but pressed on anyway.

"Our friend, he brought it back with him. Or it hitched itself to him, and we think he had control of it for a time, but something happened."

"Does this have to do with Court's parents?" Dani asked. "Or his brother?" The elders were all struck dumb. Her friends and the detective were also taken aback, and all eyes were on her. "Does Court even know he had a brother? He's never mentioned one to me. Does he know what happened to his parents?"

"He was a baby," Aster said. "No. We haven't yet told him."

"You saw the picture then," Elden sniffed.

"You knew about this," Dani said. "You all knew, and you've done nothing. And people have died, and Court is… is…"

"We couldn't do anything," Glen said. "We were sick. We were dying."

"Then before you got too sick," she said. "You knew about this thing and…"

"You don't think we tried?" Elden asked, his voice loud and eyes fierce and narrow. "I searched for that goddamn churchyard every free chance I could. I knew our friend wouldn't tell us where it was; he was protecting the shittin' thing. But I looked, ready to load some buckshot into it as soon as I could."

"How hard can it be to find an old church?" Blue asked.

"It moves," Elden mumbled, turning away.

"It what?" Bullocks said. The disbelief was evident on his face, his wide eyes and completely bemused expression, as soon as his head whipped up.

"He's right," Aster said. "No one knows much about it now, but it was an old church way back when, during the settlement of the area. The first settlers are buried there. But it's a local legend. You're walking in the woods and stumble upon it, but maybe you come back to bring a friend and it's no longer there. It's in another part of the county. Its ground is tainted."

"I found it," Dani said. "Last night I found the churchyard."

"I've heard some of my patients talk about it," Lena said. "I didn't believe. Then. Now…" She shook her head.

"There's a lot of this story what's going to be unbelievable," Glen said. "But it's true."

Rong was leaning against the wall, typing on their phone. Jada edged up to them and peeked over their shoulder. "Research," Rong whispered, hiding the screen from her view.

"So how do you find it, then?" TJ asked. "If this church changes locations, how do you find it?"

"By accident, like I did once when I was a boy," Elden said, "or if it has something you want, or need. It's why Dani was able to find it last night."

"And you think Court's there?" Blue said. The incredulity in her voice was thinly veiled, and Dani wondered, especially after Elden's volatile pushback, how long before emotions exploded.

"So, we load up," TJ said. "We get our guns, and we go find this place, because we all want to or need to or whatever, and we blow whatever has Court the fuck away and pull him out of there."

"Language," Glen said.

"If he's still alive," Dani said, and sank back into the recliner from which she'd half-risen, the tears flowing. God, did she truly love him this much? She must, and she touched her stomach and rubbed it absently, deciding then and there she wouldn't rest until Court was back in this house.

"We believe he is, sweetie," Aster said, and walked over to Dani and wrapped her arms around her in a hug. She then lowered herself onto the hearth and held Dani's hand, her head bowed as if in prayer.

"It ain't easy, killing it," Elden said.

"How do you know?" the detective asked.

Elden nodded to Dani. "She asked about his parents, our kids. His brother. We tried once. We failed." With those last two words, he bowed his head and appeared to close his eyes, his lips pressed tightly together.

Glen resumed the storytelling then, his voice low and somber, his tone even, his stare vacant, as though he could see only the memory.

It had come for Court's older brother, first. They'd found him out behind his parents' house, by his swing set. Their friend, the one who'd brought it from overseas, had been in the hospital for a week recovering from a coronary event. Whatever he'd been doing to keep it at bay, with him in the hospital it must have gotten free.

"It began stalking them and calling out for Court especially. He was just a toddler, and he ran out into the woods because it was calling for him. He'd been staying with us at our old house."

Everyone felt the shift. Not that they'd been gathered for anything joyous, but as the elders relived the memory, Dani felt closer to the churchyard, the creature, and death, than she'd felt since arriving.

"I got to him in time," Lena said. "Before he crossed into the tree line. But I still remember feeling it, smelling it. Looking back, I think the churchyard was close that day."

Glen reached over and took his wife's hand. "We decided we needed to do something, so we loaded up my son and left Elden's daughter and Court with Lena and Aster, and we drove out to find the churchyard."

"And wouldn't you know," Elden said. "We found it."

"Bullets didn't work. We shot at it, but it was too quick. It... got behind us, and before I knew it, it had killed my son. Court's dad." Caught in the memory, Glen's eyes teared up, and when he looked up and saw everyone staring at him, he forced a smile. Not a smile borne of happiness or contentment, but one meant to show some form of strength. "Eviscerated him," Glen said. "And then it was gone."

Aster squeezed Dani's hand, cleared her throat, and looked up. "It came here. To this very house. And found its way inside. We tried to hide with Court, but it rampaged through the rooms. Shredded furniture. Punched holes in the walls. Angie went after it. I told her not to. I told her to get back with us and look after her baby, her remaining child, but she wouldn't listen. She pulled one of Elden's rifles off the wall and charged after the thing and fired on it. But it got her."

"Why didn't it get Court?" Dani asked.

"Because our friend showed up," Glen said. "He found Aster and Lena and said he scared it off, but…"

"But," Lena interjected, "I remember hearing him saying something. He walked into the house like an exorcist and shouted a single word, and then it was gone."

"Do you remember what he said?" Dani asked.

"*Qissa*," Lena said. "We looked it up. Took a long time to find the word, but I never forgot it. It's Arabic. It means, story—or epic fable."

Dani noticed when the four grandparents exchanged a shared glance. "You know what this is," Dani said. "You know what this thing is."

"We do," Glen said.

"It's a ghoul," Rong said, and now it was everyone's turn to look in their direction. Dani noticed the grandparents nodding.

Bullocks removed a textbook from his inner coat pocket and dropped it on the table. Dani had noticed him cradling something, favoring something large and heavy with his left arm, under his coat pocket. "You should read Chapter Five," he said. That the book's cover was spotted with what she just knew to be blood forced Dani to look away, nausea sweeping over her. Still, she'd read the title.

Blue stood up, shaking her head and hugging herself as she stalked away. "I can't!"

Jada reached for her. "Blue!"

"I'm out, Jada. Dani, I love you, and I love Court, but I can't. A ghoul? A fucking monster? This is too much."

But rather than leave, she sank to the couch as Jada, who'd been sitting on the other end, slid over and wrapped her arms around her. Dani realized that what Blue had vocalized, they'd all thought.

"You've seen it," Bullocks said to TJ and Britta. "The tape that young mortician showed us…"

"That boy," Lena said, her eyes alight with understanding from where the book had come and what the stains on the cover really meant.

Bullocks nodded sympathetically. "I'm afraid he's dead."

"What boy?" Elden asked.

Aster clearly started to fumble with her words in an attempt to explain how Lena, and she, for that matter, knew him, when Blue spoke up.

"But a ghoul didn't kill Chuy," Blue said, her voice the loudest, and she was crying, and even though Jada reached for her, she pulled away and stood up. "Jesus fucking Christ, you guys! We were in a bar day-drinking, and now Chuy is dead. And not because of some fucking monster. He's dead because some racist redneck asshole shot him in the face with a shotgun."

"Yeah," Rong said. "I was there, remember?"

Blue nodded through teary eyes, and she walked to them and wrapped them in her pink cashmere sweater. They took the hug and relished in it. Dani heard Rong whisper a thank you to Blue.

A slight buzzing noise filled the room. Bullocks drew his cellphone from his coat pocket and tapped the screen, then raised the phone to his ear. "Hello." He froze, listening, his face growing pale, and the attention was drawn back to him. "Okay. I'll be right there," he managed finally, and shoved his cell back into his coat as he met all their gazes. "I have to go."

"What's wrong?" Aster asked.

"Are you okay?" Dani asked.

"No," he said. Then, "The sheriff," he muttered before trailing off. If he were aware of muttering it, no one could tell from the lost, haunted expression. He turned to each of them, mouth open in shock, before he uttered a hefty, world-weary sigh, and exited the home.

⊂⊃

As familiar as the dark and the cold of these Ozark winters were the accompanying smells, skimming through the air like a stone across the river. The burning of leaves. Similar, but stronger, the snuff castoff of a wood-burning fireplace, engine oil, diesel and char smoke from a passing semi or dump truck or tractor. These things mingled under the gunmetal sky as Bullocks exited his vehicle, as tape stretched the perimeter and what remained of the uniformed deputies—those who'd been off duty or out on patrol—busied themselves while also shouldering the forlorn. They would have time enough to mourn, so Bullocks snapped them awake, taking charge instantly. Soon, more sirens whirled in the distance. One of the city cops called the state troopers and before long, even more cops were on the scene, processing and debating and asking Bullocks a lot of questions—because he was now the highest-ranking member of the sheriff's unit. He directed the newcomers to the patrolman who'd walked in on the scene, and the poor kid gave his statement to a fresh set of faces for the umpteenth time while huddled under a blanket looking white as a sheet, his hair matted with sweat, his lips trembling, his stare vacant. Bullocks stood nearby, but by now he'd memorized it. A glance at his watch told him the state boys had arrived at a little after three, which meant he'd been here for over three hours, and it felt like he'd only recently arrived.

Coming in from his shift, the young patrolman had tried the door, but found it locked, so he used his key. Yessir, in retrospect it should have been odd that all the blinds were closed, but he wasn't looking at all the drawn windows in the moment because he figured someone had mistakenly locked the door. So, he opened it.

The smell hit him first. Then the obtrusive silence. Then he saw the spackles of blood, and as he pressed further into the building, he saw more. Bodies in weird positions, unmoving. Faces bloodied 'til they were unrecognizable.

A local patrolman and a state cop approached. They'd found a couple more bodies, they said. Bullocks' ears were ringing, and his head felt as if it were wrapped in a pillow. This had been going on since he got the news and even now, hours later, it hadn't improved. One of the deputies and his wife, back at their home, the patrolman was saying. Another brought him the prisoner sign-in sheet for the day. He glanced at his watch again when he noticed the shadows lengthening and the sun behind the clouds at its brightest spot over the western horizon. If he stared at it, he could make out the diffused orb glowing white behind a translucent shelf of gray in the overcast sky. His phone verified the time, said evening was upon them. An alarm bell rang in his head, but he couldn't make sense of it. Time was passing so quickly.

There was only one name on the sign-in sheet. "Am I to assume Mr. Willette is deceased as well?" That he silently hoped for this was only outweighed by the concern that no one had listed Clem Willette's name in the catalogue of the deceased.

The deputy fidgeted. "Not exactly, sir. Mr. Clem's cell was… well, open. There weren't no sign of him."

The ranch home was five or ten minutes away, given this traffic. Of course, he'd put on his siren, but the people of this town, while obliging of emergency vehicles, were still slow during their evening commute. And this place was small enough and there were enough of them—he knew he could take even longer. But he might already be too late. They might already all be dead.

INTERLUDE NINE

The Tale of Salt and Iron

Once upon a time, three gods walked the earth. Of all the many gods, only a few occupied time here.

The god of the earth was a benevolent being who only waged war with the gods who threatened the people he loved.

The god of the sea loved to claw at the god of the earth. He swallowed up great civilizations and warped earthen tools until they were ruined.

The final god was the god of death. The gods of earth and sea both gave life, as did the gods of fire and sky. They were unified as the life givers, despite their other squabbles. The god of death stole from each of them. The god of death was as powerful as the gods of earth and sea, and they knew it. He walked with impunity across the earth, taking when it wanted, causing grief and loss with but a smile, using the gods against each other in its own machinations and for its own enjoyment.

The god of death threatened all of creation, and the other gods knew this would destroy the world, so they devised a plan. They saw how the god of death birthed the demigod of evil, and how it spread. They knew if they could control the demigod, they could keep life flourishing.

So, the gods of earth and sea teamed up to battle evil and death, and they combined their resources. They found, in the end, salt—which combined minerals from the god of the sea—and iron—which combined earthen minerals—best repelled the demigod of evil and so helped stave the thirst of the god of death.

They realized they couldn't stop the god of death, nor its offspring. But to hold it at bay, that was enough. All they needed was the salt and iron of the earth and sea to keep death back.

The End

CHAPTER FIFTY-SIX

*E*ver-darkening shades of gray again overtook the town. The house. The vast night marauded with the wintriness to bar the townsfolk inside. At the Oscar farmhouse, the group looked up from their conversations about the book the detective had brought and noticed the hour had grown late, delivering the cold and dark. This was normal for this time of year; they were only surprised by how quickly the afternoon had passed. None of them detected anything else ominous pressing in on them. No portent alerted them to what was coming.

Lena took notice of Glen's yawn and sat back, stretched, then with her hands on her knees, pushed herself to standing from where she had been sitting with Glen and Dani on the couch. Dani reached to help in getting Glen up, but spry as ever, he thanked them and stood up briskly, staring down at the book, opened to chapter five and the wood engraving that had caught the mortician's attention, and then the detective's.

"What is it?" Lena asked.

"It fits," Glen said. "What we saw. What we know of it. It fits."

"Yes, dear," she said, patting his back.

When Lena yawned, Glen said, "We need a break. Nothing's going to happen tonight. We best all get some sleep and start fresh in the morning. You coming with us, dear?"

Dani felt the beginnings of a headache, a dull ache, like the back of her skull was a vise. There had been a lot of words and plans this afternoon, and worry was voiced in a plethora of ways. They were all drained, and no one was surprised when Glen made this announcement, yet she still shook her head. "I'm going to see if one of the guys can drop me off later," she said.

He pointed to her pocket, indicating the key. "You let yourself in, sweetie. We'll be asleep."

"'Guys' is insulting," Blue said, but no one paid attention.

Glen shook Elden's hand as Lena hugged Aster then waved to the others. The door was shut behind them and they walked to Lena's Avalon, but Glen paused before walking around the hood to the driver's side, dangling the keys in the air for her.

"You feel like getting us home, Nana?" he said. "I'm a bit wiped."

She unzipped her purse and began to dig. "Got my own. I'm surprised the man who has to drive everywhere is asking."

"Actually, I want to save my energy," he said, and winked.

Her cheeks flushed. There had been a time he'd been this frisky, but they had been so overwhelmed by heart issues and feebleness, illness and weakness, she'd nearly forgot about it until now. All at once, the old feelings had returned, of them not much younger, but filled with more energy, before the disease and the wear and tear of old age had consumed all their stores of energy. She shifted into reverse and angled the car down the hill, toward the town.

They were little less than a quarter mile away, down the hill and by the single-wide Elden rented out, when thunder ripped through their world. The windshield exploded; glass shards sliced into her face. The vehicle careened and the wheel jerked out of her hands, spinning, hurling them into the ditch. Her face slammed against the steering column as the seatbelt caught her, snapped against her torso as though she'd been hit with a ball peen hammer. Glen's passenger side window imploded. The ditch caught them like a concrete barrier, crumpling the hood. Her vision went blurry and sounds and sensations melted into each other, the hiss of steam, the heat of fire. Something dripped down her forehead onto her cheek as bursts of pain peppered her body like flak.

"Glen," she said, reaching for her husband. He was mumbling something. Blurrily, she could still see the windshield had a large hole in the center with cracks spiderwebbing, and the world beyond, the ditch, the steam venting off the engine block was a kaleidoscope of images. *God, was it about to blow up?* Glen knew these things, not her. Lena pulled at her seatbelt and thought, what a waste, as it and the airbag did little to protect them, but at least neither went through the windshield when… Her thoughts began to clear. "We were shot," she said aloud.

"Lena," Glen said, his voice weak. She reached for his hand and grasped tightly. "You okay?"

"I'm fine," she managed, but she knew she didn't sound fine.

Through the dark, the smoke and swirling images, she met his eyes. Weak and hurt, his face was cut by the glass, as she was sure hers was. "You okay?" he tried again. She thought he hadn't heard her, or maybe couldn't register what was going on, and this terrified her.

She tried to nod, but the movement caused the pain to cascade like a wave, sloshing from the base of her neck to behind her eyes. Her left shoulder burned, wrenched from the crash.

Something large landed with a thud on the roof with a thud. Both Glen and Lena looked up as the metal screeched under the weight.

The driver's side headlight still worked but shined only into the grass of the ditch and skimmed the lawn of the trailer.

The being crouching on the hood looked like a man. It was dressed in the clothes of a deputy sheriff, though the clothes were bloodied and torn. The face, shrouded by shadow, bent to them, its jaw unhinged, opening wide. Rows of canines and incisors glinted in the night light, shining like ivory daggers. It stretched a long arm toward them, through the hole in the windshield. Blue and gray, impossibly long. The nails stretched to claws and made a sickening, flesh-tearing sound.

"I am *Umm ghulah*," it said. Its voice sounded damp and when it yanked its arm back, pulling the windshield free of the frame so that nothing separated it from the two passengers, Lena gasped and froze. Its breath or its scent or both reeked of grave rot. "I was Marid. Was driven insane by the comets when God forbade me from delivering the stories of heaven to your prophets. I was made sick. Now I return you to your sickness." It dug its long claws into Glen's chest, twisting its head, losing all semblance of humanity in the night, now some bald and bent gray creature with bile-colored eyes that glowed like starlight, a wide mouth and sharp teeth with acid for saliva, exhaling a breath like sulfurous fog across Glen's face that plumed through the car. He coughed once then clutched his chest, and winced, but her husband did not tear his eyes away from it. It snarled defiantly, searching for a sign of fear and, receiving none, it leapt off the vehicle and bound into the pasture and darkness, and Lena was alone with her husband, the night, and encroaching sounds of sirens. Lena wondered who would have called the police, never once thinking it could be the detective returning to them because he had realized what Clem's plan was when he escaped or that he would be in league with the creature. Glen, pale under blood and shards of glass, fluttered his eyes, and he looked from where he clutched his chest, and there was pain and grief and horror in his eyes, and fear. Glen was dying again.

"I'm sorry," he said.

CHAPTER FIFTY-SEVEN

*L*ast thoughts. We all have them. They stick with us after the fact, accompanied usually with "What if I'd done…" or simply acting as tags for the last thing we remember processing in our brains. Did Jada have any regrets in the last seconds of her life when the wooden door exploded inward and they saw the face of the man who'd murdered Chuy, and he turned the shotgun on the young Asian lady and pulled the triggers to both barrels, and her head seemed to vaporize as blood splattered on Britta and Blue and TJ?

Did her spirit realize it was dead and say, *Damn, I should have ducked when the doorknob jiggled*, or *I should have run when we first heard the shot down the street?*

Britta could only manifest a single declarative statement before buckshot tore into her flesh as Jada's head burst apart, and blood soaked into her clothes and her skin with bits of grey matter. "*Sweelorgeesus*" and in her mind she saw her children, and TJ playing with the kids as they grew up, and then Chuy and the detective showed up behind him saying it had been a sting operation and they'd been successful and then Court showed up and he and Dani kissed, and all was okay and…

Her head slapped against the corner of the table; her world went black, and her thoughts silenced.

Blue saw a white man, salt and pepper hair, a Baby Boomer, skinny but strong, toting a shotgun. When he pointed it at Jada, Blue thought about stepping in front of her friend, like it would make a difference, and anyway before she could think of moving, buckshot raked her thigh, her arm, her torso, and Blue felt Jada's blood on her face and the pain and shock of it all sent her back into the wall.

Elden's clearest moment came with the gunshot outside, off in the distance. He'd risen to listen for another and turned his head toward the front door. Instinctively he'd raced to it and checked the locks; both the deadbolt and the doorknob lock were secure.

Aster's clearest thought came as the doorknob jiggled a minute or so later. She had started to rush toward the door but was held back by Elden, who'd grabbed her and Dani by their shoulders and dragged them back toward the kitchen. Aster's mind raced to find the location of the nearest gun. In her periphery, the strange little Asian boy moved toward them, passing in front of Jada.

CHAPTER FIFTY-EIGHT

Clem turned in place, scanning the room. The only thing his father left him, besides the drinking problem and the mean spirit, was the double-barreled 12-gauge Browning, 5-1 semiautomatic. It had become his favorite. Wherever he looked, he aimed the Browning held down by his hip, his right index finger hovering over its twin triggers.

The old couple were gone. The ghoul wouldn't like such delays. The first shot took out a few of the women. The wall and floor were red, and he could see bits of brain matter and skull. Similarly speckled with human goo, on either side of the headless body lay pretty girls. Neither moved. The younger one had a great figure. He'd seen her around town, but the other one, a bit square with short, curly hair, and a squarer jaw, a bit mannish, he'd never seen, and imagined she was one of them.

But where were the old couple, or the Mexican chick, or the little effeminate Asian kid, or the big dude…

The blow came from the right, sending his head ricocheting against the drywall. His eyes crossed and light flashed in his vision.

Clem went sprawling onto his back, and another blow came to his left temple, and a large man with broad shoulders and a tight haircut and big arms hovered over him. Clem realized quickly he was no longer holding his shotgun.

"Don't never let your shotgun go, boy," his daddy had said back when he was eight and they were out duck hunting—Clem had jumped at the first sound of the barrels unloading. Well, it was the sound, Clem had said, what startled him, but in reality, it was the ducks falling from the sky, their wings up with their beaks, pointed skyward, motionless dead weight falling toward the water. Their dead bodies freefalling had frozen him.

Freezing up. His biggest problem. Like when he shot the boy last night. He should have marched into the graveyard and kilt the other'n, but he froze, and so the little effeminate Chink boy got the drop on him. And tonight, he'd frozen again, and now…

The back of his skull bounced off the hardwood floor and the stars danced in front of him. He blinked but his vision stayed blurred, saw only red, and he realized he was bleeding. This was it; this guy—he'd seen him about town too, TJ something—was going to kill him.

"You're an American," his dad was saying in his ear. "I didn't teach you to be prepared for nothing. He's helping them colored folk out, so he ain't no better."

But he was prepared, Clem remembered then. The shotgun wasn't his only weapon. His right hand fumbled for the pockets in his pants as his head bounced again. This time, the stars warbled. Great black spots filled his vision. Sounds were muted. It would be so easy to slip unconscious right now, or even something more permanent, before he could get the surprise.

"Is this it?" his father's voice asked. "You gonna be taken out by some boy who'd rather beat on one of his own kind?"

"He ain't Black," Clem mumbled. Stars danced in front of him, and he tasted copper.

TJ said, "What? What, motherfucker? My fucking wife, you piece of shit," and drove his knuckles into the claylike flesh again.

"Don't matter," his father's voice said. "He's got your number, boy."

Bounce. "Yesh," Clem said, and his smile infuriated TJ.

"So which pocket is the blade, and which is the sidearm?" his father asked, and Clem felt the handle of the blade and wrapped his fingers around it, and smiled up at TJ and blew him a kiss. It was enough to give TJ a pause; the bigger man couldn't understand why this old fart would egg him on so. He lifted his bloody right fist, primed it back at the shoulder.

The serrated blade drove fire into his abdomen, cutting through intestine, stomach, spleen, and kidney. Blood spurted, drenching the knife handle, warm on Clem's hand. TJ paused, wavered in his punch, then doubled over, clutching his guts as he curled into the fetal position on the floor.

"Dammit," he said, his voice strained. "I had him. Dammit." And then he thought of Britta and their kids, and he muttered, "I'm sorry."

Clem rolled over onto his side, spit up blood, rose to his knees, then braced against the wall and stood. The Browning lay on the kitchen floor. He limped towards it, forced himself to bend down though, as he did, his head swam and went black. He found himself fumbling around for the gun, but he was able to reach it, stand it up, and lean on it, his head clearing, his other hand still holding the knife. This he jutted back into the sheath in his pocket, and he shifted the barrel to his now free hand to be able to reach into his left pocket. From there he drew a Glock .9 mm.

TJ rolled onto his back, his vision blurry from tears a"nd pain. He could still make out the handgun that pointed at his forehead and the smiling bloody and bruised old man who braced himself on his double-barrel shotgun like it was a cane.

"You was a good boy. A worker. But you went and fell in with this bunch. You thought you had my number." He whistled and spat blood and half coughed, half laughed. "But I got your number right here."

"Fuck you," TJ said, but most of it was blood.

"Maybe in your dreams, you faggot," Clem said, and pulled the trigger. He watched for a minute as blood began to trickle out of the hole in TJ's head and pool on the hardwood floor.

CHAPTER FIFTY-NINE

The light on the pole in the calf lot dimly illuminated the laundry room in a soft yellow, brightened the sky, the barn, the calf lot behind the house. *That would be nice*, Dani thought dreamily, her mind unable or unwilling to process what she'd just seen, though what exactly *that* was she didn't know, except that perhaps it meant she were elsewhere. They could run. Might make it to the shed behind the house. Probably not down to the barn. Rong and Aster held each other tight. Dani had pulled away from them in their retreat down the hall, and now looked on as a spectator no longer invited to the event. Elden had broken away from them too, pulling his own 12-gauge off the wall, then shielding them as they retreated by aiming the barrel in the direction from which they'd come. There came a hard-left turn, then another. Elden ran into the bedroom at the other end of the short hall and returned a moment later, pumping shells into the gun. Dani noticed a .22 rifle hanging on the wall over the dryer and thought she had seen a Smith and Wesson revolver during their retreat. Elden must have had guns all over the house, and he must have had ammunition scattered about for all of it.

Ssh, Elden motioned, then aimed the shotgun forward, toward the door to the hall. It was the only opening to the back part of the house. A single report rang through the house like a banshee wail summoning death for all within earshot. She whimpered a bit at the sound. Footsteps on the linoleum drew near. Dani's breath caught, but she couldn't control the shivering. When she glanced back and saw Rong and Aster, they stared at her wide-eyed and pale, their breaths shallow. Elden, still aiming his shotgun forward, backed down the hall toward the rear bedroom. *Oh, Rong*, Dani had time to think.

The door opened. Blocked the hall. The attacker stepped in from the darkness. An older white man, his face bruised and cut, a bloody rivulet trail down his chin, aimed the barrels of his shotgun at them. Dani glanced at Rong and saw their pupils constrict, rage on their face. The man asked, "Where's the old man?" and then the blast came. But not from this man. From behind the door.

Clem's chest exploded from the inside out, his blood splattering on the walls, the ironing board, the hangers and rod and wire shelf. Bits of wood splintered as the door also exploded, organic shrapnel slicing through him. His shotgun dropped harmlessly to the floor as he sank to his knees, then pitched forward. What was left of the door swung shut as Elden stepped forward and surveyed the scene, the barrels of his own 12-gauge smoking.

"You all okay?" he asked.

No one answered. They couldn't. They stared at the bloody mass in front of them, the blood streaming out of his chest. Aster and Rong, holding each other, scurried backwards as the blood pooled at their feet, as if afraid the blood might burn into their flesh.

"I…" Elden began, then dropped his gun and clutched his chest. Dropped to his knees. He had looked so strong, for the moment. So determined. But just before he fell, his face had gone ashen, and it had frozen, and he looked as though he might be having a stroke or a heart attack.

"Elden?" Aster said. "Papaw?"

A dark figure stepped over him from behind, like a puppeteer revealing itself. It stretched a long claw over his back. Aster screamed and Rong clutched her, but Dani stared. Saw it for what it was.

"Lost in his dreams again," it said.

"You're it," Dani said, a shiver running up her spine from fear, but also a flush of anger. "You have Court."

"I am *Umm ghulah*," it said. "I was Marid. Was driven insane by the comets when God forbade me from delivering the stories of heaven to your prophets. I was made sick. Now I return you to your sickness."

Dani thought she saw a gleam of light on the creature's teeth. And then it was gone, retreating into the darkness. As Aster and Rong rushed for Elden, Dani gave chase, racing down the hall. The back-bedroom curtains billowed in the night breeze. Tiny shards of broken glass crunched under her shoes into the carpet as she crossed to push the curtains aside. The sky above was pitch as the night was deep, and a cool wind blew naively across the back of the house, an ersatz peace like an ill-timed prankster. She knew, from this feeling, that it was gone. Totally and completely gone. No peace could exist in its presence, so this quiet, serene feeling must signal the monster had returned to its lair. She caught a sob in her throat and nearly crumbled to the floor.

Sirens brought her back. What had she been doing? Caught nearly in a faux nirvana. A dream. A dream without Court. At the sound of a familiar voice, she turned. For Dani, all this happened in a matter of seconds. The truth was it didn't take much longer.

Dani found Rong at Elden's still body, not wondering right then where Aster had gone. No, this was chaos, and her ears were humming, and her head was spinning. The walls were like a merry-go-round, like clockwork hands, twisting, twisting into the nether, and they gelled together to provide a labyrinth of nightmares, forcing her to fumble forward, forward, into the kitchen, then into the living room now painted in blood, where the detective stood and the bodies lay.

"Detective Bullocks," she said, her voice odd even in her ears.

"You okay?" he asked, leading her outside. She choked down a maniacal laugh, not sure how to answer. "Clem Willette escaped jail today. I realized after shooting that kid yesterday, he might come back up here for the rest of you. I think he was working with the creature—"

"I think so too," Dani said. Then, noticing the empty drive, added, "The truck is gone."

"Whose?" Rong asked, exiting as EMTs hoisting a gurney quick-stepped to the back of the house. The cream walls were splattered with crimson, darkening to a blackened purple, as more EMTs sorted through the scattered remains on the floor. The house had been invaded by people in different uniforms shouting acronyms, adding to the chaos Dani had hoped was over. Were they still the recognizable friends of Dani's and Rong's, hidden underneath the disfiguring masks of blood and carnage? What resembled the woman named Britta reached up a hand weakly, her fingers trembling, and brushed Dani's own fingertips as she was carted past.

"The Oscars'," the detective said.

CHAPTER SIXTY

Lena rubbed her temple and winced, settling on leaning her forehead against the cool metal of the truck's passenger side. When the... *thing* had leapt away into the darkness, she'd followed, limping slowly at first up the road both because she wanted to make sure the emergency vehicles saw the wreck and because she was so damn sore. Her ribs felt shattered, and her breath came in labored gasps. When she saw an ambulance stop and the paramedics begin to tend to Glen, she hurried on. Police cars weren't far beyond.

As gunshots rang out at the farm, she quickened her pace, not carrying a weapon herself, but sure the farm was where she needed to be. In the distance she heard two more ambulances. Limping, holding her side, scanning the house for signs of life, she reached the drive, heard glass shatter, and thought she saw something bounding through the calf lot behind the house, toward deeper pasture. The left leg weak, she dragged it across the gravel, praying for more sound. There were lights on in the front room and the kitchen, but she couldn't see anyone moving and she heard no signs to support the idea anyone had survived.

What if they hadn't? What if the ghoul had killed them all, and now with Glen hurt and Court still missing and… if she were the only one left, could she face it alone?

She leaned against the pickup truck, then looked over the side. Bags of salt and rebar still lay in the bed from a mission incomplete by Glen and Elden. The thought came to her as the door swung open and Aster stumbled out, blood splattered on her clothes, tears in her eyes.

"Oh Lena," she was saying. The two women hugged with Lena whimpering just a little. "It came back. Got Elden."

Lena nodded despite the pain shooting up her neck. "It got Glen too. Someone shot at our vehicle, and I wrecked." They looked over her shoulder down the hill to the cop car and ambulance. Others sped toward them.

"What are we going to do?" Aster asked.

"Get the pickup keys," Lena said.

"You should rest—" Aster began.

"We'll go where Dani went."

"What if we're wrong?"

"I can't just do nothing," Lena said and straightened a little. The pain shot through her, but she didn't give into it. She could not let the pain win now.

❦

Aster steered the truck towards the side road Court's car had been found on, going faster than she was comfortable. In the passenger seat, Lena produced a handkerchief from her shirt pocket and dabbed at the blood on her forehead, every touch triggering a fresh pulse of pain, the mirror under the visor her only guide.

"Dammit," Lena said.

"What?"

"My purse, still in the car."

Suddenly, she began to weep. The few words she muttered sounded a lot like 'Glen' and Aster understood.

When Lena quieted, Aster said, "It was Clem Willette. Shot at you, came to the house."

"The ghoul was with him," Lena said. "Aster, how did we let it get this bad?"

"We didn't," Aster said. "This ain't our fault."

"He hurt them, didn't he?" Lena said then, her voice a whisper. She snapped the visor up as her shoulder screamed at her for such a careless action, and she stared out the window through the pitch as the truck pulled onto the county road and parked on the shoulder.

Aster shifted to park and shut off the ignition. "Yes." She paused, and Lena imagined Aster was wondering how to proceed. She must have settled on truth and brevity. "TJ's dead. The Chinese girl, she's dead too. I don't know about Britta or the other one, but there was so much blood, and no one was moving."

"And Dani?" Lena asked, looking over at her.

Aster nodded. "She's fine. So's the boy."

Lena shook her head. "What are we going to do?"

Aster hiked a thumb over her shoulder toward the bed of the truck. "Elden shot Clem Willette, killed him before the ghoul got him. So, we're going to finish the job they started. It's what we're going to do. We're going to stop this thing."

Aster stepped to the bed of the truck and as Lena followed, she saw the provisions. Glen had told her how he helped Elden load up the rebar and bags of salt.

"We don't know where the church is or how far we'll have to walk," Lena said.

Aster nodded. "Ought to be a rubber mallet in there, somewheres," she said, and opened the toolbox lid. The toolbox itself spanned the width of the bed and had been bolted in. Lena opened her side.

"I've been in a car accident and look like I'm ready for the cemetery, and we're both old women."

"Yep," Aster said.

Lena found the mallet and drew it out, holding it up despite the various pains coursing through her, wincing to get Aster's attention.

"We'll carry what we can," Aster said, and, with a grunt, she hoisted a bag of salt out of the bed of the truck.

Lena found with her left hand she could lift out a piece of rebar. It was corkscrew iron and densely heavy, but manageable, even at nearly five feet long. Setting it against the side of the truck, she pulled out another, and managed them both, with the mallet, well enough that she could follow Aster into the woods. Like Dani before them, Lena could feel something drawing them. It was the same feeling she'd felt when she'd chased toddler Court into the tree line so many years ago, and when Dani had described it to the group earlier, Lena had recognized it. Yes, she was in pain, and yes, her body screamed at her every step of the way. But Lena refused to listen.

The church appeared to them through the thickness of the night, first a few tombstones and then the building itself. Lena dropped the rebar and helped Aster to open the salt, and the two women picked up the fifty-pound bag and began spreading the salt over the ground.

"The book said this would work," Aster said, but she didn't sound sure.

"We'll find Court," Lena said. She'd heard the doubt in Aster's voice and knew what she was worried about, because she worried about it also.

"It touched them," Aster said. "And they got worse again."

"I think they're linked to it, somehow," Lena said. "I think their health has been linked to fighting it."

"By who?" Aster asked. "God?"

They finished sowing the bag and returned to the truck, grabbed another bag and more rebar.

Lena didn't answer. She thought this thing had a better understanding of what they called God than they did.

After one more trip, they had six pieces of rebar on the ground in front of the church entrance. They drove the posts into the ground with grunts and the mallet and were nearly finished when they heard a great commotion of screaming metal out from the direction of the road. Lena hit the last piece one last time and shook it to make sure it was sturdy. Satisfied, she looked up to find Aster was gone.

※

Pushing through the trees, Aster saw the hood of the truck laying on the pavement, the engine spewing steam like a hot spring geyser. She could no longer see Lena or the church behind her. Great gashes like torn strips of flesh scarred the truck. The heavy toolbox, once bolted to the bed next to the cab, had been tossed in the road, the box busted into pieces and the tools scattered about like organs. All four tires were flat and hissing air.

"Dear Jesus," Aster said. Something blurred past, knocking her into the driver's side of the truck, the jagged metal stabbing at her back and shoulder, and she slumped to the ground to avoid both getting cut and another attack. Blanketed by the dark night, standing over her, the ghoul smiled. It turned its head like a dog, studying her, then knelt.

"You are horrible," it hissed. She tried to shut her eyes, to look away, but its fingers grabbed her chin, and she could taste the grave on its breath. "You know evil. You know wrong because you are wrong. You failed. Your husband, Court, all of them. You failed and you are going to die knowing the badness in your heart has led to so much suffering."

Aster closed her eyes as it raised a claw when from the tree line, she heard Lena scream.

CHAPTER SIXTY-ONE

Whatever shroud had been draped over Aster's crumpled form evanesced at Lena's arrival. Desperation and fear forced Lena into a fast, painful limp. She attempted to kneel, but her body shot fire through her various wounds. Still, she could see well enough, even in the dark, that though Aster's eyes were closed, she still breathed.

"You think you can block me?" The voice called from the darkness. "Keep me out of my home! I can still get to the boy, stupid woman." Lena looked up and around, but there was no sign of the creature. Around her the trees stood vigilant, helping the night to conceal everything.

"We've got you trapped now," Lena yelled. The sound of her elevated, angry voice frightened her. It had been years since she'd allowed her anger to manifest so. "We'll come back for you."

The thing made a sound Lena assumed was a laugh: a dry noise, a mix between a cough and a screech. "I will remove the iron and the salt, silly thing, and then you will never find us. Besides, now you're all alone."

Breathing heavy, Lena considered Aster, still unmoving. She thought of Glen. Aster had told her the damage Clem Willette had done. She'd told her about the ghoul attacking Elden. The boy was okay. So was Dani. But everyone else… Dark thoughts shrouded her. Lena knew, deep down, it was not lying. Worse than that, she feared it had already won. Her thoughts shifted then to Court, and she felt on the verge of tears.

Lena heard what sounded like laughing and then the shifting and scurrying sounds of the underbrush being disturbed. As the sound faded, it gave way to the beating of her own heart…dangerously fast. With a terrible groan and columns of pain exploding up her spine through every point on her body, Lena forced herself down until she sat by Aster. A cursory check told her the spine and neck were undamaged, so she worked with heavy sighs to raise the unresponsive head and supported the other woman.

"I'm here," Lena whispered. Aster moaned. Lena felt in her coat and found her cell phone, then dialed.

"Detective Bullocks. Yes, I know. I'm sorry. We're at the old access road where they found Court's car. Send an ambulance. Aster is hurt."

CHAPTER SIXTY-TWO

Time didn't move. It was always dark, and it was always dank down here. Down here was cold, lonely. Court passed the time sleeping and reciting poetry. Whitman, Wordsworth, Keats. Then perhaps Ginsberg, Carlos Williams, Thomas. Dickenson and Plath. This was how time moved for him. Sleeping because he could do nothing else, and his mind, slogging through fear and doubt, exhausted from trying to quell those fears with comforting words with which he'd grown close, would finally force him to shut down, until some random noise, a far off drip, or the return of the creature, the click of its claws and—more than its sound—its smell came too. The smell of the grave, of the rot on its breath.

Now, as he recited Yeats, he heard a new sound: digging and disrupting soil, above and off to the left, the sound of the earth spilling away nearby though he couldn't see where, and then the familiar clattering of the claws on the chamber of bones.

"*With the hot blood of youth, of love crossed long ago; / And I took all the blame out of all sense and reason, / Until I cried and trembled and rocked to and fro...*"

"What say you?" the thing grumbled, crawling along the walls in the shadows towards him.

"It's a poem," he said. "'The Cold Heaven,' by WB Yeats."

"You're scared," it said, and the clacking of its nails stopped. He could smell it near him. Rank like carrion flesh, coppery and sugary and buttery like it had snacked on something fat.

"I was, I am. But I'm also tired, and hungry and thirsty, and angry."

"Sleep," it said, "and I will bring you food."

"I don't eat what you eat."

"Then sleep and when you wake, I'll bring what you eat."

"I've slept! I still don't know what you want from me. I want out!" He stood, his legs wobbly, no sturdier than a scarecrow off its pole. The creature stood. It approached, standing under the torchlight, hunched over. Its flesh a grayish-sallow color, with blue veins scarring across the surface, its limbs impossibly long and gangly. Its ribs showed, its face under a bald scalp, with yellow eyes and a wide jaw filled with teeth, as sharp as the claws on its hands and feet.

"Qissa," it said.

"I don't know what that is!"

"Tell me a story," it said. "Qissa. Or poem."

"Why should I?"

"Because. You hide, pretend. Drink. You think you don't come, so they don't age. But that isn't how you keep me away. It means you'll miss them when they die."

"Keep you away? You think you're Death?"

"I am as death is. I devour all. I will devour you as I have devoured them."

"If you hurt them!" He swayed uneasily, knowing full well in this state it was an idle threat.

It walked towards him, strutting like a gorilla and pounding its chest. "You'll what, eh? Iron is strong. Your grandmothers thought so also, and tried to keep the *ghula* away, but I still found a way inside."

"My grandmothers are here?" But it had used the past tense, and this sent a fresh wave of fear through him.

"They were, but I found a way inside. Death always finds a way inside."

"You aren't Death," he spat. "You're a scavenger. You eat the dead, like a vulture or a fly. Too weak to hunt, so you take the easy prey."

It raked a claw across his face, hard enough to knock him back, and he smacked his head on the stone floor and saw stars. It kneeled over him, twisting its jaws open, saliva from its open mouth reeking of grave, drooling down on his nose and lips, its sulfurous eyes burning through him. It took his chin in its clawed hand like one might examine a peach and turned his head in inspection.

"Stings," it said. "But you won't die. No. Not unless you keep refusing. But with qissa or poems, you will live a long life. A happy life." It bent closer to him. Smelling him. "Qissa helps me sleep. Now you sleep. Sleep and when you wake, you will have your food."

It palmed Court's face and squeezed its fingers into his skull. He could smell rot on its claws, the stale blood and torn, festering flesh under its nails, and then it slapped his head down against the stone. Court's vision blurred and he was vaguely aware of the thing even closer, its ear to his chest (but it didn't have an ear, but a tiny hole in the side of its skull where there should be ears), and then it rose and mumbled something about the storyteller still alive ("good, good") and as it crawled away, claws clicking rhythmically, and Court's vision again went black.

INTERLUDE TEN

The Tale of the Poet's Dream

Once upon a time, there lived a poet who wrote his dreams. For years, he dreamed of his parents even though they were dead, and he wrote down his conversations with them. Some years later, he'd dream of his grandparents in the same way, but morning always came the same.

The darkness of the dream, the settled stillness of night, the cool air filtering through his room, brought a deep resonance of peace and drawn breath from where he lay, his head nestled into his pillow, the blankets pulled tight around him, on his side with knees drawn and arms folded in front of him. He never wanted to wake from these dreams.

So, morning came cruelly, its gilded light or its bluish light (depending on the time of the morning and the season) broke his sleep and woke him to a world in which they were gone. It didn't matter how pleasant the morning tried to be. In his younger days, he might've awakened still drunk from the night before, or to his automatic coffee maker filling his apartment with the smells of freshly brewed Colombian roast. As he got older, he wished to be awakened by the sound of a baby crying or the feel of his wife's bare foot caressing his shin, or her thigh upon his, or the smell of breakfast meant to rouse him. Temptations meant to rouse him and pull him away from what the slumber promised: to see those he had lost once more.

So, unresolved in this, the poet wrote about the dreams and about the mornings and about the feelings of temptation and about the pleasantness of sleep and about the good intentions of the morning and the selfishness of the night, and in his private times (the shower, his office at school, his office at home, on the toilet, driving his convertible, time alone with the baby who couldn't possibly understand), he wept. Torn between the draw of the night and the morning, he wept. Torn between his love of those who'd gone before him and of those who needed him now, he wept. He wept and he wrote.

The End

PART FOUR

Only One Strike

CHAPTER SIXTY-THREE

When pacing had proven ineffectual in staving off her thoughts, Dani jutted her hands in her pockets and approached the window. The waiting room was dark and fairly quiet, the glass partition filtering out most of the room alarms and beeps, even the overhead pages. The room reeked of ammonia and was a bit too cold. In her left pocket was the familiar bulk of her cell, but in her right, she felt something misshapen, hard, metallic and thin. The Dillons' house key. Dani squeezed it. Framed in the window, the landscape cloaked in darkness, no moon or stars to offer any relief outside, and what light existed inside reconfigured the window into a dim mirror showing only the long shadows on her face and hiding her eyes in deep, dark sockets.

They'd lost. She realized it now. Court was gone and this thing, this ghoul or whatever it was, was gone too. Letting go of the key, she reached up and touched her stomach. The ramifications of losing seemed more terrible now.

If she even kept it. Perhaps the stress would keep her from carrying the child to term, or perhaps this ghoul, if it had been hunting this family, would come and claim the next generation. This thought, initially a fleeting divergence of a mind chasing a string of logic, now seemed all the more probable. It was settled, then. Even if her family disowned her, she couldn't stop this thing and she couldn't keep it from taking her child, so she'd spare her child. She'd do it herself.

And this thing, tied to the family as it appears to be, might know what you robbed from it, and come for you anyway.

This seemed as likely. *Madre de Dios*, she thought, and then she thought of her own mamá, and her own papá, and wondered if this thing wouldn't stop. It would come after the Dillons first, but then it would find the Oscars—and now that she was connected to them, it might target her family. There may be no end to this thing, and this thought frightened her most of all.

An irrational part of her hated them then, his grandparents, for not divulging any of this to her, to Court. It was their fault he had been abducted, and their fault all this death and carnage had happened. This calamity lay solely on their shoulders. She took a deep, regretful sigh. All well and good to let your emotions run wild, but the truth was, even if they had told her and Court, there was probably little if anything they could have done. There's no way she would have believed such a story, and it still would have probably gotten to Court.

She turned her back on the outside. Rong was slumped in a chair, sleeping with their right cheek propped on a fist and elbow on the armrest, like a kickstand for their face. She hated them for being able to sleep, even as she knew this wasn't true. Their body probably shut down, as they'd been through a lot also. Rong was stoic; whatever they felt was buried inside. How they must be processing the death of Chuy and now the others she could not begin to guess. A couple of seats away, Lena sat, staring at nothing, her face pale and washed of color save for the forming bruises and inflamed flesh around angry cuts where glass had sliced into her.

"Why didn't you warn us?" Dani asked.

Lena blinked then looked at her. Rong looked up, instantly alert. "What?"

"This thing was tied to you and the Oscars and you didn't warn any of us. You didn't tell Court. And now he's gone, and people are dead, and your husband and Mr. Oscar are dying again. And it's your fault. Yours and Glen's and the Oscars'. You should have told us."

Lena stayed where she was settled and kept her gaze on the floor. Dani felt like a child who'd tried, though was too young, to successfully admonish a parent.

"And would you have believed us? Some supernatural creature had targeted our family and killed Court's parents and his brother when he was a baby?"

Dani didn't respond. She felt foolish as Lena echoed her previous realization.

"We thought it was gone, Dani. We didn't know it was lurking. It had vanished for years. We didn't know it was being contained. We didn't find out until you did. And when we did find out it was back, Glen and Elden were dying—and when they got better, we tried to call Court back, to tell him."

"And now he's gone."

"But what do you think we owe you?" Lena continued. "For all we knew, you were some fly-by-night affair. Some fling he'd toss aside or who would toss him aside after you were done. We talked to him. We skyped and texted and kept up with our grandson. He'd mentioned you but hinted at the… lack of seriousness of your relationship. Oh, don't get worried, dear, he didn't betray any of your confidences or provide salacious gossip, but we raised him, and we could hear it in his voice. He wasn't sure about you, and you weren't sure about him."

Did Dani owe her an explanation then? Again, her hand rose to her belly.

"So even though we talked, we weren't convinced you'd come. You sure surprised us." Lena turned and took a few steps, dropped her head, and then turned back. "Well, you surprised me. Glen seemed to know. He knew you'd show up. He always seemed to know."

"I know we were tenuous," Dani said. "But right before he left, we..." *talked, planned, had it out.* "...Things are different. I..."

"You're pregnant," Lena said.

Dani stammered. "How did you...?"

"I'm a grandmother," Lena said. "I've had friends who are mothers and grandmothers. I can see it on you."

"I didn't come because... I only took a test at the farmhouse."

"I know," Lena said. Her gaze softened. "It's why we let you in. Glen always knew. Even Aster, I think. Why they didn't want to keep you or your friends in the dark anymore. And I can see now that you and Court aren't as tenuous as you both thought." She smiled. "You probably never were."

Dani allowed herself to smile also, and to think about Court. "I was scared. I was this type of person... someone who wanted to be independent."

Lena sighed. "Well, I'm still getting to know you, but my grandson, I think, was scared too; he was distancing himself from us. Sure, we talked. But he was pulling away. He probably found it too painful to see us getting older, to see his grandfathers wasting away."

"He was a womanizer and a drinker, a partier," Dani said. "I'm not casting stones. I did my share of partying."

"It's irrational," Lena said, "but some people think the best way to stave off death is to run towards youth. Like Peter Pan."

"Or Dylan Thomas," Dani said.

Lena put her arm around Dani in a hug and then touched her belly. "But running away isn't living, sweetie. This is. I'm sorry for what I've said to you in the past." Dani surprised herself when she hugged the elder woman, and Lena wrapped her other arm around Dani. They stood embracing for a time until the doors slid open, and Aster wheeled in wearing her pants and a hospital scrub shirt, her wheelchair pushed by Detective Bullocks.

Rong rose and joined them as the group came together.

"Aster!" Lena exclaimed. Aster struggled to her feet and reached a blue-veined hand to her friend's, smiling brightly despite the pain on her face. Solace, Dani thought, could transcend pain.

The woman looked worn, and held onto an IV drip of morphine that fed into her left arm, but smiled nonetheless. "I'll be okay."

"You ready to tell me what happened out there?" the detective asked, and so the women told him, first about the farmhouse and the car, and then about their journey out to the church. When they finished, Bullocks shared what had happened at the sheriff's office.

Aster looked away and Lena bit her lip, a single tear rolling down her cheek. "He was an old friend of the family, was in Glen's Sunday School class and served as a deacon with him," she said of the sheriff. Aster affirmed she and Elden had been on a first-name basis with him as well. They allowed for a moment of silence before the detective spoke again.

"It certainly has weakened us. But I still want to find it. We have to stop it."

"Look how much it's weakened us," Rong said.

"But Court," Dani said. The desperation in her eyes finished the thought for her.

"We don't even know where Court is," Bullocks said.

"He's somewhere in the old church," Dani said.

Lena and Aster nodded. "The *ghula* said as much when it attacked us," Lena said. "It said it would find another way in… to him, and it would get rid of the salt and iron so that we couldn't find the church again."

"Unless we want to find it," Dani said, but if anyone heard her, they did not acknowledge it. Still, as she jutted her hands in her pockets again and began rocking on her feet, as the fingers of her right hand curled around the lone key, a plan was forming.

The sliding doors to the waiting room hissed open again as the doctor entered, a grave countenance on his face. Immediately Aster's eyes filled with tears and Lena put a hand to her mouth.

"Clem Willette did a lot of damage," he said. Not a hint of whimsy in the comment, only forlorn sadness. "Your husbands are stable, but I'm afraid I was right; I *was* afraid their conditions, while certainly appearing miraculous, would be only temporary. I don't know how much longer either has."

He allowed them to process the information in the ensuing silence. Two nursing assistants in pink stood on the other side of the glass doors, looking in like peeping toms.

"Lena, Aster, why don't you go to them?" the doctor said finally, motioning to the aides.

The women nodded and squeezed each other's hands. Lena offered Dani another hug even as the detective patted her shoulder, and then they were gone.

When they had turned the corner, Rong asked, "What about our friends? Blue and Britta?"

The doctor, tight-lipped, looked at each of them in turn before speaking. "They are both still in surgery. Each one caught buckshot in the torso, and it tore up their insides. It's touch and go, right now, but we'll keep you informed." His next words came as he turned to leave, thought better of it, then faced the three again, this time focused on Bullocks. "Detective, make sure these kids get some rest. Leave your numbers at the nurse's station and we'll call you when there is more news."

Bullocks got on the phone as the doctor left, delivering a litany of cop-speak to whoever was on the other end. Dani felt the weight of it all settle on her. She heard "sheriff's office" and "bodies" and "Little Rock." Rong placed an arm around her, guided her to a seat. "Tow trucks. Two. Plus a wrecker… something to scoop up the remains of the pickup."

At this, Dani shot out of her seat and ran up to him. "Detective," she said, "Can you drop me off at my car? I want to pick it up."

"Hold on," he said to the cell, lowered it. Studied her. "I don't think that's wise." His cold, dark eyes squinted. "You ran off last time. You…"

"I'll have Rong with me," she said, and looked at her friend, who nodded. "I want my car. I won't go to the church. You can watch me pull away, or leave a patrol there, whatever you need to do."

He sighed, his broad shoulders heaving up and down. Into the cell he said, "Tow the truck and the Dillons' car. I'm taking the girl to pick hers up. I want a regular patrol on the road."

❦

They were silent on the way out to the farmhouse. The most audible sound was the way the gravel in the drive popped under the tires as Bullocks parked the vehicle. Dani exited the passenger side and saw the driver's side window roll down as she opened the back left door to let Rong out. A cool air greeted her, a soft breeze winding through the yard up from the barn. In the distance, a cow mooed. The roar of a single engine rose from the bypass. A neighbor was burning firewood in the fireplace, from the smell that carried along the zephyr.

"Dani," Bullocks called to her, "I'm going to follow you to the Dillons' house."

She'd expected his distrust. In fact, she was surprised she'd gotten this far. The engine sound changed as he shifted to park.

The night air was thick and wet; a low fog as gray as a shroud crept along the road and hovered over the ditches on either side, snaked past the fence, and obscured the pasture beyond. There was no sound, save for the detective's running engine. Everything felt alien, like he had dropped them off on another world. No birds or squirrels or hoofed things crunching through the dried and dead leaves and grass. Whichever of the herd had mooed had been swallowed up by the night. Gooseflesh ran up her forearms. It wasn't exactly cold, but there was a chill in the air, prickling the fine hairs on the back of her neck and along her arms. A glance at Rong told her they felt something too. She unlocked her car doors, and they climbed inside. When she'd turned the car around and saw the detective's headlights in her rearview, she spoke.

"It's still here."

"I felt eyes on me," Rong said.

As they pulled into the drive, the detective's car stopped behind them in the street. Idling. Waiting. *Fine*, Dani thought. She had every intention of going inside. She lifted a hand in a wave when the key clicked in the lock.

Once inside, she locked the front door. She made a beeline for the Dillons' bedroom, pausing only to flick on the den's ceiling fan light, through the downstairs bath, then pushed open the accordion closet door.

"What are you doing?" Rong asked. Dani fell to her knees, pushed clothes on hangers around. Reshuffled shoes. When she stood, she stared at the cool leather in her hands, feeling the weight and balance. *The blade must be sharp*, her father had said, so many years ago, before he'd taken her guitar from her and set it by the workbench.

"For the agave," she mumbled. "Oh, Papá," she said. Her name for her father and Court's for Glen. Dani stood and turned and showed him what she held: Glen's machete in its leather sheath.

"A single blow," she said.

CHAPTER SIXTY-FOUR

Rong reconnoitered to make sure the detective was indeed gone after a brief wait, and not in fact lying in wait to trap them should they try to leave. His drive next door was empty. His house, dark. The street offered up no evidence of another vehicle. They stepped out onto the Dillons' porch, leaving the lights on inside. Dani handed Rong the house key with the express instruction to return to the house after to preserve the illusion.

Rong accepted the key but didn't move toward the car. When Dani saw this, she faced them. "C'mon. I need you to do this."

Rong looked down to the sheathed machete in her hand. "Why don't we get the detective to go with you? Or let's go back inside—I'll get a gun."

But Dani had seen them back at the farm, when the old redneck was shooting up the place. Rong had been nearly frozen. Aster had to drag them both down the hall. Instead of embarrassing them by reminding them, Dani said, "You said guns wouldn't kill it."

Rong looked down. They were trembling.

"It's okay to be scared, Rong," she said. "I'm not asking you to go. I'm not asking anyone else to put themselves in harm's way. Not you or the detective, who, let's be honest, would find a way to put the kibosh on this whole idea."

"If something happens to you, too, I couldn't live with myself, Dani. I can't lose another friend." Their shoulders were shrugged, and their head lowered. Dani wanted nothing more than to cry with them. Hold them and let it all out for their friends. Chuy. Jada. *Jesus fucking*—she thought, then forced herself to straighten her spine and compose herself. There would be time enough soon, but now was not the time for mourning.

She smiled and reached with her free hand to grasp their shoulder. "And I can't lose Court, and if we do nothing, we lose him. We lose another friend."

Rong seemed to consider this, then nodded. Slowly, they turned for the car, the weight of the keys jingling in the palm of their hand.

As Dani reached the passenger side, she added, holding up the machete, "If anyone asks, tell them I made you do it. I held you at knife point."

They both smiled.

CR&O

She directed them past the road, back to the farm. The shed in the calf lot was unlocked. Rong stood watch in the doorway as Dani pulled the chain for the lone bulb dangling from the rafter, the soft glow of a used, grime-covered 60 watt the only illumination. Unsheathing the machete, she touched the blade. Sharp, serviceable… but could be sharper. The grinder sat at the end of the workbench nearest the shed door. She tried to recall what her father had showed her, so long ago. She hadn't protective goggles or gloves, saw neither hanging around the bench, but there were so many things hanging within reach. Elden had all manner of tools and trinkets. Finally, she found a pair of work gloves and slid them on, the fingers of the gloves cold and stiff with disuse. She checked that the grinder was plugged in, then turned the machine on. The wheel spun, a gritty sound like a tire whose rubber was all used up. Sparks flew when the blade touched the wheel. It came back to her then, how to hold the blade and sharpen it. She heard her father's voice, even smelled his cologne. In this shed, though, his wasn't the only presence, for the building itself belonged to Elden, and the machete to Glen, and as she sharpened this weapon, they were as present as her father, guiding her hands.

After, Dani and Rong cruised the bypass until they had estimated a turnoff nearest the service road, and Rong killed the lights, pulling onto the shoulder to stop only long enough for the passenger side door to open and then close before pulling away again. The bypass was nearly empty of traffic, and Dani watched them pull away as their lights only returned when the vehicle was near highway speed, and she started into the tree line.

CHAPTER SIXTY-FIVE

Bullocks had not, in fact, trusted them, but he hadn't the luxury or the time to babysit, either. As he walked back into the hospital's lobby, he ticked off the facts as he knew them like an accountant taking stock of his ledger: 1) state troopers confiscated the sheriff's office; 2) the bodies of everyone killed at the station and at the farm were in transit to the state crime lab in Little Rock; 3) Dani and Rong were at the Dillon house, safe as… No longer nose-blind to the hospital antiseptic, Bullocks took a big whiff and pushed out the simile, because Clem Willette had shown at the farmhouse that houses weren't safe. The thought of trying to find the churchyard crossed his mind, but it wouldn't be smart to go it alone. The short list of people he could take with him flashed over him when his cell rang, and at first, he thought it was the nurse's station down the hall, probably even the same middle-aged woman who'd acknowledged his arrival, calling. Too fucking lazy to walk a few steps, he thought.

"Bullocks."

"Detective," it was the nightshift switchboard operator. She had this nasal, saccharinely sweet voice, a sound that could cut glass. He'd only worked with her a couple of times since his arrival, but he'd recognize her voice anywhere. "Mr. Hammersmith said there was a commotion out at his farm. Swears one of his calves are missing. You feel like fielding this call?" Her voice trembled and she sounded weary; he knew she was close to the staff and had worked the dispatch a number of years, and he couldn't imagine how she pulled herself away from mourning to come in and do a job like this.

He sighed. There wasn't time for this bullshit, and if it were anyone else but the old farmer, who sat on the town council, who was friends with the sheriff, who'd helped the sheriff back Bullocks' hiring to the rest of the council…

"What patrolmen are on duty?" he asked, catching himself as he'd nearly asked which were left, and when she told him, he said, "Send Curry." *Fat ass needs the exercise anyway.*

Bullocks hung up. None of this was her fault, or Curry's for that matter, so he shouldn't take it out on them. He was so damn frustrated. With himself, mostly. Chased out of Chicago and retreating from Fayetteville, this was his last chance. If he weren't stuck here in this hospital waiting room, he could stop this. There was nowhere else to run. There was only one thing he should be doing.

The cell again. This time it was Curry's direct number.

"Detective," the patrolman said when he answered, "I was on my way out to Hammersmith's when I saw this light-colored sedan you said to be on the lookout for."

Dani, goddamn it. Out loud, he said, "Detain Ms. Morales and I'll come pick her up."

"It's not her," Curry said. "Some Asian kid driving it."

Around him, alarms started to sound. Bullocks stepped into the hall to see a flock of scrubs entering the side-by-side rooms occupied by the two old men. Orders were yelled out, and he saw Lena and

Aster each pushed out into the hallway where they clung to each other.

"Detective, you hear me?" Curry's voice echoed in his ear.

"Jesus," Bullocks said. "Lock the car. Bring the kid to me here at the hospital."

Dani, he thought, pocketing his cell, *What have you done?*

CHAPTER SIXTY-SIX

She used the flashlight app on her cell to guide her, but in the low light and in the deep forest, it only helped her avoid the more obvious underbrush obstacles. The pines and oaks were plentiful and easily seen, but vine-like thorn plants jabbed at her legs, and crawling roots, snaking along the ground, snagged her feet with each step. The fog made things worse. She wouldn't have seen these things without it, but she might have sidestepped a lot of it.

After Rong dropped her off, Dani had entered the tree line, machete in one hand and cell in the other. Walking as straight as possible, she estimated the distance to the access road, then again, the cross-distance into the forest where the churchyard had been the last time. But the only thing to greet her was the mud and clay forest floor that slicked the soles of her shoes, and the vines and thorns and brush of a reticent forest intent on impeding her path.

From her right came a flash of light; she turned to follow it, realizing the forest still had something to say. It appeared again in the distance, accompanied by muffled voices: two men talking. She thought better of calling out. There weren't many, if any, she'd like to alert to her presence, so she pocketed her cell and moved as stealthily as possible until she stood behind an oak, able to see the county road and two tow trucks with the shattered pickup already loaded. A scrawny guy with a mangy beard was pulling chains around the rear tires of Court's car while a heftier guy in overalls secured the fasteners on the bed of the truck.

"I'm telling ya," Mange was saying. "Ol' Clem finally went batshit."

"I don't think he could kill everyone at the sheriff's office with so many people there," Overalls said with a huff, locking down the straps. "Someone would have stopped him."

"I heard he was hopped up on something. I heard he snuck in a pistol and got the guard to open the jail door for him."

"Only thing Ol' Clem's been hopped up on is the hootch," Overalls said, now wiping his plump hands on the denim of his uniform like a giant toddler rubbing his belly.

"Didn't his daddy run moonshine back in the day?"

"So they say."

Mange walked to his truck and activated a lever under the bed, and it rose, lifting the remains of Elden's truck. Overalls meanwhile picked up a piece of the front bumper and threw it on the back of the tow truck. Mange shut the machine off, letting the silence return, but he was looking right at her. Had he seen her? She readied herself to run.

"You hear something?" Mange asked.

Overalls stopped. Ear cocked like he thought he was a collie. "Only the sound of a guy who don't want to work. Get a move on. I got a case of Bud calling my name."

"It's creepy out here," Mange said.

"You been listening to too many hill stories," Overalls said.

"My cousin saw it once," Mange said then. "He was out in the deer woods south of 5 on a night like this and he came across it. Said it was all there, from the tombstones to the old church with the cross hanging like it was about to fall down over the double doors. He said one of the doors was open, and he heard something from the inside, calling his name."

The two men were silent for a moment before Overalls busted up laughing. "Bullshit! Tanner, get your ass in gear," and Mange Tanner tried to offer a laugh in response, like he was kidding, but even Dani could see from where she stood that he was frightened.

As the tow truck started hoisting the car again, Dani took the opportunity to slink away, sure the sound of the motor would drown out her footsteps. She retreated the way she had come. Counted her steps. Tried to remember the last time she had been out here, and when nothing appeared again after she'd walked twice the distance, she stopped and sank to her knees, dropping her machete.

Lena had said the cars anchored the place. The salt and iron had too. But it wasn't enough. It wasn't enough and now Court was gone. Tears began to stream, not out of fear or weakness but out of anger. Her face reddened and she clenched her fists, digging her nails into her palms. The machete lay in front of her on the ground, like an offering, still sheathed. She felt blood in the palms of her hands and kept clenching, letting the tears fall. This fucking thing had Court and it wouldn't let him go and it was afraid. Afraid to face her. It…

"Dani."

She opened her eyes, filmed with the tears of frustration. The voice had carried along a zephyr, through the fog and the trees, and to her right, the fog bank parted. As the fog receded, a tattered, cracked tombstone appeared. Dani could smell a hint of decay in the air, a touch of mold in the dankness. And then another tombstone. Backlit as if a spotlight shone on them, or as if the very fog itself shone with an unnatural light. Wiping her eyes, Dani snatched up the machete and stood, pushing forward as the mist cleared more, and more of the churchyard revealed itself until finally the old church itself began to materialize through the fog. *Once upon a time…* she thought, pressing on, the machete held tight in her grip, believing she was prepared to face the monster and rescue her beloved.

Dani sidestepped around the tombstones. Approached the double doors. Indeed, one hung open, held on by only one hinge, it seemed, as the cross above dangled by a single nail.

"Dani," the voice called again, from inside the old church. The steps were wooden and cracked, and beyond the threshold smelled of things festering and damp and musty. She drew the machete from its sheath and dropped the leather casing on the ground.

"You'll get it when you come back out," she whispered to herself. Then up the steps—one foot then another—and between the two doors.

Inside the portico, light streamed in through the windows: nothing artificial, but as though the fog outside had luminescence and now shined into the great building in moonlit shafts. Through the broken windows, where the fog could penetrate, small, bright clouds seemed to gather, and though the shadows hung heavily still in the abandoned building, the light coming in was enough for her to see.

Inside looked much like an old church might, with two rows of pews and a wooden pulpit up front, raised on a dais, a small tabernacle in front. Of course, everything in here was rotten and dust-covered from years of neglect.

From the portico she entered the sanctuary proper, and from the narthex, she could see the whole room. Windows, mostly busted out or boarded up, lined the walls along the side aisles. She began down the nave. One step. One more. Up the risers to the chancel. Palms sweaty. Blade impossibly heavy. There was a door behind the choir seats, but she found it locked, and holding firm. Hoping she'd overlooked something, she turned to face the sanctuary and saw the shadow of a man sitting three rows back.

She jumped.

The man rose, walked to the nave. Faced her.

"Glen?" she said, a quick smile flashing across her lips before she remembered he should be in the hospital. She leapt off the dais steps only for him to vanish, and this only compounded her fear. She glanced around desperately, realizing that real people don't vanish. *Not real*, she corrected herself. *Living*.

Her heart sank. Interminable sadness swelled within her. The thought of saving Court, of succeeding, seemed so desperately impossible. Perhaps this vision meant Elden was gone also, and she looked up, wondering if he'd appear next. But it was Glen, again, who stepped out of the shadows by the wall between the side aisle and the chancery. Appearing solid and decidedly un-ghostly, he curled a finger soundlessly, and when she approached, he vanished again. She ran her hands along the wall, the paneled wainscoting, worn in many places, which stretched around the perimeter of the room.

"It's a wall," she said, and brushed her fingers along the wainscoting as she looked around the sanctuary again. When her fingers found a brass handle, she realized what stood here only was made to look like the wall. It was in fact a door.

And it opened.

On the other side, a hall, and off it several more doors, leading to what might have been dusty classrooms or offices adorned with cobwebs. The first door on her left revealed a small room with a couple of schoolhouse desks, one overturned. She didn't bother with the others when she saw Glen appear at the end of the hall in front of the last door. Pulling it open revealed only a closet, until she saw the stairs leading down underneath the building.

No light reached down there. From her pocket she pulled her cell and turned on the flashlight again. "Down we go," she said, and took a deep breath.

The rickety, termite-rotten stairs creaked under her weight as she descended the passage, her hand tracing along the stained and spongy whitewashed drywall as a guide. She stepped into an earthen cellar underneath the church. As she shone the light, she saw the room wasn't very big, and great stone blocks served as the building's foundation; these were cracked and chipped and seemed as tenuous as the rest of the building. Glen stood off to one side, near a deep shadow, a frown on his furrowed brow. As she approached, the shadow resolved itself into a hole large enough for her to duck into. Her light revealed a tunnel, angling down into the earth at a shallow slope. The smell was stronger here, mixed with root rot and decaying things long since buried, the sweet and sickly and syrupy cluster known as death.

The vision of Glen smiled at her in his pleasant way, with the crow's feet around the eyes crinkling up and the upturned corners of the mouth, and then he vanished into the shadows, and Dani was alone. Down the tunnel, she saw no end to the blackness, and a cool hollow wind blew up from underneath, carrying with it the scent of the deeply interred who had not quite returned to the earth. Shining the light from her cell and gripping the machete tight, and with another deep breath, she began her descent.

CHAPTER SIXTY-SEVEN

When Court first heard his name called, he looked up, and through the dimness of the chamber of bone, he saw his grandfather. Elden Oscar stood ten feet away, his mouth opening and closing soundlessly as if he were speaking with a mute button on or trying to breathe. Court reached out to him, but the old man shook his head. Court, who'd been sitting with his knees bent and supporting his forearms, worked against numerous aches, empowering himself with curses and groans under his breath, to stand. This was a vision. A ghost. *Dear God*, he thought mournfully at that realization, his heart aching so tangibly the pain rose in his chest. He knew he could not do this without his grandfathers. The old man turned his back, shoved his hands in his pockets, hunched his shoulders and paced, looking down at the stone floor. As he walked, the sound of his footsteps increased, until Court could hear him clear his throat.

"You taste blood, son? It's my fault."

"Papaw," Court said. He limped over to him. He put his hands on either bony shoulder and squeezed. "Papaw, nothing is your fault. If anything, I owe you."

The old man shrugged his shoulders out of his grandson's reach, chuckled, and stepped away. "What do you owe me, Court? I tried to keep you safe. I love you, boy. You may not know it, but I do."

"I do know it," Court said, "because you don't say that word a lot. You don't say a lot, but you show it. In your actions."

"Taste the blood," Elden said. His voice, with those three words, sounded like a record scratch, and there came a kind of baying. A sound like screaming, but not from human lungs.

"What?" Court asked.

"Hard work," Elden said. "A man's sweat and blood at the end of the day."

"Where's Papa?" Court asked. Around him the chamber of bones shimmered, as if it had been coated with shellac. Something was wrong here. Court could feel it, but he couldn't put his finger on it.

"Showing her the way. So, you can both defeat it. You know, I always told you money makes the world go 'round."

"'What's the number one thing?' you used to ask me," Court said, and held up his index finger.

"Well, you get it by hard work."

Court blinked. He couldn't breathe; copper and salt and thick offal choked him. He was no longer standing, but on his back, the hard stone floor pressing against his spine. The thing hovered over him, its weight like a lodestone and crushing the air out of his lungs, one hand pinning down his chest, the other shoving chewy viscera into his mouth. He gagged.

"You can't forget the stories, Court. They's as important as how hard you work." Elden stood behind the thing, leaning over it. There was no indication in his gaze or his words that he saw Court's predicament.

Court thrashed helplessly on his back. The creature shifted to sit on his chest, using both hands to force the chunks of the bloodied meat down his throat. "Help me, Papaw!" he cried, choking up as much as he could, scrambling for breath. He tried to spit it out, tried to wretch it up, but there was a small part of him that he would never admit to anyone ever that was just so hungry, and he craved the juices and tender tearable sinewy raw muscle shredding between his teeth.

The old man spat. "I'm trying to, boy. Sometimes the hard choice means doing something you don't want to do. But it still has to be done."

"Pap—!" but more handfuls of the thick and chewy mass in his mouth, the foul juice sloshing down his chin. The taste of blood.

Elden said, "No, son. It's not *like* blood. It *is* blood. Now, you remember what I said." He vanished into the chamber walls.

An animal screamed, but Court's was louder, and blended with it, and the two sounds melted together. "Don't go," Court wept. More raw meat, and the scream of the animal faded to its own silent plea. It was merely a tease, Court realized. Seeing his grandfather like that. Just a reminder that he was alone and probably going to die.

Red gore caked everything he saw, and sank into his eyes, and poured slowly like syrup down his throat, and he kicked and thrashed and sat up, even as the *ghula* leapt back. He raked at his eyes, his face, his mouth. Spat. In the dim light he saw his hands covered in the dark, crimson liquid, heavy with weight like ink. At once he heaved, then vomited at his side, again and again, his eyes watering. Only then, when he had nothing left inside, did he draw his gaze toward the baying, whimpering animal at his feet. A calf lay on its side, breathing hard. A back leg twitched spasmodically. Its tongue lolled out of its mouth, its upturned eye focusing on Court. Pleading in its own way, and Court felt terrible for feasting so readily and wished he had the power to save it. A patch of fur had been ripped away and a substantial hole chewed in its side. The animal didn't have long to live.

His eyes jumped back to the creature. The thing met his gaze with its yellow eyes. Court pushed himself up off the floor and found purchase with bent knees, so it appeared he crouched or knelt as though to spring at the monster if only he had the strength to spring. His mouth hung open and he breathed hard, but he matched its defiant stare and quoted, "and what I want to know is how do you like your blue-eyed boy/Mister Death?"

It also crouched, but its coiled and spring-ready posture looked strong and eager to meet the challenge, and it clicked its claws on the stone floor like a battle-ready snare beat.

"Qissa," it demanded, showing its teeth.

Sometimes the hard choice means doing something you don't want to do. "No," Court said. "No Qissa. No story. You can take the rest of the calf."

"Qissa!" it shouted, slapping the stone with a flat, empty sound that failed to echo.

"No!" Court barked.

It slapped him, hard, slashing its claws across his other cheek, mirroring the still-bloody marks it had tattooed earlier, and again the back of Court's head thudded on the hard floor of the chamber. But instead of stars he saw images, Polaroid snapshots from his life. Times he'd spent with his grandfathers. Catching worms or crickets for fishing. The detritus and offscouring debris that gathered in the water gate over the creek that ran through the farm. Splitting logs. Hauling hay. The smile on Papa's lips as they launched the canoe, sledding in the winter, Christmas gatherings around a tree, Thanksgivings at the dinner table.

The time he and Elden had gone to sheetrock the back-deck ceiling of a rental house; Elden had driven while Court stared dreamily out of the passenger window, until they arrived at the property and found the driveway empty. No sign of the guy, down on his luck, who'd agreed to help, who had been working as a painter and general laborer on the property for a few weeks now.

Elden and Court had exited the truck, perplexed, then walked around the side of the house to find the back patio stacked with several layers of sheetrock, but the tools Elden had left in a nice toolbox next to a red-brick column were gone.

"He took them," Court said.

Elden had jutted his hands in the pockets of his overalls and stared out to nothing, beyond the raised clothesline hung in the back yard.

"Maybe."

Court clenched his fists and spat. "Maybe? Fucking *maybe*? Call the police, Papaw!"

"And what did your Papaw say?" the *ghula* asked.

The chamber of bones shimmered behind the skull of the thing crouching over him. He could feel its cold, stiff femur, its coarse goose-hair and gray, fatty flesh as it crouched over him.

"He said maybe the fella needed the tools more than we did."

"He was weak," the thing hissed.

"No," Court said. "He did the right thing. Not the easy thing."

"And what is the easy thing?" it asked.

"Giving up," Court said. Had he just done the same thing, then? Telling a story when he'd been so adamant against doing so. He told himself he had been tricked into it. The creature had cast some sort of spell, but that wasn't true. He saw now, laying here on the stone floor, what the hard thing was. What he was supposed to do even though he didn't want to.

The *ghula* leaned in and smiled, the worst thing he'd ever seen.

CHAPTER SIXTY-EIGHT

Glen's stiff fingers did not return the grip of Lena's fingers. This is how death would come: taking the strength, then, slowly, the breath would carry the life out of Glen's body until there was nothing left but memories and the moments the various photographs over the years had captured. She held on tightly, her head sunk in supplication, eyes closed. But then Aster called out, though Lena, in the fugue state caused by grief, heard no alarm.

The cold, clay-like hand which she held suddenly flexed, and the fingers curled around hers; when Lena, who'd been deep in prayer with a God she'd thought she'd known most of her life, realized what was happening, she looked up into Glen's smiling face.

Tears came instantly. There was more time after all—her real prayer, what was hinted at under the whispers for strength to accept the loss and God's will—she could have her husband back and have it not end like... this.

"You came back," she said, as somewhere back in her mind she realized that Aster's cry suggested Elden was back also.

"I get a little more time with you," Glen said.

They held hands for what felt like a long time, staring at each other, smiling at each other, until Glen let go to push himself up in bed.

Rong rushed in then. "Mr. Oscar's awake," they said.

Lena smiled. "Wonderful. Where's Dani and the detective? Do they…?" but she stopped when she saw Rong's face. Something had flickered across their eyes: worry or fear. "What is it?" she asked.

"They're gone," Rong said. "They went to find Court and stop the ghoul."

Glen struggled to sit up. Lena tried to steady him. "No," he said defiantly. "No. The damn fools. Get themselves killed."

"Rest," Lena tried, but as Glen struggled, as the alarms started going off as he pulled out the IV and yanked off the leads for the heart monitor, as the doctor and two nurses rushed in, Glen was adamant.

"It ain't there…We got to finish it, Lena. We do. We need to be there to get Court."

"No," Lena said. "I was hard on that girl. Part because, well, I'm not proud to admit that part." She dropped her eyes, but he quit struggling. Sitting up, he was in a position to look down on her, but she saw in his eyes what she'd always seen. Love, patience, consideration. "But also, because you and I both know what that thing has done to Court's previous relationships."

He squeezed her hands. "That's why it has to be us." His voice, his eyes, pleading, but Lena shook her head.

"No. She is different. Our time has passed. This is her fight now. If there is any hope of saving our grandson, it lies with her. I realize this now. This is her fight."

The doctor said Glen's name to get his attention and the fight left him. He slumped his shoulders and sat back, and the nurses returned the IV and replaced the leads, calming the machines. He did not release Lena's hands, however. Glen looked at her, offering the thinnest and weakest of smiles. The worry had not left him. She could see it in his eyes. Worry plagued her too, but it was truly out of their hands now, so all they could do was wait. Hold hands and wait.

CHAPTER SIXTY-NINE

Dani raised her hand to a thick root blocking the path. A tangle of thinner roots also curtained down. So little light existed here that it appeared the passage ended in a dead end, and if not for the air seeping through, the noxious breeze slipping between the strands of root, she would have believed she reached the end. But she could feel it. Not strong, certainly, but there. Just enough to hint that the passage went on.

Clutching the handle of the machete, she stepped back to a little more than arm's length and swung the blade. The tangle of thinner roots fell, and the blade made it through the thicker about halfway before getting stuck. She needed both hands to rip it free. Still, its inability to cut wasn't due to its sharpness but more her strength. So still holding onto the handle with both hands, she adjusted her stance and swung again. The great root fell, and the passage opened up in front of her. Dani stepped into the flicker of torchlight that illuminated the bone-covered walls.

Moisture caught in her throat, tasting ferric; the whole room was slick with dew, which only seemed to enhance the sugary smell of decay. Court lay in the center of the room, blood splattered over his face, his clothes. And more than that. A pile of entrails, thick chunks of meat and gristle and near him, the source: a calf, dead now, laying in a pool of blood which still flowed out of the cavernous hole in its side.

She rushed to Court, kneeling. Her fingers pressed against the vein in his neck, and she found a pulse. She wiped away the blood in his eyes and parted his lips after setting her blade down. There was breath but it was shallow. Great lacerations in various degrees of healing marked his cheeks. His eyes opened, blinked stupidly in the low light. His mouth worked soundlessly.

"I'm here," she said.

Instinctively he ran the tip of his tongue over his lips. "Trick. Dream."

"I'm not a dream," she answered. "I'm here." *Dreams*, she thought, don't smell. Not like blood and rot and piss and shit, all of which she detected now, nearly recoiling. She would never tell him, if they made it out, in just what state she'd found him.

"We heard you," he said then.

She cocked her head. The one word caught her—we. She looked up and around, then back to him. He was more alert now, his eyes wider, and what she saw in them was fear. The torchlight didn't reach through all the shadows, and somewhere in the dark, she heard the clicking of nails on the bone-covered walls and heavy, heavy breathing. Almost like a growl.

She said, "We have to get you out of here."

She pulled at him, and to his credit, he tried to stand, but he was slow to rise and acted more like dead weight. She pulled a little too hard and he cried out in pain. He clutched his ribs, but even underneath all the calf's blood, she saw the extent of his injuries. Her arms hooked under his, she hoisted and grunted, cursing silently his inability to assist.

"Go," he tried, using what sounded like all his breath for the one word.

"I'm not leaving you," she said.

"Dani," Court said, breathless. The word sparked something in him; she was here with him, *for* him. His muscles began to work. To help. Under his own power, he was able to help her help him stand. The pain worked itself into knots on his face, the only sounds he could produce the grunts and sighs and near-screams of pain, but he was able to assist.

Once up, she supported him, letting him lean on her with her arm around him. His head lolled and his eyes closed, and he nearly sunk off her shoulder, but she slapped him in the face just hard enough to get his attention and shouted his name.

"Can you move?" she said, nearly yelling.

His eyes opened wider, and he tried for a nod, then took a step. It would be slow going, but she was sure they could make it.

The ghoul emerged from the shadows, effluvial rot on its breath. Its legs bent and it hunched, lowering its bald head so its yellow-slitted eyes glared, its great maw wide, showcasing razor-sharp teeth. Limbs long and lanky—but strong—the whole of its form a sickly gray like boiled meat. Even its claws were gray, save for the tips, stained red. *Its claws*. In its claws it held the machete, with one hand cradling the handle and the other gently caressing the blade.

"So, you know rules," it said, not looking at her, but consumed with the blade. Could the thing smile, and was it doing so now? It was toying with her. Challenging her.

"One strike," she said, repeating what Glen had told the all just hours earlier. "I get one strike to separate your head from your body."

"He brings me qissa." It looked up at her then, meeting her eyes with a challenge she could feel. She was taking him from it, and it was ready to fight.

"He's mine," Dani said. She wanted the courage to sound in her voice, though she wasn't sure it was there or, if it were, that it peeled out of her throat effectively. She ushered Court sideways to a section of bone wall and propped him against it, never taking her eyes off the creature. Sure, he wouldn't fall over, she stepped towards it.

"Then you must strike," it said, and tossed the machete toward her, and then it leapt.

Dani managed to grab the handle out of the air, but as she did, she saw the monster in the air also, claws out, angling down on her, its mouth wide with sharp canines that dripped with slavering hunger. She lunged back as it landed and swung the blade in a full arc, connecting with the neck just above the shoulder, her arm as stout as soft rubber as the blade sunk in, not unlike when she hit the root, and saw the creature fall backward. She released the machete's handle and rushed to where Court leaned.

Her arms around him, she knew every time she touched him screamed in pain. He stiffened or reflexively pulled away as he sucked air through his teeth, but he held on. It took her a minute to find the tunnel. Finally, in a deep shadow, she saw the remains of the root system she'd cut through to reach him. It was in the distance and easily lost. No wonder Court couldn't find a way out. They moved together, as quickly as possible, Court limping along but seemingly growing stronger, as if the will to live had returned and now powered him beyond and through the pain. Of the creature, if the blade had severed the neck from the body or if she'd merely wounded it, she wasn't sure. She only hoped they had time to leave.

"Qissa." They stopped and turned, the ghoul already on its feet, a snarl on its lips. The blade swayed, dug deep into its neck, hanging down toward its chest.

The ghoul limped towards them, clearly in pain, lifting one claw to the wound as though trying to hold itself together. "Qissa," it mumbled. "Hungry. Food will fix. Qissa. Hung… Food will fi…" It stumbled. Fell face-first. Still. Quiet.

Dani helped Court hobble towards the opening. "Come on," she urged. He was weak and shuffling, but they were closer now.

A sickly gray hand reached up. It rubbed its injury and when it pulled its claw away (perhaps it was a trick of the light, though Dani didn't think so), its wound seemed to be healing around the blade. The gash was shallower; the blood had stopped. It flexed both sets of claws, its knuckles cracking and echoing through the chamber. The creature bared its teeth.

And then it charged.

From behind them, a gunshot rang out. The sound echoed throughout the chamber deafeningly. The ghoul's shoulder exploded, bits of grayish flesh splattering into the darkness. Dani and Court whipped around to see Detective Bullocks rushing toward them, but a growl alerted them all back toward the monster. Having rocked backward, it stood nearly erect, its neck's wound a healed scar, and tossed the blade at her feet. It flexed its knuckles, great crackling sounds Dani felt in her own joints. Its eyes, shining yellow orbs without definition, like blind headlights illuminating everything in front. Its teeth, long and jagged arrowheads, dripping with pink. A forked tongue flicking out mindlessly, tasting the air, hunting for their scent.

"I am un-Ghula! I bring death! I *eat* death."

The threat was a horrific proclamation, but it had lost all meaning with Dani. For Court, in bracing himself, reached absently for her waist, her stomach, reminding her what she had brought along. Not only the machete.

"Jesus," Bullocks muttered, rushing to their side, taking Court under one arm to help, nearly dropping him when Dani stepped forward and relinquished her hold, bending to pick up the machete.

"Eater of death," she called out. "We're supposed to fear you? You are nothing but a scavenger. You don't stop death. You don't erase life. You are *nothing*."

The ghoul's shape morphed in the dim reflection of the bone walls and torchlight. Its gray hide tanned, spotted fur sprouted, and its nose blackened. Though it didn't share the ears of a hyena, it bellowed out the beast's maniacal laugh, its claws raking across the bone floor, its jaws unhinged and wide. It pushed off with its hind legs and leapt at her again.

Dani swung, burying the blade deeper in the creature's neck, dark, sweet blood fountaining out of the wound. The blow knocked her back off her feet, and she released her grip on the handle, but she recovered quickly, bracing herself for its counter-lunge. The ghoul had fallen to the ground in front of her, howling and yelping, scrabbling for the weapon. *Not good enough*, Dani realized. Its hide was tougher than she imagined. Squatting, her thighs burning, she braced herself. The claws raked at the air, and it turned its face to Court, its visage caught between a hyena and the monster it was. "Help…" it muttered, reaching for him.

Dani took the moment. Lunged for the blade. But as her fingers curled around the handle, there came a low growl and the creature's balled fist smashed against her cheek, pitching her backwards. Her skull slapped against the chamber wall. Instantly numb, the world swimming around her, sounds muted. Her name, screamed by Court, drawn out as if heard underwater. Her wobbling vision was slowly consumed by a tunnel of black, as in front of her the thing stood, still trying to remove the blade. The last thing she saw was Court and the detective, rushing into view before she slumped down, eyes closed.

INTERLUDE ELEVEN

The Tale of the Lonely Patient

Once upon a time, there was a patient who was in the hospital and he had to stay many days to resolve his medical condition. He spent the days reading the paper or reading his Bible, staying confined mostly to his room.

He wore green-patterned pajamas, and a thin robe and matching slippers when he ventured down the hall, when the nurses came to see him, even when the doctor visited. The robe he wore because his mother had given it to him, and he wore the other things because he was told they matched the robe. One day, a nurse of about fifty, plump, with auburn curls and deep gray eyes, walked into his room and patted his thigh. He jumped a little at the intimate touch, and to this she only smiled something like a mother doting over her kid.

"You single, ain't ya?"

"Yes ma'am." She'd removed her hand, a good sign. Still, he couldn't imagine where this conversation was heading.

"You doing good, walking and all?"

"Yes ma'am."

She nodded, pleased with herself.

"I don't mean to be impolite, but what's with all the questions?"

She took his left hand in both her own and squeezed and shifted her position on the bed, so the mattress jostled under her weight, and she said:

"I want you to meet someone. Now hush hush, listen. If you feel strong enough, make your way down to the cafeteria tomorrow about six. I'll introduce you."

The patient smiled and waved his hand. "I'm okay."

The next day, the nurse returned and helped him out of the bed, and he followed her, hand in hand, up to the commissary on the next floor, where a gaggle of young women in nurse's uniforms laughed at a table, some private joke isolated from the rest of the world. Between them there were cups of coffee and cake and pie, and some discarded dishes of real food and half-eaten salads.

The older nurse said to the group: "This is Glen."

And though all the nurses turned, he noticed one in particular, and her fair skin and dark hair and blue eyes.

"Hi," Glen said.

"Hi," the nurse said. She was dating someone and not looking, and besides, Glen was older than her by a few years, she could tell—but there was something in the way he wore the pajamas and robe, tacky as they were. She smiled.

❦

In those first few weeks, she wasn't sure why she kept seeing him. She had a fella who worked hard selling insurance, though she wasn't serious about him. With Glen she wasn't serious either, but he intrigued her, and he was a loquacious sort. She felt butterflies when she knew she was going to see him, not with the other guy. When Glen came around, she found herself laughing more at things he said, smiling more.

Then one day he took her to meet his family. He was the oldest of four children, and both his parents were there, and she was so nervous. As they pulled into his parents' drive, she shivered. The front screen door was closed, but the inner door was open. His two younger sisters played out in the yard. They laughed and giggled and chased each other, their youth infectious.

He stepped out and called, "Where's Bobby Carl?" and she knew, from his stories, this was the name of his brother, the youngest child.

Laughing and smiling and lost in their own revelry, both pointed inside.

"Come on," he said, holding her hand, but when she hesitated, he quit pulling and turned. He had dark hair, like hers, but with a widow's peak, and a full face and bright, sparkling blue eyes that shined even more when he offered up his crooked smile. "It's okay. They'll love you."

She knew right then what he meant was he loved her, and she never felt so secure.

The End

CHAPTER SEVENTY

Soft mud in hair, dampening the back of her shirt, her jeans. Light behind dark lids gave a pink hue. Voices fading in.

Court: "How's your hand?"

Bullocks: "I'll live. What you did, it probably saved lives."

"No," Court said. "She's the hero. I... I failed us all."

"She's waking up," Bullocks said.

Dani opened her eyes. The world came into focus. They were outside. Through the treetops above, she saw blue sky and could feel the sun's warmth and the crisp dawn air. She couldn't see the birds, but she could hear them. It had been so long since she'd heard the chirping, since anyone in this town must have heard it, the sound was alien at first. She blinked a few times and looked around; she saw no tombstones, no old church.

"Where," she started, but God, her head hurt. Her temples throbbed and there was a sharp pain at the base of her skull. Still, she was moving.

"Vanished," Court said.

Her vision cleared more, and she looked at him, kneeling in front of her. "The ghoul?"

"Dead," Court said. "You'd started to black out, but while it was on the detective you got to the machete and... finished the job."

"What?" she asked. Her head was fuzzy; words sounded alien. What did he mean she finished the job?

"It didn't take much," he explained as the detective helped her to her feet, and she in turn supported Court by putting an arm under his shoulder as he leaned on a tree nearby. "The machete had already done most of the work." Dani's shoulder, the one responsible for driving the blade, was so sore she didn't think she could lift it above her head. A steady throbbing soreness pulsated up that arm and down her torso, rippling across her body.

The detective stalked off through the trees, not looking back.

"I was afraid I'd never see you again," Dani said. There was so much to tell him. She wondered where and when to start.

"Me too." Court chanced weight on his left leg. Winced.

The walk to the road seemed shorter in the light, even though both could only limp along. When they arrived, Bullocks was already off his phone, waiting for an ambulance.

Court and Dani held each other, leaning against the detective's car, staring back at the tree line. Passing between them in the silence were all the things they would eventually say, and all the things that had happened, and even the answers to the questions Dani had considered but not fully asked either Court or herself. Like did she really save them? What happened down there? Dani's head throbbed. She was sure a healthy bruise was knotting the back of her scalp, but they stood in silence, in the moment, just relishing that they again were together.

CHAPTER SEVENTY-ONE

Sometime later, a tall, lanky World War Two vet dressed in overalls and a ball cap, accompanied by a shorter, broader Korean Conflict vet and a twenty-year-old non-binary Chinese college student walked into Dean Garson's office in the concrete encapsulated walls of Kimpel Hall at the University of Arkansas. They had a request. They entered the office despite the secretary's attempt to keep them out. The dean, at his desk, hovered over papers, the row of bookshelves lining the wall from floor to ceiling serving as his backdrop, barely looked up as the three entered, though he showed his dissatisfaction with the interruption immediately with the sourest of expressions and a huff of annoyance. How they had come to their knowledge, the dean couldn't know, but they were all aware of his hypocrisy. They didn't seem to focus on his interactions with the young male grad student, but they were more concerned with how this might affect his wife and how it had affected his engagement with his staff.

"How goddamn dare you!" the dean had tried to protest.

"We're not one to judge," Rong said. "You love who you want, but we don't think your wife would like the attention you're paying to your grad student. Brad's his name, right?"

"If you think you can waltz in here and blackmail me…"

"Love who you want," Glen interrupted. "Like your faculty can love who they want, right?"

Dean Garson was seething. His cheeks were flushed and there was hate in his eyes. He stood over the desk, stiff-arming his weight over it, but none of the three were impressed. The impetuousness of these three riled him and he wanted to ask who they thought they were, but with this last statement by the shorter vet, Garson knew at least who'd sent them.

"So that's your angle? Fighting Professor Dillon's battles."

"Faculty senate probably won't look kindly on a dean or a tenure-track professor sleeping with a student," Glen said, "but at least Dani isn't a current student of Court's. Now, the three of us," and he pointed to himself, Rong, and Elden, "are going to Dani and Court's wedding. What'll happen to your marriage and your position if it comes out you're engaged with a student currently under your instruction?"

The dean waved his hand to end the thought; they allowed him the pause and watched him take several deep breaths, then straighten himself, and then his tie. He looked from one to each of them, huffing short bursts, his nostrils flaring.

"I don't think the faculty senate needs to know about any of this," he said finally.

Elden smiled. "We'll send Court your regards," he said with a grin and a wink, and waved at the man as the three filed out.

☙❧

The Aveo pulled up to Rong's apartment, and they got out but didn't walk away. It was nice to look up and see blue skies. Though their time the previous fall in Rapps Barren was relatively short (only a few days, looking back on the whole ordeal), the smothering clouds had seemed to last forever. They'd ridden back with the windows rolled down, this early January afternoon with warmer-than-average weather. Still, there was a little bite in the air, and Rong shivered on the sidewalk.

"I've always had a fear about the South," Rong said. "You hear stories as a minority, and I think a lot of them are true. But I'm glad to have met you guys. Court talked about you a lot. He's lucky."

Through the passenger side window, Elden extended a hand. "You're a good kid. Court and Dani are lucky to have you as a friend."

"Take care," Glen said.

Rong knew then this might be one of the last times they'd see them. In fact, it would prove true. Rong would see them once more at the wedding, but they wouldn't get a chance to speak. Only nod from across the room.

Glen rolled up the windows and pulled away, Elden taking one more opportunity to wave out the window. Rong stood in the warmer afternoon on the sidewalk outside their apartment and watched the Aveo drive down the block, turn unceremoniously around a corner, and like that, the two old men were gone.

CHAPTER SEVENTY-TWO

The apartment was cold because it was a loft and had no central HVAC, only wall-mounted units like she'd seen in hotels, so it did little to knock at the cold that seeped in from the outside this February morning. The wall unit in the living room sounded like it was running at full blast. She rose to find Court had already left for work, a rose in a vase on the table, with a note saying, "Just because." Buzzing from the seating area drew her to her cell phone on the coffee table, where she'd left it sometime the day before. She saw it was one of her bandmates.

"You love this band," the drummer said.

"I love playing and I love teaching," she said. She was on track with her schoolwork. She hoped the baby's arrival would coincide with summer, so she wouldn't have to miss her last semester before earning her MA. The head of the music department had offered her a teaching position contingent on her completion.

"Well, I don't guess I could see you rocking a mic or a guitar right now."

"How about this: one more gig, once I pop this kid out, like a final sendoff."

"Sounds good," she said, though she knew this would never happen. It sounded nice to offer up some kind of closure.

She hung up and poured herself some orange juice, then sat at the kitchen table thumbing through the pictures of her and the band, the pictures she'd posted on Instagram spotlighting moments during their performances. There had never been an illusion, as far as Dani was concerned, that they'd ever make it big. Maybe the others thought so. Maybe with a different singer, they would. For her it was a release, a means to pay the bills while in school. The band didn't get in the way of her studies. It was a fun, novel way to use her talents, and it allowed her to blow off steam in the process. So, she felt sad to say goodbye to it, but she never once had the feeling she was missing out. She had no regrets at this point in her life, and she was happy with her decisions. Court made her happy. This life made her happy.

What she missed was the damn coffee.

CHAPTER SEVENTY-THREE

The table was small, occupied by Rong and Blue. Blue's right arm had long since healed, as had the marks on Court's face. She sipped her beer and Rong sipped water, and Court, though he'd never tell Dani, sipped a pint of beer with a healthy head. At the table were two untouched glasses: one held a mixed drink as Jada would have taken it and the other one of Chuy's go-to cocktails. The food came, but no one touched anything. This was the first time since the wedding they'd gotten together.

"Ceremony was nice," Blue said.

"Thank you," Court said.

"How's Dani?" she asked.

"Good. Taking it easy. She's ready to pop." He took another sip of beer. "Thank you both for coming today."

"Of course," Rong said.

They talked for a while. Rong had gotten word they were accepted into an engineering research project at the University of Michigan to begin the following fall, a graduate program with a decent stipend. Blue had plans to go out west once she'd finished going through her aunt's things. The funeral had been another horrific event to fill out the past few months. The cancer had taken Blue's aunt not long after the group had returned from Rapps Barren. Court didn't blame them for leaving. Maybe with time, each of them could work through or repress everything they'd seen.

"How are your grandfathers?" Rong asked. Outside, the overcast sky threatened snow, something northwest Arkansas hadn't experienced to any real degree in a decade.

"They are so sweet," Blue said.

Court shook his head. "Not doing well. We don't think it'll be long now."

"How's your friend Britta?" Blue asked.

Court shrugged. "She has her kids. TJ's funeral was rough. I feel like we've all had too much tragedy lately. But she's healing and getting stronger every day. She still visits with my grandparents."

He finished his beer, ordered another, savoring the taste of both, for when he returned home, he knew he'd have to abstain again. Dani had told him he could still drink, but since he'd learned she was carrying his child, he hadn't wanted to. So, the promise he made to her was as much for him as it was for her: he wouldn't drink anymore. The painkillers prescribed as the scars healed on his face helped numb him in place of the alcohol; these he moderated, fearing another addiction. But then Blue called, not long after her aunt's funeral, after they'd had the wedding and had returned from the honeymoon, and Dani had wanted to go, but she was so sick. All this and the spring thaw was knocking on their doorstep, and while it had only been a few months since TJ and Jada's deaths and the events in Rapps Barren, it was already feeling like a lifetime ago. The invitation was there for him to imbibe again, but as he did so, and as he savored the taste, the subtle flavors of the local craft beer, the specialty hops, the hint of gold and something citrusy, it couldn't get its grip on him, and he knew this would be the last beer he'd ever have.

When he returned home that evening, he held his wife as they looked through the house listings their realtor had emailed to them, as a late season snow blew in, delaying the thaw a little longer.

CHAPTER SEVENTY-FOUR

Court's office in Kimpel was hot those the dog days of summer. He had come in to get some work done while Dani stayed at home with the infant on the promise he'd watch their son later so she could get some work done also. Court was sipping coffee he'd gotten from the campus Starbucks across the road, when the knock at his door came.

"Jesus, it's hot," Rong said, showing themself in. "And you're drinking coffee."

Court motioned to his computer. "New syllabus. I'm teaching a new Craft of Poetry this semester and I finally got the text in."

Rong helped themself to a bottle of water from the micro fridge in the corner of the room and plopped down in the spare chair on the student side of the desk.

"How are you?" This seemed like a weighted question, and Court took some time to answer. Absently he reached up to his face. The scars had long since healed, but some days, Court realized, he could still feel them. It was about time for another trip back to Rapps Barren.

"Fine. Absorbing it all. The good and the bad. Hits all at once, you know."

Rong nodded. "How's Dani, the baby? I was hoping to come see you guys before I leave town…"

"Yeah, the big move. UM and the big project. Nervous?"

"Kind of," Rong said with a shrug.

Court smiled. "They're good. She's at home with him now. We've got his nursery finished."

"I like your new house," Rong said.

"I do too," Court said, then sipped his coffee.

"Can I ask you something?" Rong said after a moment of silence. "About your grandfathers?"

Court nodded.

"I asked them, as we were all driving over to confront the dean, how they knew. They didn't answer me. Did they ever say anything to you?"

Court downed the last of the coffee and considered the cup, turning it around in his hands. "After the ghoul touched them," he said, his eyes never looking away from the Styrofoam container, "and they were slipping again, both admitted to a kind of awareness. Like before, as they were going there, to the other side, they were numb to it, but this time around, they weren't. They could feel everything, could feel themselves slipping away."

"This is what they told you?" Rong asked.

Court shook his head. "No, more like I was there, listening in, but the conversation was between them, for my benefit. But they were in agreement."

"Did you ask them about seeing them below the church?"

Court nodded. "They both knew that they had to do something, make those last few moments count. They didn't have the words for it, but what they described sounded like out-of-body experiences.

Papa knew he was guiding Dani down through the church as Papaw knew he was talking me through…"

Court tightened his lips until they were white. Dani had told Rong what she had seen down there, and given the blood and the dead calf, Rong could only guess what Court had experienced, though Court refused to talk about it now.

"But how did they know about the dean?" Rong asked again after a minute, hoping to pull Court away from those memories.

"Best we can figure, in those moments so near death, they were made aware of information, and whatever powers that be allowing them to come back, let them bring their knowledge with them so as to do one more thing. For me. They always did for me."

He was sure Rong could see the tears in his eyes. "They never asked for anything in return, and they always did for me."

Rong stood and tossed their plastic bottle into the small recycling bin by Court's desk. Court's window provided a good view of the green lawn, and they watched them for a moment. A few students passed by: a girl in short shorts, and a skateboarding guy with long hair, and a couple of frat boys in polos and khaki shorts.

"You all packed?" Court asked after a minute. Rong pretended not to see when Court wiped his eyes.

Rong nodded. "I leave tomorrow."

"Michigan will be a big change," Court said.

"Yeah," Rong said with a nod. "Hopefully no monsters."

They both laughed. "Hopefully not, old friend," Court said.

They held out a fist, which Court fist-bumped, then said, "Take care."

"You too," Rong said. And they walked out to enjoy the warmth and sunshine, the day and the summer, and life.

FINAL INTERLUDE

The Tale of the Grocery Store Visit

Once upon a time, there lived a farmer. He dedicated a small plot to vegetables, but he specialized in raising animals on his one hundred and ten acres, and while he bred mostly cattle, he had a pen for horses and one for pigs and a henhouse with an incredibly obnoxious and possessive rooster.

But while the farmer had his plot of land devoted to tomatoes and some cucumber and lettuce and a row for onions and another for carrots, these grew seasonally, and he was hungry most of the time. He wasn't great at growing collard greens, for example, but he loved them with some cornbread and black-eyed peas (corn and peas and beans also gave him all sorts of trouble in his garden).

He also liked milk, but he didn't raise dairy cattle. Instead, he sold a lot of the yearlings born to his stock of heifers and his Brangus bull, and once a year butchered a steer for enough meat to last through the winter (more than enough when he also butchered a fattened hog and a couple of chickens), but he didn't have a dairy farm.

So, because of this he went to town every week. He climbed in his pickup truck and drove down the road past his rental house. In later years, the house would be condemned, and then razed and a cheap single-wide would be placed on the plot and it would earn him a reasonable and steady income, along with his other rentals and side jobs and farming.

He passed the sanitation place and the recycling center that employed the challenged people like his deaf sister, and the Epoxyn plant where they made fireplace hearths, turned north on College and followed it to its junction with the state highway 62 snaking through town, 'til he came to the local grocery store.

His grocery list never changed: the aforementioned veggies hard to grow in his particular garden, some cheese and milk, some biscuits, canned SPAM, bologna, and sliced white bread.

"Can't live long with such a diet," the short woman said. He'd seen her pretty regularly on his Sunday evening runs to town. She liked potatoes and, when the season was right, watermelon.

He pointed to the one in her basket. "It's a good 'un."

"Might eat it tonight. Slice it up for me and my ma."

He shot a glance to her left hand and saw the ring, bright and gold, on the one finger what told him this conversation couldn't go any further.

"Only you and yo' ma?"

She followed his gaze and blushed instantly, her right hand grabbing her left, her fingers twirling the ring as she smiled sheepishly. "Yeah. I'm sorry. I…"

He frowned. He could tell she wanted to say something maybe difficult for him to hear, but he wanted to hear it anyway. "It's okay," he said. "I didn't mean to upset you. I… I seen you here nearly every time I come to town."

"A lot of people come to town to do their shopping on Sunday nights."

He jammed his hands in the pockets of his dingy overalls and nodded and looked to the tiled floor, did a quick shuffle of his feet. "Yeah, but I seen you."

He heard her sigh, and he looked up to see she was still twirling the damned ring. *Just leave and take my bags of groceries back to my farm and forget this mess*, he thought. Maybe next week he'd shop at the new shopping center that had only recently opened. They had a section specifically for fishing and hunting and the like, on top of groceries.

"I wear it to remember," she said as he turned to push his buggy away. "I guess you don't know, but my husband died last year. He was working on his boat and got electrocuted. Well, the shock sent him into the water. Officially, he drowned."

"I'm sorry," he said. He could think of nothing else, but all of a sudden, he didn't want to push the buggy away. He'd heard about the guy. It was purely an accident. He'd been found by her brother of all people, who was late to get off work to come help him at his boat dock. She'd been sound asleep when the sheriff came to tell her.

"It's me and Ma now. We live in her house on 3rd Street."

"You still love him," he said. The question was enough for him to turn the buggy around.

"I probably always will," the young widow said. "But I can't stop my life for someone who is gone. I've grieved a lot this past year. I want to be loved again. I want to have a family." Her blush deepened another shade. "I'm sorry. This is too intimate a conversation for the bread aisle at the local grocery store."

"It's fine," he said. He reached for her hand and felt a jolt when she let him take it.

"You were in the war."

"Europe," he said. "Mortar platoon. I came back with ear damage."

"I'm sorry," she said, not pulling her hand away.

"I was lucky," he said. "Most of them didn't make it. The few who did came back worse than me."

"You work for the school district," she said. "You got the big farm up the road. I heard the city approached you to by some land to build a park for the kids."

"I'll probably sell. They want to build baseball fields."

She smiled. "You like baseball?"

He smiled. "Played as a kid."

She squinted a looked at the contents of his buggy. "You like fried green tomatoes? I make a mean batch."

"Naw," he lied. "Can't stand them."

It would be the first meal she'd cook for him.

The End

EPILOGUE

Dani couldn't remember the last time she had slept a full night. Still, a couple of months after her son had been born, with Court sawing logs in their master, she stood over the crib one particularly cold autumn night and watched her baby sleep.

What raced through her brain was a summation of her life. A little girl flying a kite over hills laced with daffodils. Stirrups supported her legs as searing cramps, like peristalsis on steroids, threatened to rip open her vagina as though it were a worm hole opening to a new dimension. She dove into a lake, her hair cascading around her, tickling her back, until she rose and took in breath. She saw the ghoul, lunging for Court's neck, and she stabbed forward.

Their son bit his fist and, wincing his eyes shut, kicked his little legs. David's a bit restless, she thought. He mewed, perhaps in response, a psychic reply to his mother helicoptering over his crib.

I am still a guitarist, she thought. *I am a teacher, like his father. I teach sound; I teach music, where his father teaches words, and sound, and vision. I teach the ear where he teaches the eye.*

The boy cooed and kicked and stretched. Dani reached down and caressed his cheek with her finger. Around her, the darkness encroached. She fought against feeling suffocated.

"Your grandfathers wished for you. Before they passed, they swore to protect you. If you see them, smile, little precious one. Because they love you."

Tomorrow, she would leave him to teach and tutor and play the guitar, and she was excited; the thought made her immensely happy. But it would also mean she left this little guy, and this saddened her, but she knew he'd be in good hands with Court, who had the day off from everything except fixing them all dinner and working on a new poem.

She whispered. "He loves you. He loves us. He won't ever put us in harm's way. He is a good father."

CR&O

Thanksgiving Day spit blustery snowflakes that blanketed the grassy areas and slicked the streets, the first snowfall of the season and the first significant snow in almost a decade in Rapps Barren. Court, with wife and baby in tow, took the curves gently. The SUV handled the slippery conditions well, and though it took them a little longer, they made it safely to the drive.

Court unpacked his family and then the turkey, and Dani and the baby were greeted by doting grandmothers and their plentiful kisses. The four of them sat down for a meal, leaving two place settings for the men who'd been the world for each of them.

"It's been calm," Aster said as Lena cut the pecan pie after lunch proper was served. "Detective Bullocks didn't even try to go for sheriff, though we both encouraged him."

"Didn't think this white town would want a Black sheriff," Lena said.

Court shrugged. "Worked in *Blazing Saddles*." This garnered a little laugh from each of them, which caught him off guard as he thought the reference was too young for his grandmothers and too old for his wife.

"They're good," Dani said of their friends when Lena asked. She expounded on the big moves and how they heard from Rong and Blue sometimes.

"Britta and the kids are…managing," Aster said.

⁕

After lunch, they braved the cold, piling into the SUV and driving out to the cemetery by the funeral home. The baby bundled up, Court carried him in the infant car seat and shielded him from any wind, with Dani at his side and the grandmothers flanking them. Orange and red and yellow artificial flowers had replaced the purple and blue from the summer.

"They did good work on the headstones," Court said. He didn't mention it but seeing Lena's name next to Glen's minus a date, and Aster's next to Elden's also missing the same crucial piece of information, unnerved him. A shiver raced up his spine, and not from the cold.

I miss you Papa, he thought, reading Glen's name. *I miss you, Papaw*, he added, glancing at Elden's. What he wouldn't give for them to have known his son, for them to still be here. He knew it was greed and he knew he was lucky to have them for the time he did, but he didn't give a shit. It wasn't long enough. Truthfully, if he'd had them another twenty years, it still wouldn't have been long enough.

Still, there was an inescapable truth hanging in the air, like honeysuckle in April. As much as he'd missed them, as much as he'd cried at each of their funerals, and despite the frightful turn of events drawing them back from death's door—the last terrifying adventure—he knew this: their return enabled him to move ahead with life, with a son, with Dani, and with his grief. He was no longer frozen, no longer with his head in the sand. Rather, he was processing every day and engaging life. As if to remind him of this, his son reached up, stretching a finger toward him looking like the painting on the Sistine Chapel, like his son was reaching for God, so Court bent toward the finger and kissed it.

Three plots next to them held family Court had never known, though he felt the loss of his parents and his older brother all the same. He saw in his grandmothers' eyes how much they'd lost, and their pain upset him. *As much family below the ground as above*, he thought, and the seeds for a new poem were planted.

❧

That night, he dressed in the living room of the farmhouse, leaving Dani to rest with the baby, asleep in the crib. As careful not to alert Aster, as he was his wife and child, he took a flashlight from the corner cupboard in the kitchen and checked its batteries to find it worked well enough, even if the lens was cloudy.

He trod across the yard and into the calf lot behind the house. Passing through the barn would be the easiest way to get from the calf lot to the main pasture, and the barn allowed him a reprieve from the biting cold before he exited and trekked across the snow drifts and rolling hills until he came to the fence that separated his grandfather's land from the forest beyond.

He found a wooden brace post and was amazed at his age he could still climb it. The woods shielded him from the worst of the storm, but it was still bitterly cold. The arctic wind coiling through the trees nipped at his exposed ears and nose, and his lips were numb. He hadn't walked far, thankfully, before he saw the first tombstone. And then another. And another. And then through the falling snow and the night, his flashlight fell upon the old church, her image slowly revealing itself like a tenuous lover.

Inside, it was warmer, the storm whistling around the eaves. He shed most of his outer garments and laid them on the back of a pew. The air in here was musty, but hadn't it always been so? As he descended, first into the cellar and then underground, any hint of winter dissipated. The chamber of bones was still sticky, and warm, not cool like in those warmer months, like when he was trapped here. He still didn't like to think about it.

The torches still blazed. There still existed something fetid in the air; in the darkness nails clicked on the bones.

"Do you still eat?" he asked.

"Qissa," the voice hissed, and he supposed since there had been no sightings of it nor reports of graves being disturbed, maybe this was how it was satiated in the interim.

"Remember," he said. "I won't be able to come back until next month."

It crawled on all fours out of the shadows, sniffing the air and eyeing him, then circled in place and sank to its haunches, curled up in front of him. It closed its yellow eyes and huffed. "Qissa," it said again. Court thought of his wife and child and how David might have inherited a gift he didn't want, and then Elden's words to him. Sometimes the hard choice meant doing what you don't want to do. He hoped it would be a long time before his son would have to make the hard choice.

Court cleared his throat. "This one is called, 'The Last Tale of the Storyteller.' Once upon a time," he began, as the story came to him. "Once upon a time, there was an old man whose job it was to tell stories. He'd been telling stories for years, long before he was old…"

The End

ACKNOWLEDGMENTS

I want to thank my wife, Kerri, for believing in this vision and supporting my writing as well as the creation of Sley House. I couldn't do this without you, sweetie.

To KA Hough, whom I met prior to Sley House, who has been an outstanding editor. We are so honored to have you on board.

To the Sley siblings. You miserable bastards.

To my grandparents:

While, at the time of this publishing, we still are fortunate to have both my grandmothers, it has been several years since my grandfathers have passed. I was lucky enough to know both men for a long, long period. But their deaths came also with the death of my stepfather over a period of three years, from which I don't know if I or my family has ever recovered.

As Court found with his grandparents in the novel, it was hard watching them grow older. I am thankful for the years that I had with them, but I still miss them every day. Writing this novel has been cathartic. There is so much of my Papa in Glen Dillon, and so much of Papaw in Elden Oscar. They were far from perfect, but if someone is looking for that kind of novel or memoir, they'll have to look to another writer. All in all, I think every day about what they taught me: the value of hard work and doing what you love, the importance of kindness and gentleness, the strength that comes with education and the wisdom that comes from living, the power of tact and morality and doing right by others.

I miss you Papa and Papaw. The world isn't the same without you.

ABOUT THE AUTHOR

JR BILLINGSLEY has been publishing short fiction for nearly two decades. His MFA allows him to teach, but he considers himself a writer first and foremost. When the two publishers who picked up his first novel both closed their doors, he had the bright (and somewhat naïve) idea of starting his own publishing house. Since then, Sley House has put out anthologies, novels, radio dramas, collections, and continues to grow. He lives with his wife, son, and their yellow Lab, Shadow in Northwest Arkansas.

ALSO FROM SLEY HOUSE

NOVELS

A Mind Full of Scorpions
(Eyes Only, Book One)
JR Billingsley

Ground Control
K.A. Hough

Bad Form
Joe Taylor

Persephone's Escalator
Joe Taylor

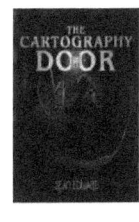

The Cartography Door
Sean Edward

Black Echoes
JB McLaurin

ANTHOLOGIES

Tales of Sley House 2021

Tales of Sley House 2022

Tales of Sley House 2023

Tales of the Sley Siblings

STORY COLLECTIONS

Melpomene's Garden
Curtis Harrell

Observations and Nightmares:
The Short Fiction of JR Billingsley
JR Billingsley

See more at https://www.sleyhouse.com

Milton Keynes UK
Ingram Content Group UK Ltd.
UKHW041305210924
1775UKWH00001B/1/J